[A collage of overlapping handwritten letters, postcards, and envelopes]

Top letter:

Kate my darling —
If you could see us now! Picture do y...
... out mirrors ...
draw ...

Left-edge letter:

Saturday
June 1937

Turdy to a
mormous
te you
gentlem
of yell
e all
nte
on

Ship postcard (Cunard):

CUNARD R.M.S. "SAMARIA."

Dearest Family —
The first of March is he...
and would that you could se...
this minute. We are...
up in...
on...

"Gray Top" letter:

GRAY TOP 1926
HESTER, NEW JERSEY

July 28th

...v Katie —
...so glad your letter...
this morning —
...was starving
for news

Barcode label:

D0053495

Envelope (center-right):

SOUTH POSTAL STATION
BOSTON.MASS JUL 16 —AM 1925

Miss Dorothy Meserve
"Gray Top"
Chester
N.J.

Lower-left letter:

Then I rush to a meeting of the C.A. Board.
Here I find quite a different type of woman
—behold→
This may be Helenka
or Iti, or any of us.
The general idea is the same.
After this I rush to supper and swallow what
is there. I won't call things by any names
because I know you want to eat your
dinner with a good appetite, and I hate
to take away your desire for food.
Anyway, at 7.20 I am at the station
taking the train into Philly to see Walter
Hampton in Macbeth. Quite a different
looking creature now, am I, from the
beefy, athletic, organized college girl. You
might even say I had feminine charm?
Ah well, don't get too stuck up.
Tomorrow morning when the
bell rings eight, you'll be walking

Lower-right letter and envelope:

27 EAST 69TH STREET
NEW YORK

Dearest dearest D:—
...the whole world...
dreadful...

NORRISTOWN OCT 23 1940

Philip B. Kunhardt Jr.
Groton School
Groton
Mass.

The Dreaming Game

ALSO BY PHILIP B. KUNHARDT, JR.

My Father's House
A New Birth of Freedom: Lincoln at Gettysburg

WITH DOROTHY MESERVE KUNHARDT

Twenty Days
Mathew Brady and His World

WITH PHILIP B. KUNHARDT III AND PETER W. KUNHARDT

Lincoln: An Illustrated Biography
P. T. Barnum: America's Greatest Showman
The American President

Dorothy Meserve Kunhardt
in her early college days

The Dreaming Game

A PORTRAIT OF A PASSIONATE LIFE

Philip B. Kunhardt, Jr.

RIVERHEAD BOOKS

a member of Penguin Group (USA) Inc.

New York

2004

Riverhead Books
a member of
Penguin Group (USA) Inc.
375 Hudson Street
New York, NY 10014

All photographs are from the author's personal collection.

The author would like to thank the families of Katharine Strauss
Mali and Franklin P. Adams for granting their permission to use the
letters printed in this book.

Library of Congress Cataloging-in-Publication Data

Kunhardt, Philip B.
The dreaming game : a portrait of a passionate life /
Philip B. Kunhardt, Jr.
p.   cm.
ISBN 1-57322-294-1
1. Kunhardt, Dorothy Meserve, 1901–1979.   2. Authors,
American—20th century—Biography.   3. Children's stories—
Authorship.   I. Title.
PS3521.U66Z63   2004   2004042185
813'.54—dc22
[B]

Printed in the United States of America
1   3   5   7   9   10   8   6   4   2

This book is printed on acid-free paper. ∞

BOOK DESIGN BY AMANDA DEWEY

For my beloved wife, Katharine

ACKNOWLEDGMENTS

My children—Philip, Peter, Jean, Sandra, Sarah, and Michael—read this book chapter by chapter while it was being written. Maybe inflicting all this reading on the six of them was my way of staying close to them over the past two years, yet Lord knows that wasn't necessary. All six of them gave me inspiring bursts of encouragement along the way—letters from Maine, e-mail from Massachusetts, telephone calls from New York City. All Philip had to do was hand me his good suggestions; he and Peter and I have been working together for almost two decades now, making television documentaries and companion books on different aspects of American history. Even though my offspring seemed at times like a single, united force, still I must mention two of them separately for their special contributions to this book.

Sandra Basile, my second daughter, a fine writer and artist who lives in Rhode Island, already knew a lot about Dorothy Kunhardt, having studied her grandmother's work and written about her. At the very start, I asked Sandra to edit each chapter as I wrote it, and she did so with loving intensity and a skillful pencil, offering perceptive suggestions for additions and for deletions, too. Inevitably, some of the insights into my subject came from Sandra as she worked tirelessly over my original manuscript as if it were her own.

Always a presence was my second son, Peter, who gave me his many good ideas on what worked and what didn't. Hardly a day goes by when Peter and I do not see each other or talk on the phone. He is doing what I tried to do for my mother—make aging easier.

Of course, non–family members also helped me complete this project and get it into print. Joan Caron, a longtime colleague and friend, was the person who made sense out of my scrawls and typed version after version as I made changes. Joan had plenty of practice already, having coped with two of our television and book projects over the past decade. Other members of the staff of Kunhardt Productions helped organize a huge picture file on my mother. I am especially grateful to Sabin Streeter, who was asked to cast a cold eye on the manuscript. He did, and the result was some painful but necessary cutting and reorganization.

I want to mention Fred Mali, a godson of my mother's, and his wife, Lucretia, who read the manuscript for accuracy, gave me permission to use Fred's mother's letters to my mother, and opened up the Mali family photograph files.

Esther Newberg has represented the collaborations of Philip, Peter, and me three times over the past fifteen years. She liked this book from the beginning and knew to match it with an old friend, Cindy Spiegel at Riverhead Books. Cindy did the final edit herself, and, assisted by Susan Ambler, oversaw the look and layout. To all of you I send my deepest thanks.

Acknowledgments

Finally, I want to return to a family member: Katharine, my wife of fifty-four years, and the mother of our six children. She was the first to read every new page of this book and she was the glow that kept me going. Without Katharine, there would be no biography of my mother, something both of us felt was important. For she and I, together, have benefited from that life, and so, we hope, will generations to come.

Introduction

Dorothy Meserve Kunhardt among her books
in her Morristown, New Jersey, bedroom

O N A J U L Y M O R N I N G in 1939 my mother walked into the offices of Harcourt Brace, in New York City, carrying a small book she'd put together by hand called *Pat the Bunny*. She left it with an editor who later turned it down because she thought it would be too difficult to publish. "It is really a toy manufacturer's job," the editor said, before adding that it was also "by far and away the best little children's book I have ever seen or dreamed of."

My mother's little book would go on to reshape the children's publishing industry. *Pat the Bunny* was a true original, the first book aimed at babies and tiny children. It was the first interactive book, one that had actual things on each page for the tiny reader to play with and do. It became one of the best-selling books of all time, still sells close to 200,000 copies every year, and is published in countries all over the world. *Pat the Bunny* also changed my family. You might say it rescued us from the grips of the Great Depression—and it forever defined my mother in the minds of most people.

But Dorothy Meserve Kunhardt was much more to the people who knew her than simply the author of a small pink children's book. She was an amazingly vibrant woman possessed of a wild imagination, unique perceptions, vast strengths and passions—as well as dark complexities and lonely insecurities.

My mother never kept a diary. However, the only record of the racetracks of her mind and the speedways of her emotions lies in her writings, especially her letters, which were directed mainly at two people: her husband, and her best friend, Kate—Katharine Strauss Mali. My mother and Kate Strauss met in 1911, in grade school, and after twelve years of school together they became compulsive letter swappers for the rest of their lives. When my mother died in 1979 at seventy-eight, her last letter from Kate was on her bedside table, and I discovered many more tucked away in a green straw case close by. Kate died six months later, in 1980. Maybe a year went by before I got a call from her husband. "Uncle" Harry asked me to meet him at the University Club in New York City not far from where I worked. When I spied him waiting for me, he was holding two large boxes. He sat me down and told me he had brought me all of my mother's letters to his wife, spanning the time from when they were both teenage girls to my mother's last years, before she ceased to write at all. Opening the boxes, he showed me row upon row of envelopes addressed in dark ink in my mother's familiar curling script and stamped with the dates on which they had been mailed along with the location of the post office that handled them. They were all filed in the order in which they had been written, hundreds upon hundreds of letters stretching back to the early part of the twentieth century. They have provided me with a unique insight into a deeply passionate woman. Instead of relying on memory alone, I suddenly met my mother on a wholly new canvas as her own private words helped paint an inspiring self-portrait while she challenged the life around her.

Her first letter to Kate was written at seventeen:

Dear K,

I love you all the way and if I and a pen and paper were only more efficient, you should know it. As it is, guess and I know you'll guess right.

"I've read every one of them, three times over," Uncle Harry said to me. "I've studied them enough. Now they're yours." Abruptly, he handed the letters over as if he didn't want anything more to do with them, as if he were ridding himself of their secrets. When I got the boxes home and began reading, I soon saw that the two friends had shared the most intimate details of love, marriage, childbirth, ambitions, and sorrows. They had traded secrets and advice as each grew into middle age and beyond and raised a family of her own, but they had never given up the open, lavish friendship of their youth. My mother's letters would begin with "Dearest" or "Katie, my own" or "Angel," and were often signed with Kate's special name for her—"Dodo." Punctuating many of them were explosions of eternal love. Neither had known anyone else back then, whether family member or friend, who thought in the same rarified way, whose moods and passions matched hers, and who stirred her to open up and confess her deepest feelings. Some letters were almost startling to me in their intensity—like these lines my mother sent Kate after their college graduation:

It is getting to be a chronic state with me that I want to write to you. But if it is a vice, I yield. I am as weak as water—write me soon, thou pearl of all oysters.

Absolutely anything could be said in the privacy of these girls' letters—their adoration for each other could be expressed openly. Their fears, their loves, their battles, the foibles of their families, their self-proclaimed pettiness and their insecurities, the rush of life—all were grist for their mills. And everything they wrote was to be private, just between them; at the ends of many of their early letters, the girls ordered each other to "Burn this" or to "Destroy immediately."

As I read these letters, my mother's early life began to open up to me and I became aware of qualities of hers that I couldn't have known or had hardly noticed as a son. I found myself drawn back years and years into her past and was increasingly consumed by a desire to study it all and to write about it.

This had happened to me before. When my father died in 1963 at age sixty-two, I missed him a lot. Five years later, after surviving a heart attack at the age of forty, I felt compelled to write a book about my father. It had something to do with the close call I had undergone. In the weeks of recuperation I became obsessed with my roots, with my childhood, especially with the simple, decent life my father had led, and I found myself asking what lessons I could learn from his life, what I could borrow to make me a better father to my children.

Following my mother's death, sixteen years after my father's, I knew I wanted to write a book about her, too. She deserved one, this romantic youth who transformed her innocent self into a woman of the world, the author of a truly revolutionary children's book, the mother of four, grandmother of eighteen, worshipped wife, devoted daughter, and, for me, an extraordinary collaborator and friend.

And it wasn't just her heyday I wanted to investigate, it was the mystery of her final years as well, when the bold glow of life seeped away, when her dream of a perfect existence was suddenly clouded and cracked and she reached for artificial tranquility to quell her ghosts. It would be hard, at first, to see behind those waning years, I knew—to see my mother as she once was. First, a veil had to be lifted.

And then, hadn't she asked me straight out to write about her? It was after she had read the book about my father. "He would have loved to read it," my mother told me. "He didn't know you felt that way about him." Then she looked me straight in the eye and asked, "What about me, Philip? You hardly mention me in your book." "Of course I do," I replied. "I'll write about you more thoroughly, though, someday."

Two years after my mother's death I had retired from my job as editor of *Life* magazine to write books, and soon after my meeting with Uncle Harry I began assembling all the material from my mother's life that would help me tell her tale. In addition to my mother's letters to Kate were a host of Kate's letters in reply, carefully saved. I also had hundreds of letters my mother had written to my father and his back to her. And I had the evidence of her writing career stored away in dozens of cardboard boxes—her first drafts, her artwork, the thousands of pages of notes scrawled out on yellow legal paper, her rave reviews. I wrote some chapters, then stopped, not knowing exactly where to go next. Maybe I was not ready to write about her yet, I told myself; she was still so alive and complicated in my mind. So I filled some old suitcases and boxes with the letters and notes and photographs and carried all of it back to the attic for another day.

I actually tried to start the book two or three more times over the next fifteen years, but there were always more pressing projects, other books with built-in deadlines that got in the way. Then, about a year ago, in the early spring of 2002, I pulled out all the 1920s letters to and from my mother and father, along with the correspondence between my mother and Kate, in order to immerse myself in her early life, to really start exploring. But many of those letters, stored so long in asthmatic attics and dark cellars, were now covered in mildew. Handling them, breathing in their contents along with their spores, touched off a lung infection in me. When my coughing and breathlessness refused to get any better, I was hospitalized, put on oxygen, and eventually diagnosed with pulmonary fibrosis, a disease which, the doctors told me, I had had for years and which had just been waiting to be inflamed, a disease that has no cure.

This turn of events galvanized me into action. Now I tell my doctor, as I undergo three shots a week of experimental interferon, "Just keep me around until the book is finished." He says, "I'll try, but hurry." And so, a quarter of a century after my mother's death, armed with the letters, now copied onto clean sheets of paper, as well as with a thousand other sources to her soul I have harbored over the years, I finally set forth on this long overdue journey.

1.

Day's End

Letter writers and best friends, Katharine Strauss
and Dorothy Meserve (in stripes) sit back-to-back
in their college living room.

For Dorothy (Dot, as her family addressed her, or DM as she was called by her friends) the summer of 1923 was an endless banquet of weekend house parties on Long Island, in Connecticut, and in New Jersey. That was the way many of the recent graduates of Bryn Mawr College were entertaining themselves, constantly in and out of one another's houses over the weekends, hoping lightning might strike with the young men they had gathered round them. Dorothy Meserve and her band of eligible young ladies were celebrating their newfound freedom by spending almost every waking moment making lists of the guests they might ask to their parties, gossiping, dreaming up meals the family cooks could concoct, and imagining activities strewn with romance. It was a flirtatious reverie of garden parties, teas, open cars, pretty clothes, and chaperones.

Dot's best friend was Kate Strauss. They had first met as young girls at the Brearley School in New York City, then went on to be roommates at Bryn Mawr College outside of Philadelphia. Kate was brilliant, swan-necked, striking-looking, and wealthy. She had been raised in a self-reliant, austere family that guarded its emotions. Dorothy was plain-looking, quick-witted, flirtatious, from an outgoing, loving family, and only moderately well-off. Early on she distinguished herself as a budding philosopher-poet and it was not long before the two girls became inseparable.

Although Dorothy's marks at college were unremarkable, she was adored by her teachers because of her quick, unpredictable mind and her searching, outgoing nature. Hers was a mind fascinated by the human animal in all its costumes, all its guises. She lived her ideas most fully in her head and in the wild imaginings of her heart. Often, when she was alone, she played a game of letting her mind ramble wherever it chose to go, taking this road and that path and usually ending up at some preposterous intersection.

A friend remembered, "She's more people's best friend than anyone else there is." But Dorothy also struggled with black moods and insecurities, and it was her roommate, Kate, who best understood her complexities. "All her relationships were intense, ranging from fierce to passionately tender," wrote Kate:

Who can detect the source of enchantment? Some of the genii that attended her were dark, some were quicksilver, but where she was there was always magic.

Dorothy and Kate were sure they were different from others, that they were almost the same person, and that they felt things more deeply and therefore realized more pain as they made their way through life. But they were convinced that their heightened sensitivity would pay off for them someday.

"I can't help thinking, Kate," wrote Dorothy:

that all this agony of mind and yearning of heart that we seem fated by some queer turn in our mechanism to go through, when other people find their little corners and are quickly happy—must be going to bring us to a better place, and a little higher gratefulness when we find it.

During that summer of 1923, whenever Dorothy and Kate were not together they wrote to each other incessantly.

"Angel, I love you," my mother addressed her friend:

And what do you think, Wright has asked me to go to the Harvard-Yale races this weekend and "spend the following Sunday with us." Who "us" may be I know not, but am duly thrilled and flattered. By the way, write Billy a good one and catch him. All men are worth our attention. Be nice to the least and if we're good little girls some day the greatest will pop around the corner and surprise us. Now write me, scoundrel. I love you and must hear from you or die.

The "greatest" had not yet appeared for either Kate or Dorothy but their code phrase for when he did was "Day's End." Those two little words would herald the end of the search for the perfect mate for one of them. It was all part of their secret language. They were each other's agent and coconspirator in a great game—a great male-chase. Forced to decline one of Kate's weekend invitations, my mother mock-raged:

Fate, your name is mud, and I hate you, you have mangy hair and black teeth and your eyebrows are falling out. Well, Kate, do this for me, anyway—tell Hugh what a super divinity I am.

Toward the end of that year of release, Dorothy attended a wedding house party in Providence where she met a twenty-three-year-old New Englander who would one day become my father. Although each was intrigued by the other, they almost passed in the night, never to meet again. Dorothy had her mind on the round-the-world cruise Kate's family was sending the two girls on. Phil was attracted to Dorothy but made up his mind that she was too much for him to handle.

As 1924 got under way, the two girls, along with Kate's fifty-eight-year-old Uncle Fred, set sail on their extravagant voyage aboard the SS *Samaria,* which would cross the Atlantic and circle the globe by way of Egypt, India, China, and the Panama Canal. The four-month-long trip was a milestone in the lives of both of these wide-eyed girls. And for my mother, through her letters back home, it served as a kind of writing class in which she tried to make her life come alive on paper.

Dearest Mother and Father,

The sun is bright and warm and shines on me as I lie in my steamer chair and write my first letter to you. I just realize now that I count up, that I have fifty-six thank-you letters to write for farewell gifts and steamer letters. These first days have been terrifically cold and extremely rough, seas on the average of twenty-five feet high. We have been spending the most delightful lazy life in the world. In the mornings we sleep in our warm little beds until 10 a.m., when the crisp and polite stewardess comes in and presents us with the menu. She brings in the trays and we eat and then read in bed until about twelve thirty when we get up and take nice salt tubs and dress for lunch. Yesterday afternoon K and I went up to the gymnasium and rode on the electric camel and swung on the parallel bars which quite exhausted me. We really have done very little exercise for months, outside of dancing. Speaking of dancing, they had the first dance on the boat last night, but the ship rolled so that one could hardly walk straight, let alone manage some fancy steps.

Upon reading Dorothy's early letters to Kate, and those written aboard the ship to her parents, I could tell already that my future mother was no shrinking violet. She had a mind and a will of her own and when she wanted to do something, she did it, no matter the consequences. In the same way, when she decided not to do something, she stuck firmly to that decision:

Last night K and I decided not to get drawn into the silly, wasteful life of the steamer which does nothing but pass away the glorious time of the day. The first days we were here we had a taste of it. We met all the dozen young men who are running around this boat and we played bridge all day and danced in the evenings. But last night we talked it all over and decided that that is not what we are here for. These four months are probably the only time in our lives when we will be able to think absolutely peacefully, and read, and write, and sketch, and do all the delightful things of life that one so rarely has a chance to do. We began our new resolution last night by coming down after coffee was served, changing our dancing clothes to sweaters and walking skirts, and going far up into the bow of the boat to watch the stars and the dark water.

While growing up, since I was both fascinated and terrified by girls, I wondered about my mother and boys. From her letters, I learned that they were a part of life for her, a necessary ingredient, but one she didn't quite understand yet, an ingredient that could be played with or put aside when the soul sought more refined delights.

February 3

There is an endless number of stray old ladies and just as many stray old gentlemen on this boat, and they are just beginning to pick each other up and cling for dear life. Then the younger generation of men aren't as bad as we first thought them. I should say there are about twelve young men on the ship—"useful men" as I would call them in my little black notebook, and while they are not what we are used to at home in the way of attractiveness and general fineness, still, men are men—and we can't get along without them.

ON FEBRUARY 12, the *Samaria* left Italy for Egypt. The trip was only two weeks along, but my mother and Kate had already visited Madeira, Gibraltar, Algiers, and Naples, and my mother said she felt as though she "had spent a month in each of them." Algiers in particular seems to have struck her:

It does give one a shock to walk along the street which is filled with veiled Arab women and Arab men in long, white robes—streets which are so filthy that the worst parts of Naples seem pure and stainless in comparison. It really is perfectly thrilling to sail into the port of a strange country and intensively live for four or five days in an entirely different civilization.

In Egypt, the girls took a train from Alexandria to Cairo, and then made a special excursion to Luxor, to visit King Tut's newly discovered tomb. My mother told her parents that they wouldn't recognize "the big, fat, brown girl" that she was becoming. Days later, from India, she sent a vivid description of a Parsee funeral:

> They worship one God but they worship him through the five elements so when a Parsee dies, his family dress him in clean white linen robes, put him on a stretcher and carry him at night to Malabar Hill and the Towers of Silence. When the family has gone, two men take the body into the tower, take off its clothes and leave it exposed. Perching all over the tower, waiting, are hundreds of huge black vultures who descend on the body and finish all but the bones in twenty minutes. Then they hop back to their roosts and wait for the next meal. The bones that are left are dropped into a lime pit and are dissolved—so that not one of the elements is defiled by the rotting of the body.

Having circled the globe once myself, I know what a trip like that can do. It can make you shed the past, like a snake leaving its skin behind, revealing a new person. Only a year ago, while still at college, neither Dot nor Kate had wanted to let go of the charmed life they had been leading, a rapturous mixture of close companionships, intellectual flowering, and arguments into the wee hours over the meaning of life. Now all that was behind them; the high seas and ever-expanding world were opening their eyes to how delicate life was—and how fleeting:

> We travel over the sea toward Manila. Tonight there will be an April Fool's dance on the aft deck from nine to eleven. It is ages and ages since I have written you—but it is all the fault of the

tropics—everything is. Heat is a demon that comes up and blows its hot breath on you one moment and you sink back. The next moment it clutches you, and you are more feverish and excited than you ever remember being before—and then it blows its breath again and the very blood is soaked from your veins and you sink back listless. Another passenger—quite an old lady—died the other day from the heat. It was quite casual. I know I must sound brutal to you all who live in a northern climate, and I would never have believed the truth about the equator had I never been there. But honestly and truly, the tropics mean hysteria and weakness and madness beyond all control. One never does what one ought to do or what one intends to do—and what is more, one is tolerant of everything. Nothing surprises or shocks anyone here. Everyone drinks too much and makes love too ardently, and stays up too late at night because it is too hot to lie down in one's bed and sleep.

Although her letters home never revealed enough to make her parents anxious, Dorothy was obviously having a fling on shipboard. Given her flirtatious nature, it would have been hard for the handsome young officers aboard, especially one called Mac, to overlook her. Although Kate was never far away and surely kept things straightforward, it was my mother's first real romance and it left her yearning for more:

It is four o'clock now—and my special officer gets down from the bridge, and I have a date with him. He is really quite a darling boy. I think you would like him.

By mid-April, the girls were in China, the part of the round-the-world trip that would forever haunt Dorothy with its fierce beauty.

From the circumscribed life at home, so beloved yet so obvious, Dorothy was suddenly thrust into a land of mystery—so different and challenging and bizarre that for as long as she lived, she would never get over it. The spectacle of China would become part of her poetic landscape:

We have been traveling from Shanghai since eight o'clock yesterday morning and we won't get to Peking till after midnight tonight—so you see we are taking quite a little flight into the middle of China. This train carries a whole extra car full of soldiers armed with rifles and bayonets, in order to protect us from robbers and insurrectionists who might attack us. It makes it quite exciting to retire into your compartment and hear a guard pacing up and down the corridor outside your door all night.

Spring has come to China. You can't imagine the beauty of the country that I see from my compartment windows as the train whirls us along. Our trip is almost over—in one way it seems years, and in another it has gone like a flash. My old life seems dim and unreal, and I am meeting so many strange people—people of the world who have traveled and have poise and can talk well and have a very different outlook on life. It is absolutely the most priceless thing that could happen to anyone—to sail around our great huge world and see the millions and billions of people who live on the different continents in an entirely different way from what we know as life—and think and believe things that we never even dreamed of. It ought to make us tolerant and wise and much more able to work out a little course of life for ourselves when we get back.

My mother's letters stopped here, with only Japan and Hawaii ahead, and the trip ended in an emotional whirl—with the two girls crying in happiness and my mother missing every moment of the incredible journey for months afterward, especially the times with Mac, the young purser who had pursued her throughout the voyage.

"Gosh, I never would have believed it possible," she later recalled to Kate:

> but I suppose you can't see a person every evening and part of every day for three months and enjoy it—and then expect to forget immediately. I would give a lot if tonight I could go out to the swimming pool on the forward deck and see him standing in the half-darkness in his stiff white shirt and ridiculous short dress-jacket and hear him say, "Good evening, Dorothy—shall we go out on the prow?" O the devil—and yet I'm not sorry, I'd do it again a thousand times. And I couldn't like him as much even if he were entering into my shore life—it was just that unreal dream-life on ship where true gentlemen arise—whatever the land world may call them.

As a young boy many years later, I heard stories of my mother's famous round-the-world trip. In her bedroom she kept a large, black photographic scrapbook the steamship line had made up for her. No matter how hard I searched for her face in those pictures, I could never find it. Later, I came to realize that the steamship company had produced the same album for every passenger, using pictures from similar trips made in the past. But here I was introduced to the pyramids of Egypt, the Sphinx, the Taj Mahal, and the Great Wall of China. My mother had brought back jewelry from her trip, too, especially amber, and she kept it in the top drawer of her bureau along with piles of exotic kerchiefs with gold and silver threads. Jackets from Tangier with coins dangling from the lapels hung in her closet, along with a blue emperor's robe from Peking, peaked straw workers' hats from the rice paddies, tiny cloth shoes from Japan, and other curiosities that had struck my mother's fancy along the way.

The experience had been so lofty and so awe-inspiring that even though it had taken place years before, my mother kept referring to the trip and its wonders, almost as if she had visited another planet. The trip had helped shape her dreams. Even as an old lady, so many years later, she treasured its symbols—especially the jewelry. She would handle the beads over and over, fondling them, their very presence calming her and reassuring her that yes, she was still the same person that the great journey had shaped.

BY JUNE OF 1924, my mother had settled back into her post-college life, joining her family at their summer house in Chester, New Jersey, where she was busy with an ardent admirer named Carl. But nothing felt right. In one of her daily letters to Kate, fifty miles or so away on Long Island, she confessed:

> Carl has been out here this weekend and I really don't know what I think or feel. I am such a disgusting girl that to put it crudely to you who are the light of my life—he is the third man that I have let kiss me in two weeks—only George and Larry were playing and Carl isn't. He is in dead earnest which makes me feel all the rottener.

Still, however rotten she may have felt, she was twenty-two—and her feelings for this Carl were serious enough to initiate some talk between them about marriage:

We have talked it all over and of course it would mean ages of waiting until he stops studying and tries to make some money, and then even after, it would be struggle, struggle. But that wouldn't make any difference if I loved him, of course, but Katie, I am so dulled and hardened and softened and my view is so warped I guess, that I can't get the slightest kick out of the whole thing. He is filled with strange and wonderful longings and splendid ideals—the kind we used to have—the feeling that love is sacred and life is beautiful. While he is planning achievements and all sorts of splendid things with the sky as the limit, I sit there as unmoved and practical as the kitchen stove! It's damnable! I loathe myself. Life just stretches ahead with nothing in it but boredom and hosts of people who will never understand.

Clearly restless, my mother was soon rid of Carl and setting her sights on an apparently dashing seminary student named Erdman, "Erd" for short. She planned to ensnare him at a Fourth of July house party of her own in Chester. Making the guest list, she suddenly remembered the young man she'd met in Providence just before leaving on her round-the-world cruise—Philip Kunhardt, my future father. Always on the prowl for new male playmates either for herself or for her friends, Dorothy promptly sent off an invitation to Phil, having mapped out the pairings. Kate would be with Tex, Dena would be with George, Helen had agreed Derrick was a perfect match; another great Bryn Mawr friend of my mother's, Aggie, would be hooked up with Phil; and she, the hostess, would have Erdman all to herself.

Looking back, it's interesting to me that my mother was inviting my father to this party of hers for the sake of convenience, not romance. She had not been very impressed by him when they first met. To Dorothy, the cherubic-faced, heavily-muscled, overly polite Phil was an unknown quantity. He wasn't a part of her New York party scene. Born and raised in Massachusetts, he was a New Englander. And he wasn't worldly in any sense. Rather, fresh from his graduation from Harvard, he was eager to start the job that had been waiting for him all his twenty-three years—at his father's woolens mill in Lawrence, Massachusetts. Indeed, my mother first thought my father to be nothing more than a big, likable baby, still tied to his family, his private school life, and his college.

Nonetheless, Phil was interested in Dorothy right from the start. Soon after their first meeting, he had nervously written her, knowing she was about to embark on her round-the-world trip and sensing that this energetic and articulate woman of the world was far beyond his reach. He described the weekend they'd spent at the party in Providence as having been "like a dream," and he told her he liked her "infinitely more" than she liked him. Then he reluctantly bade her farewell—and I don't know if he thought he'd ever see her again. When he got her invitation the following year, he was thrilled at being remembered, but clearly still nervous. His reply to Dorothy was filled with self-deprecation:

> The only time you have seen me was at a rather jumbled house party and on a train ride to Boston. So you don't know what you are getting in for with this mill-working, "childish" bum.

He signed off with a rather stiff "Sincerely, Philip B. Kunhardt." Still, he came to my mother's party and apparently had a good time. A week later, he wrote a grateful bread-and-butter letter:

> You were all so blooming nice to me when I was quite a dumbbell of a guest that I am very thankful. I thought all the ladies of the party were "knock-outs."

Phil also liked Erdman whom he called "a very sound egg," and he asked Dorothy for his address so he might write him.

My mother liked Erdman, too. So much so that by mid-summer, she had been influenced enough by him to seek out a job in Manhattan taking care of underprivileged children in a church group (she explained in a letter to Kate that four days a week she commuted to the city from Chester "to rule with an iron hand eighty howling children"), and she was leaning toward taking courses at Union Seminary herself.

Fortunately for my father, this romance was causing alarm at Dorothy's home—serious alarm. Her parents were concerned over their daughter's fervid frame of mind, over her attraction to a future clergyman, and especially over her social service job and her leanings toward the ministry. Her father, Frederick Hill Meserve, had his own reasons for concern. He had suffered terribly when, as a boy in Colorado, his minister father had suddenly deserted his family to become an itinerant preacher. Frederick had never forgiven him. "He told us that God would provide," my grandfather once said bitterly. "Well, God didn't provide!" After spending years helping support his mother and three younger brothers, Frederick held a dim view of the ministry as a profession and did not want his eldest child taking that route, either for herself or through marriage. Edith, my stately grandmother, was also adamantly opposed, not because of the religious factor (which she silently applauded, being a devout churchgoer herself), but on the grounds that Dorothy was much too young to know her own mind; after all, she fell in and out of love almost overnight and, therefore, no young man should pay any permanent attention to her. With all that in mind, Dorothy's distressed parents decided to ship her off to Paris with an old maiden relative for nine months and pray the situation would straighten itself out.

On September 7, 1924, my mother wrote Kate about the sudden change in plans:

Never, never, never did I think I would be writing this letter to you, but let me in tears break it all in one fell swoop. As things stand now, I sail sometime during the first week in October for France—where Cousin Nell and I spend the winter in Paris, I studying literature and art at the Sorbonne. It was all decided about two days ago, in a flash. The family want it terribly and I am still so stunned that I don't quite realize what it all means.

The following week, she wrote Kate again, now under the spell of her strong-minded parents, and resigned to her banishment. All the independence she had built on her round-the-world trip earlier that year had vanished, and she was a little girl again, doing her family's bidding. She sounded almost pleased that she was being saved from a potentially unpleasant situation. And, at the same time, she was professing very different feelings about Erdman from those she had expressed before:

You know, it's so funny—human nature, that is. I gave in and said I would go away to study art in Paris—when it nearly kills me to leave everyone again, and when my whole heart was set on getting a social service or a political or some sort of a job in New York this winter. I said I would finally, because mother and father were really so brokenhearted over the things I had chosen to do—and because it was only a year of my life—and I thought for once I would try out the old-fashioned idea of letting the parents' desires count for something. Now the family has forgotten quite

how it happened and sincerely believes that it is sending me because I want to go—and at great sacrifice to themselves—and
sometimes rather as though I were a bit hard-hearted to leave
them again. Which makes it difficult. But I won't and can't change
now. I really will have to go through with it, though words can't
tell how my heart is in New York.

As for Erdman, I loathe and despise him. Listen to what the
man has done to me! You may perhaps be aware that he and I have
been quite intimate this summer. Warm friends, we might say.
Well, I wrote him a *long letter* when I first heard of the plans for
me to go—explaining just why I was giving up my future in social services, etc., and a week or so later, I get a *postal-card* (of all
rude things) saying, "I am so used to being surprised by you this
isn't much of a shock. Hope to see you before you go." It seems
to me that it would have been kinder and more gentlemanly to do
at least as much as my friends did, take the trouble to write a few
words in acknowledgment—but no, not Erd.

Dorothy had yet to learn that it would take more than an outburst of
loathing to dismiss someone she thought she loved. She could now turn
her attention to the man of whom she had thought little until now. It
seemed she was beginning to change her opinion about Phil:

Helen's house party went off this weekend with a bang—eleven
damsels and swains—and a riot every minute. Phil was the nicest
out here—he was simply darling, and so very thoughtful for the
older people—and very interesting to talk to—I never got a
chance over the Fourth to know him, I was so engrossed in pur-
suing Erdman.

Phil, in turn, wrote Dorothy after this party—no longer calling her by her school friends' nickname, DM, but for the first time using her family's name for her—Dot:

"You certainly were very nice to me," he wrote:

Here it is, only three times I have seen you and I feel as though I know you quite well. I don't usually work that fast; maybe it's because you are such a ready listener, and any fellow is conceited enough to like to hear himself talk.

His letter concludes with the enticing: "Why the deuce do you have to go off to Europe, anyway?" But romance would have to wait. My mother ignored my father's last line, and sailed off with her rheumatism-wracked Cousin Nell down the Hudson on October 4, 1924.

Among the many letters that awaited Dorothy in her cabin was one from Phil, written on Harvard University Graduate School of Business Administration stationery and addressed to the SS *Minnetonka* at Pier 56, N.Y.C. It was carefully composed by my father because it was important to him that this exciting new acquaintance remember him during her stay in Europe and come home wanting to see him again:

Well, you are off! The band has finished playing, and the weeping women have left the rail. Manhattan island slips away and you go below to your stateroom to find my humble offering at the bottom of a mighty pile. Judge it not by its size, but by the quality of the good wishes with which it is sent. I can see you in a couple of weeks. There you are, clad in some glorious Parisian conception, leaning upon the arm of a handsome gallant entering the Opéra or the Comédie—for it is a part of your education to attend the

French theater. Be sure, however, to choose your escort well. He must not be some high-minded, unpractical minister of the Faith, but rather some young captain of industry. I shall keep you no longer. Run to the top deck and catch a last glimpse of Sandy Hook. Or better yet, open that bottle and munch on a fig while you really enjoy yourself reading a letter written by a twisted hand.

OUT ON THE HIGH SEAS of the Atlantic, my mother tried to write:

I had an idea that simply drove me wild until I got it on paper— and then when I did, I walked to the blunt end of the ship and threw the pages into the deep, which was too nice a death for them.

In her deck chair she thought over her life and became determined that there was something lacking in her character. She would use France to improve.

"Now we'll see what Dodo can do about herself," she wrote Kate:

while she is far away in France. This is Friday and we land early Sunday morning; then begins a new life, in a way, and I am re-solved not to just wait for it to seize and mold me—as I might have a few months ago—but to see my objective and have the strength to form my days as I want them to be.

Then my mother admitted that she was still in the grip of her affec-tion for Erdman:

Damnation and hellfire, I can't forget him and it is painful, to say the least. Every day I tell myself—you are a fool—you have simply got to get over this. But nothing happens—yet! Of course, it's early in the game, and we have often said, time and distance will do anything. They'd better get busy on this job, however.

What different circumstances Dorothy found herself in, compared to those of her trip with Kate earlier that year. Then, she had wallowed in freedom and friendship, in an ever-changing panoply of exotic sights and sounds, and in having little or no work except writing home. Now she was on her own in Paris, watched over by a strict and aging relative, intent on cramming some real learning into her head, and having a radical change of heart as well. At least the memory of Erdman seemed to fade as my mother contemplated the kind of art she hoped to study. She sought the classes that might bring out a talent she felt she possessed but had so far only crudely displayed in the humorous stick-figure drawings of people she had rendered for her college yearbook:

This morning I went to four *ateliers*—studios—to see the different methods and teachers and results. Each studio seemed to lodge itself in the most tumbledown and dissolute spot possible. One was almost like a hayloft, and had to be reached by a ladder, and all of them cried out poverty and art. The general scene in each was this—a group of about thirty students, men and women, standing before their easels in the process of painting, or drawing in charcoal some poor nude woman who was either sitting or lying before them in a strange contortion. The unbeautiful received as much concentration from the artists as did the beautiful, and men and women squinted at and measured and devoured every detail of their bodies.

Dorothy had never seen anything like this before in her life. In all probability she had never seen anyone naked before, save her little sister, Helen. Certainly not her mother or father, who both meticulously closed the bathroom door when they privately bathed and dressed. Now, here were human beings parading around without a stitch on and paying absolutely no attention to their nudity. My mother was taken aback and at the same time thrilled by what she had seen:

> I bought a pad of sketch paper and some soft pencils, came home, locked myself in my room and spent the early hours of the afternoon standing in front of my mirror, stark naked, making pretty pictures of a Dodo that one seldom sees—thank heaven.

Soon my mother was hard at work studying the history of art during morning sessions at the Sorbonne, and drawing nudes in three different afternoon studio classes.

DM was wide-eyed over the naked models used in her drawing class. They were women, some fat, some thin, some pretty, some ugly. But one day a huge black man appeared on the scene:

> This morning at the studio all was going merrily and I was making a stunning picture of a white-skinned girl with black bobbed hair. Suddenly, in walked a big, well set-up Negro, and the man who is in charge of the studio nodded to him and said, "Ah yes, we'll have to take a vote on whether we want you for next week." He told the man to undress and called in the others, who were painting another model in the next room. They all crowded in and stood in the doorway—men and girls, all in their smudgy smocks. The Negro stood right up by the white-skinned young girl while we judged. He took off his shoes and socks and funny high-waisted trousers and collar

and shirt—every article, one by one, and then sprang up on the stand beside the girl—a superb, brown figure in all his muscular strength and hairiness—and we all voted to take him . . .

Incidents like this were helping Dorothy get over Erd:

Now that my work keeps my silly self so busy, in between times I don't give myself a chance to think at all. I go to cathedrals and I sit by tall pillars and look at the gorgeous lights in rose windows and watch candles flicker before sleepy wax figures. I suppose if I let myself remember certain things, I could still be in agony, but I don't, and I really think it's going to be all right.

Romance even became entertaining again. For Kate's edification, Dorothy continued to describe examples of the male animal: "Why is it that some people are like sparks that fly and crackle and others are like—wet toast?"

Describing another visitor, Dorothy was scathing yet perceptive:

Poor girl, I don't think she has a chance. She's a saint, but has none of the charm men want, none of the faults and the divine zip. In other words, I don't think she would "click" anyone.

Meanness like that was confined to her letters to Kate. Each could be just as catty and hard-spirited as she wished on paper to the other, but they were never that way when they were with anyone else:

We agreed, didn't we, that we would be horrid about people only in our letters to each other, but never to anyone else. Well, I've kept to it so far, not that I've really had much testing yet, but up to now I've been as dovelike and as much like a baa-baa lamb as I could possibly be.

When a young man Dorothy didn't like insisted on coming to dinner with the aim of taking her out on the town dancing, the evening was spelled out in detail:

I met him downstairs and told him before Cousin Nell arrived that I was awfully sorry but my cousin did not allow me to go out unchaperoned, so we couldn't dance that evening. He was about to argue when CN sailed in, looking perfectly regal and cold as an iceberg—purple velvet dress and heavenly white hair. I resolved not to let CN leave us alone for a second all evening. I simply hated him. He wanted to sit on the sofa and talk to me in a low voice, but I got out the crossword puzzle book and made the three of us work over it together. He was mad, but sat beside me while I held the book. CN got out a dictionary and began to look up some words. Once, while she was engrossed—and the dear thing is as blind as a bat and as unsuspicious as a baby kitten—he reached over, took a hold of my arm with one hand and put his other over my hand and pressed it. I simply shuddered—however, pretended not even to notice that anything had happened, got up and went over to sit on the piano stool. Then he didn't go and didn't go for ghastly hours, and when finally he rose, he said to CN, "Aren't you going to let me take her out sometime?" CN is terribly softhearted and she sort of stammered. But I was frightened she would relent and said, "You see, Cousin Nell, I know just how you feel—you hate to restrict me and yet you know that my parents have never allowed me to go out alone with a man, even in the afternoons. It's rather hard but I know you'd feel happier if we respect their wishes." He looked at me as though I were an idiot. I didn't go to the door with him. Ugh— Kate, you know, we may be wicked girls when the climate or the circumstances lay the scene, but we have pretty darn super-high standards for men and ideals of them. There are men—such as we know them, with all their noblenesses and their failings—and then there are beasts. Heaven keep us from the latter.

IT WAS INEVITABLE—Dorothy's old flame Erd would sooner or later acquire a new love and word of her would surely travel across the Atlantic. When the fateful news finally arrived in a letter from another friend, Dorothy was surprised that it didn't throw her. That meant, she figured, that she was truly free of Erd's spell, especially now that she could see his faults so plainly.

"The new girl had just been out on a wonderful party with Erd— theater, dancing afterward, etc., and he evidently made it pretty exciting for her," my mother wrote:

It's his darn physical attractiveness and his peculiar flash of mind. Of course, he told her about all the little girls' hearts he had broken (omitting yours truly, I believe, for safety's sake) and confided his hopes and aspirations and danced like a god and looked at her with his periwinkle blue eyes—and the poor girl is miserable, I can tell. He's just playing with her for an odd moment as a relaxation from the Bible, but she is allured in spite of herself. I'm sure he has no intention of being serious with her any more than he had with me—and if she could just come over to Paris for a month, she'd thank her lucky stars. Because here the kick fades,

and from what is left you know that never, never, never would it
work—he's too thoughtless and ministerial and impractical—
not counting the coarse streak in him which we all admit.

Back home, Kate was having a few man problems of her own, and
through the mail was seeking help from her friend in Paris. The two had
been giving each other advice for years, each setting very high standards
for the other. It was almost like preaching. Now it was Dorothy's turn
to restate what they had chosen to believe, to caution Kate from taking
second best and making a mistake from which, my mother was sure, it
would be difficult for her friend to recover:

I read every word of what you said about Don with the greatest
interest. Don't do it, Katie—hold on and on to the bitter end,
which I hope is not going to be bitter at all for either of us, but
glorious. I know now I'm never going to take anything which
could have a suspicion of being second best—it's going to com-
prise all my highest dreams, or else not be at all. I can't imagine
Don doing that for you. I have this weak and selfish feeling now
that if only I had the right person to share things with I could
bear—and also dare—anything.

AS IF TO GROUND Dorothy's twinkling Paris life and her speculation on
future bliss, an occasional letter from Phil arrived. He was attending Harvard Business School and coaching the freshman football team. Dorothy
had written him and although he had heard she was "blue," he didn't believe it because her letter bubbled over so. Her vivid description of her life-
drawing class with its naked models sounded to him like a "slave market."
And her invitation to meet up when she returned to America was enticing:

What a poor nut you are—if you will pardon me for saying so—
for ever doubting I would like to return to Chester in the future!
I honestly think it was a way of fishing. Well, you have caught
your fish this time, and if you could only pull the long line in, he
would lie flopping at your feet.

Phil then carefully explained the workings of his father's woolen mill
and just what the mill overseer was—a boss who was in charge of two
hundred workers in the weave room. The current overseer was more
than seventy years old, he explained, and his father had offered the job
to him. "I have many fears but golly, I hope I'll be up to the job. Pray for
me to make good."

I have no idea how my mother felt about the details of the mill—I
doubt, though, that she was much interested. It was my father's "niceness" that struck her, as she told Kate:

I've had a nice letter from Phil Kunhardt, rather childish, but
straightforward and wholly refreshing, so full of solid niceness.
Nothing has given me as much pleasure in a long time.

Although the pursuit of a man and marriage were never far from
Dorothy's mind, Phil was not yet an important factor in her scheme as
she waited for "the supreme moment, when it comes, of your ultimate
choice of a husband." To Kate, she wrote:

As Christmas comes along, I, of course, long more than ever for
New York. But, strangely enough, for a manless New York. I
haven't given Erd or George or Larry or Carl or Bob or any one
of those worthies a thought since a week ago today, just about. I
have glorious Paris and every reason to be happy, and nothing to

keep me from coming home when I want to. I won't be pitied, when I'm to be envied. I have almost everything. Why weep because at the age of twenty-two and twenty-three, we haven't attained life's crowning joy? Oh, why weren't you a man, darn you—or why wasn't I?

To celebrate New Year's Eve, my mother and Cousin Nell visited the Rodin museum. Later, she described for Kate how the sculptor's works had deeply stirred her:

I noticed that all the marble Rodin had carved represented the love of men and women so beautifully and tenderly that it almost hurt me to look—as it was meant to, I suppose. When we got out, Cousin Nell said in a cold and rather shocked and suppressed voice, "Did you notice," and then she said just what I noted above. And I thought, how lucky it is that I have had some of that divine love—tasted in little sips—for short times—and never really has the joy been supreme, as it will be when the right person comes. But at least I can respond to things such as Rodin's pure and glad white figures, and not shrivel up inside me as Cousin Nell does—disappointed, alone, shocked by this young beauty. It's not that I shall do again the things I have done—but I regret nothing, nothing, nothing. I'm only grateful for every moment I have had—even for Mac on that dark evening in Singapore.

In another letter Dorothy referred to creaking, rheumatic Cousin Nell again and warned her friend:

Sip every minute of golden youth while you have it, Kate. Age is a cold, pitiful thing, if it isn't a warm and glorious one, and there's always just the chance that things will slip up and it will be the former.

Looking at Cousin Nell, my mother felt conflicted—on the one hand, she was sorry for her aged companion; on the other, she saw her as an example of what a vacant wreck a loveless life could leave behind:

Her frozen spinster life has made her into something utterly uncompromising, with standards and desires that are as high and as low as her life alone has made them. I have become accustomed now to living with her day after day—and never telling her anything I think—except the everyday chaff. For instance, the other day she was reading a book—a normal book—and out of a clear sky she put it down and said, "Oh, I think this lovemaking is all too disgusting. Why can't we multiply from spores, like leaves and trees?" (or some other such unscientific remark). I always laugh at things like that and say, "Oh, no, I don't think that would be any fun at all." And then she with her purest, arctic air will say, "You're a strange child, Dorothy. You've a lot to learn." Silence. Silence. And then we'll talk about what we think there will be for dinner. My theory is this: This winter will show me one thing among many. One has to marry—to live forever with—above all, someone with whom one has tastes and thoughts and desires in common.

EVEN AS SHE was enjoying her life and her art classes, my mother was struggling with the idea of being a writer. She had been:

trying to write something other than letters—a story, perhaps—but alas, although I worked eight solid hours on Sunday here at my little desk, I destroyed everything in rage at the end. I'm simply rotten, that's all there is to it—but, still, I'm burning with a strange fever to create something—and I can hardly eat or sleep for the heat of it. Isn't that a joke—I don't think I've ever really felt that way before.

Then on January 11, 1925, she finished a poem. "The Dreaming Game" consisted of nineteen four-line stanzas, and told the story of a girl and her friend Nicolette. The poem was an ode to my mother's great friendship with Kate, a friendship born of innocence and nurtured by their shared passions and curiosities and their adventure to the Orient. It also reflected DM and her unique way of thinking.

As little girls, the poem's narrator and Nicolette play what they call "The Dreaming Game":

Then both of us will close our eyes and let our memories
Just drift away and come upon whatever thing they please,
And I may think of prune juice, and summer clothes and trees
And you may think of paper boats and why one has to sneeze.

Then one of us will call out "Time"—you may have reached
the sea
While I may be in Switzerland just learning how to ski—
You'll tell me then I'll tell you, and that will be the game
Our Dreaming Game, she called it, and we've always kept
the name.

As the poem continues, the years pass and the two little girls grow up and drift far apart—yet they still play the game and now write their dreams to each other:

I'm in China and it's springtime and the rice fields are all green
(I am starting from the rice field, Nicolette knows what I mean)
I'm dreaming now of temples, with roofs of shining gold—
The priests are wearing jeweled robes, so stiff they will not fold.

There is incense in the temples, there's a laughing Buddha there
And the candlelight is shifting on the lacquer everywhere.
It makes me think of amber, glowing honey-warm and clear—
And rickshaws—and the devils that the little children fear.

Massive walls that clamber over all the treeless mountaintops—
A woman with her feet still bound—she walks in little hops—
Gigantic coolie hats of straw, with saucy pointed peaks
And beggars whom a quarter would feed for twenty weeks.

My mother ended her poem with snow falling on China in winter. And the final stanza brought her story full circle, and gave it meaning:

With snow, my lovely Nicolette, is ended this my dream
For snow, like many things, is not what it would seem:
It's only water in the end—my dream has vanished too—
But it will never leave me quite; for it has gone to you.

My mother was pleased enough with her China poem that she sent it off to her parents to show she was accomplishing something, and also enclosed some of her figure studies. Her father, who was footing the bill for her and Cousin Nell's trip to Paris, received the verse on January 26, 1925, and began a letter of reply which would be written in fits and starts over the next few days. An amateur poet and an author in his own right, the kindly, firm, opinionated man started out by admonishing his daughter for her letter pagination:

Dear Dot,

First, why can't you do as I have asked so many times and write your letters on sheets numbered as book pages—and not backward and forward. A woman who can't write straight letters is far worse than a man, who doesn't generally know much any-how. Second, I quote, "I now want to come back where I belong and begin to lead a normal life of some sort again." But as you did not lead a normal life before, that word *again* disturbs me. There is substance for a large juicy sermon here. You must look Mr. Re-form in the face and not gaze at his back hair. What I really have in mind is that measly church-visiting business. Your mother says, "Pish tush, it does some good." I say, "Tush pish, it does no good." My philosophy is perhaps different but I am convinced it is right. Sooner or later people with responsibilities come to my opinion.

I continue at lunch. Sooner or later you are to use your knowl-edge. Bryn Mawr. World. Paris. Sorbonne. Art. People, etc. Even if you marry, you will still hope to use it—or stagnate. Why use it? There are two answers: I) To earn money II) To kill time if you do not need money. If a female marries she will have her hands full if she is sensibly normal. If she does not marry she will be more or less misanthropic (more so as time goes on) or she must work or go mad—too many go mad because they can't find the work. Me, I prefer marriage, provided the wife does not have to be a breadwinner or suffer because the natural breadwinner is slothful or incompetent.

You sneer at my ideas and turn up your nice elegant nose at my advice. I don't care. I shall go on in my own way trying to publish to a select audience some of the things I *know*.

As for painting, I had no clue you would learn about it, or that you would be a painter. But if you find that you like line better than color, you have got so much to the good. Both take a lifetime of practice and only the few get practiced enough in a short lifetime to amount to anything whatever. The life class is largely piffle as you will see in retrospect. One out of a hundred can ever get any art out of it, although the other ninety-nine make screaming copies. There is more demand for line than daub. After all, the demand creates the supply, and no sensible person learns to draw who does not see in the future a market price for his wares.

The drawings are here. For quick work, they are interesting but not marked as "excellent." Better than I could do, which is not high praise. You could not have done it when you began, however, and the drawings show the "style" of the atelier. Many thanks.

Up to this point in the letter, Dorothy must have been extremely disappointed at her father's harsh criticism, his lecturing tone, his unbending stiffness, and the practical, financial lens through which he looked at her experiences in Paris. Frederick adored his daughter but he saw her slipping away into the kind of loose and undisciplined attitudes and actions he abhorred. So he would put her straight. Fortunately, he had some kinder words as he drew to a close:

But the jingles about China are a different story. They are not polished enough to publish, but they carry a story, and have vision or imagination. I got deep enjoyment from them. I still think you can sling a wicked pen and get some enjoyment too. Enjoyment from working, whether in words or line or teaching or even typewriting comes in proportion to the recompense. Ha! I can see you sniff—Pop's materialism! Wait till you have four good-sized spenders to support. Wait till you learn by experience! Forgive my bad scrawls but I really have had to write this in specks and spots. Love to Nell.

Affectionately, Father

Reading this letter from my grandfather when he was fifty-nine, to his twenty-three-year-old daughter, made me realize anew how much they needed each other. In hopes of his blessing she had sent her best accomplishments for him to judge. And judge he did, as he loved to do, pulling no punches. Later in life their roles would reverse, with my mother in command and her father seeking her blessing. But even then, the need each had for the other's support was just as strong.

FOR MARCH and half of April, Dorothy toured Italy with her mother's relatives, marveling at the towns and amphitheaters, "whose stones cry out from past generations," and describing the oranges as "galumptuous." Yet she was restless. Often she was constricted by her older and more conservative traveling companions:

I can never let down and be my natural foolish doubting self about the world. I can never jump on the bed and shriek, "What is life? Give it to me, oh, Allah!" I must always say, "I think we had better wear hats into the dining room, this is a big hotel and I think it is a little nicer."

Calling herself a "piece of proverbial driftwood," she wrote to Kate: "Isn't it astonishing—one can never escape from anything one has done."

On the Italian Riviera:

The sun is hot and I could tell myself that I am at peace and completely happy. Well, I am—and ought to be—but there is something in me that burns and hurts and longs for something it can't name. I suppose when that burning thing goes out, one is old and life is over.

From Casino, my mother wrote to Phil of her mounting nervousness about coming home soon and, upon her return to Paris, there were letters awaiting her from Cambridge explaining that she was probably just scared to return home because of all the decisions to be made. My father, in turn, was excited about the decisions looming in his life. In one of her letters, Dorothy had coyly tossed out what she called one of her truly difficult decisions—choosing between Mr. Smith and Mr. Jones for marriage. Phil replied that he'd like to see them. He would be in New York City during the summer ahead, would have easy access to Chester, and, "I shall be interested, purely scientifically you understand, in watching the progress of Mr. Smith and Mr. Jones."

Phil couldn't meet my mother's ship when it docked in New York in early May, but he wrote, "I am very, very anxious to see you again."

Dorothy must have been anxious, too, for she was able to arrange to accompany her father on a business trip to Boston and Phil was treated to dinner and the theater and "a peach of a time." He thought her father to be "a corker from way back," and for the first time his letters began to talk seriously about his affection for her:

> I want to tell you how seeing you again has so filled my heart with joy that it has kept bubbling over at different times today in chuckles and chortles of mirth.

By mid-June Dorothy was confiding to Kate her latest thinking on love:

> You've got to marry someone who understands not only the conventional happy side of your life—the life all our little friends have lived—but also the mystery and the passion, the restraint, the fury, the calm, the lure, and the subtleties of things that you and I have just begun to guess at. I do believe it is possible to fall in love with quite a range of people—witness me. But I truly am sure that there is also in the world that old fairy-tale "one love," that belonging togetherness that brings rare happiness.

Kate realized what Dorothy did not yet—that her friend was falling in love with Phil. After a Fourth of July weekend house party in Chester, she suggested that underlying my mother's plans for all their crowded parties was, "the subtle intent of having enough people to cover your and Phil's tracks." Dorothy, in turn, gradually began to concede what was happening:

> I feel like a bedraggled and soiled woman of the world beside him; not only could he disapprove of a great deal in our lives, but

also it would not interest him. He hasn't enough background to see points of resemblance between our pasts and his. Therefore, he would rather think of fishing and riding and football and dogs and business, than Europe and the East and people, as we do. He would kill me in a week, I guess, physically, because he has the energy of a racehorse and is relentless in what he thinks girls ought to be able to do. However, he is an exceptionally fine boy and I think a lovable one; I'm not sure yet. Not that he has made it necessary to write you Day's End, but I have a feeling, just from nothing at all really, that in the future, sometime this summer, he may fall in love with me.

During the Fourth of July weekend, probably while they were sitting on the pillowed glider on the great porch at Chester on Saturday evening, Dorothy let it slip that she cared for Phil. And he whispered something in her ear. Was it "I love you"? By July 8, three days after he had left Chester, Phil wrote:

If your letter had not come today I should have been a wild man. When I saw it on my desk, I was almost scared to open it—for some crazy reason you do like me and thought quite highly of the glorious evening I spent with you on the porch.

Dorothy confessed to being stricken with unhappiness, weeping for hours. "You must know," Phil wrote back, "that every great happiness is arrived at through a good deal of struggle and pain." And then, finally, Dorothy having made it clear to him that she really and truly cared for him, for the first time Phil could write honestly of his emotion:

Dot, Dot, how can I ever really tell you that you've moved the very core of my soul? The sea roars in, phosphorous white, and the storm rolls up dark and ominous, but you and I sit together with splendor about our heads, the splendor of a mighty love.

I VISITED CHESTER often in my youth; I'll get to that later in this story, but right here I must jump ahead, past my birth, to a hot summer's Chester day when I was little and my family was spending a weekend with my mother's family. When it was hot at home, we could always swim in our old stone pool, and I remember I was complaining at not being home now, it was boiling so. My mother took me by the hand and led me down the long lane and through the cornfield and into the trees beyond, and pretty soon we came upon a little brook. I took off my shoes and waded and even found a deep hole beneath a tree stump where I could stand in the cold water up to my shorts.

My mother was gazing about a glade nearby, wandering out of the trees to a little field, letting the long grass whisk at her skirts, and commenting on how the sunlight lit the leaves. She seemed to be searching for something. When I emerged from the brook and followed her, my mother told me, "This is where it happened. Right here on this spot. This is where Dad and I got engaged. He needed a little help bringing up the subject of marriage," she continued, and then trailed off.

For a moment, I tried to picture the scene back then, but I couldn't, and soon I'd almost forgotten that I'd been shown this grassy spot, so sacred in my parents' lives. But remembering it today allows me to draw a picture in my mind as I read my mother's Day's End letter of July 27, 1925, to Kate:

Now, here comes something which I still don't believe is true. I think I'm writing in a dream from which I shall soon wake up. See if you think it sounds real. I am engaged to Phil. Oh, Katie, I'd give anything, anything, to have you here now to tell you all about it. But from what I can gather out of my dazed condition, here are the facts. We took a walk in the woods—a long way— and at the end of it we stood in a little field, with cedar trees around, and sweet fern, and the afternoon sun just lighting the underside of all the leaves. He asked me if I would marry him. Well, the long and the short of it is that we talked it all over this weekend from every angle. He loves me very, very much. And strangely enough (strangely only because I thought my heart was stone forever), I love him.

2.

"The Most Fortunate Two People on Earth"

Phil and Dorothy on their
Virginia honeymoon, April 1926

M Y MOTHER WAS STUNNED by her sudden engagement. This was what she had been dreaming of for years, finding the right person with whom to spend the rest of her life. But this right person had materialized so rapidly—and in the form of a young man whose qualities had not been high on her list only a few months before—that even with all her presence of mind and her usual tight grip upon her world, she was thrown for a loop.

"It's something quiet and suddenly strong, and it's come all at once," she tried to explain to Kate:

Can you believe it? I can't. He gave me his gold football, which I must keep well hidden from my family. Katie, I know if you could have been here, you would say it is making no mistake. I don't know what he wants such a worn-out, used piece of goods like myself for, when he is youth, ideals, and freshness personified, but he seems to.

The sudden turn of events was thrilling to my father. He had long hoped that he would meet the perfect girl and that they would fall in love, but Dorothy was beyond anybody he could possibly have imagined. He was not deserving of her, he kept repeating.

"I have been appalled ever since last Saturday at my utter unworthiness for such a blessing," Phil wrote Kate. "But as DM said with a wonderful twinkle in her eye—that was for her to decide."

On receiving the news, Kate had immediately responded:

Dearest, dearest, beloved DM,
I wish you were here so that I could see you and touch you and make sure you are as happy as I want you to be. I do so utterly want you to have heaven on earth, my adorable elfin Dot.

Just a week after his proposal, my father was back in Chester, and after an intense discussion between the lovebirds it was decided that Phil should speak to Dorothy's father and mother, "under vows of secrecy." My mother wrote Kate all about it:

Well, last night he did it. Father was darling! Mother was awful— ranted about and said under no circumstances must there be an engagement, that Phil didn't know me, that I was the most changeable girl in the world and had already thought I was in love with a dozen men and he might as well know it now. She called Phil a mere boy and said he couldn't possibly know his mind—was really quite insulting, I felt. However, Phil was very contained and courteous and said of course, if Mrs. Meserve felt that way it would have to be left as she wished for the time. As he said to me afterward, it doesn't really make any difference to us what we call it.

Similar opposition to the union was gathering steam at the Kunhardt estate in North Andover, Massachusetts. When Phil broke the news to his parents, neither was happy. Their principal objection was the fact that he made almost no money and was in no position to support a wife and family. But there were other reasons, too. Phil's mother, Martha Kunhardt—"Mingie" to her children—had been suffocating her younger son his whole life and didn't want him leaving the nest, even at twenty-five. His father, George E. Kunhardt, who would be known as "Guppa" to his grandchildren, had been teaching Phil the woolen business since he was a boy and saw marriage getting in the way of his master plan. Phil's older, more independent brother, Jack, had married without his father's advice or consent, and the sudden intrusion of love had certainly interfered with Jack's single-minded dedication to the firm. If George E. could help it, Phil wasn't going to follow that same route. In August of 1925, George E. wrote the Meserves to that effect and, soon after, Dorothy conveyed the letter's contents to Kate:

A very discouraging letter came to Father from Mr. Kunhardt, miles long—typewritten—very open and frank—very clear in what he felt about it all. He said he ought to make his standing known—it was that he wished the young people had waited longer before they engaged themselves, that he was not at all in favor of the idea of wedding bells for Phil for a good many years yet, that business was driving him wild with worry and it would not even begin to hold its own for three years.

Earlier that year, Phil had been offered the job of assistant dean of the Harvard Graduate School of Business. Even though the field of education would have been an ideal profession for the convivial, studious twenty-four-year-old, his father had put pressure on him not to take it and to work instead for the family business. Just as he had browbeaten his son into working at the mill during his school and college summer vacations—one summer learning to weave, another in the carding and spinning departments, still another in the dye-house, and others in the cost department and the general office—now Guppa made it clear that if Phil wanted to inherit his part of the family business, he'd better come aboard upon his graduation from Harvard. In contrast, Jack took a strong stand in favor of the dean position, writing Phil a long, thoughtful, and persuasive family demur:

> In the first place, you went to Groton because your family sent you there. The same with Harvard. This is a family-owned business. You have been brought up in it. I am in it and everything tends to draw you into it. Now you have been offered a job entirely on your own merits, with no influence from family or tradition. Assistant dean in the best school of its kind in the country. For heaven's sake, take it. Don't let Father decide the matter for you. To get out of the rut of Groton, Harvard, business school, and a family mill, take the dean's job and make good. It is a job you have earned and one you deserve.

Everything seemed to favor this exciting new offer, especially since Phil could work as assistant dean for two years and then return to the family business if he so chose. Still, whether it was dreams of money and business glory or an inability to strike out on his own, he allowed himself to be manipulated by his tough father into a world whose details would eventually stultify his brain. And now his father was also attempting to keep him from the marriage he so desired.

But there were some reasons for hope. Even though Dorothy's mother had been so opposed, Phil was taking courage in her father's kindly acceptance of him:

> Remember how your father spoke, how he seemed to understand how we feel, and knew that we weren't children, but have minds of our own and love each other with the strong, pure, and lasting love of early manhood and womanhood? This is no mere passing fancy of a thoughtless college boy and a flapper, but has entered into the very core of our beings, and that is why it has such a noble, such a holy, touch to it.

Fred was on their side. Maybe he thought back to his in-laws' initial opposition to his own engagement. Maybe he was just wise in human assessment. In any case, he invited my father to lunch and brought out a fresh burst of joy from Phil to his fiancée:

> He is really the best man that ever lived in this world! You may guess that I met him shaking in my shoes; and when, after we were duly seated, he stated that he had taken advantage of me and asked me with an ulterior motive, I came near slipping under the table.

But there was nothing to fear. Fred had spent the last week working Edith over so that now she, too, was an ally to their cause and would welcome Phil to Chester "with open arms."

Kate was another strong supporter. Immediately upon getting the word from Dorothy, she had written Phil a kindly letter of congratulation on his great catch. And as the one-month anniversary of their engagement neared, Phil and Dorothy were also buoyed by a letter from Jack.

"It has come to my ears that Dad does not want Dot's and your engagement announced," wrote Jack:

> Pardon an unsolicited opinion, but here it is: announce your engagement whenever Dot wishes. It is a shame and disgrace to connect love and business in the same judgment of a situation. Love is enduring, and above such embarrassments as the making of money and the fleeting success or distress of business.

Although Phil felt obligated to his father for everything he had in life, this was the moment, he agreed, to break free of his father's whims, and he promised Dorothy the engagement would be announced by November.

But then he hesitated. He put the confrontation with his father off. Autumn approached but there were still no mutual family visits and no engagement announcement. From the Harvard Club in New York City, he wrote Dorothy:

> Another waking to empty-armed yearning has strengthened me in my resolution to go up to North Andover and talk to my father as man to man, not as browbeaten youngster to his lord and master. I must speak that way to him or I shall never get out from under the cloud. I shall try to do it in a way that won't make him blow up, but whatever the consequences, I am going ahead. I think that you may really start thinking of January, for I am going to marry you then, my dear love, if I have to move heaven and earth.

As for my mother, the months that followed Phil's proposal and her acceptance were a blur of excitement and anxiety. She was well aware of the quandary into which Phil had been thrown, but instead of coming unstuck as her mother warned she would, her intentions only became firmer. Weekends and sometimes weeknights, Phil turned up at Chester, where they could sneak out on the porch after dinner and hold hands and kiss. Then he would disappear back into the city to his job as a salesman of woolen goods in the New York headquarters of his father's firm, spending his nights in a garret on Eleventh Avenue in midtown that the company rented for its frequent visitors from the Lawrence Mill. An almost daily stream of letters from Phil told Dorothy over and over how much he loved her and how miserable he was when they were apart.

Even without the Kunhardts' blessing, my parents started to privately inform their close relations and friends of their plans. Dorothy must have been struck by the intensity of feeling her future husband elicited from almost anyone receiving the news. Garry Norton, Phil's best friend from Groton and a Harvard roommate, was "turning handsprings," Phil told her. Bobby Bradford, Phil's other Harvard roommate, wrote to Dorothy directly, asking whether she, in such a short time, could really appreciate "this great, big, lovable, wolfhound puppy who has been playing and working with me for the last five years." Phil's younger sister, Hildegard, who was studying at Vassar, thought her brother to be "the most sympathetic, understanding, many-sided person that ever was." She wrote Phil, "I always compare all men to you and they always fall so short." Phil's idol, the founder and headmaster of Groton School, Endicott Peabody, known to everyone as "The Rector," wrote: "I am glad for you, dear Boy. My love and congratulations. I also congratulate Miss Meserve. Tell her by this choice of hers she has obtained one who will be steadfast and true."

Dorothy's future sister-in-law, Jack's wife, Joan, wrote to Dorothy from Ilkley, in Yorkshire, England, where her husband was being schooled in Scottish wool design and weaving techniques. "One doesn't generally congratulate the girl, I know, but if the lucky man happens to be a Phil Kunhardt, one does."

All agreed, mixing Phil's solid and true qualities of character with Dorothy's quixotic brilliance and sensitivity could make quite a brew.

"Dearest love, it comes over me more and more what a good working combination we are going to make," my father wrote in one of his almost daily epistles to his future bride:

> Our ideas on the basic things in life are identical. In other ways, we should make good counterparts for each other (that gives me an easier job than you, because you are so many-sided and I am not); in situations of understandings between people, emotions and prejudices, and all that side of personal relations you have the rarest insight and ability. In situations more impersonal, perhaps requiring rapid action, I believe I can help.

ON OCTOBER 30, my father mailed off a carefully written letter to North Andover, telling his father that he planned to marry Dorothy in April of 1926. He was sorry if this displeased his father, but his mind was made up. He listed the reasons why, and said he would soon be up for a talk.

Two days later, in the privacy of his library, George E. Kunhardt began composing his answer. If Phil pursued his present course, his father saw "nothing in the future but disappointments and anguish and perhaps worse":

First of all, I am very positive that it is not for the best for a young man to persuade a young woman to marriage unless he can support her in a measure that she has been brought up to regard as necessities of life. In your letter you refer to a generous allowance from Mr. Meserve. Such an allowance to Dorothy should be hers for luxuries and charities, not for maintenance expenses.

This was a "very trying time" in his life, George E. said, with ill health coming on top of the economic decline of the family business. Phil's present salary of $1,800 a year could easily just vanish. Even if it didn't, it might take years for his son to prove himself and make a higher salary. "I have much faith in you, Phil," his father concluded, "but it will take time and I think April is far too early for you to consider marriage." George recommended postponing the event until the spring of 1927, instead—a year and a half away. He also had suggestions tailored for each member of the young couple:

You, Dorothy, make a study of some useful occupation to which you will devote your time and thoughts this winter and you, Phil, in the assurance of Dorothy's love, let that strengthen and encourage you to your best efforts to equipping yourself for real work and real responsibility in a vocation you have chosen and a heritage that your father has spent the best of his life for all his children.

He signed his letter, "Affectionately, Father."

Two days later, on November 3, Phil's mother tried to soften the blow and yet support her intransigent husband:

In regard to your letter to Dad which he showed me—it was a sweet, lovely letter from a son to a father but I fear you have not convinced him. He loves Dorothy, but he wants to give you a good send-off and this he does not feel able to do. You must know what the business situation is, that there is a chance now of failing. In talking to Dad try to consider his side, too. After all, the decision is for a lifetime—a few months do not count so much.

Phil's younger sister, Hildegard, thought differently:

What has Dad written you now—something discouraging, no doubt. Hell's bells, anyways! He's the darndest man. I suppose he can't be changed now. Of course, he's a wonder and all that but, golly, I think he's narrow-minded.

Days later, my father went to North Andover, made it clear that he was not going to back down on the April date, and left. It had taken him four months to work up the courage to stand up to his judgmental and controlling father. It took a few more weeks for the Kunhardts to acknowledge his decision. On November 30, his mother wrote:

You must realize, Phil dear, that we love you and Dad was only giving you his advice. Of course, we are going to gracefully accept your decision to be married in April.

Very few words on paper were exchanged between the families after the capitulation. Christmas came and went. Dorothy celebrated with her family in New York and Phil returned home to undergo his final Christmas festivities in North Andover. Although his parents had dropped their opposition, they seemed withdrawn, in sharp contrast to the high spirits of Phil's siblings, who were enamored of Dorothy and couldn't wait for the wedding bells.

Invitations were mailed to over six hundred people on March 16, a mere three weeks before the wedding date—Saturday, April 10—and during that time a steady stream of presents began to arrive at the Meserve home at 148 East Seventy-eighth Street, including a two-hundred-piece silver service in a lined mahogany box from Dorothy's parents, a number of Liberty bonds from the elder Kunhardts, a check from Kate for a later purchase of antique chairs, and a magnificent desk from Kate's parents. In all, there would be 429 presents to the bride.

Just ten days before the wedding, my father had not yet settled on a honeymoon spot. One of his Harvard roommates, Bob Bradford, from Boston, came to the rescue by suggesting a riding farm in Trevilians, Virginia. Phil's letter requesting reservations was answered in the affirmative—"fifty dollars a week per person, including room and board and saddle horses."

The wedding was held at 4:00 p.m. at the Madison Avenue Presbyterian Church, followed by a reception in the ballroom of the ultra-chic Colony Club. Because Dorothy's mother was a confirmed teetotaler, having taken an oath as a young girl never to let her lips touch liquor, nothing stronger than fruit punch was served. As was normal back then, no photographer was present, so there are none of the pictures of wedding scenes to which we have become so accustomed—the bride and groom with both sets of parents, with the bridesmaids and ushers, cutting the cake, or dancing their first dance. The only photographs to commemorate the day were taken weeks earlier in the Fifth Avenue studio of the Misses Selby, where my mother posed in her new knee-length, creamy white satin French wedding dress with its full lace train, and her fragile antique lace veil.

Six days after the wedding, writing his new father-in-law from their Virginia honeymoon hideaway, Phil shed a little light on the events of the wedding service which, at Dorothy's request, had excluded the word "obey":

Never have I beheld anything so lovely as Dot when you led her towards me down the aisle last Saturday. My heart was filled with such a great and enduring love and such a mighty thankfulness that, while we were being married, my one prayer was that I might be worthy of this beautiful girl you were giving me, might serve and protect her and might make a success of life for her sake. I feel sure that the Great Spirit hovered over us and blessed us as we stood up there together.

One of the most vivid of lasting impressions of the wedding that Dot and I have is your expression as we turned around to go down the aisle. It is a very wonderful thing for a boy to see such an expression upon the face of the father who has just given away his daughter. That you could be so happy in giving Dottie to me is one of the greatest compliments I have ever received. I shall always strive to bring about the expectations you have of me.

For her part, Dorothy wrote to Kate from the riding farm in Virginia—"an old ramshackle farm," as she called it, describing the honeymoon:

We had to run like hunted bunnies to catch the train—and we just caught it by the skin of our eyelids. We got to Washington about five and went to the Mayflower Hotel. The next day we deserted the bright lights of the city for this divine spot in the country. To-day I am in bed with the curse—nasty old blight—and the fruit trees are in blossom; the sun is warm enough to have burnt us both to a crisp. We ride over the hillsides together all day long, or walk in the pine woods—and are terribly, gorgeously happy. There really is nothing else like it in the world, Katie, the utter joy of companionship with the man whom you love and with whom you are going to spend your life.

Phil is quite the darlingest, most thoughtful person I could ever have imagined. Every time I look at him I am terribly proud to think that he belongs to me. We lie on pine needles in the sunlight in the woods and watch the clouds go by and he tells me how much he likes Dorothy and about all the books he has read and the things he has done and the dreams he has dreamed, and the things we are going to do together. He is very wonderful, Katie.

IN MAY, fresh from her honeymoon, my mother wrote Kate in Paris describing her new life and its new priorities, painting a vivid picture of my parents' first days as man and wife:

You wouldn't believe *I* was *I* if you saw me now. Here it is in a small nutshell. At 7:00 a.m. the alarm clock rings and we both leap up from a dead sleep. Phil dashes into the kitchen and puts on the coffee. Then he rushes back and spends a good twenty minutes snorting and blowing and roaring in an ice-cold tub and shower. I am supposed to have given myself a lick and a promise and jumped into an article of clothing or two. Then I come in and set the table with all its numerous little dishes and salt shakers, egg cups and whatnots that I've always used but never knew existed—you know how it is—then I concoct various materials so that when Phil comes in at ten minutes to eight looking like a shiny May morning, he will find waiting for him coffee and cream and sugar, toast (very hot), butter and honey, cereal, two boiled eggs, and bacon.

At 8:30 he leaves for business and then I set to like a streak of lightning or whatever else it is that works speedily, and by eleven o'clock I have finished washing the dishes and cleaning the pots and pans and the kitchen in general, sweeping and mopping the floors, dusting, and oh, I forgot to mention making the bed—I'm still a bit clumsy at managing such a great unwieldy object. Then I wash and iron any little things like handkerchiefs and good underclothes or Phil's socks and stow them away. Then I depart for the big outer world with a market basket under my arm, and come home laden with all that the best chain stores can provide.

We are really getting along beautifully. Phil came over just then and had to have his head rubbed, he's just like a pussycat. How I wish you were here to play with me.

During that first spring and summer of marriage, my father was traveling a lot, trying to sell his family's woolen goods to customers in Rochester, Chicago, and Philadelphia. His notes back to Dorothy alternate between plaintive bleats about being separated and avowals of eternal love and celebrations of their new domestic life together. One nighttime departure from Grand Central made him envision her just above his train in the tunnel:

Right now we must be going almost under you as you lie upon your little warm bed where you were so darling, sweet, and loving to me. Good night, my little wifelet. May God bless you and keep you. And may He grant that I may always live nobly for thy glory, my sweet.

In a letter from Rochester, Phil called Dorothy by a new name—hers, spelled backward—yhtorod—part of the private, intimate language the young couple was developing. In another letter from the road, he referred to himself as "your Mowgli," a name Dorothy had begun calling him, after the man-cub raised by wolves in Kipling's *The Jungle Book*.

Most business trips were discouraging, producing very few orders, but some days my father was caught up in his work:

I am right on the "firing line" getting to know our biggest customers and handling the cloths from their original conception. When these men come to New York I shall be able to show them how we have developed their ideas. In fact, I am now in on everything. The more I can learn this way the sooner I shall be able to contribute definitely and the more worth I shall be to the concern.

Back home, my mother was settling into a new life—a life very different from that of the world-traveling artistic dreamer she had been fast becoming over the past two years. Even though she had always envisioned that her Day's End love affair would deal with great truths and moral insights, she did not seem taken aback now to be learning that marriage was mostly made up of the plain and the ordinary. Yet, she seemed happy. To Kate, she wrote:

I spend most of my time knitting socks for Phil. It has become a perfect passion with me now to keep my husband in stockings. He went off to the office this morning in a pair of green woolen masterpieces created by my own ten fingers, and four steel needles. I hope he doesn't return all blistered this evening. I know if he did he would swear it wasn't the socks, it was just the great heat of the New York sidewalks which has sizzled through the shoes. He gets more angelic every day, Katie—you simply wouldn't believe how nice mortal man can be.

In September came the first mention of pregnancy, and the name Mowgli took on new significance. From Baltimore my father wondered, "How is Mowgli? Kicking?" Two weeks later, with Dorothy in Chester with her parents, he elaborated, writing from a desk in New York's Harvard Club:

I often think of my little baby in his dark warm home and wonder that a little thing like you can be so plucky as to face it all with the smile you do. When he or she is here we shall be immensely happy. But now with all the unpleasant kickings and changing of a most beautiful form you have more nerve than all the fellows on a football team put together.

I am writing from the same corner where I penned an incoherent scrawl last summer just after you first showed me that you might care for me. What a glorious change to now. Dottie is my wifelet, and her love is swift, hot, wonderful, limitless whereas before it couldn't even be guessed at.

Soon, my mother was describing her pregnant state to Kate, charting her morning sickness, which she had decided to call seasickness, and urging Kate to find someone to marry soon: "Being married is really all that mortals in this world could ask of joy and content—at least being married to Phil is."

Still, not far from the surface of marital joy, my mother's old urge to write was percolating. She had no idea what she wanted to say or what form her written words might take, but she knew she was not willing to have marriage and children obliterate the need to create. In her final 1926 communication to Kate, she reflected:

You and I both know what fun it is to build things out of words. You do it far better than I. I can play with jingles, you could toy with greater inventions of the mind, if that's what it is that makes them. Our poor Bryn Mawr constructed round-the-world-molded minds—they ought to be able to afford us some amusement, now that traveling days are done.

ON JANUARY 21, 1927, nine months and eleven days after her wedding, Dorothy gave birth to her first child—my sister Nancy. The Sloane Hospital for Women on Fifty-ninth Street charged eleven dollars a day for the more than two weeks she was confined—payable in advance—plus a twenty-five-dollar delivery room fee and eleven dollars a day for a nurse. As soon as she could put pen to paper, my mother wrote Kate:

The baby is just three days old this minute. She is very funny-looking—I like her. They'll only let you gaze at her through a glass door like a cucumber in a hothouse, but I must say, that's the most becoming way to view her, due to her extreme youth. She has a sandy complexion, light hair and blue eyes. What would you make of that? Phil and I expected nothing less than an Ethiopian and here we have something that is almost the color of a Swedish waitress. However, they say everything about her will change, so there is not really any use noticing what she looks like now.

After Nancy was brought home, my mother set up house. Maids were a perceived essential. Even though Phil was making a stingy salary, life without help was unthinkable to the young couple. My mother had lived with cooks and maids her whole life, and my father had been raised on a three-hundred-acre estate simply bristling with servants: not only women to run the twenty-eight bedrooms but barnsmen to care for the buildings, groundsmen to keep the massive lawns and fields clipped and the lake clean, gardeners to tend the beautiful boxed-in beds of roses and every kind of summer flower, and a chauffeur to keep the automobiles shiny and ready for any trip George Kunhardt might order up. When my parents first moved into their Eighty-second Street flat in Manhattan, they needed only a temporary cleaning lady, but with the arrival of Nancy, a cook was engaged who was expected to act as a serving maid and a cleaner, too. My mother, showing little sensitivity, wrote Kate of the new help she had just acquired:

The new maid, Ida, pronounced Eeeda, is too idiotic to be allowed even to breathe alone. She is really so dumb that she would probably feed Nancy eggshells and soup if she were left to her own devices. To be literal, she starts to cook a steak at three in the afternoon and serves it at seven with a proud smile. She heats little chocolate cakes until their tops are all runny and soft, then she turns them upside down on a plate so that they stick nicely and passes them with their bottoms turned to the ceiling, helplessly. A butter knife embarrasses her, a finger bowl makes her giggle, crumbing the table sends her into hysterics—and I have to lead her from place to place and in my best sign language say, "Scrub here," "Sweep here," "Dust the spiderwebs away here." Husband and baby and house and maid are wonderful possessions—but they are binding—the old freedom to leap to your side at a moment's notice is gone. I love you—I love you—and it is only this business of cooking the baby's cereal and doing the family laundry which is so new to me still that it drowns out other things I want to do and mean to say.

One of the things Dorothy was hoping to receive from Kate in the not-so-distant future was a Day's End letter. On the same pages where she had talked about baby's cereal and family laundry, my mother also warned Kate not to impetuously scuttle another budding romance:

Don't, for the love of St. Peter, slap his face and say some deadly thing just at the crucial moment. Show him what a nice, darling Katie you are and the rest will do itself. You certainly have been foolish about crucial moments up to now.

It wasn't long before my parents found their apartment too confining. Phil had been introduced to a high-level woolen broker named William P. Jenks, who owned extensive property and houses outside Morristown, New Jersey, and who was willing to rent Phil a small, clapboard house at the base of a large hill about ten miles from Chester.

In February, with Nancy less than a month old, Phil was in Philadelphia trying to sell woolen goods to old Kunhardt customers there and writing to my mother about the country house outside of Morristown for which he had recently contracted with Mr. Jenks:

Our little apartment where we lived our first real bit of life together is darling, isn't it? But our little place in the country is go-

ing to be even sweeter. My, but you are wonderful the way you
look forward to it, when you don't know just what it is going to
be like. But I can guarantee to you that you will love it, love having your own house, and love having your baby and maybe your
hublet in it.

"The beauty of the hills," he wrote her:

the glory of the starry skies are all brought into one image—your
lovely self. Everything in heaven and on the good old earth that I
have loved and worshipped since I was a little boy.

THE MOVE TO the house in the country took place in the spring of 1927
but even so that autumn was a particularly difficult time for my parents.
Phil's father sent him on a month-long business trip to the West, to visit
wool buyers in Cincinnati, St. Louis, and Chicago. It was a test to see if
Phil had enough background, perseverance, personality, and salesmanship
to woo some of the toughest customers in the land in a dwindling market.
From the start, it was a losing battle. Because of the Kunhardt name, my
father was greeted warmly in each city, but sales were not forthcoming and
the trip was lonely and torturous. Phil would climb off the overnight
sleeper, make his way to the hotel room reserved for him, and immediately
unpack, setting up a semicircle of framed photographs around a central
chair where he would sit and smoke his pipe and write his letters home and
never lose sight of his two girls. "My room is like a little home with my
darlings looking at me from all around." He was particularly entranced
with one of Dorothy's posed, pre-wedding portraits. "I love that picture
so much, for it looks at me just the way you look at me, and my heart turns
over. It's my favorite for it says to me, 'Come to me, my own boy.'"

It was a hot September (air-conditioning would not be standard in hotel rooms for years to come). Phil washed his socks and underwear in the hotel sink with Lux soap flakes and spent hours naked in front of fans, trying to dry the sweat from his body. To while away the time between appointments he read *Life of Thomas Carlyle*. A few days before Dorothy's twenty-sixth birthday he ordered her a sweater to be sent air-mail from Peck & Peck. He also sent along a check for six dollars to pay for four hair appointments he wanted her to have and, trembling on the actual birthday night, he arranged for his only telephone call home for the entire month: "I have just put the call in and I can hardly sit still. It is six o'clock here and seven with you. I figure I shall get you about seven fifteen. I do hope it all goes through all right." As soon as the call was completed, Phil returned to his letter: "Six minutes have gone now and I had you and now you are gone. I could hear your sweet voice so well. God bless you, my own."

Throughout the trip, Phil received at least a letter a day from Dorothy, sometimes two or three, long letters of cheerfulness, love, and encouragement. He was the greatest salesman in the world, she told him. He could do anything he wanted to: "Just be your own marvelous self and use your peppermint eyes." Phil wrote back each night, telling her that she didn't know what she was talking about but, "tell it to me anyway." Her letters lifted his spirits and gave him the courage and self-confidence to go on. Sometimes her confidence in him plus a successful day put Phil on top of the world:

I positively know I can do well in this business. Only it takes a long time of preparation, of learning how to handle men, of learning how and why others are succeeding and failing. It takes time to mature ideas, put the whole composite together, and lay your finger on the secret of success. It takes time to wait for your chance and to grasp it when it comes. I have the power and the energy to do mighty things.

But such optimism was usually followed by misgivings:

I have a frightful hangover this morning from sitting up until after twelve last night writing you a lot of rosy-colored bunk. In the cold light of day a lot of what I remember saying is a bit youthful and visionary—a good deal of tommyrot.

My father was always dissatisfied with city life; he needed trees and birds and stars and fresh air—and his wife:

I think of our little place over there in the country and what fun it will be to get back. I think of myself thrashing and puffing and doing silly things about the place, while you so dainty and pretty, think that I am crazy. I think of how I shall chop our firewood, and of how after cutting up a couple of pieces I shall not be able to do any more without running down to the house to kiss you.

Thoughts of home made Phil realize how lucky the two of them were, especially when he compared their new circle of friends in Morristown to the bunch of Chicago socialites he had occasionally been seeing:

They are very attractive people but they all drink like fish and throw money around like fools. I really think we are in an unusually simple and happy crowd. All these people seem to be striving for some excitement to make them happy. In contrast, I think how really happy people are over any little thing. We are in a bunch where we fit, darling, and we are lucky.

"A long lingering kiss to you, dear," he ended his next-to-last letter:

I shall sleep with you next week. We shall be together once more. All my love to you, dear, the holiest, purest most unselfish love; as well as the maddest burning passion.

My parents wrote to each other whenever my father traveled during those first years of marriage, and sometimes their tender language was vivid in detail; they seemed blissfully united physically and, when parted, wished to remind each other through the mail of that bliss: "Dear girl, I want you now in my arms, pressed close, you warm and quivering thing that sets me all aflame."

I WAS BORN on February 5, 1928. It was noon on a Sunday. Like Nancy, I came into this world at the Sloane Hospital for Women on Fifty-ninth Street, which boarded me for eleven dollars a day for twenty days, charging ten dollars for "Use of Operating Room for Circumcision," and nine dollars a day for the private nurse my mother always told me was such a hellcat she wouldn't let anyone even touch me. The nurse growled at my grandmother Meserve when she came in for a visit, she snapped at my mother whenever she meekly asked to see her baby; even my father could not get me out of her clutches. They said for weeks I was beet red and screaming every waking minute. My father, being a loyal Grotonian, wired the school about ten minutes after I was born, and heard back from the Rector two days later:

My dear Phil,

It will be an honor to have the name of Philip B. K., Jr., inscribed upon the register of this institution. I send my hearty congratulations to father and mother and my blessing for the newborn. May he leave this world many years hence the better for his having lived here.

Affectionately yours, Endicott Peabody

George E. Kunhardt sent his congratulations a week later, from his vacation spot in Hawaii, saying he was delighted with the news and was especially pleased at the wise choice of a name.

Three days after my birth, Dorothy wrote Kate from her hospital bed:

Small Philip is just three days old now, to the tick of the clock, and he is very sweet—a wonderful little son for my big Philip, and not through any cleverness or even extra exertion on my part. I am feeling marvelously well, not an ache or a pain anywhere, and it really is true that a second baby is only about half as much to be dreaded as a first one. It was the comparative quickness of the whole thing which was a blessing. And last time I remembered it took quite a while—this time I rack my memory and already the whole day has faded completely away—and in its place is little Phil.

Oh, I want to see you so, Katie. Next Monday I am allowed the first visitors and I have a hellhound nurse who even snaps at Mother when she pokes her head in the door, and who will poison anyone who even [asks to] pick up the baby. I have barely laid eyes on him, but even a glimpse told me I would like him.

Kate was still unmarried, still playing the field. It was almost as if she treated Dorothy as still single, too, for she poured out the kind of intimate detail she had always exchanged with her childhood friend. She once wrote Dot:

What I want to be is carefree, careless Kate, enchanted with summer days, in love with life and happy gracious friends—what right has John to crash in and blacken everything and tie life into hard knots and beastly problems?

He didn't ask me to marry him, yet we talked and talked of it as though we'd been told we had to do it. He doesn't relish the thought of matrimony any more than I do, but he seems to think we should.

I don't want to marry John. I think he's a great brute, unattractive almost, not very kind, dominating, dissipated—nice picture?—but I have the most horrible feeling of having been lassoed by fate. Dodo, do I have the strength and courage to throw off the noose, and what will become of me if I do?

The year after my parents' wedding, my mother began pressing for a romance between her best friend and Harry Mali, who had graduated from Groton two years ahead of my father and was in the woolen business, too. "I hate writing letters that will have to be forwarded," Dorothy wrote after having tracked down Kate, who seemed to be always on the move:

Most words sicken and die if they are not read within twenty-four hours of penning. Except yours. They could come to me after months of cold storage and I would have the same quickened joy with them. I have written Harry about the twenty-ninth. He grows momently more charming to me and I hope with you it is the same. If not, write to me and I will explain to you how bad you are and how blind.

Dorothy had been working on Kate ever since her own marriage:

Kate, I simply yearn for you to find someone. I keep turning over in my mind whether that someone could not by any slim chance be Harry. There is nothing really wrong with him, he is very fine, he is cultivated, educated, traveled, has family background, the wherewithal to support you, offers life in New York near your family, among your friends, would not restrain you in any way from developing your talents, and he would be only too proud and grateful that you were his wife.

Af first, Kate wasn't buying Harry Mali at all. At one point she wrote to Dot, "I think he lives on another planet." A few months later, surrounded by men who didn't entrance her, Kate told Dot, "Ye gods, what's the use of beaux if you haven't got one you want to marry." In still another letter to Dorothy, Kate had almost given up. "I don't know how I feel about Rummy or Harry or Al or any darned man on earth. I don't think I care two pins about any one of the whole bunch." After running into an engaged couple she knew, Kate "came home so blue. Lovebirds, lovebirds all about, and never a mate for me." From France Kate wrote, "It's funny the way when you have the best of everything you can still have a little ache of emptiness."

Kate certainly had the best of everything. Her letters to Dorothy told the story of a pretty, young, extremely observant and discerning college graduate dancing about in a world of privilege on the lookout for a husband. Her days consisted of waking late, servants, baths, tennis, shopping, luncheon with friends, recitals, naps, talk. Her evenings were consumed by dressing for dinner, cocktails, theater, after-hours dancing parties, and, of course, carefully served four-course meals. There were cruises to take, Europe to be jumped over to, and beauty everywhere to be explored.

FOR MY FATHER in 1928, business was still in peril. Because of the inconclusive selling trips, his father now decided that what Phil needed in order to eventually take over the sales office of the company was a lot more grounding in the basic art of making fine woolens. And where better to get that kind of education than the very place Phil's older brother had visited, much to his benefit, in 1925? The University of Ilkley, Yorkshire, England, the world capital of textiles.

By late summer, plans for the trip had been laid. Setting sail in early October on Cunard's RMS *Laconia,* my mother and father had a joyous crossing drinking a good deal of wine, rolling the babies by the hour about the deck, and winning the prizes for Fancy Dress at the ship's ball. "Phil also won the potato race," Dorothy wrote Kate:

> and oh, there is a surgeon on board who is the blackest devil of all beguiling devils. He is Singapore—and all things dangerous and nice rolled into one. Came to see a cold in Philip's eye yesterday and spent an hour alone with me in B44 telling me that he and I were *en rapport.* I opened my blue lips and said I did not understand. Whereupon he grew all tense and mysterious and said, "I am a man, you are a woman, we are alone together, what need for words?"

Coming upon a letter like this was no surprise to me; it only emphasized what I observed for myself off and on during my childhood. My mother was a born flirt but of a different kind than the usual eyelash flutterer. She used her mind instead of her body to make herself alluring. Ideas, humor, irreverence, sarcasm all spilled out of her and soaked her victim with suggestion. Men were startled and amazed by her as she stabbed at their vulnerabilities, and after an onslaught it was hard for a male adversary not to think something sexual was up. It was. But it wasn't. Dorothy had a come-hither twinkle, yet nothing was behind her sparks. Watching her enchant some poor schoolteacher or editor or visiting poet or just a plain Morristown husband, I came to realize she was naturally seductive, but quite innocent, or as innocent as an accomplished cerebral tease could be.

IN THE NEXT few months, writing to Phil from Massachusetts, George Kunhardt instructed his son on his mission in England in letter after letter:

I do not attach much importance to your going through any mills in England; that in the main is not what you are after. It is cloth, construction, design, the way of doing things and the meeting of men that is the important thing for you.

You are not over to acquire information as to what may be the present tendency of trade. You are over just to broaden yourself and to return at the end of possibly six months, aged by perhaps two or three years.

I look forward to your development, the gaining of inspiration, your return to us, and the planning, if possible, of our whole selling organization upon a more up-to-date basis.

I think you will find that when you do get back you will have a real job cut out for you.

Even though Herbert Hoover had won the 1928 presidential election in a Republican landslide, the George E. Kunhardt Corporation was doing poorly. "Our sales for the whole year amount only to $2,502,284," my grandfather wrote. "They are the lowest they have been at any time, notwithstanding all the hard times after the war. This kind of history must not be repeated." Business was so bad by Christmastime that my grandparents had to move out of their big North Andover house and set up quarters in the eleven-room guesthouse next door, which cost much less to heat and run. With the help of Warne, the houseman, my grandfather set himself up in a large upstairs room with a radiator, made a dressing room, moved a desk in, and felt it "quite homelike." That December he also opened a savings account in my name with a fifty-dollar deposit.

Guppa's Christmas would be spent alone with Mingie, and he hoped not only to be back in the big house Christmas hence but also to be surrounded by his new grandchildren, two of whom were now in England. Well before Christmas, my grandparents had received a hand-drawn card by my mother showing my sister and me and a nativity scene with a poem:

> This sending our love across the seas
> And blowing a kiss by every breeze
> Is a very nice game to play.
> But after all, say whatever you please
> For a Christmas hug and a Christmas squeeze
> England is dreadfully far away.

In December, Kate visited Dorothy and Phil. On January 3 of the new year, 1929, Dorothy sat by a fire in Ilkley and wrote her recently departed friend:

Dearest my Katie,

Lexie (our nurse) is away for over a week, and I am slightly frantic from having Philip wake each morning at five and from too much sitting children on pot-pots and giving them porridge to eat. My, they are angels, though. Nancy has learned about fifty words all of a sudden, and uses them in a new way that makes me think she may never need to go to college. Philip is much better these last weeks—goes crawling around like the west wind and any day now he will cease to be a four-legged animal. It seems a shame, one has so many years of two legs, so few months of four, and who knows that we weren't meant to be on four. Phil worked right through the holidays in a storm of energy and eagerness to get home again—railing at all the lazy English who have put up their feet on soft velvet cushions and plan to sip tea for six weeks. For Christmas day we never saw a soul but dear each other.

On board the RMS *Caronia* on her journey home, Kate was in a different state of mind. After a week with my parents at Ilkley, she had convinced herself that she was an integral part of their love for each other and that her presence completed a perfect triangle. It was another way of fending off marriage a little while longer, and it indicates to me that excessive kindness of the kind my mother and father had dished out could turn out to be cruelty in the long run. Kate wrote from the ship:

We three are completely united in a miraculous love. Three has always been a lucky number except in human relations where it has invariably been a count of gloom. But God is good. You two are so perfect with each other that it would be happiness to me just to see you together. Besides that, by some trick of generosity you make me share—so that I never feel like a wistful outsider. When we are all together, I am more happy than at any other time on earth.

My parents' happy life in Ilkley came to a sudden close in late January, when my father was mysteriously stricken with a painful kidney ailment. The pain in his back was so intense he howled. Foreign doctors were called in, and extensive testing began, but when no solutions were come by, it was decided that the family would rush back home so that Phil could be treated by the world-famous expert internist, Dr. Lord, of Boston.

Lying in a private room in an elite wing of Massachusetts General Hospital, my father, despite his as yet undiagnosed pain, became concerned with the financial implications of what was happening to him. He was making $4,800 a year now from his father's firm, but even if he received a raise, it would be completely impossible to go back to the house in Morristown, as its rent would go up to $1,500 a year in June. Phil had, sometime in the past, been offered a very lucrative job by a Judge New, which he had turned down in order to stay with his family's firm. "This is all most distressing coming just at the time of Judge New's proposal," he wrote my mother at her family's house in New York:

> Just by walking across the street from our office, I could put our troubles to an end, put us in a position to be of help to our families if they needed it, put money in the bank for our children, and be able to think of more children. I think Father should know of it some way. He thinks that I owe everything to him—as I do a great deal—but he has no idea of what I gave up to stay in the firm. He should know what others think of me and that I am not just what he has made. It might enhance my value in his eyes.

From his sickbed, Phil wondered if Judge New's offer was still open or, if not, could be reopened. He begged his wife to "Please find this out!" But nothing came of it.

February 1929 was an inconclusive month with Phil in the hospital in Boston and my mother, Nancy, and me in my mother's family's house in New York City. A constant chain of letters connected my parents as they exchanged their hopes and fears. One day Phil was having his lungs x-rayed, the next he was swallowing barium for X-rays of the intestines. The pain persisted. Mr. and Mrs. Jenks, my parents' landlords in Morristown, had written to invite Phil to recuperate, if need be, at their winter place in Wyoming. Phil was fighting against "the terrible depression born of being away from" his Dorothy. The letters flowed between Boston and New York, his informational, hers inspirational. Each was filled with the frustration of being apart. Only once did Dot break down from her high level of expression: "Curse is over and I feel wonderfully and I miss you like hell." Phil was more discreet, "I think of your warm little self getting into your cold little bed and wish I could be there to act as your hot water bottle."

But the problem of money hung over everything. Money—how would they ever make enough of it to survive and, in the future, to flourish? One idea for supplementing their income was initiated by Dot's father, who had offered to begin turning over to his elder daughter his enormous collection of Abraham Lincoln and Civil War photographs. Money could be made from the collection, but Phil wrote Dorothy that she had to decide whether she wished to make a serious avocation out of American history, one that she would maintain through life: "So search your mind carefully and see whether you wish to give up any possible vague ideas of drawing, painting or writing, and directing your energies along these lines."

Money-making schemes were constantly on my parents' minds, along with how to cope with a rich father who lived on an enormous estate, vacationed in Hawaii, was currently trying to economize and therefore absolutely refused to pay either of his sons a fair wage.

"I have already written you of this dark German outlook that seems to be prevalent in my father's mind," Phil wrote Dorothy back in New York:

> There is no explaining it—it is there and must be faced. The other night, Jack and Joan were up. On leaving, Mother remarked that Joan, with five children, looked tired. "Yes," said Father, "poor girl." And he meant it. Yet by paying Jack a decent wage he could lift them right out of most of their troubles! Curious, isn't it? Quite by accident I learned the other day that to bridge over his period of sickness and bad business, Father made large loans on his life insurance—$130,000 of which are still outstanding. I imagine until that is paid up, and maybe further because of habit, the same ideas will be dominant.

My father had convinced himself that if he were one day in control of the firm, he could make a go of it: "In the long run it is the place for me because in your own business you can make ten times as much as working for someone else." So it was now a matter of approaching his father with their needs and applying pressure, if necessary.

But the approach would have to wait. During the first week of March 1929, my father underwent major surgery—a radical operation in which his left kidney was tied off, leaving him with an ugly, wide scar starting high on his right shoulder, running down and across his whole back, and ending up near the belt-line on his left hip. On March 11, Dorothy wrote Kate from my father's hospital room:

Phil adores your flowers; thank you my darling Katie. He is much, much better and it is so wonderful to see him lying there smiling with his brown eyes after all that pain. I am confident that everything is going to continue to go well, and that no second operation will be necessary. Phil has never been sweeter or more magnificent. Some people show up well in the face of danger—is it not so! I am a miserable coward, Katie. I'm not a bit brave and I honestly don't know what I would have done if anything had happened to Phil. The doctor told me the operation ought to take an hour and a quarter. Phil was on the operating table almost three hours, and I was alone the whole time. Not that I wanted someone. Mrs. Kunhardt came in later in the morning and said she would be in again in three or four days. When Phil was still under ether, he asked if his mother and father had been there all during the operation, and if they had been worried. I told him yes, they had, and they had been terribly worried. He seemed very happy. He doesn't remember asking now. It's funny what our selves grasp at in time of need.

A week later, still writing from the hospital, Dorothy described my father's recuperation to Kate:

Phil got out of his bed today and walked halfway across the room and sat himself in a wheelchair—it was magnificent! The doctor says the operation is definitely a success and I am returning to New York tomorrow . . . He leaves the hospital next Saturday for Hardtcourt for a month of sunny air and sleeping twelve hours a night.

Hardtcourt, the name of the Kunhardt estate, was a word made up out of the last five letters of the family name with "court" stuck on for good medieval measure. Even the guest house was beautiful, with ample room, but having seen her husband through his difficult operation, my mother was not invited to stay for my father's long-term recuperation. Instead, she returned to her family's town house in New York City. The decision was not hers—and she resented it.

"Listen to my sad tale," she wrote Phil:

and please give me a great deal of sympathy. These are the weeks, of all weeks, that we should have been together, leaning on each other, being happy together. Sometimes I think I am a silly fool to have just grit my teeth and borne the separation and thought I was brave to be doing it. And at moments like these I say it never should have had to be—these days have been stolen from us and we can never get them back. A few moments ago in despair I called Lawrence 7340. Mingie answered. I said, "Hello, Mingie, this is Dot." She said, "Well?" Then there was quite a silence and I said, "I just called up to see how you all were and to send my love." She said, "Hasn't Phil written you?" I said, "Yes, but," etc., etc. and the conversation went on. Really Phil, I know I am a little cad to write you this—and probably Mingie didn't mean anything at all but kindness—but my feelings aren't as insensitive as they might be and I am so tired of being treated as though I were some hostile outsider—or better still, some riff-raff of absolutely no account. After all, you are their son, and I am your wife, and it would have been such fun to be made much of and enthused over and loved. I could just weep. If only I had you here to hold me in your arms and explain it all away and tell me how un-understanding I am, it would be all right—but here I am so longing for you and things seem pretty cruel.

My father had decided himself to go back to his childhood home to get his strength back. In doing so, he allowed himself to revert temporarily to the dependent, dreamy state of his youth. He left the hospital on a Sunday, with George William Busby, the family chauffeur, carrying all his things down to the Lincoln. Arriving an hour later at Hardtcourt, he settled himself in a downstairs room in the guesthouse where the family was living now.

When his parents returned from church, the three of them paid a visit to the big house and Phil rested there while Mingie and Guppa walked up to the teahouse and then down to the lake. "It was beautiful sitting out there," Phil wrote Dorothy that evening:

> the wind blowing across the lake and humming through the pines, the sun pouring out warmth, and the birds singing all around me. I felt like I did when I was a little boy back from school on Easter vacation for the first day, nothing to do but sit somewhere on a fence rail and listen to the birds, sniff the wonderful spring smells, and bask in the sun.

In Phil's mind the boyhood he had spent on the Hardtcourt estate was charmed. He had been lovingly brought up by the chauffeur's English wife, Annie Harper, who was the Kunhardt governess and riding instructor. When Annie had married Busby, George E. had given them a lavish reception on the estate, and they had been in residence throughout Phil's childhood, along with their son, Philip, named after my father, their favorite of the four Kunhardt children.

In 1905, Phil's father had built the mansion and dozens of outbuildings on 300 acres of rolling Massachusetts countryside, containing whole farms and bordering on Lake Cochichewick with over a mile of waterfront. Modeled after nineteenth-century German baronial estates,

Hardtcourt, fashioned out of brick and oak with yellow brick walks and drives, was completely self-sufficient; its farms raised different crops; there were pastures for a herd of Guernsey cows, a breeding barn for Morgan horses, a three-acre vegetable garden, a ten-car garage, an electricity generator and refrigeration unit, a blacksmith shop, two resident carpenters, a pipe system that brought water from the lake up the hill to the big house. There were also smaller houses that slept over forty workers and guests sprinkled over the vast countryside.

When Mingie desired a formal garden a professional gardener, hired from Kew Gardens in London, designed twenty-five-foot flower beds with a long path between them leading to an open-air oak and brick Japanese teahouse. When it was decided to build a guesthouse with a pool, Italian masons were brought across the Atlantic to lay the hand-painted tile for the border as well as the tiny white tiles for the pool.

It was not the kind of life Dorothy had dreamed of, and in her few short visits to Hardtcourt she must have shuddered at the thought of possibly inheriting the place someday. And I know she wondered how Phil, after growing up in these surroundings, could possibly be the kind and simple man he was. However, every once in a while my mother yearned for a less solitary life.

"Wherever I go in New York," she wrote to Phil, "people are discussing brilliant plays and the latest books and wearing lovely soft clothes, and I feel all dull and dowdy and lonely and of no account." But it was not size or pretension she craved, it was the elegance and aesthetics of the city's artistic community.

I VISITED HARDTCOURT when I was a child, and I remember Mingie placing herself on the little electric seat that took her up the stairs, and Guppa trying to amuse his grandchildren by popping out his glass eye.

Fifty years later, I began visiting the place again, an abandoned shell of its former self but still formidable, taken care of by watchmen who tried to keep teenagers from breaking any more windows in North Andover's fenced-off, favorite target. I arrived with a daughter, Sandra, and my two oldest sons, Philip and Peter. We were let in by Philip Busby, the child of my grandfather's chauffeur, who, in retirement, still lived nearby, cherishing the past. It was dark inside, the great stairs loomed in front of me; there was the fireplace, big enough to walk into. I found the internal phone system in the pantry—there were the name tabs for servants to answer to: Mr. Kunhardt, Mrs. Kunhardt, Jack, Harriet, Philip, Hildegard. One of my sons removed a small piece of the heavy, imported wallpaper from the dining room as a souvenir. We were happy to emerge into sunlight after an hour of submersion in the past. I tried to imagine my father living in this Germanic castle as a boy and wondered how he had survived it.

Even though the Prince of Wales once visited Hardtcourt, as did President Taft, all was not well within its gloomy walls. Both my grandparents drank too much Scotch and wine and lost help regularly because of evening tirades. During the weeks my father was recuperating, he witnessed an explosion on his mother's part which cost the family its latest cook and butler. To my mother he described his stay at his old home as comparable to the life of a goldfish:

Not a moment by myself, constant interruption if I do try to read or write, constant bickering. I have been doing even less than usual because I have been spending much time in the kitchen and pantry. I really think it is fortunate for Mother that I came back, for I have taken much of the heavy work off her hands—otherwise she would have to have done it all. Tomorrow a new couple arrives, someone else to swear at.

Fortunately, Phil's worries over his soaring medical expenses, made even higher than expected by the use of some of the most renowned and expensive doctors in the world, had been eased by his father's intervention. My grandfather had offered to cover everything, even the staggering fee of $2,500 for the kidney surgery. Phil told Dorothy that his father promised to:

> send me back not one penny poorer from this operation business. Dad stood at the foot of my bed, speaking of paying around $3,000 as though it were nothing in exchange for having me well. Really, I felt terribly at having misjudged him so. I should have realized that he would do everything but that he would wait until the end to say so. It's my fault for not knowing him better.

Dorothy was overjoyed to have her husband on the mend, with an examination by his doctors indicating that there would be no after-effects. And now, with the knowledge that her father-in-law would assume all the medical costs of his illness, she could hardly contain herself in the letter she wrote him:

> Darling, darling, I am so full of joy. We seem to be the most fortunate two people on earth, everything works out so perfectly for us. If only you knew how I am feeling ever since your examination. It means that you will be well after all your terrible long illness and we can start out on a new life together with carefree hearts. Only it will be far more glorious than our starting out three years ago— though that was beautiful enough. Now I love you with a deeper love—a love that makes me cry out for you miserably when you are not by my side—a love which takes my breath away for very

blissfulness. Phil, why aren't you here so that I can throw myself into your arms and be crushed there and tell you that I adore you?

In another letter, Dorothy referred to Endicott Peabody, Phil's headmaster at Groton:

Do you remember what the Rector said to me the first time I met him? He said, "One of the biggest things about Phil is his absolutely and never-changing loyalty to the things he has loved." I often think of that—and sometimes when we say un-understanding things about our family at Hardtcourt, I feel terribly because I am fearful that I have led you to be disloyal. We mustn't be.

Before finally coming home to Dorothy on Saturday April 21, Phil restrained himself from boiling over at his father for having consciously scheduled a Kunhardt Corporation board meeting on his wedding anniversary. Within days, though, Phil had regained his normal optimism and was overflowing with big ideas about his future.

"I hate this being associated with a losing business," he wrote Dorothy:

and I long to get in and make it earn money. More than that, I want someday to be in a very important executive position—not just the head of the selling organization of a small mill—but the head of a great chain of mills and retail stores organized to sell the products of those mills. In other words, my ambition is infinite. I want to build up something better than anyone else has, something like a General Motors of the clothing business whereby we can give the consumer a better article of clothing for less money. I am so afraid I may miss my opportunities, that someone else may beat me to it, and that twenty years from now I shall sit back in a salaried position and think what a failure I have been. You must help me, darling, to the utmost.

Such flights of guarded optimism never lasted long for my father.

SOMETHING MUST HAVE been happening in the life of Kate Strauss that had passed Dorothy by, for on June 10, 1929, Kate wrote Dorothy this seemingly casual letter:

It's fun to be busy. I have been. Golly, so much has happened since I saw you. For instance, I am engaged. At least, I think I am. I have been trying all morning not to write to you because I thought it would be such fun to tell you and Phil together, and watch your expressions. Anyway, if you breathe it to Phil, remember it is so secret that I am not sure of it myself. And I'll hang you by the neck till you're dead if you tell anyone else.

When Harry asked me if I liked emeralds I nearly died of fright. I am terrified he'll call me up this evening. Perhaps he's forgotten what happened last night. I *hope* he has.

Harry hadn't, and later that year the two were married.

3.

The Grim Spectre

Dorothy holding the author as an
infant in the spring of 1928

T HE CRASH ON WALL STREET in 1929 and the downward spiral of the Great Depression sent the woolen industry, like so many other industries, into a series of hard times. My father was often discouraged—if not outright bitter. Coming into his own at a time when careers were being derailed and business was floundering made him believe it was he that was unsuccessful. "Oh, Dottie," he wrote her from Cleveland in the midst of a late 1930 "hell of a trip":

the market is depressed beyond words. They almost die when they hear a woolen man is calling. You say someday we shall have money, but I don't see it. I'm just a flop in business—useless, useless!

My brother, Ken, was born in January of 1930, and that added to the
stress although it also brought joy. Just months later, my mother was
writing encouragement to my father in Chicago:

Somehow I have a premonition that this trip is going to be a turning point for good. I felt so proud of you, dearest, when you
stepped on the train and left me. You great big thing, so darling and
so wonderful-looking, all full of life and energy and push. Nothing
is going to stop you from getting ahead. I really have a terribly
strong feeling that everything is going to come out beautifully for
us. It is a great position of trust to have you out there dealing with
the concern's greatest customers. And oh, Phil, dear, just hang on
doggedly, you know what it means to us. Try to write very good
full letters back to your father, and please don't belittle your own
powers. Let him realize he has the cleverest young man in the
woolen business for a son and sooner or later—I wouldn't be surprised if sooner—he will see that you are valuable. I am pinning a
lot now on the fact of his half-promise that next fall he will retire—
and if he only takes Uncle Jim, too, we are certainly started on the
upward path. I think you are perfectly right (although at times
when I am very tired I just allow myself to be foolishly dejected) in
saying that we must hold on and tide over these hard months.
Don't you worry, darling, I am much nicer inside than I seem to be
outside and often when I seem to find fault and be a poor sport I am
really thinking just the opposite way down deep and agreeing with
you completely. I am a bad, stubborn girl. Remember what I told
you on the station platform. I love you—frightfully, desperately
much. You and I—together and never, never separated—are going to attain wonderful heights and have glorious, glorious times.

But the "glorious times" did not come. The Grim Spectre came instead. "The Grim Spectre," Dorothy explained, "is our own pet name for ghastly financial worry. It just seemed sort of humorous to call it that." Things were so bad that, by spring, Dorothy and Phil were exploring a bold new living plan. What they devised was this: They would sublet the Morristown house for the summer, starting in June, and borrow a place to live on the Maine island of North Haven where Phil's best friend, Garry Norton, summered with his parents and siblings. There my mother, we children, and our nursemaids would settle and live as cheaply as possible on low Maine food prices and no rent. Phil, in turn, would move to his in-laws' summer house in Chester and for the three summer months he would work in New York, spending nothing but his train fare to and from the city. He would also search for someone to sublet the Morristown house in the fall, in the hope of finding a less expensive winter home, but with the idea of someday moving back to the little house at the base of the hill they loved so. It was a frantic plan from the start and would be jarred and complicated by turns of events that neither of my parents could have foreseen.

"Oh, how I hated leaving you yesterday afternoon," Phil wrote upon returning to Chester after dropping off his family in the tiny island community of North Haven, Maine. "How terrible it is to be apart. But we are doing it for each other, so that we can stay in our little house. Oh, what bitter misery, though."

At the office, my father had to do his own job as well as that of his Uncle Jim, who was ill and unable to come to work. Aging, old-fashioned James Knapp was Phil's mother's brother and longtime head of the New York sales office, the job my father badly wanted.

From Maine, letters of encouragement and professions of love showered on Phil's lonely, hot existence back in the city:

Phil, I do love you so terribly much. There never could be a more wonderful, adorable husband than you. I love you and am trying every day to be a better wife for you. I wish I were near you to encourage you in this awful fight for money for us to live with. I have been thinking of a lot of ways I can save next winter—little ways—but they will help. I am doing my best up here and if only our past bills were paid I would make headway.

Even though my parents' bank account was practically empty, Dorothy had come to Maine with two nursemaids in tow—Esther and Elizabeth—allowing her to be free of her three small children whenever she felt like it, free to go marketing or swimming or sailing or out to dinner. Nursemaids came before groceries and made life bearable. And despite the financial stress, Dorothy was comfortably sliding into a social life with Garry Norton's family—his mother, the grande dame of the island compound, which included the two cottages the Kunhardts were borrowing; Garry's sister Lucia and her husband, Allan; and Garry's brother, Kim. Almost nightly Dorothy was summoned to the main house for a long dinner and much friendly talk. She was cautiously loving it.

It soon became obvious to Dorothy that the free summer at the Norton island hideaway had some strings attached to it. First of all, it meant being genial company to the old lady, listening to her outpourings about her life, and being careful to not really respond except for neutral words, smiles, and an occasional exclamation of surprise. Second, it meant being a companion and confidante to Mrs. Norton's daughter, Lucia. Third, it meant being an interesting and responsive single woman at the dinner parties Mrs. Norton gave for her many friends—people from the island, and those cruisers who dropped in from their yachts for a night or two.

"By the way, Mrs. Norton has some very unique impressions of your boyhood and youth," she wrote my father:

She says that you always found the fare to come to North Haven difficult, even in the old days, and that when Lucia visited you she found the house a palace and the grounds regal. Also, she couldn't understand why you never were allowed to come to New York. Funny how one's affairs are talked over even when we least think it.

Garry, on a weekend visit, also reminisced about his close friendship with Phil at school and college.

"Garry said that you had always been a big successful hero in school," Dorothy wrote:

that you always seemed so strong and wonderful and on the crest of the wave—that in athletics you swept everything before you and everybody loved you. Also, you were the only boy at Groton who had taken a real army training course and would be commissioned if the war went on. Also, everybody knew about Hardtcourt and was just holding his breath to be invited there for a weekend. Garry says he has never forgotten the thrill the first time you asked him. He said you were by far the most glamorous person in your form—outstanding in so many ways. Darling, you are so humble that you never picture yourself to me at all as anything but a little boy with darling peppermint eyes, and I just have to imagine so many things.

One of Dorothy's July letters to Phil discussed the Morrows, another family who summered on North Haven. Anne Morrow, a close friend of Lucia Norton, had married the world-famous aviator Charles Lindbergh, and Lucia was convinced, as Dorothy quoted her, that the marriage Anne had made was a terribly difficult one: "How rough he is and how stubborn and how ill he adjusts himself to people and how Annie is growing white and thin struggling over him—and how much in love they are with each other." But for all the passing cheer, the main subject of my mother's letters was money and how broke they were and what they could possibly do about it:

Mrs. Norton and I have spent today in Rockland, shopping. We find that the prices are one third to one half of what they are here and we laid in a big supply of everything. I had to make a big out-lay of money but I couldn't have gone through the month here the way things were.

Here was a young couple from affluent backgrounds and with the prospect of a substantial inheritance someday, who had never budgeted their expenses. They had married and started a family on a limited income but they had assumed that fate would see them through and so they could, until then, live very much according to the custom of their upbringings—their tastes calling for the best in everything, always having help, renting an expensive house in an upscale community, having children at will, using the finest doctors, owning two cars, entertaining their friends, and jamming as much weekend fun into their lives as they could.

These attitudes and problems were, I think, not uncommon at the time, especially among my parents' social set. In mid-July my mother asked Mrs. Norton—who had had her ups and downs, too—about what was described as "the theory of living inside one's income." This theory, or question, it seemed, was obsessing my mother. She wanted to know "whether it was better to worry along and bluff things out till good luck came or whether it was better to go into hiding for two or three years and then emerge." Mrs. Norton's answer was definitive.

"She chose the latter by all means," my mother wrote:

unless you needed the social acquaintances with whom you dined and wined in your present community as aids in your business, as stepping stones to bigger things. But if you didn't need them for business reasons, leave them for a little and when you come back with money "the whole world is at your feet." Those were her words. Mrs. Norton said that many times in their early life they made temporary retreats, and even when the children were in school and college, and she wanted special sums of money to send them abroad or some such, she would give up her big house, and her servants, and go and live with Mr. Norton in a hotel for a year. And all her friends would say how queer, and she wouldn't see them for a space, and then bang, she would have the money she wanted in her hand and be really happy again, and she could snap back into the old way of living in two minutes. Mrs. Norton said this is the one time of our whole lives when we really can "retrench" because our children are so young that they don't know whether the little boy they are playing with is Henry Morgan or the butcher's boy and they can just grow and live and the little family will knit itself very close together and the children really don't need much besides good food and care and the companionship of their parents and each other.

Of course, the answer Dorothy would get to her question depended upon to whom she was talking. Three days later she tried out Mrs. Norton's daughter, Lucia:

Lucia opened up her heart and confided to me many things about Allan, Garry, her mother, and all kinds of things. She is just as human and fallible as the rest of us, and I have always before been rather afraid of her. I asked her what she thought about people living beyond their incomes and just betting on the future as opposed to cutting down, doing one's own work, and living within one's means. She was of the opinion you used to have, that it was better to live as nicely as one could and hope for the best. She also said, which I disagree with, that she thought two people living together and doing all the work and never seeing their friends went horribly stale and something beautiful between them died. I think she is wrong and that it is just up to us to keep ourselves alive and interesting to people, and nothing could die between us, everything will just bind us closer together. We have enough education and background to go a year or so without people and plays and football games and dances, however much we may like those things.

By mid-July my parents had already agreed to continue to sublet their Morristown house, move to one of the nearby, less desirable towns—either Princeton or Orange—and get rid of their nurse, but not their maid. Up until now they had been making ends meet with wedding-present cash, the elder Kunhardts' gift of bonds, and a few loans which were almost used up. Even Dorothy's parents couldn't help them anymore—Fred Meserve's savings had been almost wiped out by the crash and now, on his $14,000 salary, he was struggling to keep his head above water. The Kunhardt mills were almost at a standstill, as was almost every industry in the country. Unemployment, breadlines, foreclosures, and panic marked 1931, with President Hoover unable to do much about any of it. From the protection of the island, Dorothy wrote Phil her reactions to their proposed new fiscal life:

The only big thing I am sorry for is that it means you and I can practically never play around together, and go out calling, and driving, and get off to a football game at Princeton. If we have no nurse I simply will have to be at home with the children every minute, and conserving my strength at home as best I can. We couldn't expect Elizabeth to stay alone in the house and do all her own work and look after the children, too, it isn't humanly possible and the children would be badly neglected. I know how exhausting it is, having had them today. But, if we were to keep a nurse, there would be hardly any saving in moving and we would still have two big mouths to feed. No, the only thing to do is to accept the first plan in its entirety. I really can do the children if we are sensible about it and try to do absolutely nothing else, but how I hate the idea of not being able to go to call on the Crosses with you, or drive to the Kinneys, or go to a barn dance, or the Seth Thomas Christmas tea, or to swim at the Jenks, or any of the nice things we used to do. Are we foolish to stay near enough to all of that so that we shall see it all going on without us and so that it will tantalize us? Or do you think we can do as the Potters have done, simply withdraw, and let people come to us if they want to see us. I think we can, but what is far more important, I think we have to. I know we could never bear Main Street in West Orange, so I think this is pretty nearly the ideal solution.

Back down in the steaming city, Phil was left with the job of finding someone to permanently sublet their house, getting that person approved by his landlord, Bill Jenks, and then searching out a place to live until the financial storm blew over. He had visited the town of Princeton, a possible alternative, but had found it "flat, hot, and tawdry." Very quickly, though, the money was running out:

We are spending a hundred dollars a month more than what we get and that doesn't count clothes and school. We have enough to go just about to the end of the year. Then we can't borrow again, and I am certain I won't get a raise. So what shall we do? I am filled with all sorts of wild revolutionary thoughts, of insisting on Uncle Jim's being fired, or of looking for another job. We simply have to cut expenses some way. I am at my wit's end and just feel beaten, and hate my work.

IN LATE JULY of that year, my father drove to Maine and spent a weekend with us. Sometime in those two days Dorothy let her worst fears be known—she was late with her period and was pretty sure she was pregnant.

The worried couple talked far into the night, trying to come up with a solution. An abortion was one way out. Even though abortions were illegal, they knew married women who had had them done and doctors who performed them safely. They also seemed to know how to go about arranging one and the cost of it, but Dorothy was loathe to go through with, to her, such a ghastly medical procedure. She suggested to Phil that, instead, she try to induce a miscarriage.

Phil agreed reluctantly. What Dorothy had proposed—something she had heard from a friend or a doctor about quinine and hot baths— did not sound like a risk to her health at five or six weeks pregnant. Once back in New York, he wrote:

I expect to hear from you in the next day or two whether your efforts have been successful. If they are not, darling, don't make yourself sick by trying too hard or by worry. Just get as strong as you can so as to go through with it in a happy frame of mind. We shall swing it one way or another and we shall be happy that our family is growing.

Not willing to accept Phil's "somehow it will all work out" philosophy, my mother started promptly on her treatment:

Last night I took ten grains of quinine and a very large dose of castor oil and a hot bath. Needless to say, I am not feeling very well today. I have just taken ten more grains of quinine, and am about to go and sit in a very hot tub; so you see, I am doing my best. I will write you the result.

The following morning she sent another letter, first describing how there were men out on the water working on their broken float—"It sank yesterday when three hundred-pound barrels of oil for the Lindbergh plane were landed on it"—then moving on to her self-medication.

"I have just taken ten more grains of quinine," she wrote, explaining that her ears were ringing and her mind had stopped working:

and I jump clump-clump whenever I can, and have had one hot bath just now and am about to go to the village and buy a douche-bag as a last desperate measure. It all makes me feel so horrible that I don't see how it can fail to be successful. A douche-bag costs five dollars, but that is cheaper than a child.

The next morning, Dorothy noted that, "The Lindbergh plane has just gone over our house, starting out on its trip to China." But what she really had to convey was her shakiness and growing desperation:

I have just taken ten more grains of quinine, making a total of forty now, and am about to take another big dose of castor oil. It makes me very shaky and weak and I have buzzing in the ears. Perhaps I'll have success today. If not, I hope I haven't hurt anything.

My mother believed she was doing all this mayhem to her body for Phil's sake and for the sake of their children, for their schooling and clothing. "I continue to think of last weekend with delight," she wrote:

It certainly is blissful when we are together. I only hope I can fix this little matter so that I won't be a drag on you this winter and so that we can have a chance to pull ourselves out of debt.

On the last day of July, the home remedy was still not working. Unable to dislodge the fetus, my mother had, instead, exhausted herself, irritated her kidneys, created a sharp pain in her back, and thrown herself into dejection:

Now that this last news is definite, and we really are going to have a fourth child by April 10, our sixth wedding anniversary, the decision remains whether we will have the operation or not. I know in what desperate straits we are financially, and I think we will have to very carefully measure benefits and drawbacks. The benefits are: we shall have our fourth child and completed family by the time I am thirty and you thirty-one, they will all grow up together and be more companionable to each other than if we strung out the last one, they will all go to schools and colleges at about the same time and give us far more freedom and time for travel and whatnot together than if we had them of diverse ages. In fact, the big things in favor are that it will be nice to have a completed family of four, and to have it done, early in life.

But the things against us are that we are already $1,800 in debt and we cannot lay our hands on the $1,200 to have the baby (doctor and hospital costs, etc.). Also, it will mean that this winter when I should be well and strong to help you face this business crisis, I will be rather dragged down and not be the buoyant support you need. (Although I would try.) Also, we would be an increased burden on and worry to my family who would have to assume command when the baby arrived. Also, it would mean increased regular expenses probably in the way of a nurse, as it would be much more work to do baby's diapers, etc., etc.

In fact, looking at the arguments dispassionately, it would seem to me to lean toward the operation. If so, I ought to come down to New York immediately (saying to the family that it was for the suspension of the uterus operation) and have it done quickly. Mother could come right up here and assume command—I don't think it would be more than a week in the hospital or that it would cost more than $300 altogether.

For perhaps the first time in her life, my mother was making a tally-sheet decision based on finances and fear rather than on desires and hopes. Here she was looking squarely at the figures and reading them in black and white, with no room for gray.

"Sweetness," she concluded:

I wish we were together. I love you so terribly and am so happy being married to you that I can't think of any greater bliss than this life of ours—hard fight though it is for a living. You are not to worry about me. This seems a bad time just now, but ten years from now it will all have worked out beautifully and we will look back on it and see how closely it all bound us together and how happy we are.

When Phil opened her letter and found out she might be damaging herself with the "medicine," fear spread through him. He ordered Dorothy to give it up, they would survive somehow, her health came first. They were like two children talking back and forth, neither one able to be realistic about the situation, each concocting a fiction concerning the future, unwilling to admit they were flirting with disaster. My father justified letting his wife go ahead with her dangerous "medication" by believing that she knew what she was doing, and that holding on to the way of life they had established thus far was worth almost anything. Dorothy justified her actions by making herself believe that she must do practically anything to help her husband during these terrible times. The depth of her panic at their financial situation can be measured by Dorothy's resolve to end her pregnancy no matter what, even if it had to be done by the hospital procedure she had formerly refused. With Dorothy on the verge of racing to New York for a conventional, although illegal, abortion, to be conducted in a hospital, her home-remedy procedures finally resulted in a miscarriage. On the morning of August 2, having already telephoned the news to Phil, she was able to write, without mincing words:

Well, we are successful in what we tried to do, and I know you are as glad and relieved about it as I am. I do feel a little as though we had killed a son or a daughter, but it had to be, and now we can go ahead with the fight and have much more chance of winning than if you had had this new burden. I just can't get over how lucky we are—and just when we had given up hope. I'm glad I succeeded for you in what we tried to do. Now we can go on with lighter hearts. I adore you with every bit of me.

Phil downplayed his distress at losing a child but confessed financial considerations had won out. "I can't help but admit that I had a little pang," he wrote:

to think we would not have a new baby. But it is much better as it is, for we must send Nan and Philip to school and we would have been weighed down with terrible debts. You were certainly courageous to do all that you did. I pray you have done yourself no permanent harm.

My mother's physical health was never very good and disrupting her insides certainly didn't help. But it was her mental health that must have been affected most. She loved human life; she adored babies especially. Having to snuff out the possibility of a person in her womb must have greatly saddened her. In any case, it was a turning point. Never again would she feel invincible.

THAT AUGUST, talk of the pregnancy vanished quickly, as my parents' letters began to focus on Uncle Jim, who stood in Phil's way in the New York office, and on my grandfather, around whom everything revolved. "The one-man rule of terror," Dorothy called George E., "and there is no hope of changing things so late in his life."

Through his brother, Jack, Phil had been pushing his father to get rid of Uncle Jim and put him in charge of sales. My mother was forever awaiting word that the move had been made. "Of course, the great danger is that Jack will cease to push the matter," she wrote Phil:

> having done his bit, and your father will settle down into the old routine again, and put off what, of course, is an unpleasant job. If that happens, I don't know what you can do about it. It means, most probably, sitting and waiting for a death or an earthquake.

Accustomed to having her way, or at least to holding the reins, Dorothy tried to help manipulate her husband into a more powerful position in his family's firm:

> I shall help you in every way I can—I promise you, dearest. You can count on me. When your father communicates with you and writes on the subject, as he must do—he can't just ignore it entirely—please let me know all that he says. It hurts to think that he hasn't complete confidence in you. But it doesn't hurt deeply because I simply feel that he is the one who is making an error in judgment and, after all, he is old and worried and not very well, and he just hasn't the vision to face the music and change things. He needs to be shown and he will be.

Finally, my grandfather swung into action. Uncle Jim was called to Lawrence from his summer home on Vinalhaven (another island in Maine, right next to North Haven), and told that, because of the disastrous decrease in sales, his services would not be needed in the autumn season ahead; that for the time being, anyway, Phil would be in charge of the selling operation. Jim could go back to Vinalhaven and stay there with his wife, who was not well. By benching his brother-in-law only for the next selling season, George E. was leaving the door slightly open so that he might be brought back if Phil didn't succeed. When Phil heard from his father about the painful confrontation, it was not by dictated or typed letter as he usually communicated but in Guppa's almost unreadable handwriting which Phil then copied word for word and sent off to Dorothy.

"He shook hands with me when he left," George E. wrote of Uncle Jim:

> I think he felt dreadfully about the whole matter, and of course he realizes that it is not only a question of remaining away now, or until October 15, but probably remaining away for the entire spring season and possibly the ensuing fall season, if not for good and all.

However, just to make certain his son would not applaud this turn of events too loudly, George E. suggested Phil use Uncle Jim for advice— thus making sure that my father would never feel comfortable in the presence of his Uncle Jim again:

"Please do not feel too elated over the decision I have arrived at," wrote my grandfather:

> I must confess that I am not altogether satisfied that we have made the right decision. Mr. Knapp's experience is an asset to the company and as long as he will have to get a return from the company, the company might get the advantage of his experience.
>
> He did not make any personal remarks as far as you were concerned. He did at one time start to talk of disloyalty, but he stopped short and started talking of something else. He thought, in the end, with your active experience not covering much over two years, that the company was running quite a risk in throwing the responsibility of merchandising its spring product entirely in

your own hands. Possibly he may try to have a conference with you. Of course, if he does, you will treat him courteously, as he is still the vice president of the company. My brother-in-law has been with us his entire business experience and is deserving of a great deal of consideration.

My father had been placed in a no-win position. Now he had no idea how to act. In a pique of anxiety and confusion, he threw himself upon the mercy of his wife. "Get a reply back to me as quickly as possible," he wrote Dot:

for I feel fairly sure that Uncle Jim will turn up during the week. Think well when you write. If necessary, excuse yourself from everything for a couple of hours, get your mother to take the children, and give me a reply upon which I can act.

As soon as Phil's desperate letter arrived, my mother wrote back:

I have thought a great deal about your letter and your father's. If we could have foreseen the method he would use we could have prevented many things which are a great pity. It was done cruelly to you and cruelly to Uncle Jim, but there is no use blaming your father or being angry, because you are going to have to work *with* and not against him for the remainder of his life, and what is done is done. I am so glad you are going to talk with your father and Jack this weekend. Avoid misunderstandings. I think you will probably come away from North Andover much relieved, as when your father gets over the strain of the two days Uncle Jim spent with him, and when he sees for himself that your attitude is quite the contrary to "elation," I think he will be more of an ally to you and a rock for you to lean on.

As for Uncle Jim, I strongly advise you to commit yourself in no way in any letter to him. Wait until you see him, in the meantime writing him an affectionate note, saying nothing. When you see him, make his slipping away less hard and hold his friendship, because if this thing is well managed now he will not return and you will have your big opportunity and win. He knows this deep in his heart but you must tell him these things.

Then my mother turned her considerable powers of inspiration upon her husband.

I am so very proud of you and trusting in you. You are going to make a good spring season, even though it seems it would take a miracle to do it. You are that miracle. Believe in yourself and never lose heart for a minute. One thing about you is that you don't get flurried and dashed by small things going wrong—you keep your eye fixed on the whole and have a grand sense of proportion . . . Your father loves you and trusts your ability far more than he will ever show. He is queer and will hide his approval when he can. But you know he is a darn clever man with a head that is still crystal clear, and he would never have made this move without thinking a good deal of you. We just have to discount his crabbedness. I think you will be much more at ease about the whole matter after this weekend.

My mother ended her long letter with an acute observation on the business jungle and what it did to the weaker of its members, like Uncle Jim:

The war of business is a stern, uncompromising one, and the weak are bound to fall by the wayside. In the long run, this is all going to come out well for you, but just now we must work toward making the falling a little less hard for the weak. I send you all my thoughts and my love—and shall wait anxiously to hear from you.

Armed with her advice, Phil resolved the matter with his father in North Andover that weekend, and true to Dorothy's intuition, the old gent acted much more sympathetic and loving than he had in his frosty letter.

Uncle Jim himself acted well, too, sending a courteous letter to my father, reluctantly handing over the reins:

Your father will probably advise you that he wants me to postpone my return. He told me you wanted a free hand in going out for spring '32 and handling the business. While it was quite a shock to me to be told I might hinder more than help by being in New York at the time of openings, you can bet your last dollar I wouldn't intentionally crimp your style and would be the first to congratulate you if our line would sweep the market, as I certainly hope it will.

Flushed with success, my father now needed his wife's mind to switch gears and tackle a business problem that called for creativity. The firm was putting out a new lightweight wool weave that cried for an appropriate moniker—some kind of Mediterranean name most likely, nothing with the word "tweed" in it, for that suggested warmth. Rather, a catchy term for a cool, summer-weight fabric. "I thought you might think one up," Phil suggested. My mother's answer came speeding in the next post:

"The name I suggest for your new cloth," she wrote—jumping at the chance to help in a concrete way, and adopting the language of the profession as if by osmosis:

is Monte Carlo Cavalier. My reasons are: Monte Carlo is a place which gives to the man who is buying this low-priced suit an immediate feeling of swellness, heat (and therefore one would have to wear cool clothes), dash, style, raciness, and basking about in a warm climate. The name of the cloth—Cavalier—is designed to give to this middle-class buyer the idea that he is a gentleman, a courtly, fashionable gentleman. Also, the two names offset each other; while plain "Monte Carlo" might be too spicy for the average man on the street to risk buying, "Cavalier" gives it a tone of old-time knightliness. It is not a specially original or clever name, but it might take the fancy of buyers if well advertised. Or do you think that it ought to be something snappier like "Monte Carlo Special"? That would indicate lightweight and that it was a weave especially invented. Maybe that sounds too much like an ice-cream soda. A much cleverer name would be "Monaco Cavalier." Monaco is the little kingdom of which Monte Carlo is the capital, but the trouble is, the average man will not know that and it will mean nothing to him. Or do you want something tricky like "Monaco Tropico"? Here I am just wandering on.

Her "wandering on" hit pay dirt in New York, and Phil promptly informed her that her last idea, "Monaco Tropico," was excellent and they would in all probability use it. "You have a wonderful little head on your

shoulders and a wonderful heart inside," he wrote her. It was the first time
Dorothy had truly helped Phil in his business. It wouldn't be the last.

Not all of my mother's correspondence that summer centered on
money, abortion, and business. Her children were becoming more and
more interesting to her. Whereas before, references to us were largely
limited to "the children have all come piling into the house and are being little hoodlums at their lunch and I must go and help," now we were
starting to become real people and a source of entertainment and wonderment. It was the beginning of endless perceptive notes about her
children and their every move, notes which my mother would file away
for some kind of future use.

"This morning," she wrote, in mid-August:

> Nancy came down to breakfast very angry because the shoulder-
> straps of her swimsuit were flapping and Philip began to smile
> teasingly at her. I said, "Eat your breakfast quickly, Nancy dear."
> Philip said, "Nancy's not a deer." Nancy, at this, was infuriated
> and said, "I am a dear." "You are not a deer," said Philip. "I am a
> dear," shouted Nancy. "You're not a deer," said Philip again, en-
> joying himself hugely. "I am a dear," screamed Nancy, spitting at
> Philip in her rage. "I am—I am a dear!"

On the weekend that Phil had been in North Andover confronting his
father about Uncle Jim, Dorothy jotted down how her two older children
had dealt with Sunday church on the island. She had warned the children:

> to sit absolutely silently and not move a muscle. At the end of fif-
> teen minutes they had wriggled so, and smiled so wickedly at all
> the people, and kicked the cushions one kneels upon so many
> times, and Philip, during a prayer, looking too sweet for words,

had held out his arm to me and said in a perfectly loud voice, "Tickle me!" Imagine the words, "Repent all you that have sinned" and then this fleshy, "Tickle me!"

AFTER MY FATHER was put in charge of the sales operation in New York, talk in the textile world became focused on a coming strike that would force the Kunhardt mill in Lawrence—which in good years had grossed $3.5 million—to the brink of bankruptcy. George E. had experienced strikes before; more than once over the years he had been driven to work through streetfuls of angry strikers. But now the situation was worse. As the Depression deepened, strikes were taking place all over the country and unemployment was ravaging the land. And even though George E.'s employees considered him reasonable and humane, in the public mind he was lumped in with the industrial tyrants who kept mill workers at poverty level and detested the labor movement. By early October an industry-wide strike loomed, as my grandfather's correspondence related:

October 5, 1931
Dear Phil,
The row has begun! At noontime the help at the Wood Worsted Mill struck, and all walked out.

October 8, 1931
Dear Phil,
I am sorry to report that they have caught us! Immediately after paying off last week's payroll, half a dozen youngsters dropped work in the card room and stampeded through our weave rooms and our spinning room, with the result that the whole card room went out.

October 19, 1931

Dear Phil,

I came to work early this morning and was opposite the Pacific Print Works at five minutes past seven. It took me from then until twenty-eight minutes past seven to get to our mill door. As one old fellow in the card room said, "People on the street were as thick as the hair on a dog's back, and all bristling." The concentration of pickets kept other mills from starting up at all. I rather think we are in for quite a long siege.

As circumstances headed more and more wildly out of control, the George E. Kunhardt Corporation's creditors moved in to take the reins of the company. From now on, the Bank of Manhattan Trust Company and the State Street Trust Company of Boston would have representatives on the premises at Lawrence, guiding curtailment of expenses and the company's every move. Salaries were immediately cut, my grandfather's by $6,000 a month, his sons' by $1,000 a year.

Now, more than ever beset by financial worries, my mother was determined to defeat what they called the Grim Spectre by doing whatever she could to "pull us out of the hole we are in." Writing was certainly a possibility. But writing what? And for whom?

4

Lucky Lady

Lucky Mrs. Ticklefeather is one of the characters Dorothy
created in a series of books she wrote and drew for children.

M EMORY WORKS in strange ways when it comes to visualizing the looks of a parent who has long been dead and buried. For instance, even though I have not seen him in the flesh for more than forty years, I have no problem calling up a picture of my father—he is always just as I remember him in the first decade of my life, in his thirties, strong and in charge. He is working in his garden on a summer's day, wearing nothing but khaki shorts held up by a wide leather belt, with a red L.L.Bean handkerchief looped over the belt at the hip, ready to be whipped out to mop up forehead sweat, of which there was always plenty. He could have been hilling his hollyhocks or snipping a few sweetheart roses which he presented to my mother each day as if they were jewels, or he could have been checking his bees behind the flower bed that ran along the northern side of his garden, the border of which undulated out into the grass, turned gracefully, and swept back in again.

It would have been the morning when my father was watching out for my little cousin Felix who, stricken with infantile paralysis, wore iron braces on his thin white legs. Flixie, as we called him, had been plunked down on the lawn like a crab next to my father to help him work. As my father dug in the dirt with a spade, Felix plucked out handfuls of weeds, making little piles. They talked about the weather and the garden and then, by mistake, the little boy suddenly broke wind. Turning red with humiliation, he squirmed and looked away. My father smiled and winked and said, "That's okay, Flix. Working men fart," and thereby elevated a crippled boy to the status of a man. I can see the light in my father's eyes, the casual, easy way he made us all feel good about ourselves.

This memory exercise is not so easy and automatic when the subject is my mother. She has been dead for twenty-three years now but when I call up her image, I first have to determine the stage of life that I wish to recall. Unlike the memory of my father—who never seemed to change either in age or setting—my recollection of my mother comes in a variety pack, a half dozen different ages with a face, a voice, a gesture, a setting to go with each. Her final stage, that of a scowling, bent old woman with tubes for oxygen running into her nostrils, was how people saw her in the late 1970s, how, unfortunately, our youngest two children still remember her—they knew no other Dorothy except the one that flitted between tilting flights of imagination and then slitted her eyes and ground her teeth in despair.

How different from my first memories of my mother. In her early thirties I remember she had a romantic look—feathered hair, sparkling eyes—and her mind was always darting about as she led the conversation, keeping everyone amused, making her husband proud, and constantly surprising her son. She was still young then, with three children, and was living in the country, completely isolated from the sophisticated social scene of her youth. Was she to be relegated to a life on a wooded New Jersey hill with no neighbors except birds that she hated and bees that she couldn't quite bring herself to hate since they were such a constant and persuasive mystery to her? Was she to accomplish nothing on her own?

My mother knew she was talented. Kate told her so over and over. And who, after all, would have been a better judge of Dorothy's writing talent, who was closer to her soul? Kate had been brought up a sensitive Quaker who thee'd and thou'd members of her family, and she inherited her parents' rage for the arts, especially literature, and their addiction to elegant language. Although filled with a missionary zeal to contribute good to the world, Kate wanted above all to be a writer, in particular a playwright. But no matter how hard she labored, her offerings came out slightly wooden. Her best friend, on the other hand, had a fresh, peppery style which filled Kate with both admiration and jealousy. It hurt her, too, when Dorothy was too quick with her, or ununderstanding of her words or critical of her writing. "Be a little more gentle," Kate implored, "and my love will be a little more easy."

My mother was thoughtless at times, yes, but that mostly stemmed from her peculiar way of looking at life, her insights and passion, her abounding curiosity, and her itch to get on with things. Her letters were lyrical, punctuated by acute powers of observation and an ability to tell stories and describe people and the world in vivid, fresh ways. So what was she to do with all these scattershot and unfulfilled talents? She had to think of something, and that something had to make money—the George E. Kunhardt Corporation was headed for extinction. There was a sense of impending doom in the house.

In the end, she settled on writing—a decision that began to coalesce in the early 1930s, when she helped start a new and ultraprogressive elementary school on our hill. At that time, the one private school in the area seemed painfully dull and old-fashioned to many of the bright young parents in the community. My mother and her friends wanted a school

that truly cherished children—their imaginations and their love of life—
as well as the endless potential of their minds. So my mother took a course
at the Bank Street College of Education in New York City, to help her get
a firmer grasp on how children's minds worked and on her feelings about
their education. Her notes from back then show how she was learning that
repetition and special sounds are basic to a child's way of thinking:

> Philip was eating Toast for his breakfast.
> Crunch, crunch, crunch went the
> Toast in Philip's mouth.
> It almost made Philip deaf to hear
> The munching, to hear the crunching, to
> Hear the scrunching of Toast in his mouth.
> How Loud it is.
> Crunch. Crunch. Crunch. Philip always has Toast
> For his breakfast.
> Crunch. He always has Toast for his supper, too.
> Breakfast Toast is a Noisy Toast. It is scrunchy, crunchy Toast.
> Supper Toast is Quiet Toast.

She was also learning to be as specific as possible.

"Come, let me wipe your mouth," said Philip's mother, and she
wiped his mouth on the elephant in the middle of the bib, and
then she took the left-hand corner of the bib where the pig was
and wiped his mouth on the pig. "Oh, mother, I like animals,"
said Philip. "How I wish I had a real live animal to live here with
me. If I had a real live animal," said Philip, "he would sleep on
the floor beside my bed and I'd be so quiet in the morning not to
wake him. I wouldn't even sing out loud. I'd just sing inside me."

The Mt. Kemble School in Morristown was founded on the basic principles of the Bank Street School. Both believed that "certain sounds of permanent happiness can be best established in early childhood and need to be continued as part of daily life." After much study and talk among those in the Morristown community who backed the idea, three women with Bank Street backgrounds were hired to help establish the new school. My mother was listed as one of the original governors, along with my father as treasurer.

After the first year of operation, which consisted of eleven tiny pupils plus a teacher, my mother was asked to write a description of Mt. Kemble and a mission statement for its official pamphlet. In doing so, she demonstrated how deeply involved she was in questions of early childhood education:

> For so few children, the equipment, the care, the devotion, all that
> has gone to enrich their days, has been lavish (she wrote). Lavish
> is an offensive word, and just here, an extraordinarily fitting word.
> The children have benefited in proportion to this lavishness.

The idea behind the school, she said, was to make each child's "seeing of things a keen seeing, and their hearing and smelling keen hearings and smellings—their power of touch a sensitive one. We want each child to feel in himself, his work, his play, his social relations, his whole life, a response to his total environment."

My mother went on to describe how this all-important response was nurtured through trips to a dairy farm, a chicken ranch, the coal yards, a blacksmith shop, and other centers of activity in Morristown. The children came back to the school and were allowed to re-create what they had seen and understood. She detailed their other activities as well:

Each morning there has been an hour of play outdoors in the sunshine with large outdoor blocks, a jungle gym, sawhorses, boards, and boxes with which to construct their garages, their boats, their aeroplanes, and their shops. Here is the spirit of invention and gaiety.

Each day they stand at the easel and paint with watercolors in bold free strokes pictures of whatever is in their minds.

Each day they model in clay.

Each day they tell stories.

One morning a week the children have been given an hour of rhythmics. They skip and jump and run as though they had within them some very special joyousness.

No reading has been taught to these five- and six-year-old children. They will start in next fall and learn by the method which teaches children to read whole sentences first, then words, and last of all letters. An acquaintance with the subject of arithmetic has been made this spring, the children mastering simple combinations of such concrete things as blocks and graham crackers.

At the end, my mother wrote: "We are sending our sons and daughters to the Mt. Kemble School, hoping they will learn that the heavens are flaming with stars—theirs for the seizing."

In my early childhood, when I was old enough to go to school, I would jump down our three porch steps, run past my brother Ken's chicken house, kick some gravel in front of the garage, and lope up the steep path in the field that led to the huge house lent to the school by Mr. Jenks—so high on the hill it gave us all the feeling, my mother thought, of "far-up-in-the-heavenness." I spent my first years there in what might well be called play. Ever since, my feeling about working hard has been associated with playing hard. It was, at least in part, my mother's unique mind that balked at the idea of reining in the fantastic imagination of a child at play. But my mother could also be lighthearted about this unusual school. Once, to make sure no one thought the workings of the school were normal, she put together a pamphlet called "The Outrageous Untruth about Mt. Kemble School," complete with hand-drawn, cartoonlike figures. Its premise: A child of Mt. Kemble watches Farmer Kreemdrinker's cow being milked and then expresses the experience of having seen a cow milked, first in blocks, then in carpentry, in song, in clay, in dance, and, finally, in storytelling. The final page had a stick-figure pupil spouting, "I saw a cow, I saw a brown cow, I saw a brown cow with brown eyes, I saw a brown cow with brown eyes and a brown neck."

Somewhere along in the process of helping start this school, my mother had become obsessed with how children's minds worked, especially what made them laugh. She had started keeping files on humor, on who found what funny and why. Every time one of her children said something humorous, she would write it down and file it away. She kept all her children's earliest drawings and paintings and studied them to see how they would illustrate people and places and ideas. She was learning that children were fascinated by other people's misfortune, that exaggerations—sometimes even grotesque distortions—struck little funny bones, that unexpected happenings brought on hoots of glee, that strange sounds and names provoked laughter, and that rhythmic repetition was appealing to little minds. She was learning, too, that situations in a story must not be too new for children or they would be confusing and the children would not recognize the everyday situation on which they were founded. Better to begin stories just a little removed from the commonplace and go from there. And children's drawings—how strident and to the point and colorful and simple!

By 1931, with the school only two years old, my mother was thinking about writing for children—maybe writing something outlandishly humorous. After all, Kate thought Dorothy had a "rich, rare strain of lunacy." But it was all still in the thinking stage. In what would become her signature approach to any writing project, she was collecting raw material, conducting research, learning as much as she possibly could, and covering all angles analytically before committing pen to paper. Later in life, when she and I collaborated, her incessant research would drive me mad—to the point where I would have to demand that she stop researching and write.

In June of 1932, Kate extended an invitation to Dorothy to visit with her later in the summer in a cottage on the grounds of an exclusive mountain hotel in the Adirondacks called the Ausable Club. Kate's husband, Harry Mali, would be there on weekends, but, still, it would be a relaxing, intimate time for the two women to catch up on all that had been happening in each of their lives, and a time, possibly, for Dorothy to experiment with some writing with Kate beside her to inspire her onward. My mother replied days later, clearly revealing the stress of her life:

Dearest Kate,

Of course, I am terrifically thrilled at the thought of Ausable and you. My prolonged silence has meant this: that for the last ten days I have had neither nurse nor cook as I have given up a nurse for good and let Esther go, and Elizabeth has been away on half of her yearly vacation. Children and housework and cooking com-

bined have been quite a job, and I haven't been able to do anything but just keep right at it. You should have gazed upon me ris-
ing in the morning, getting breakfast, dressing the children, and
whisking Phil to the 7:47 train, locking the house and taking the
children with us, of course. And so on. Well, it's over, fair Elizabeth has returned, and merely three children to care for seems like
idleness.

I think the first of August would be a better time for us to go.
Midges are hell. As to Elizabeth, I had planned to have her here to
make Phil comfortable in his aloneness, as he wants to come out
here every night. But I think I can manage to get someone to take
care of him and live here in the house and it would certainly give
me more freedom up there in the mountains to have her—as
without her I won't be able to go a step without Nan, Phil, and
Ken and will be completely tied down, all day and all evenings.
She is an ideal combination cook and nurse, and I think it would
add to our happiness tremendously to have her. Let me know if
there is going to be room for her. I won't say anything to her till
I hear from you, but in the meantime I'll be looking around for a
substitute here and working out whether I can swing it or not. It
seems silly to be thinking of pennies so much, but you understand. The mill is virtually closed and the Lord knows what the
next few months hold.

In early August, my father drove us and our nursemaid, Elizabeth,
north to the Adirondacks. There, Dorothy spent a productive two
weeks with Kate, talking and writing. By the time her vacation was up,
she had actually finished a manuscript, a prototype for a children's
picture- and word-book she titled *Junket Is Nice.*

Above the handwritten text was a dashed-off drawing of an old man eating something out of a large bowl. At first, the bowl had been filled with gooseberries (and the original title was *Gooseberries Are Nice*) but right there on the first page of the manuscript wherever the word "gooseberries" had appeared, it had been erased, and the word "Junket" substituted. Junket was the name of a brand-new puddinglike dessert made with a special rennet tablet, to be mixed with milk, sugar, and vanilla.

"Once there was an old, old man with a red cap and red slippers," the story began:

> He was sitting at a table eating out of a big blue bowl. He was eating Junket out of the big blue bowl. The old man ate and ate and ate and ate. More Junket and more Junket and more Junket and more Junket, until at last people began to be very much surprised at how much Junket he was eating and they began to come and look at him because he seemed to be such a very hungry old man. So people and their friends began coming to look at the old man eating his Junket.

The manuscript was thirty pages long, each page with a primitive sketch done in black crayon, with the old man's Santa Claus–type cap and slippers done in red, the bowl in blue, and some yellow scattered about. People kept arriving to watch the old man eating his Junket and as soon as all the people in the world were there, the old man suggested that they try to guess what he was thinking about while he was eating his Junket. First he gave them a big hint by telling them three things he definitely was not thinking about—a cow and a rabbit and a spider. With that help, the people started to guess—a turtle, an elephant, a pig, a bear, a giraffe? No they all were wrong. But look, there just happened to be a giraffe resting under a tree nearby. The giraffe jumped to his feet and before a single person could make another guess the giraffe walked right up to the old man and said, "Old man, it is very easy for me to see you are thinking about Junket."

And the word "Junket" took up a whole page of the manuscript in Dorothy's big printed letters. The giraffe was right, and as a prize the giraffe got to lick the bowl. The story ended soon after with the old man getting ready to leave for home.

It was a crude beginning, but my mother began to revise it. Sometime after her return to Morristown, she changed the giraffe into a little boy on a tricycle (based, she always said, on me). Unfinished, unpolished, graceless, still, the manuscript had the bare bones of a different kind of book for children, different from the average children's books of the time, whose stories and language were logical and which were illustrated with elegantly professional pictures. What Dorothy's *Junket* needed now was a heavy injection of absurdity in both story and illustration.

Dorothy worked hard on her manuscript in September, and in October of 1932 she submitted a rewritten and illustrated version to Charles Scribner's Sons. The drawings were no longer crayon sketches. Now they were done in bold strokes with India ink and colored with watercolor. They filled the pages playfully and dynamically, using empty space as artfully as drawn space. The old man was capless, bald, and smiling, and had grown an enormous, curly red beard. The little boy wore shorts and he and his tricycle cast a shadow, giving dimension. The world of people resembled a field of ants. The guessed-at animals were now each embellished with absurd characteristics. The old man's hints about what he was not thinking about were "a walrus with an apple on his back," "a one year old lion blowing out the candle on his lovely birthday cake," and "a cow with her head in a bag." Some of the guesses that inevitably brought on "WRONG!" from the old man included "a daddy longlegs holding up his foot for the sun to warm it," "a pig seeing how many minutes it takes for a cold bath," "a hippopotamus with all the lights turned out laughing at how hard it is to see other people on the sofa," "a pelican pretending he didn't hear anybody call him," and "a rabbit wondering if there can be a bunch of grapes tied to his tail."

In the end, all the foolish, anonymous people are out-guessed—not by a hard-to-identify-with giraffe—but by a clear-thinking little boy on a tricycle who comes out of the enormous crowd made up of everybody in the world. Of course, the little boy gets to lick the bowl. And the whole world is mad that he is right:

All the people in the world were very angry and they stamped their feet and while they were stamping their feet they said "Oh dear it isn't fair for a little boy to have all that fun licking. Why we were just guessing all those old guesses for fun when we knew it was Junket all the time."

The book ends with the old man hitching a ride home on the back of the little boy's tricycle saying over his shoulder, "Oh my oh my oh my oh my oh my but Junket is Nice."

In a stroke of imaginative genius, my mother chose to hand-print the text rather than having it set in type. The hand-printed words themselves seemed to come rushing forward and then were suddenly stopped cold by a giant WRONG, sped on again, filled with repetition and rigmarole. It was as if a child had hand-lettered the text and dreamed up the simple drawings.

Scribner's turned the book down. It wasn't that they didn't like it, it was because of the country's economy—the time was 1932, the depth of the Great Depression. On November 2, editor Carol Hinman wrote:

Dear Mrs. Kunhardt,

I am sorry to write, that try as we might, we cannot cooperate with you in publishing *Junket Is Nice*. I do want you to understand that we like your work tremendously. In fact your story has more freshness and originality than anything that has come into the office since I have been with Scribner's. But, as I told you before, the problem was to reduce manufacturing costs until it was profitable to sell the book at a normal price. This we could not do if we were to print in color. And frankly I think your work demands color. For these reasons, we are regretfully returning the manuscript to you today.

I hope you will take the book to someone else who may be able to solve the manufacturing problem. Why don't you submit it to Miss Louise Seaman (at the Macmillan company) who is wise and able and I believe will appreciate your work. Miss Seaman would be the first choice and after that Doubleday or Knopf. If there is any way I can help, do let me know, for certainly *Junket Is Nice* should be on someone's list. Even if we can't publish it, I'm glad that we had the fun of seeing it.

Instead of taking Carol Hinman's advice, my mother next approached Harcourt Brace & Company in person, with her manuscript under her arm. This time she got a positive reception. Yes, the editors would like to publish her *Junket*, but, again, it was much too expensive to reproduce as it was. The illustrations used all the primary colors—red, blue, and yellow—plus black. Please, they asked, could you redo your drawings with black and just one other color? My mother must have blanched at the thought. Her illustrations might have looked simple enough, but each one had required hours of research, torn-up sketches, and the calling up of courage to produce an image of professional quality.

It was simply a terrible struggle for her to draw. Many years later, my mother recalled her difficulties:

> I remember holding a page of the dictionary against the glass of the window and tracing a lion. That was long ago, for my children, and now it's a multitude of grandchildren who make their demands, and they are specific. "It's such a trouble for you to draw, grandmummy," they say tactfully. "Why don't you just write the words and let a real person make the pictures?"

Dorothy was convinced that she could never create her *Junket* illustrations a second time, but her book had been accepted so she bluffed her answer. Yes, she certainly could draw new illustrations. She had no idea how, but . . . As soon as she got home that night she filled the bathtub with warm water and, in a fit of inspiration and frustration, threw the manuscript into the tub. The watercolors rose to the surface in clouds of blue and yellow and red. The India ink held fast. When she wrapped up the swollen pages years later to put away for her children, she wrote a note to go along with the package:

> I first did these pages in five colors, using my children's paint box. Harcourt Brace accepted the story with the command that the pictures be redone in pen and ink only—color was too risky an investment for an author's first work. As I could not, in a million years, have made these illustrations a second time, I took a great

chance and dropped the whole book into a full bathtub. Luckily
the pages did not melt, and when ironed were usable.

The book had a style all its own, capturing the language and speech
patterns of children, as well as a wryness and a wisdom which showed
through the pages. It looked different, too. It was oblong in shape, the
colors were black and red, each page was bordered with red, the text was
hand-printed, and some words were larger than others and emphasized
by capital letters when the little boy guessed right. Six letters spelling
out Junket screamed across two full pages. Dorothy even wrote out the
copyright in her own bold capital letters—1933, Harcourt Brace & Co.

Junket was an instant success. It was published on September 17,
1933, and the reviews were uniformly excellent. But one, written by
the famous *New York Herald Tribune* columnist, curmudgeon, and wit,
Franklin P. Adams, helped propel my mother into the stratosphere.
Adams stumbled on the book and loved it—loved it so much he wrote a
review in the *Trib,* parodying *Junket's* style:

> Once there was a new, new book with a red jacket and a red cover,
> and a man who had on a blue shirt and a yellow tie saw the book
> with the red jacket and the red cover in a book store, so he went
> into the store and bought the book and took it into his white
> house that had three boys and one girl in it and two dogs and
> two cats.

Along the way, Adams ventured that *Junket* had "the greatest sympathetic simplicity and the most poetic and affectionate imagination"
he'd ever encountered—"and I don't except *The Story of Little Black
Sambo* or *Alice's Adventures in Wonderland.*" The review closed with a

command: "Read it every day before supper. So every day before supper the man read the book, and if you guess that the boys or the man
ever got tired of it you are WRONG."

By Christmas of 1933, sales of *Junket* had skyrocketed. Heavily promoted through radio and print ads, the rectangular red book was not
only on Franklin P. Adams's holiday list but was also on the *New
Yorker*'s (E. B. White's wife, Katharine, wrote that the book is "exactly
what children like"); and on the *New York Times*'—"It has the delightful absurdity and exuberance that characterizes true nonsense." *Vogue*
said, "Children swoon over it." Virginia Kirkus wrote, "A silly, delicious
story which you'll have to read until the youngest knows it by heart."
Publishers Weekly even announced a December guessing contest with
cash prizes as further promotion of *Junket*.

My mother was finally, for the very first time, making money on her
own, and by doing something she loved. She felt very lucky. Even
though *Junket* was priced at only one dollar a copy, and her royalty per-
centage was very low, the checks from Harcourt made all the difference
in our lives. My father was so pleased and proud of his wife's success
that he went around smiling. It never crossed his mind to be threatened.
All he could talk of was the brilliant creature to whom he was married.

In her own way, Kate was also caught up in her friend's newfound
success. Although she'd had one of her poems published in a little magazine, her desk was littered with rejection slips and now, as if to keep
away bad news, she was concentrating on a long-range project—a play
about two young women on a round-the-world cruise, surrounded by a
lot of odd characters. Kate liked to read aloud and then discuss what she
had written while Dorothy chose to hide every one of her words until
they were in print. In a letter written on May 28, 1933, Kate was starting
to show a little understanding of Dorothy's reluctance to show a work
in progress:

Can you and Phil come to us over the Fourth of July? Do bring what you have written if it's in a state where the human eye won't wither it. I never used to understand why birds wouldn't go back and sit on eggs that humans had handled. Now I know.

In the fall Kate thanked Dot for sending a first-edition copy of *Junket Is Nice* with an inscription from Aunt Dorothy to her godson Freddy:

I had already ordered one copy from Mr. Macy's and will get still more to give and show to other people. But Freddy's own is his most treasured possession. To Allen it is simply "Book" as, indeed, it is to me, too.

"Book" to me is the trumpet of a new stage for all of us. (As we have shared so much despair and indecision, I now shamelessly share in the pride of authorship.) I hope you are very proud, my Dorothy—not only of the inspiration that makes the book so poignant but of the "drudgery" which gave it its rhythm and landed it in a good publisher's hands.

WHEN MY MOTHER realized that she could be a successful children's book author, she decided to take over part of our attic and turn it into her workroom. With my father's help, she set up a desk and some lamps and was ready to go. Whenever she could escape up there during the day she did, and we could usually hear her chair scraping the floor at night or early in the morning as she wrote her books with a feverish hand. In the winters she wore extra sweaters, even an overcoat, in her tiny, freezing hideaway, but in the hot summers she stripped down to her slip and tied handkerchiefs around her wrists to keep sweat from smattering her manuscripts.

I think my mother stewed and struggled more than she actually wrote. Sometimes she would come down from her attic office without having put a single word on paper. Because she wanted to do everything perfectly, she had a problem finishing projects. And it wasn't just a writing problem. Our house was filled with tiny half-sweaters that she began to knit when she heard about her friends' new babies. Whenever she painted a piece of furniture, she would lose interest in the process and our father had to paint the second half of it. And I still remember how she never finished the flag for my club—The Wolf Pack. She promised to do it and told me she had a wonderful picture in her mind of a fierce wolf. I kept saying she could just make a small sketch of the wolf she envisioned on a scrap of paper, just so I could enjoy thinking of it while I was waiting. My mother said she had it in her mind and she wanted to surprise me with the wolf's full terribleness. For a few days she sewed a black strip around the sides of the yellow cloth we had picked for the flag. She sewed a little more a few days later but then she stopped. I found the red spool of thread she was going to sew the wolf with and the material all folded up together in her bottom bureau drawer under her attempts at knitting, along with a very ancient copy of *Little Red Riding Hood* with a marker at the fiercest wolf picture. I knew right then that she'd never finish my flag. She meant to, but she had thought about it enough. And in her own mind it was done and she was tired of it. Her imagination was darting and vivid and she didn't like being bogged down with practical details.

But when an idea caught hold, there was no stopping her. The words came dashing out of her pencil, accompanied by frantic sketches of what she wanted her characters to look like. At times, she would write an entire book at a single sitting. No line was sacred—nothing she had first written couldn't be scratched out or changed or discarded. She was always trying for the right words, exactly the right sounds, and in the white heat of creation her mind outraced her hand and left scrawls behind on her big yellow pads. But those great bursts of inspiration were never for naught—her ragged first drafts, no matter how rapidly laid down, caught the essence of the books to come. Her initial sketches were unreproducible, merely guidelines, but they always captured the ideas she was after and those first expressions on a character's face, as well as his or her bizarre actions, could be seen in the final, finished product.

Way before the excitement over *Junket* had calmed, my mother's fertile mind was hard at work on a second book. As a child, she had been taken to the Barnum & Bailey circus and had even been introduced to Zip, P. T. Barnum's original, aging "missing link," who still performed in the sideshow. As soon as we children were old enough to survive the crush, she led us to Madison Square Garden and the hectic joys of the circus. There were times when she brought just one of us along— Nancy or me or Ken—to record our reactions and delights by jotting down our words verbatim on a tiny pad of paper in her purse. (I still have the ring I pulled off the finger of the 1930s Ringling Brothers giant, Jack Earle, who bent down from his sideshow platform, extended his ring finger with its prize, and scooped up my quarter all in one motion.)

The circus was a familiar and fantastic place to her and it was here, under the big top, that she set her second book for children—the story of Little Peewee, the circus dog. Her illustrations alone were worth the price of admission—the tent, the elephants, the exaggerated red-and-yellow performers (the giant consisting of just his ankles and shoes). Each image burst out of its frame as she masterfully played with composition and space.

The book told the story of the star of the big show—"the teeniest weeniest teeny teeny teeny weeny weeny weeny little dog in all the world"—Little Peewee the circus dog. Everybody loved Little Peewee. But then one day he began to grow. And he grew and he grew and he grew. Until he wasn't small at all anymore. In fact he was just like any other plain, ordinary dog. So, of course, he had to be dismissed from the circus. Everybody cried to see him go, from the clown to the fat lady, to the man on top of six tables, to the snake, to the giraffe who swallowed a ball, the goat on a burning bed, the lady hanging by her nose. But wait. Stop all those tears. For Peewee suddenly began to grow again. And he grew. And he grew. And he grew—and then the circus man said, "Oh my dearest Little Peewee now you won't have to go after all because you are so lovely and big you are just the very dog for my circus." Instead of being displayed in a tiny, tiny box, now Little Peewee stepped out of the biggest box in the world, and could not squeeze into the two-page spread, to the acclaim that he was the "hugest most enormous dog in the whole world" which made Little Peewee "very happy indeed."

The story of Little Peewee, which was titled *Now Open the Box,* with its hand-printed text and wildly bold yet deceptively simple drawings, also took the country by storm. Once again, Dorothy had a hit. At home we had no idea of what was going on. Our mother was seldom around. Caught up in success, she searched everywhere for ideas for future books. No longer did she feel stuck in Morristown. From the nation's capital, staying at the Mayflower Hotel, she wrote Kate:

Here I am alone in big Washington—on a pilgrimage—working in the Library of Congress on an idea I had for a book. After two days of slaving I am very discouraged and mixed up—there really isn't a single thing in this world that someone hasn't already done, and done pretty well. It's annoying beyond words. I think I shall go home and take care of my husband and children again.

This anxiety, however, did not slow her down. The following year—
1935—was a banner year for my mother. On the heels of the success of
the story of Little Peewee came two more Harcourt Brace publications:
Brave Mr. Buckingham and *Lucky Mrs. Ticklefeather*.

By today's standards of what is politically correct, *Brave Mr. Buckingham* definitely wasn't. The story revolved around a little boy named
Billy, who was scared of having a loose tooth pulled. So his kindly Uncle
Alexander told Billy a story, about an American Indian named Mr.
Buckingham, that made being scared of such a little thing as a wiggly
tooth seem silly. Instead of being made of blood and flesh and bones,
Mr. Buckingham was made of Nugg. Which was fortunate, because he
was always having the most terrible accidents, like falling into a hole
while trying to catch some bees in a bottle, and having his ear cut off by
a jaggedy rock. But brave Mr. Buckingham just smiled a brave smile and
said, THAT DIDN'T HURT. Those big words were accompanied by a picture of the smiling red Indian in his headdress and little grass skirt, with
one ear missing—no, there it was, lying on the ground beside his foot.

As the story unfolds, Mr. Buckingham loses a foot to a vicious-looking
fish; an arm to a huge pair of pincers; another foot to some crazy-
looking machinery; a leg to an open stove; a hand to a saw dropped from
an airplane; the rest of his arm to a pistol shot; the rest of his leg to a to-
boggan accident; his other ear to a collision with a flagpole; and finally
his body to a truck whose driver had mistaken Mr. Buckingham for a log
in the middle of the road. Each time, a reduced Indian told the aston-
ished reader, THAT DIDN'T HURT. In the end, Mr. Buckingham was just a
head, contentedly being fed strawberries by his granddaughter.

After Billy had heard his uncle's funny story, he, of course, allowed
his wiggly tooth to be pulled and, when it popped right out of his
mouth, Billy smiled a brave smile and said, "That didn't hurt."

Lucky Mrs. Ticklefeather, which followed, had no macabre overtones.

It is the story of a sweet, old, eccentric lady who loves sunflowers and whose best friend is a puffin named Paul. When Paul disappears, she sends a policeman after him, who collects almost everything but Paul along the way—from a suspicious-looking pillow to a bottle of milk of magnesia. He finally finds Paul, with a sunflower in his mouth, just about to have his head chopped off by Mr. Buggles for the Thanksgiving meal of Mr. Buggles's fifteen children. The policeman quickly trades Paul for an enormous fish and takes him home to Mrs. Ticklefeather. From then on, Mrs. Ticklefeather sits beside a huge vase holding the sunflower, with Paul the Puffin on her lap, "and every little while she put her arm around Paul and she gave him a tight hug and she said 'Oh, what a LUCKY LUCKY LUCKY LADY I AM!'"

"*Lucky Mrs. Ticklefeather* is a *Junket Is Nice* type of thing, but, I think, better," wrote my mother. "It is a mystery story for young children, as there is a considerable element of suspense and surprise in it. At least, I hope there is."

IN JUST THREE YEARS, my mother had become enormously successful with her off-the-wall stories for children and, because of them, her world was expanding. She wrote Kate about how silly her sudden celebrity was:

I write one idiotic little nothing, have it published, and the world is at your feet. Success of any kind that brings publicity, brings admiration—you need make no effort from then on; people run to you. It is ridiculous, but it is so.

Through Franklin P. Adams, Dorothy had made some connections in the New York literary world. Adams had insisted on meeting her, was entranced by her girlish looks and her quicksilver mind, and tried to do something about her low royalty rate. "I called up the Authors League," he wrote her in 1934:

and it is as I thought. There is no law to compel a publisher to pay more than one tenth of one percent; but it is the custom to never pay less than ten percent on the list price. When the author also is the illustrator, the royalty might be larger: or the illustrator gets about $400 for the drawings. It is obvious to me that you have been gypped; and that it may be too late to do anything about that book. But not about the next one. You should join the Authors League, 9 East 38th Street. The annual dues are $25, and they may be paid quarterly. When you come to town, or before, call up or write Miss Luisa Sillcox, Secretary. I talked to her this morning, and she knows all about it. She said that Alf Harcourt was plausible. I know that, and I know that he would chisel the pennies off a corpse's eyes, and think it good business. Donald Brace is decenter at heart, but also thinks that business is business. Miss Sillcox says that she would like to see your contract; and I know that you can't fight those birds without some organization. You have got to fight them, too. First, they hate publicity, which by God they will get from me if they don't treat you better; and second, there aren't many authors like you that make actual money for a publisher and are latent gold mines.

FPA.

Adams also tried his hardest to romance my mother. Once, at his house, with his wife and children away for the day, he suddenly appeared half dressed, which so frightened my mother (she much later told her daughters), that she straightaway fled back to her car and

Morristown. She was obviously intrigued by him, though, and said as much to my father whose jealousy was immediately aroused.

What made Adams so fascinating to Dorothy was not his hawklike face, craggy looks, and mustache, but his lifestyle, his friends, and the aura of wit and sophistication that surrounded him. After all, his column, The Conning Tower, had been for years the leading voice of sophisticated humor in America's humor capital. In the '20s, it had made him the extraordinary sum of $25,000 a year—just for being arch and highbrow as he ranged over what was going on in the high-society circles of New York. His group of friends consisted of some of the most celebrated American writers of the age who, famously, met at the Algonquin Hotel's "Round Table," including Alexander Woollcott, George S. Kaufman, Marc Connelly, Edna Ferber, Robert Benchley, James Thurber, Dorothy Parker, and the founder and editor of the *New Yorker,* Harold Ross. More than once, Adams brought my mother as his guest to a Round Table gathering. Later in life, she confided to her daughters that Dorothy Parker, probably miffed at the inclusion of another woman, had behaved rudely toward her.

The fast banter around the table, the wit of so many *New Yorker* and Broadway stars, the literary conversation, the ingenuity, and the attention any guest got from the regulars made a deep and lasting impression on my mother. The experience made her start dreaming that she, too, could be a part of this high-powered, sparkling scene, if she could only produce something of the same excellence on an adult level that she had already achieved for youngsters.

My mother envied the poet Rachel Field, who had proved she could enchant adults as well as children. She saw Gertrude Stein's *Autobiography of Alice B. Toklas* and Virginia Woolf's *Flush: A Biography* on the adult best-seller list and she thought she could emulate them with her own fictionalized autobiography, telling the story of the marriage of a

young couple and what happens when a tragedy befalls them. Something serious and worthwhile, after all the lighthearted absurdities of
her children's stories. When she wrote Kate in April of 1935, she was already deeply involved with her idea for a novel: "My mind is struggling
so to be on higher things. It resents very much and takes with bad grace
being forced into iceboxes and linen closets."

Iceboxes and linen closets were foreign matter to Kate, but pregnant
now for the third time, she was feeling sorry for herself. "I rather enjoy
hating practically everyone in sight," she wrote Dot in the summer of
1935:

> I'm terribly lonely and there's not a book I want to read any-
> where, and there's a smell of paint remover all over the house be-
> cause of some floors being fixed. I know, I know, my Dorothy,
> I'm damn lucky, feeling the way I do that I don't have to cook and
> look after the children and exert myself and snap out of it. But let
> me moan—it's such fun being discontented after a lifetime of
> grateful appreciation.

Even through this blue period of pregnancy, Kate found it remarkable that Dorothy could jump from wife and mother to creative author,
and still keep her sanity. "You have to add one personality to another to
do it," she wrote. "And that, to begin with, is a terrible strain. You have
to jump from one chair to the other, always keeping them both filled."
But aside from wondering at the "fatiguing" part of Dorothy's existence, Kate had only admiration for what it produced. "Your books are
delicious," she wrote. "But much more than that, they are new. You
have not used an old pattern in them at all. The rhythm is a new one."

For Dorothy, even such praise from her friend wasn't enough. She
felt absolutely driven to write a novel. She craved an adult audience and

the special acclaim of that achievement. But it didn't come in a flash of inspiration as had been happening during the last three years. By mid-May of 1935 she wrote Kate of the agony she was going through on this new path of endeavor:

I am in complete turmoil and upset over the organizing conception of my book. It will be a good year, as I feel now, before I write the first word. And I may never. And if I do, it may be no good. But I have to, have to try. I am going away tomorrow to lock myself in a hotel room in New York for a week and simply think how this thing should be written. As you may guess, I'm almost insane. And if I break the high tension now, I'll never get it back. I feel like an awful fool—probably I'm reaching for the moon. You understand how I feel—Desperate!

5.

Bramblebush

The house on the hill in New Jersey. Dorothy did most
of her writing in a tiny office on the third floor.

Throughout the 1930s, when my mother wasn't working in her attic room or in an office she later rented on the square in Morristown, she vanished into hotel rooms in the city to work by herself without the myriad duties of mother and wife to get in her way.

For the purpose of stirring the muse she once wrote a story about one of her tries at city solitude. She called it *A Week-End of One's Own*, a humorous curtsy to Virginia Woolf's extended essay *A Room of One's Own*. The story was a self-mocking, tongue-in-cheek account of her own literary aspirations. Written in the first person, it is a scantily clad autobiography, grandiose in its self-deprecation. Dorothy named herself "Star," a successful author of books for children, who yearns to write something sparkling and important for adults.

The story begins with Horace, Star's husband, making a suggestion: "Darling, I thought you could just go away for the weekend and write something really good, I positively know you have it in you, you are so talented, everybody says so." And when Horace said "something really good," he, too, meant something for adults, because "there is no money in juveniles." "But I can't think of anything to write about," Star protests.

Star takes a room in the Pennsylvania Hotel and continues to think about what she might write, her thoughts punctuated periodically by her fears of being a "rank amateur" and by phone calls of encouragement from Horace:

> After that last phone call I worked even harder than ever. I struggled, yes, you could say struggle, because it was a struggle to think of something really good. I did think of quite a variety of different subjects and lo the afternoon had slipped away before I had even the vaguest idea.

As she muses on plotlines and characters and scandalous, amusing topics, Star's thoughts drift again and again to "something near my heart"—her successful book for children, *Three Rabbits Went Hippity*, and how it called out for a sequel, *Three Rabbits Went Hop*. But then Star remembers there is no money in children's books and the family's money situation is grim and so she returns to her musings on ideas for adult fiction:

> And then suddenly my eyes rested on the little table before me, and I gazed and gazed and all I could think of was that table. Almost as in a trance, I took up one of my new pencils and wrote the first words I had written all afternoon, and they just came, it wasn't as I had planned to write them at all.

O table, is it fun to be a table?
Or is it
Not fun
Just standing there that you can't be able
To get
So very much
Done.

Exhausted, Star calls her bachelor brother and joins him for dinner, the theater, and a nightclub. When she gets back to her hotel room at 4:00 a.m., there are telephone message slips everywhere:

In practically less than ten shakes of a lamb's tail I heard Horace beating on the door. I rushed to unlock it and in he staggered, gaunt, wide-eyed, trembling. "I thought you were dead, darling," he gasped.

After a few romantic hours together, they happily head home and during the drive Horace asks Star what exactly she has written during her creative hours alone. She reads him the poem about the table.

"What is that?" Horace asks.

"That is what I wrote," Star answers.

With that Horace suddenly loses control of the car, which spins into a ditch.

This little story about literary hopes, writer's block, spousal over-attentiveness, and creative whimsy fit perfectly with my mother's high-spirited, experimental mindset during her first rush of children's books. She was confident enough to make fun of herself and the whole business of inspiration and accomplishment, yet the same subjects could not be dealt with so playfully in the crucial year ahead. It was one thing to make fun of the difficulty of writing for adults, quite another to tackle serious prose directly. But she was determined to make a name for herself in adult fiction. She was thirty-four years old and probably thought it was now or never.

The inspiration for her novel was a brand-new venture unfolding in Morristown. The Seeing Eye, an organization devoted to the training of guide dogs to be eyes for the blind, had opened its national headquarters in our town, and now our streets and sidewalks were filled with a daily parade of German shepherds, their trainers—often blindfolded—and, eventually, blind men and their guide dogs walking together, practicing this new and humane method of dealing with sightlessness.

My mother was not a dog lover, but on the streets of Morristown she watched the training in admiration for hours at a time, as she found before her a ready-made, fresh, inspiring story just waiting to be told. Her book, she decided, would be the real story of The Seeing Eye, describing all the hard work of getting into the program, the qualities of calm and intuition in the chosen dogs, the difficult months of training, and how one of these remarkable dogs could change a blind man's life. But instead of a straight reportorial approach, she would transform the story into glowing fiction about a young couple whose marriage falls apart when the man is accidentally blinded and his bright, complex wife is beset by revulsion and an overwhelming desire to escape. The marriage would finally come back together with the help of a Seeing Eye dog, the perseverance of the husband, and by the awakening and rebirth of the wayward wife.

The fictitious couple would, of course, be based on Dorothy and Phil. My mother was convinced that if she could write this story, she would have a best seller on her hands, much as her first attempt at a children's book had become a runaway success.

After a vacation week in Bermuda as guests of the Malis, my sun-burned parents were home and Dorothy was in hot pursuit of her novel.

In the spring of 1935 she wrote Kate: "I have been at The Seeing Eye practically night and day for weeks. I am living and breathing it."

Kate was of two opinions:

Your ambitions seem to me, when I first hear of them, to be, as you say, "reaching for the moon." Only when I first think of them. Then the excitement and desire begins to infect me, too.

Dorothy had introduced Kate to one of the directors of The Seeing Eye, Morris Frank, and the two of them had spent hours in earnest conversation. In May, Kate wrote her friend:

I wonder if it is The Seeing Eye itself or Morris Frank's personality that makes it so enthralling? Of course, his blindness lends a peculiar poignancy to his anguish of mind; but what is really troubling him is just what we were so unhappy about ten years ago. I know what it feels like to be bursting with arrogance and quivering with self-distrust at the same time; to swear to heaven that you will have nothing if not a jewel without flaw and yet nurse the conviction that you'll be lucky to get a splintered pebble.

As her research continued, Dorothy began writing. The first chapter had the heroine, Nell, wrenching herself out of bed at five o'clock one early spring morning to accompany her simple, loving husband, Jared, on a hurry-up trout-fishing trek to a nearby stream to wade in the rushing water for an hour or two before Jared had to change into his suit and catch his commuter train. When Jared kisses Nell awake:

a sort of desperateness spread over her. Couldn't he see that the last thing in the whole world she wanted to do was get up on a cold morning and go and watch him fish? Still perhaps it was difficult to know if she gave no sign. And no sign would she give.

Later, as dawn begins to light the woods, Jared points out what he feels are startling spring sights. "Don't you love the different shades of green?" Jared says to Nell. "And did you see all the bloodroots everywhere?"

Nell pretends to like what Jared likes, but inside she is seething:

"I hate brooks," Nell thought. "I hate cold, I hate woods. I hate ferns and bloodroots. I like to think about them and read about them but not be near them. Jared would never understand that I would rather talk for hours about what is poetry and what is beauty, and what is love and what is jealousy, and what is hate and what is happiness, and what is everything, than see a sunset or hear a birdcall or pick a flower. I like to think about things. Jared likes to do them."

Right off the bat, the lines are drawn. Nell and Jared are opposites. Dorothy had not had to dig too far into her imagination for these basic qualities in her hero and heroine, for they existed openly and lavishly in their real-life models, in her and my father. She liked to read and think and tinker and take notes under a 100-watt bulb, occasionally going to the window and waving to her husband in the garden. My father liked to dig, chop, carry, and plant and every once in a while turn to the house, spy her in a window, and wave back to his beloved Dot.

Growing up, Nan and Ken and I heard it over and over again. Dad couldn't bear to be confined, whether it was by blankets at night or clothes in the daytime, whether walls were hemming him in, or cities.

He needed air, he said, and he needed earth and high trees and wind and stars and water and space—the very things our mother didn't need at all. Her perfect world was being shut off from nature's elements and walled in against the sun. She once told me she had come up with something that would give her the utmost pleasure if it became a reality. Her invention was a sleeping tube, a host of which would be available at all of New York City's subway stations, like the little lockers where you checked your bag for a quarter. In the middle of a hurried day in the city, one could inch into one of these comfy tubes, close the hatch, and have an hour's peaceful rest as the trains roared by.

My mother had set out to base her heroine on herself, but through a twist here, an exaggeration there, the fictional wife was almost evil. And, unlike the real-life partnership of an oddly-paired happy couple, the fictional marriage seemed headed for disaster:

> "I'm tired of the way Jared touches me," she said to herself. "Nothing exciting or insinuating about it. He just plain takes hold and then I always know what he is going to do. He is too good, too safe, too perfect. Jared never really takes a chance; he's so level-headed I could shriek!"

Bit by bit, my mother was building Nell's character by revealing traits of her own and intensifying them. Dorothy didn't like dogs much. Nell hated dogs: "She had been brought up to loathe them. She despised the way their hair came off on dresses." Dorothy had received a lot of amber jewelry from Phil over the years. Nell hated amber:

> When they were married Nell had told Jared she loved amber— it caught the sunlight and kept it imprisoned. Ever since Jared had bought only amber for her. Christmas, birthday, anniversary—

nothing but amber. He never guessed how tired to death she was of it.

Dorothy often complained of Phil smoking his pipe. Nell hated pipe smoke, especially in the car:

She said it was sickening to have to ride along with clouds of the nasty stuff that had already been in and out of his lungs and go- ing into her good clean lungs. Even if you don't inhale, even if it's just gone up and down your nose, I don't want it.

To describe what Nell looked like, my mother had her character stand in front of a mirror and say, in the third person, what she saw:

"It was a most satisfactory face—never full—unpredictable. When she smiled it was abandoned and merrily gypsy. In repose she usually managed to have it a wistful and Madonna face and even when she was thinking particularly disagreeable thoughts, her face found no trouble in wearing her specialty in expres- sions—that elfin, sensitive, fleetingness that is so attractive."

All her life my mother was a student of faces. Not only faces but whole bodies, and she studied them endlessly on the streets, in stores, at parties, and, often, on the train to New York City.

"There's a woman across the aisle with legs like sticks," she once observed:

really, just skin wrapped around the bone—and a corded neck. Just tight strings sticking out; that means worry and disappoint- ment. Next to her is a woman with fat legs, the kind that start in

shapely ankles and mount onward and upward into a swollen column. No one would believe a fat one and a thin one sitting on the
same seat. It sounds made up. Practically everything in life seems
made up. There's a man over there with no chin at all, just a mouth
and a neck underneath. A little girl further up the car picking her
nose and eating it. After the first bit she evidently changed her
mind and deposited the rest in little dabs on the arm of the seat.

It was easy for Dorothy to transfer her vivid, rapid-fire, X-ray ob-
servations of people straight into Nell's mind and make her fictional self
seem bright, witty, yet vaguely vulgar as well. Nothing from her own
interior monologue was off limits. Take, for instance, her "fictional" ru-
minations about attending weddings with her husband:

Jared had edged very near to Nell and felt for her hand. Taken it,
held it tight. To him it was always a new wedding for themselves,
a new consecration. He was saying the words along with the minister "For better, for worse—till death us do part." And she might
be standing there thinking of anything at all—of shocking things;
sometimes of whether the bride was a virgin; or whether the
groom would prove impotent tonight; or whether they had read
up on the art of lovemaking, courtship, the woman's part; or how
to avoid rape on the wedding night and how to achieve orgasm,
all the things you could find in that book that everyone was always getting ads for in the mail—special unabridged edition
$4.11 and it came to you in a plain cardboard box so as not to be
embarrassing.

Later, Jared described Nell's lips: "Full ripe lips for kissing—my
own wench." That sort of talk bored Nell very much:

Yes, it fell very flat with her. Indeed it amused her not in the slightest degree—not even a twinge of amusement did it give her, and she said so, coldly, and managed to make him seem boorish and he would be ashamed.

As the story proceeds, it becomes more and more obvious that this mismatched couple is coming unstuck. At an overnight house party they attend and which Nell describes right down to the anti-Roosevelt chatter, she confronts him in their bedroom:

"Jared, I suppose it would surprise you to know that plenty of your friends think nothing of sleeping with each other's husbands and wives?"

"Well, I probably should be more interested," Jared replied, "but I guess those people are missing a lot."

"But that's no answer; it's so dumb to be blind to things the way you are."

Then the accident happens. While Jared is chopping wood one day, a splinter flies into his left eye. After Jared spends hours in unspeakable pain, a doctor is able to remove the splinter but a hemorrhage has occurred, causing blindness. Nell and Jared are warned that something called sympathetic ophthalmia might occur. This means that unless the blind eye is physically removed, there is a 3 percent chance that the other eye will soon go blind as well. Jared wants the eye out, but Nell will not permit it:

Nell knew what she was thinking of, in the last analysis, was how repulsive to her a one-eyed husband would be. She did not think she could bear Jared, mutilated, with a socket there where his nice brown eye had been—or she supposed it would be a glass eye, and that would be equally horrible. Blindness, the ultimate fear, she did not consider. Three percent—that was hardly any chance to take at all. All her life she had been lucky. Imagine people staring at him; imagine sleeping in the same bed with him at night. She could not bear to have a one-eyed man touch her. And so it happened in the end they decided to take the chance, to leave the bad eye in. After it was all over and Jared found himself with no sight at all, Nell could see her own motives clearly now as she looked back—could see how sadly she failed Jared in his hour of need. But the awful part was, she knew her own motives then, at the time, too, and it didn't seem to make any difference. She went ahead and got her way.

With this one decision, my mother had turned her very human heroine into a monster. Already fashioned as vain, headstrong, and selfish, now Nell was shown to be truly wicked. My mother might have had the same instinctual reactions as fictional Nell under the same circumstances. She would have shuddered at an empty socket, would have even shivered at the thought of being in bed with an eyeless man. But would she have made the same fateful decision as Nell made? I can't imagine that. The well-being of the people she loved came first, and Dorothy proved this over and over again during her life. Instead, I think my mother was creating a young woman who was almost a mirror image of her, but a darker reflection, one who would act out Dorothy's worst thoughts and fears of herself.

DESPERATELY NEEDING MONEY, my mother temporarily put aside her novel in August of 1935 in order to write another children's book. Explaining this to Kate, she wrote:

As usual, things have been going fairly badly. Ken has had the worst attack of asthma in history this last week. It is very discouraging. He is white and very thin. Phil is tired and discouraged, and I had to give up work on the Seeing Eye project, for a while only, but it breaks my heart because I am all keyed up to do it. Instead, I must turn out a children's book for Harcourt. I am at this moment on my way into New York to lock myself up in Cousin Nell's apartment and see what a little night-and-day work will do in the way of turning out juvenile humor. I don't feel especially humorous.

Kate was pregnant at the time, and Dorothy wrote her friend:

I'm terribly happy about you having a baby—you are lucky. I wish I were. But I'll have to earn it by hard work first—maybe a year from now I can begin. Do keep on being careful of yourself. I do so want you to be well and have this baby; I can hardly wait to see it. I need to see and feel a baby.

That same year, Guppa died. I remember the phone ringing with the news. I was seven at the time. My father was on crutches, having hurt himself while chopping a tree. A large wood splinter had sliced into his leg and had become infected, and the surgical removal of the spearhead of wood had left quite a wound. He had been told to keep off the leg. My mother had answered the one phone in our house, which sat primly on a table at the door of our living room, making phone conversation a public event. My mother listened and beckoned to my father, whispering across the room that it was North Andover calling. Slowly, he came on his crutches, I guess knowing full well what was to come. He did not sit for the call. Bracing himself with his crutches, he listened for a long time and finally said, "Thank you, Jack," and hung up. The first thing he did after talking quietly to my mother was hobble upstairs to his clothes closet where he got three of the jackets to his suits. The next time I saw him wearing one there was a wide black band sewed onto the upper left arm and for the next month his hat had a band of black around it, too. My mother explained the black bands were to show everybody that he was in mourning. I remember wondering why he would want people to know.

A month later Dorothy claimed to Kate that she was in the "depths":

The Seeing Eye thing seems to have gone all to pieces. And my aardvark book for Harcourt that I had been slaving over those weeks alone in town was turned down cold by them. They can't give me a reason, just don't like it, and I must say it was a shock to me because I had worked hard and carefully, and by all reasoning, if they had liked my others, they had oughter like this. Anyway, they didn't and I am sunk. I boasted too soon to you. I haven't looked at it since, but next week am going to mail it in to some other publisher, and see what its fate will be.

October found Dorothy splitting her worry between Ken's worsening asthma and her aardvark book, which she had rewritten, done over thirteen of the pictures, and resubmitted to Harcourt Brace. To relieve her of some of her financial worries and to assist Ken, Kate had sent her friend a substantial check and Dorothy responded:

I truly do not know how ever to write you my thanks, dear Kate. But I can write them better than I can say them. If I were to see you now I would do everything that you and I both hate—I couldn't do anything but cry. I have been going around for hours with a lump in my throat. You are all that a true friend means and those are the words that I could scoff at if I didn't weep at them.

The aardvark book was turned down again by Harcourt. It must have come as a severe blow. My mother tried to deny it by writing Kate:

I don't care nearly as much for the achievement of selling one as for the money it would have made. What a dagger money can come to hold over one. I've thought about it so much and feared the lack of it so much the last ten years that I think I'm getting warped and sour.

In December 1935, my mother used some of Kate's check to take Ken to Atlantic City—hoping against hope that winter sun, sea air, and hotel rest would chase away the asthma that had been keeping him gasping for breath and absent from school more than half the time:

I got Ken up out of bed to bring him here—he was panting and wheezing and rattling like a box full of pebbles. We have lain on the beach and dug holes and built the Empire State building and eaten big meals and turned out our lights and gone to sleep each night at 8:15. He and I feel like brand new people.

Nineteen thirty-six arrived and with the new year Dorothy turned her attention back to her Seeing Eye project. Phil advised her, "assemble your material as rapidly as possible," and, "put something on paper." She must have heeded his advice for the book was completed by late spring. But her fear of failure coupled with an impending sense of doom were becoming more and more evident. She was hardly sleeping at all, just rushing to finish her book.

The title of Dorothy's novel, *Bramblebush*, became clear in a nursery song from Jared's childhood, which he sang to Nell:

There was a man in our town
And he was wondrous wise,
He jumped into a bramblebush
And scratched out both his eyes.

And when he saw his eyes were out
With all his might and main
He jumped into another bush
And scratched them in again.

"It seems to me," Jared continued, "that the bramblebush could be life, and if you just sit still and hide after the thorns scratch you, you will be blind forever, but if you are courageous enough to jump back again into life, why its very hurt and thorns will give you new sight."

"Why Jared, that's beautiful. That's absolutely whimsical of you," responded Nell with thinly veiled disdain. In the novel's bizarre conclusion, Nell becomes obsessed with the contradictory nature of her own feelings. Does she love Jared, or does she hate him? In her mind she keeps listing his habits—his freezing cold baths, his heavy breathing, his addiction to football games, the way he uses a shoehorn, his tickly nose, his growling for joy, his wearing a fresh rose each day in his lapel, his reading Thomas Carlyle and Shakespeare over and over again—taking notes on them as if he were in school, his hatred of dirty jokes, his refusal to use novocaine at the dentist, his worship of her, his old-fashioned, lavish handwriting, his too-perfect behavior, always so nice and fair about everything. Interpreted through my mother's pen and Nell's twisted mind, my father's oddities achieved exaggerated proportions in Jared.

I think my mother's financial situation was beginning to distort her perceptions as she wrote these later pages. One day, after sensing that an old college friend had looked at her disdainfully because of the faded, cheap dress she was wearing, she wrote Kate:

> It made me want to grit my teeth and say, "You wait, I'll do it, I'll get back in your world again so I can talk your language but it will be with a knowledge of another language that you will never speak or understand." This all sounds pretty crazy. All I want to do is cry. Maybe it's a mild form of the famous nervous break- down everybody else has had and you and I never indulged in.

As she rushed toward completion of the novel, sleeping little, ob- sessed with money, my mother let Nell voice her own growing fears of the harsh, judgmental literary critics who, she was convinced, waited for her out there. "As a rule when one reaches the last page of a first novel," Nell conjectures:

> one has read the autobiography of a relatively unimportant per- son. Mixed in among the confessions may be a few engaging re- marks about God, sex, or sunsets, but the chances are that the whole is infinitely more interesting to the writer's friends than to the literary world at large.

Trying to write the final chapter, Dorothy worked night and day, at one moment flushed with energy and high hopes, the next beset by dread and fear of failure. She knew that endings are particularly revealing of talent, or the lack thereof. Her story spun toward its con- clusion with a death—the Seeing Eye dog Jared gets, Daisy, eats rat poison and dies. In shock, Jared calls the Seeing Eye agency and speaks blandly into the phone, "This is Jared Cross. I'm blind again." Destroyed but not defeated, he then goes back to The Seeing Eye for a second dog, Tiarra. Instead of hating the dog, Nell now realizes that she is jealous of Jared's affection for Tiarra and jealous of how Tiarra helps him.

The final scenes in my mother's novel are weak and conventional, the happy ending too convenient, too saccharine. Nell helps Jared get a teaching job at his old school:

"Jared," said Nell, "do you remember when you sang the old nursery rhyme about jumping into a bramblebush—and when the man jumped in a second time and scratched his eyes back in again, you said that was life he had jumped back into and that if a blind person could get himself to jump back into life he would find new sight. And I said 'Pooh!'"

"Yes, I remember."

"You know, Jared, you weren't alone on your second jump."

"I know I wasn't, darling."

"I don't think my eyes saw anything before—I think they needed the thorns and prickles of the bramblebush to scratch sight into them. I love you so, Jared."

Nell waved to Jared as he went off to teach his first class at his old school.

She felt as if her heart would burst with gladness. She knew that Jared knew, just as surely as anything, that she was waving to him. Nell knew he saw her, clearly.

I do not know what happened after these final lines were written. Seeing Eye officers were anxious for publicity and surely wanted to read the book. I doubt if they ever did. I do know that sometime soon after she had finished *Bramblebush*, my mother almost scratched her own eyes out from a savage case of poison ivy. Half of the month of May was spent in bed, suffering, worrying, scratching. Much later, we were told that the book had been turned down and we were always led to believe that the manuscript was a complete failure. But neither of my sisters nor my brother nor I ever heard what publisher had read it and rejected it— if any. And no correspondence about the publishing of *Bramblebush* turned up among Dorothy's papers. The failure of the book was a turning point in all our lives, though. And I vividly remember the June morning of that summer when my mother was taken by ambulance to the Morristown Memorial Hospital.

6

My Mother's House

Dorothy and her father on the front
lawn at Chester in 1903

ALMOST IMMEDIATELY AFTER my mother went to the hospital, the three of us children were shipped to Chester, where we lived with our grandparents for the next two months. Pneumonia was one of the words we heard often. Also exhaustion. We also overheard the ominous suggestion of a nervous breakdown. At the time, I hardly knew the meaning of the words, but I did feel danger in the air. Our mother was very sick; she was coughing so hard she broke three ribs; a staggering amount of codeine and other pain medications was being prescribed; she had round-the-clock nurses. Everyone was on edge. We rarely saw our father now; our mother needed him and he saw her every day, on his way to New York City and upon his return. No one else got to see her.

My grandparents' house in the hamlet of Chester was only ten miles away from Morristown, but it seemed like an immense journey in the rumble seat of our sturdy Model T Ford, with the warm summer air cuffing my cheeks and the fresh black tar with its clean, sharp, oily smell sprinkling up from the tires like buckshot, chattering on the insides of the fenders. It was pleasant, rolling countryside, very green, filled with farming smells. I could hear my sister up front begin to sing, "I can see my house and home" as we got close to "Greytop"—that was the name of the house in Chester. Nancy sang that because that's what our mother had told us she had always sung when she was a girl coming upon the big stone and shingle house in the distance atop the hill. I remember thinking it was dumb of my sister to sing it because it wasn't her house and home, it had been our mother's a long time ago and you didn't just suddenly take over somebody else's past. But in retrospect it was an excellent choice—for what lay ahead for us was an authentic taste of our mother's childhood.

A city girl all winter, for three months each summer Dorothy was surrounded by closely-clipped lawns, spreading trees, grape arbors, and honeysuckle. Her family's summer home was a two-hundred-acre working farm with a half-mile drive past the farmhouse and up the tallest hill in Chester, New Jersey, to an elegant, unheated mansion. It had been the corporate hideaway of one of Dorothy's mother's relatives, industrialist S. C. Pullman, and was later acquired by Dorothy's mother, Edith Meserve, and her husband, along with her sister, Ella Dunn, and her husband.

My grandmother, Edith Meserve, dressed in green during the fall, winter, and spring, but changed to white in the summer. She was a big woman, tall and formidable, and she always wore a Mr. John hat—a soft, elegant slice of material that resembled a tam. Now, here she was, coming down the porch steps to greet us. The steps were steep and wide; climbing them was like climbing a pyramid. Granny's long arms encircled us one by one like a spider. Then, standing back, she shook her jewels and looked us over as she took command of her charges. First, she came at me with outstretched hand, her fingers slightly parted to use as a comb in my hair. Next, from somewhere in the depths of her fluttering, silk clothing, a handkerchief appeared and was held in front of my mouth. "Moisten this, please, Philip," was her command. After I'd spat on her handkerchief, she had a vicious little go at whatever I had at the corners of my mouth. Then she was at my sister's braids, hands all aflutter. With a shake of her head, she dismissed my brother as beyond repair. That was our welcome.

Fred Meserve, our grandfather—"Gampy" we called him—was not present for our arrival at Chester, but it wasn't long before he was home from his golf. He was smaller than Granny, always warm, tidy, and compact. He adored his wife and did her every bidding, no matter how inconsequential—partly because he wanted to endlessly show her his love, and partly because he didn't want to get into an argument. She might ask for a hanky while on the ground floor of their house on Seventy-eighth Street in Manhattan and he would plod up three long flights of stairs and return with one, only to be soon asked for another. "It keeps him young," Granny would say about her seventy-year-old husband, and it did. He lived until he was ninety-six. Back then, in 1936, we never thought he was an old man at all. He seemed ageless. In the evenings at Chester he would take us down the long lawn to the great tree and sit us down and tell us Banyan Tree stories as the dusk hurried in and bed called.

An open porch ran around three sides of the house offering elegant couches and gliders and rockers for sitting in the breeze. When it rained, the first job for Ralph, the chauffeur, was to get the heavy, rubber night-covers onto the porch furniture. Rain turned the quartz pillars yellow and the porch floor black, and the best place to be when a downpour happened was underneath the rubber covers, feeling the cold drops hit just above you and the puddles in the rubber creases filling up, completely hidden from Granny.

Inside the front door was a "great" room—so large it seemed to be half the house. Elaborate rooms ran off it. To the left was a malacca parlor, to the right a sitting room done in velvet. At the rear, past the immense open fireplace and bracketing a huge banistered stairway, were the glass-doored dining room on one side and my Uncle Woggy's bachelor chambers on the other. Upstairs, the house was divided in two. Granny and Gampy had a corner apartment overlooking the enormous spreading lawn and the cornfields beyond, and Granny's sister, whom I called Auntie, and her husband had the suite of rooms at the other front corner. In between, along a long hall, were a variety of perfectly appointed bedrooms for children and guests. It was in one of these that I was housed that summer.

Granny and Auntie, the elegant Turner sisters, had two brothers as well. One was named Wesley but he was never around. In fact, his name was hardly ever spoken, and never by my grandfather who obviously had a keen distaste for him. No wonder, for Uncle Wesley, as we grew to call him without ever meeting him face to face, was a wastrel. He was a high roller, gambling fortunes in the stock market—a millionaire one year, a pauper the next. Uncle Wesley wore diamond rings and squired showgirls about, one on each arm. He was a friend of Al Jolson's and could get front-row tickets to any Broadway show. Over sherry, my grandfather once told my father that Uncle Wesley had boasted to him that he had slept with over a thousand different women. He had kept count, along with the names and telephone numbers of the best ones, in the back of his brokerage book. After a particularly bad spell of poverty, Uncle Wesley shot himself dead on the huge rolling front lawn of the house at Chester.

Wallis, Wesley's older brother, was more reserved. But Uncle Woggy had a fun side to him; he was a good winker and a jokester. Afternoon naps were a big thing at Chester and I sometimes got to take mine in Uncle Woggy's ground-floor chambers when he was off at work in the city. I lay on a chintz-covered chaise longue with a blue cashmere robe up to my chin, pretending to be asleep when Granny peeked in for inspection. Actually, I was admiring Uncle Woggy's leather-bound books, his silver comb and hairbrush set, his patent leather slippers which he eased into each evening upon his return from the city, his moonstone tiepin, gold-tipped Turkish cigarettes, and bone-handled cane. His blue suits hung, impeccably pressed, in the deep camphor-scented closet. His red satin pajamas, blue silk robe, and endless supply of black silk knee stockings, which I found in his top bureau drawer, set me to thinking. Just what kind of a life did this quiet, balding bachelor have, living in a stylish room in his sisters' house, with stacks of *Esquire*s beside his bed, the pages creased to the Varga and Petti girl pages? And the photograph of the young woman in the silver frame? Much later, my mother told me that Uncle Woggy had had one great love in his life but it had gone unrequited and he was living out his years in elegant despair.

My room that summer was the room my mother had grown up in, at least in the summers. It was done in youthful colors—bright green and canary yellow—and had two single beds and a porch outside overlooking the great lawn. Lying there, struggling to sleep, I tried to imagine my mother as a little girl having an enormous ribbon tied in her long hair by her mother for one of the photographs in the album that sat on a table in the room. My mother was clearly her father's favorite. In other pictures in the album he was always holding her hand or lifting her up, paying little attention to her brother in the sailor suit or to her angelic-looking sister. My grandfather had sported a mustache and goatee for a few years after the turn of the century and he was always pictured in

white ducks, tie, and jacket, even for a frolic on the lawn. The little girls
wore party dresses. There was no evidence that anyone ever fell down
or skipped or tore anything or played in the dirt. But the close relationship between my Gampy and his carefully-watched, overdressed, trying-
to-please, bright-eyed first daughter, Dot, was evident from the earliest
photographs—and from the earliest stories about my mother.

Throughout her childhood, Dorothy had several bouts of pneumonia and her lungs always gave her trouble after that. As a teenager she
wore braces on her teeth, an affliction which she later described:

> The dentist had done his weekly screwing up of the gold wires
> that fastened each tooth to the cruel brace and now it was so tight
> that every tooth throbbed. Sometimes it helped to wiggle them
> with one's finger. They were all loose and movable from the
> bands straining them out of their natural course, but after the first
> relief the aching flooded back, worse than ever.

Dorothy remembered that one night her father had come up to her
room and cut the wires with toenail clippers. After a night of beautiful
sleep, the dentist put on new wires and twisted them even tighter:

> I stood the three-year process with hardly any complaint as I was
> very sensitive about my looks and felt that I was fearfully ugly to
> begin with and owed it to my mother not to present the added
> cross of jumbled teeth. Mother believed in the school of thought
> where "You look nice and clean, dear" was the largest crumb of
> praise ever given to a daughter, for fear of spoiling, and although
> I looked searchingly in the mirror at myself often, I always
> turned away discouraged and felt that I must be horrible because

no one ever told me I wasn't. As a matter of fact, I never had the button-featured pretty dimpledness of some cupidy children— my features were more the carven type that a little girl has to grow up to. I used to sneak out snapshots of myself and secretly tear them into bits.

On September 29, 1916, Dorothy received a letter from her father, who was traveling:

Dear Dot,

Fifteen! It's hard to believe that you are fifteen. You have so little behind you and so much in front of you. And it may all be pretty much what you make it or want it to be if you make up your mind not to be discouraged because of disappointments. But sometimes we come to find that what we once took to be the end of our world was really only the beginning. "It's the courage we bring to it." Mumsie and I can only start you. Then you have to keep going by your own will.

I am not writing riddles. I think you understand exactly the little sermon. Build it up on helpfulness. Keep the pesky little devils of selfishness packed away in airtight boxes. Look up. Let your vision be as wide as some other person's horizon. We have great hopes for you.

Fred Meserve never gave up trying to help his eldest child. When Dorothy was given assignments at school to write essays, her father would ask what the subject was and often he would sit up late at night writing on the subject. "He loved to play with words," Dorothy recalled:

Sometimes he would write a sonnet, using a dictionary and a Roget's Thesaurus. In the morning I would find my father's work on my plate and he looked eager and shy at the head of the table. I would read it through, embarrassed. I would say, "That's awfully good, Father," and he would be pleased and throw out a hint: "I wonder what your teacher would say to that. Maybe she might be interested." And then I would say in terror, "Oh, no, Father, I could never show it, she might think I had been getting help from you at home—she might think I was cheating. Oh, I couldn't." Then my father would look disappointed and say, "Oh, well, I just thought— well, it doesn't matter. I just did it for a little fun, that's all," and he would take back his poem and file it away in the drawer of his desk, first writing his name painstakingly at the bottom, and the date.

Once, in Dorothy's sixteenth year, she came home from school with an assignment to write a sonnet. Into the night her father secretly worked on his rival poem, really fourteen lines of writing advice to his daughter, ending with an entreaty "to tell a story that the fairies share," one "steeped in imagery."

Whether she took the advice or not, the sonnet sixteen-year-old Dorothy chose to write would be a metaphor for her early life as a writer. For she, too, as the creators in her poem, would overreach herself, having not yet learned the secret of simplicity and how to finish something started.

"The Place of Never Finished Things"

Beyond the sphere of human happenings,
Where no stray star can cast its vagrant ray,
Where winds or rainbows cannot find their way,

There is the place of never finished things.
There is a painting done in rich, deep shades
And here a poem in a lady's praise;
Light on the air a fairy music plays,
A melody that swells and softly fades
Each lacks but one completing note or word.
Their makers saw the star and looked behind
And reached for things too great for mortal mind.
They fell to earth, their clearer vision blurred,
Yet in this place a perfect flower grows
For nature's handiwork no failure shows.

Whereas Gampy was a beloved figure and could do no wrong in his daughter's eyes, Granny was the recipient of much of my mother's frustrated anger. Dorothy hated shopping with her mother, hated what her mother picked out for her to wear, hated the colors she was subjected to—browns and dark greens.

"Even the year before I went to college and all during college my mother bought all my clothes," she once wrote:

I would stand, cross and uninterested while expensive clothes were tried on and fitted. No matter how charming the outfit I would stand there frowning into the mirror and refusing to take any pleasure whatever. Finally, mother's sweetness would be exhausted. "You really are the most disagreeable girl to do things for," she snapped. "I should think you would be tickled pink to have such beautiful clothes."

"But, Mother, I would rather have any kind of clothes at all as long as I could choose them myself. Won't you please, please give me an allowance and let me go about and get my own?"

"That's nonsense, dear," Mother would say. "I should think you would be so glad to have a mother who takes an interest in your looks. Besides we can't just throw money away, we must spend it wisely, you know."

"Wisely, what is wisely?" my voice squeaked high with excitement. "Mother, how rich are we? What can we afford? I wish you'd give me some idea of what you and Father have so I can tell how much to worry about."

"Now, Dorothy, your father and I will tend to that side of things. You just be thankful for your blessings and make the most of your advantages."

Granny aggravated her daughter in other ways, too. For instance, her mottos. "Never borrow—lend, but never, never borrow," she used to say. Or, "If you can't keep your own secrets no one else will keep them for you." And she would tell her children, "Never stifle a sneeze— your great-grandmother died of stifling a sneeze, it's an exceedingly dangerous thing to do."

Sometimes, when Dorothy used to get into tantrums of weeping after an angry scene with her mother, "my father would slip into my room," Dorothy remembered, "and stroke my head and say, 'I know, I know, but you must try to see that it's the big things in life that matter— not the little ones. The big thing is that your mother loves you and wants to do her best for you. Do try to understand, dear girl, and let the little things slip by.'"

EVERYTHING WAS STILL very strict at Chester by the time of our visit. You went to bed when you were put to bed and you were supposed to stay there. Granny would bring me into the room in my pajamas after she had washed my face and brushed my teeth. She would then get down on her knees beside my bed. It took her some time and effort to lower herself because of her great height. I was expected to kneel beside her. When my hands were clasped properly and my head lowered in reverence, she would lead me in my prayers, always ending up with a blessing for my mother in the hospital. I mumbled along, but what I was really praying for in my head was for my mother to get out of the hospital and go home, so we could start living our old life again.

In my memory, Granny was always around, running things, keeping me clean, and watching over everything she could watch over. If I managed to elude her and sneak off to the vast, dark trunk room in the third-floor attic, it wasn't long before I was hunted down. Outside, the grape arbor halfway to the garage was about as far as I was allowed to stray. That was my favorite place. One side of the arbor had green grapes, the other purple. I'd lie on my back with a bunch of each and squeeze the sweet eyeballs onto my tongue. But even the arbor was not quite right. There was something too formal about the arched tunnel of carefully kept vines and their perfect bunches. I found myself longing for the tiny wild grapes at home, whose vines strangled so many of our trees.

Granny would sit with us when we ate our meals to ensure that our table manners were beyond reproach and to make sure we consumed every last bite. "Finish it up, Philip," she would tell me if I happened to be balking at some particularly unappetizing broccoli, "or we'll just sit here, you and I, all afternoon, and if that doesn't work, you'll be served it again tonight—cold!"

Granny didn't know the meaning of play, unless it was formal croquet or badminton or golf. So when she wasn't ordering us about, she would stay in her upstairs sitting room knitting and sewing and reading the stock market pages and giving orders over the phone or doing our nails. She had an absolute phobia about our fingernails. She would call one of us up to sit on the couch beside her and then she would motion for a hand. Once she had grabbed onto it, you were through. First she would attack the cuticles with her orange stick, pushing back the skin with the pointed end to make the half-moon of skin at the bottom of the nail more pronounced. She would stick the prong of her weapon under-neath the skin at the base of the nail; it was worse than any torture you could imagine. If I winced, she would hold onto my hand like a vise. "Stay still," she commanded. I knew if I cried out she would probably gouge even deeper just to show who was boss.

Next came the file—the emery board; she was a pro at that, too. Up and down she went, and then a multitude of quick, bold cross-strokes which rendered my poor, ragged nails perfectly curved. I shut my eyes and held my breath during the whole ugly process until finally she held up the row of fingers—my fingers—in front of her face to give them a final inspection. "We'll keep at them," she would say.

She didn't think she was being mean. Everybody loved her; after all, she was known for her generosity. I know she was just doing her duty as a good, clean, in-charge, Christian grandmother.

One day that summer I broke all the rules, purely by accident. I burst into my grandparents' quarters without knocking and found Granny standing stark naked in the middle of the bedroom. Here was this enor-mous woman without a stitch on except a green velvet slouch hat, her eyes wide with surprise and shame and shock, and it occurred to me, even in that frozen moment when neither of us moved, that this was an historic occasion, for it was probably the only time anyone, including her husband, had ever seen her so undressed. I knew it in my bones. I could tell it in her eyes. When I finally got my muscles to move, I darted into the bathroom to retreat. But it was not my lucky day. For there, brushing his teeth at the sink, was my grandfather and he had no clothes on, either. If anything, Gampy was more private than Granny. I was struck by his shortness and by the fish-belly whiteness of his skin except for the freckles that covered his arms, and the red fuzz hazing down his chest and stomach. Gampy looked up at me with such sharp annoyance that his hand began to shake and toothpaste smeared up into his mustache.

That night, without saying a word, Granny let me know that she didn't appreciate being barged in upon. During the nightly ritual of teeth cleaning, she held my chin and squeezed my cheeks and brushed my teeth so hard I finally couldn't stand it. I knocked her hands aside and I went for her. I was going to slug her as hard as I could. But she caught my fists in mid-air. "If your poor mother could see you now," Granny spit out through gritted teeth, "she'd never get well."

BY THE END OF JUNE, my mother was able to write her first letter from the hospital. It went to Kate:

Dear Kate,

Here is my first letter—it goes to you to say how much I have loved your letters—you are such a darling to write me often. It's funny—I don't feel as if I were living in the world at all. Nothing seems a bit real and I have lost track of time. That, I suppose, is due to the fact that they still keep me sort of doped with a morphine hypodermic every three hours. It worries me to have to have two nurses indefinitely, as far as I can see. Did you hear the funny thing I did? I coughed so hard one day that I broke three ribs and am all strapped up as stiff and immovable as Queen Victoria.

You know, when you get in the hospital you can't see anything beyond your own little routine and your own little ailments. So please forgive all these details. Nan and Phil and Ken are in Chester with Mother and she is taking beautiful care of them. Phil is living alone at home and comes to see me morning and evening. He has been a saint, doing so many dirty jobs and being so heavenly and wonderful all the time. What do you think Phil has done? He has rented a cottage on the Jersey coast at Mantoloking for the month of August. Think how the children will adore the beach and salt swimming.

Kate replied from her summer place in Norfolk, Connecticut:

When I saw your handwriting, I trembled like a girl in love. All last evening I tried not to imagine what life would be like without you. I could live without your being in the world just the way a man could go on walking upstairs carrying a heavy sack without any light on the stairs—almost indefinitely. It would really be as though the sun set every day at noon. I try to think of the many congenial people that I know—they are just acquaintances as far as the heart's deepest secrets go. When the tree was growing, its shape was made, and we grew together.

Kate and Dorothy had often discussed making their letters to each other into some kind of book. Now Kate tried to give Dot a reason to get well by bringing up the subject once again:

Do you know, as I drive about alone up here I evoke you beside me at every turn of the road. That sounds scandalously loverish, doesn't it? If we ever work up our old letters, that will be the stumbling block.

In another letter, Kate was brooding again over the possible publication of their early girlish correspondence:

It seems to me that they should be presented from some definite point of view. Only what? The real reason for adolescent troubles seems to me to be that marriage or its sexual equivalent is delayed from ten to fifteen years after the time when the body begins to feel its need. The effort made to still the clamor of this need takes all the energy out of a young person, and years go by in which he knows he ought to be doing things, but he isn't. So he begins to feel worthless and unclean and frightened. It really is too horrible to remember. When I see calm people who have accomplished miracles, I wonder whether they have never known that torture or whether they had an extra amount of it.

While my mother was in the hospital, my father gave her a beautiful copy of a book of poems by her favorite author, Rachel Field. It was called *Fear Is the Thorn,* and whether or not the title poem had any connection with the thorns of her bramblebush, I cannot tell. But the ideas that Field so vividly expressed about fear were probably close to what my mother was experiencing as her bright world seemed to collapse almost as a penalty for what she had attempted:

Fear is the thorn that guards the rose,
By unscarred hands ignored,
The ancient antidote for bliss,
The guest at the bed and board.
Fear is the penalty of love,
The heart's most secret leaven,

A subtle east wind sent to dim
The too bright shores of heaven.

She also received another gift—a Smith-Corona typewriter from her
father. Over the past thirty years Frederick Hill Meserve had made himself into the country's leading authority on the photographs of Abraham Lincoln. Although my mother never mastered the keyboard, the
present was symbolic of the professional relationship that would soon
start to grow between father and daughter, and of the many historical
manuscripts on which they would collaborate.

My mother remained in the hospital well into July. Counting the two
weeks she had been at home in bed with poison ivy, she had now been
out of commission for two full months since completing *Bramblebush*.
"It is exactly six weeks today," she wrote Kate:

> since the ambulance drove up to our house, snapped me onto a
> stretcher and rolled me here. Going home today I have a strange
> feeling. Sort of unworthiness. I don't deserve all that has been
> done for me. In a way, it's beginning life all over again, with a
> kind of second chance at living.

This letter is the closest thing to evidence that Dorothy had, indeed,
had something she would never admit to—a nervous breakdown. Complicated by both pneumonia and broken ribs, it was also a complete
physical breakdown. But now, going home, a whole life seemed to be
behind her. George E. Kunhardt had died, his family company had been
liquidated, and Phil had found new employment in New York City. The
terrible struggle for money would never be as intense again. But most
relieving of all, perhaps, was the fact that her try at a novel was behind
her, the risk taken, the failure endured. Life now, during her recovery,

seemed to stretch clean and open, a second chance—with clearer eyes and more realistic aspirations and her feet happy to be on the ground again. In *Bramblebush* she had created a despicable heroine based on a twisted sense of herself. Now she could forget about that awful self-portrait, forget about blindness and temptation and loneliness, and, instead, concentrate on getting better and accepting who she really was—a devoted wife and mother, a celebrated writer of children's literature, and a still-young woman who longed for a fourth child. As she wrote Kate in July, "There is nothing in the world I want so much now as to have a baby."

7

The Family Book

The Kunhardt family poses for Dorothy. *Left to right:*
Ken, the author, Philip, Sr., Edith, and Nancy

In the last weeks of the summer of 1936, my mother took us to the New Jersey shore while my father remained in New York, working at his new job at a small woolens firm named Samuel Hird and Sons, sleeping in our house in Morristown, and motoring the hundred miles down to us for the weekends.

It was a happy time. Recuperating by the sea, whether feeling weak or not, my mother pushed herself to give us fun-filled days. She took us to the movie *Earthworm Tractors* with Joe E. Brown, treated us to a glorious spree at the Asbury Park amusement center, and one night even let us stay up as late as we wanted to. Ken was asleep at ten, I made it to close to eleven, and Nancy, using toothpicks to keep her eyes open, always claimed she heard the twelve o'clock chimes.

My mother felt peaceful, especially about Ken, who seemed, finally, to be growing out of his asthma. But once at home on the hill, health problems still nagged at her, as her letters to Kate described:

I am still struggling with a most diabolically thorough dentist— then next Monday is the day for having my tonsils out, and shortly after that I will live again. Life stretching ahead looks very bright to me—if I can just get through these last few hours now.

A few days later, Dorothy added:

My dearest Katie—
    Well, I had my tonsils out and it's all been rather a mess (hemorrhages in throat, etc.). I have a hellish sore throat and am sipping milk-and-ice-water which feels like nails and marbles as it glides down the red lane. But I am ecstatic to have it all behind me.

Also, that October her children's book about an aardvark was finally published. *Wise Old Aardvark* was Dorothy's sixth book; her fifth, a poetic look at baby animals called *Little Ones,* had already been published by Viking.

My mother used that autumn to decide what she would write next. A note from Phil said:

I am thrilled that you have a plot in mind. If you are well enough, I think you can make a charming book about the children. Having a plot means you can be thinking it out all the time.

She was thinking all right. But there wasn't much plot connected with what she had in mind. Plain and simple, she would write about her family—her husband, each one of her three children, their dog, their birthdays, even their awful days, when no one was acting properly, and especially about the hill upon which they all lived. She might call it *My Family* or *The Family Book,* and that would be the plot—the story-less story of a family. Already, as if to restore her life after her dark days of despair in the hospital, my mother's mind was dwelling on the hill as never before.

My parents never owned even a piece of the hill we lived on, nor the houses, which we rented from Bill and Bertha Jenks starting in 1927, less than a year after they were married. First, we were down at the foot of the hill, near Route 202, but after the hard years of 1929 through 1932, Bill Jenks moved us halfway up the hill to the Fisher house, and it was here that I remember growing up in what seemed to me the wilderness. Louis the garbage man came by once a week and Charlie the carpenter was sometimes seen going to his nearby shop. The Warrens lived on top of the hill and Jerry Warren was my best, and practically only, friend. Otherwise, there were no neighbors and few visitors. For my mother, it was almost like a kingdom because of the privacy and independence it afforded her. She was a city girl, after all, and to her the hill was the frontier. When my father was away on business she wrote him every day to assure him that everything was going fine. "This is just to say," was a typical message, "that we are all well and your house on the hill here is safe with us all inside it."

Along with its isolation and beauty, the hill had a wild and dangerous side which my mother understood:

Columbus, our cat, was almost carried away by an owl night before last. I frightened the owl into dropping him when he was in the air!! He was injured—bitten in the behind—bled all night, poor thing, and cried piteously. Columbus is fine today and going to be as good as new. What with the fox barking again nights and

sending shivers down our spines with his unearthly little coughing cry, and owls swooping down to lift away our small furry
friends, our hill has its hazards.

Mostly, Dorothy stayed inside but she could look out on the ever-
changing drama of the hill as it was always presenting a new face. One
spring morning, my mother found that the hill had been encased in ice
overnight. She quickly grabbed her pencil and paper, jotting her obser-
vations from a window's edge:

> Our hill and the valley stretching away from us were shut in shin-
> ing glass. The world was fixed, silent. All morning we watched the
> hillside under its ice caress, the pine branches heavy and drooped
> to the ground, the Norway spruces swept lowest, heaviest with
> their frost burden. Prettiest of all was a dogwood in its silver cas-
> ing, its branches black and its blossoms tender pink inside the ice.
> The ice crackled and crunched under our feet as we walked, and
> when we stood still and listened there was a distant roar across the
> valley, like a thundering storm. Our eyes began to ache and we
> had to squint them almost shut from looking at so many blinding
> sparkles. Toward noon the warm sun had done what it had been
> trying to do, it had begun to loosen the country from its prison and
> it came forth like a new land, all tender and clean from its great ex-
> periences. The trees had steam rising quietly from them, the for-
> sythia and daffodils in the field looked much yellower and the
> birds came in big flocks into the trees all around the house and
> sang much louder and higher than they had the day before.

My mother saved all of our early writings, including accounts in my
sporadic "PK Paper," a newspaper that I pecked out on an ancient type-

writer and sold to members of my family. For years, I reported on life on the hill. And by the time I was a teenager, the hill had become my favorite subject for school papers.

"In the summer the hill was flushed with green," I once wrote:

The meadows were tangled with honeysuckle vines which wrestled in and out among themselves in soft, summer matting. Hot, joyful hours were spent in fashioning great caves and long passageways beneath the thick twist of vines and it was here, deep in the woods at the hidden pond, playing dare games with water snakes, that we spent our days.

That hill made an indelible mark on all of us. Take my brother, Ken, who was practically inarticulate when doing homework or talking about tough-guy things, or describing scenes he didn't care about, but who could wax poetic when he was alone with something he loved:

I call this land my own, for it holds more than just a picture. I have lived here all my life and many times have I looked upon this same sight, but never have I tired of it. This land is mine forever, because no man can take it away! Sell it, burn it, do what you may. The hill I have loved will always be here, waiting for me.

Yes, life on the hill would be integral to my mother's project. Her book would not be told, she quickly figured, from the point of view of the mother. Rather, the family and its life would be seen through the eyes of the eldest child, ten-year-old Nancy—spunky, bright, observant, outspoken, easily ruffled, but oh, so tender-hearted. This would allow the story to seem to come from the mind of a child and would contain a child's view of a mother and father in action and a girl's sense of the wildcats that were her brothers. It would also allow Dorothy to investigate everyone without directly implicating herself. My mother identified with Nancy. She had never lost her sense of being ten years old.

As 1937 began, my mother started writing *The Family Book*, and a January letter to Kate suggested she was full of ideas but having difficulty getting under way:

> I'm the kind of person that has good ideas and then never, never does anything about them. And then, this weather. I don't know whether it's been damp at all in New York but in Morristown our roofs are all leaking and our books are all green with mold and we could all scream at each other and often do. That's not true, of course; Phil is out among the raindrops digging the new garden bed. He waves a dripping hand toward my window every fifteen minutes or so.

Soon after, to her great delight, Dorothy discovered that she was pregnant. It had been five and a half years since her self-induced miscarriage. A new baby went hand-in-hand with her renewed focus on family, and waiting was particularly hard. In the meantime, she worked on *The Family Book*. My father encouraged her. "Please plan your work so that you do not get overtired," he wrote in a note. "I can see the chicken story developing rapidly."

The "chicken story," told from Nancy's viewpoint, was about the sad demise of Ken's favorite pet, and about the poignant burden of breaking bad news to a child.

> I don't know what is going to happen when Ken finds out that Chicken is dead, we all know it, the rest of us in the family, but Ken thinks Chicken is well and happy. We know that Louis the

Garbage Man chopped off her head and ate her for his Sunday dinner months ago. But Ken is still making plans for Chicken to come back to him. He was out long before breakfast this morning, fussing round his chicken yard and getting it tidied up for her return. I looked out of the window and saw him on his hands and knees picking up little bits of broken glass and two big stones, all the things he thought might disturb Chicken if she ate them. Chicken is Ken's chicken and he had to lend her to Louis the Garbage Man for the winter months because he had no real shelter that would keep her safe from winter storms, just some boards that she goes under when there is a hard rain, but even then she gets pretty soaked in about five minutes from the spaces between the boards.

"My bank has forty-seven cents," said Ken, "How much does a real chicken house cost, Dad?" "Oh, five or six dollars," said Dad. "If you save your whole allowance for one year, it would just about do it, I should think. That will be pretty hard, son."

"It will be easy!" said Ken.

Now the year is finished. Counting the time Chicken's been away it makes over two and a half years since Ken first got her and that's a long enough time to become pretty fond of a chicken.

Last night I heard Ken say, "I have enough." I heard, "five dollars and seventy two cents"—and I saw that Ken was smiling gladly at Dad. Just before I closed my door I heard, "good warm house," and "I'm not going to let her be away two winters, one is plenty." I know Dad didn't tell him, because there was Ken up so early this morning to prepare things. I guess he thinks we will all be happy to see Chicken back again. He's been telling us, "Chicken's coming home. I'm buying a real house for her." Just as if we had been missing her too. Of course none of us missed her for one teensy second because Chicken was so hard to get along with, but we never said that for fear of hurting Ken's feelings. And now her head's off, of course no one would dream of criticizing her. Ken will be asking soon for Dad to drive him over to Louis's farm and bring Chicken home from her visit. The day Chicken left Ken said "visit" to Louis over and over. He said, "Remember this is only a visit, a visit, just a visit." Maybe to Louis "visit" sounded like a word in Italian that means, "Here is a nice fat hen for you to feast on." Anyway, it's no good trying to find out Louis the Garbage Man's thoughts because way back last Spring when Dad asked him how Chicken was getting along he said, "That chicken is no good, very bad chicken, very cranky, very tough, very no-good, very bad chicken. We had to eat." Dad said Ss-Shssh—and looked to see if Ken had heard but he hadn't. He felt like scolding Louis, I know, but he just walked away because it wouldn't be any help to Chicken or to Ken. Ken's the one I mind for. I just hate Louis the Garbage Man!

I can still remember Ken's difficult chicken, the subject of one of the first chapters in *The Family Book*. As if to reaffirm her reality and to take stock of her many blessings, Dorothy wanted to record an honest portrait of our close, loving group—what we actually talked about and did, our inner struggles, our mannerisms and moods, tasks and talents, good days and bad.

THAT SUMMER OF 1937 we all spent part of July and all of August on Isle au Haut in Maine—all, except my father, who got two weeks off and then was back in the hot city again, dutifully writing us each day.

"I went through all of the snapshots on your desk," my father wrote to Dorothy, who was by then seven and a half months pregnant. "My, the children were darlings when they were little. The pictures made me realize how much I wanted Mowgli." The following day he wrote:

Take care of yourself, my dearest love. This vacation in lovely cool weather is to make you strong and well so that Mowgli will not bother you too much in October. Get all the benefit, rest, and sunshine you can.

Instead of rest, my mother was constantly trying to discover how a child's mind worked. She asked Nancy to describe particular things to her just as she would describe them to other children. Autumn leaves reminded Nan of cornflakes. She wanted to stroke trees and drink rain and catch fog and dance on spattered sunshine. She was insatiably inquisitive, especially about God. Does God need any money, she wanted to know? And if someone happens to just shoot at the air and it goes right through God, does it kill God?

Little Mowgli was seldom off our lips that summer. As Dorothy's stomach grew, so did anticipation in our house, which our mother recorded—as if spoken by Nancy—in *The Family Book:*

Ken began asking Mum at the beginning of the summer if she was going to get any fatter, and she said, "Yes." By August he said, "Still fatter? I don't see how!" And then Philip and I took him off alone by himself down the road and told him he was awful—he was hurting Mummy's feelings. So he didn't say it anymore but he used to run up to Mum every now and then and put his hand softly on her tummy and say, "How's Babes?" Mum would smile and say, "Fine!"

Ken took credit for the coming event. For years and years we had been wishing for a baby—every birthday when we blew out our birthday cake candles and on every hay wagon and every wishbone we pulled. But nothing worked until Ken held his breath while we were passing a graveyard and wished like mad. "Good old graveyard," he said later on.

Finally, on September 30, we got our wish. Gampy called to tell us, "It's a girl." Then Dad called and was so disappointed that we already knew. We got to visit the New York hospital once, but all we saw of our new sister was a bundle of blanket through a glass door. *The Family Book* picked up the story as the baby came home:

A week after Edith was born, she was brought home and we devoured her. We stood beside her bassinet and looked and looked. Everybody agreed no sweeter baby had ever been born. She was named after Granny and at first she had Granny's blue eyes. She weighed only six pounds. Gampy looked at her and said, "The nicest things always come in small packages, you know. She's perfect. She's a perfect baby. And, of course, to me Edith is the loveliest name in all the world. The father of *my* Edith wrote this into her Bible when she was little:

Edith means the blessed,
Therefore everything she needs or wishes
Shall, if good for her, be granted."

IT'S INTERESTING TO ME today to look back on *The Family Book* chapter called "Philip." I recognize only too well the little, thin-skinned redhead my mother tried to capture in words. To her, that was me at nine or ten; she kept notes on all of us as we grew and then, using Nancy's voice, put them all together:

First here are some of Philip's queernesses. He collects quicksilver from old broken thermometers and he also collects old toothbrushes of the family's whose bristles have become too soft. He keeps the toothbrushes in his bureau drawer in back of his shirts—he has about fifty at the present time. The quicksilver he keeps in a small bottle, but in a secret place so Edith can't find it and be poisoned. Whenever anybody has a headache or a sore throat naturally Mum takes his or her temperature and seven times at least out of ten the thermometer jumps out of Mum's hand as she is shaking it down and is shattered on the floor. Dad says we have lost fifteen thermometers in this way this year alone. As soon as a thermometer breaks Philip, who is ready with his bottle, gets down on his hands and knees and chases the little separate balls of quicksilver until he has them all in his bottle and they have united with the amount he already has.

Philip is apt to use "whatchamajigger" to express anything and everything he wants to say. "Yesterday whatchamajigger said why don't you ever bring your whatchamajigger to school?"

"Don't be stupid, Phil," Mum will say. "Who said what?"

"Oh you know Mum, whatchamajigger." And he will smile darlingly at Mum and let it go at that. Or it may be that he is in one of his fits of saying everything in a string of initials. "H.W." means homework. "G.D." means good dessert. "H.W.A.C.I.T.H.I.W.T.D.A.P.O.T.B" means "Have we any chalk in the house? I want to draw a picture on the blackboard." How can we be dumb enough not to understand?!

Philip has a very maddening way of leaving the room. He always turns around three times before he goes out of a door. If Mum asks him to get her the box of paints and the glass of red colored water that she has left on Dad's desk as she wants to get things tidied up before Dad gets home, and Philip says okay and starts out and then Mum looks up and sees him revolving slowly at the door—why it maddens her.

Philip's attention is a very hard thing to get at any time. Mum can explain something important and talk on and on about the details she wants him to understand but in the end he hasn't heard a word. The things he has the most difficulty in listening to are orders about taking baths and brushing his hair. Mum can tell him to take a bath and an hour later she can find him in the bathroom, still all dressed—drawing pictures with his fingers on the steam-fogged window panes.

It is hard to get very cross with Philip because of the pleasant way he answers you, even when he is in the wrong. Just today he came into the house covered all over with dried leaves, the back and legs of his corduroy pants stiff with dried mud. The mud rubbed off on about everything in the living room before Mum discovered him.

"Philip, go outside immediately and shake yourself and scrape yourself: What have you been doing?"

"Nothing, Mum."

"Tell me this minute where you've been."

"Nowhere, Mum. Really nowhere."

"You're a very rude boy. Answer me this instant!"

Philip smiled his darlingest smile and came right up close to Mum as though he wasn't afraid of her at all and as though he and she had a little secret understanding together. "Well," he said, "it may be from going down a hole."

"May be!" said Mum. "Yes it's possible. You go and change this minute!" But she looked at him in quite a pleased way as he went upstairs. She wasn't angry.

Philip is very, very tenderhearted. He is very sympathetic with animals or people that are in trouble. But that is not all—he is a mixture of softheartedness and a craving for bloody murder stories, with the body cut in little pieces if necessary. He can't find enough of these stories in books to suit him, so he spends hours in his room writing them himself to be sure they are ghastly enough.

Here is when even I say Phil is a little crazy. He is sympathetic with things that aren't alive too. He goes around and looks in scrap baskets and feels sorry for little scraps of torn-up, thrown-away paper. When the Sixth Avenue Elevated was being torn down he felt terribly sorry for it. Mum has an old muff whose fur is getting very worn out and whenever Philip sees it he says, "Poor muff." If you drop a dirty handkerchief into the dirty clothes basket on a Monday morning when the basket is empty Philip picks it out and says it will be lonely. He really is crazy on that one thing, not just merely peculiar. I can understand about animals, but with them I make myself close my eyes or think of something else or say to myself, "Well, I can't do anything to help it, can I?" But Philip has all the pain of things. I remember once Mum and he saw a lame butterfly on a spring day down in the garden. It must have had a torn wing, it was flying sideways through the air and sinking down between every few flaps. Philip followed it way down the hill through the field—and when he came back to Mum she had a long time persuading him that it didn't know it was lame, it was quite happy, really.

Today, the "queernesses" remain, although thinned by time. I still like to define things by their initials. Bloodless objects still attract my attention. And it is hard to throw anything out. I must have ten pairs of old slippers in my closet because I've walked so many steps in all of them and have therefore grown close to each pair. But today I do not revolve slowly at the door before leaving a room.

WHILE I MAY have been a little odd as a boy, my mother wasn't any ordinary mother, either—not by a long shot. Ordinary mothers ran their homes efficiently, took a long time bathing and dressing, made sure their children wore rubbers out in the rain, always had neat living rooms, and slept late on Saturday mornings. Our mother didn't know how to run a home; she had no interest in it, and she had a nurse and a cook to do that. On their days off, she had her husband to clean the rugs and cook the meals and corral us children. Our mother took no time at all bathing— she was in and out of the tub in a twinkling. She dried and dressed so fast you'd think it was a circus act—she hated wasting the limited time in her life. We were often out in the rain in bare feet; she wouldn't pay any attention. And she never slept late in her life. She usually didn't sleep at all, lying there in bed propped up on an elbow and reading book after book all night long. Not modern books, but old ones she brought home every day from the secondhand bookshop, books on every subject in the world, from agriculture to spiritualism, and she would mark the most interesting pages by inserting her own notations on little slips of paper that filled almost every book she owned.

My mother was perfectionist and procrastinator rolled into one. I guess the two went together. When she wrapped a package, the paper, the string, the ribbon, the accompanying note had to be just so and nothing less. Every word of a manuscript had to be checked over, weighed, balanced, thrown out, put back in again, shaded ever so slightly, and agonizingly okayed by her strict standards before the manuscript was submitted. After we'd go to bed on Christmas Eve, she'd go upstairs to her attic room and wrap all night, carrying dozens of presents down the back stairs at five o'clock Christmas morning and sneaking them under the tree. We were up half an hour later, waking the rest of the house and lining up in the front hall for the grand entrance, so of course she never even got out of her yesterday's clothes to start Christmas day.

My memories aren't all golden. I was punished a lot. When I shot an arrow into a box of Lux in the bathroom and the flakes made a snowstorm, she was angry. I got two hours in my room—no radio. When I crashed down the stairs and woke the baby, I got another two hours. I was always leaving things outdoors at night and when I did, it always seemed to rain. I left out my new tennis racket, my new bicycle, and my father's big flashlight. Once, I hauled my father's best tools up the hillside to a patch of bare ground where I planned my very own vegetable garden. But the garden never got dug and the tools stayed up there in the rain. My punishment was knowing how badly they felt about me. My mother could also get rough sometimes when she wanted us to look nice. She could straighten a tie and almost strangle you. She cleaned the corners of our mouths with a vengeance that matched Granny's. She combed our hair with her fingers, using her nails to make the part.

I remember the money problems, too. Everything seemed to have a price tag, and we were led to believe that we were headed for the poorhouse. It was drilled into us. My father was constantly shoving our thermostat down in winter to conserve fuel, and when the house was so cold everyone was doing his or her homework with gloves and scarves on, someone would sneak downstairs and push it up a few degrees. Long distance calls were forbidden or limited to about three sentences—what was the mail for, anyway! A light left on in a room nobody was using wasn't left on for long.

But even though money problems were often severe, my mother insisted upon going first class. Maybe that was part of the money problem. Or maybe it was her way of flying in the face of her fears. Or maybe, after her children's book successes, she thought there was plenty, and who had ever taught her to budget anyway? The fanciest butcher, the best barber, the finest schools, perfectly tailored clothes for us. In fact, it was all for us—she didn't care much how she looked, my father wore ill-fitting cheap suits, and they drove old cars. So there was nothing selfish or self-serving in her passion for the best of everything. It was for others. She had had it as a child, and so would her children. My father had had everything in his youth, too, but his wife's extravagances drove him insane. He stomped his foot and shook his head but my mother prevailed.

In my mother's pursuit of the best of everything for us, she was drawn to a popular New York City pediatrician who was all the rage in social circles back then. Dr. William St. Lawrence had some bizarre notions about bringing up children, and my mother came under his spell. She insisted on following his advice—no, his orders—to the letter. They included being careful not to give too much love to babies, feeding them on an exact schedule, and never picking them up if they cried between feedings. Little children were to be served their heavily-cooked vegetable meals on time and if they didn't clean their plates at one meal, they would be served the cold leftovers at the next. Sucking a thumb was forbidden and was taken care of by having the offender wear iron mitts at night. The iron mitts were metal devices that strapped around the wrist and thumb and made sucking undesirable.

Dr. St. Lawrence's modern ideas included frequent office visits during which my sister and I were asked to strip naked and display ourselves to him while standing on a table. He didn't touch us, he just looked us over from head to toe and that way, he claimed, he could tell a lot about our general health.

My father hated Dr. St. Lawrence and his theories. "They don't seem right," he wrote my mother. "They seem unnatural, those crazy diets and those handcuffs! Just let our children do what they want and they'll grow up fine." At first, my mother was convinced that science had come up with new and wonderful ways to better the growing-up process, and her children were not going to miss out. But my father finally prevailed on this one. After Ken had followed Nancy and me through the horror regime, my mother started saying she wished she'd never heard of Dr. St. Lawrence and if she ever had the good fortune of having a fourth child, he or she could eat and suck and be cuddled whenever the inclinations arose.

What we ate and how we ate it wasn't the only Dr. St. Lawrence cross we had to bear during childhood. Enemas were big in our house. It was very important, my mother had been told, that our bowels moved once a day—and right on schedule. We went through a period during which we actually had to show what we had done and check off a chart on the back of the bathroom door, entering the exact time that the event had occurred. We were fed huge spoonfuls of mint-flavored mineral oil to help the matter. Once, Dr. St. Lawrence wrote my mother about the blessings of cabbage and brussels sprouts, and he questioned her about my restlessness at night. "Are you sure it is not related to the bowel conditioning?" he asked. "Sometimes if there is a tendency to constipation, restless sleep will result."

Unfortunately, every so often an enema was necessary. My mother did the honors. Whoever the unlucky constipated wretch was, he or she was summoned to our parents' bathroom and made to lie facedown and naked on the little hooked rug in the middle of the bathroom floor. A hot-water bag filled with warm soapy water already hung on the back of the bathroom door. With the flick of a metal clamp, the hot soapy water flowed freely through a long black tube and into the hard rubber head that had been eased into the victim. As the water swelled up the midsection of the poor knave on the floor, the pain became fierce. Still, we were told to stand it. The idea was that when the pain was unbearable we were to yell, be released, and make for the toilet just a few feet away. We were in a Dr. St. Lawrence torture chamber and our mother was pulling the levers.

Once, I determined to be the winner in one of these bouts. I pretended to go to sleep during the process and this unnerved my mother no end. I even snored. "Phil," my mother said as she shook at my shoulder, worried that Dr. St. Lawrence's remedies were faulty and that soap had gotten to my brain. "More! More!" I exclaimed, as if from a dream, hiding the swelling pain I was feeling. "This is ridiculous," my mother finally said, twisting the clamp to "Off." I don't remember ever being given an enema again. That must have been about the time my father put his foot down.

My mother never wrote about enemas—things of that nature were below her, of no interest, and she was probably not convinced of their good sense. But she was plenty interested in our table manners and she kept copious notes on how badly Ken and I acted at meals, especially unsupervised meals. One day, she sat down and put all those notes together in a chapter of *The Family Book* called "An Awful Day." I remember our antics in the dining room drove Nancy crazy and made my mother very nervous and angry, while my father seemed oblivious. He just kept on eating and said, "I think they'll grow up in time, my dear. Remember your manners, boys! Can't you see you're upsetting your mother and your sister?"

THE FAMILY BOOK, like *Bramblebush,* never got into print. Some of it never even got typed. It certainly was never submitted to a publisher. My mother was off on other projects, but *The Family Book* served an immense purpose. By studying her children intensely and trying to capture their unique and peculiar language on paper, my mother was researching the alchemy of a young family. She had already explored the world of nonsense in her early children's books. Now the focus was on the real. No fairy tales, no adventure stories, no faraway lands and high seas. Instead, here were stories set at the kitchen table or in the front yard. This would prove to be her real genius. Armed with information garnered from the microscopic inspection of her children, most especially of her newest and youngest one, my mother was on the verge of breaking wholly new ground in the world of books for young people.

8.

It Squeaks!

Nancy and her toy rabbit in 1928—the
inspiration for *Pat the Bunny*. Dorothy
created the book a decade later for
her youngest child, Edith.

INSTEAD OF STAYING in Morristown for the summers, my parents always felt they had to get away on a real vacation. In 1938, the trouble was that they couldn't pay for one. My father was staggering along at his new job, not knowing if it would last, nervous about taking even a single day off, and my mother had not earned anything for several years. Back in the grip of the Grim Spectre, my parents worked out a summer plan that would cost very little. Dorothy, the three older children, and baby Edith would visit Mingie at her big summer house in Sugar Hill, New Hampshire, for part of July and all of August, with Phil showing up on weekends and joining his family for the last two weeks. The whole summer, therefore, would be practically free of cost, and Phil hoped his mother would get to know his children for the first time.

Dorothy agreed to this long visit, but only if she could take work with her. Summer vacations were favorite times for her to get her writing done. The children were occupied during the day and there was usually plenty of help, relieving her of dreaded housework. Lilly, our nurse, accompanied us to Sugar Hill to take care of ten-month-old Edith. My mother brought a suitcase full of work, and on weekends my father either took the train from New York to Littleton, New Hampshire, or drove up. It should have been an ideal time for some creative action. It turned out to be anything but.

Everybody seemed to have forgotten that Mingie, instead of being a kindly widow, was a fierce, domineering old lady—just as she'd always been. Now that her even stronger-minded husband was dead, she made certain that she, and she alone, was in control of everything. By agreement of Phil and his three siblings, Mingie was living on her children's trust money, left to them by Guppa's brother who had become enormously successful in the steel industry. Mingie had been spending freely and giving no account of her runway expenses. She had not only taken a large summer house in an exclusive New Hampshire town but she was also attended by a constant companion named Miss Sullivan and a chauffeur, a cook, and two maids who waited tables and kept the house clean.

Mingie had never liked my mother. She was jealous of her mind and seethed inwardly that she got so much of her son's attention. After driving Dorothy up, spending the weekend, and returning to New York City in late July, Phil already knew in his heart the vacation was not going to work. "Oh, dearest girl," he wrote:

> I am worried that you are not going to have a happy time at Sugar Hill and that all the effort of going up there will be wasted and the contrast with the attitude of your family will be very bitter.

Dorothy would inevitably compare Mingie to her own generous and kind parents, and Mingie's impetuous and thoughtless nature would be magnified. "Do not let our children be too upset by Mother speaking harshly to them," Phil warned:

> She is not very well and does not realize what she says or how it sounds. She is difficult at best, as she is always so sure she is right. It makes it very difficult for me to discuss any financial question with her without heated feelings. It is practically impossible to point out to her the disparity of her accepting such a large part of her children's trust funds and making them feel obligated to her if she returns any part. Imagine a single person, living on a $20,000 basis when all but one of her children are finding it difficult to keep up their families. Keep your courage up, dearest, and don't take things too hard. I shall not leave you there for more than two weeks more.

With less than a week of the visit to Sugar Hill over, Dorothy was writing Phil about the lack of food in the house, especially for Edith, and my father was ordered to go to a store in New York and ship her dozens of jars of baby food. We older children felt starved after our meals with Mingie but if we complained, we could expect a serious scolding from our mother. She had decided to hold her tongue and put up with anything the old woman did or said, and she was able to keep her composure even when Mingie got into a fight with the owner of Rock Pool, the one place where we could swim and, in a huff, canceled her membership.

Dorothy vowed to herself that her letters home, so as not to upset Phil, would not include descriptions of the indignities she faced, but she found herself less and less able to control her pen. On July 27 she wrote:

> Mingie said last night that if I would use my bean once in a hundred years it would be better and she didn't know how you ever got on with me. Phil, I know you say she doesn't mean it, but I

don't see how a human being can get away scot-free with being so rude and cruel to others; there is no one in the world even to say anything to her to check her, we all just stand around and are silently attacked and crushed time after time. She is as unbridled and undisciplined as anyone could possibly be. When I woke this morning, the baby was talking and I heard Mingie say to Miss Sullivan, "I suppose now I have to listen to that all through another day." And when Philip came to say good morning, she said she had been wakened by him calling out in a nightmare and did not get to sleep again. What shall I do? Yesterday at lunch she said the children ate too much, they were plain hogs, and she was going to get a trough and let them eat out of it all at once in the barn.

My father read my mother's complaints and sympathized but when he arrived to spend the weekend, he was surprised to find his mother in an exceptionally pleasant and controlled mood, sweet to his children and loving toward his wife. Then, as soon as Phil disappeared, the tyranny began again.

"I really am miserable," Dorothy wrote:

She really doesn't like me. I want to live my own life, think my own thoughts, do the things I want to do when I feel like doing them. If only you could be here—you act as a buffer between me and Mingie. I try to be sweet and polite but I just feel bitter inside. If I felt well, I think I could make this all better but I am extremely tired and nervous. I am nervous from watching the children like an old cat and yet if they get scolded by Mingie that makes me feel even worse so I am always picking on them.

Phil wrote back advising my mother not to be disturbed by his mother's bitter tongue. "Let it, if you can, roll off like water off a duck's back. Now keep well, keep your courage, and if possible do some writing. I shall type it for you."

He was hoping and praying things would start going more smoothly between his mother and his wife, but he was soon to find that the tensions had accelerated.

"We were sitting alone last evening," Dorothy wrote:

> when she suddenly said to me that she had never seen anyone with such a perpetual disagreeable expression as me and why didn't I make some effort to turn up the corners of my mouth once in a while. She said, "I certainly have much more to turn down my mouth about than you; what you need is just to give a little thought to your blessings and stop picking on your children all the time." The reason my mouth has turned down is because she has made me unhappy. I thought I'd made an effort at jollity when she said you were devoted and I said, "He likes me!" and she said, "That's what you think, but he won't for long with that face!"

Finally, the explosion occurred. "The worst has happened," my mother wrote:

> There has been a blowup at lunch today and now Mingie is in her room and I don't think she is going to speak to me again. She expects me to come in and apologize to her and I just will never, never do it. I can't.

As the meal had progressed, Mingie had been berating Nancy and Ken and me for the way we were sitting at her table, sitting far forward in our chairs when we should be sitting with our backs firmly pressed against the backs of our chairs. Our mother brought up the fact that Mingie's favorite grandchild, Flixy, sat with his back nowhere near the back of his chair, an off-the-cuff remark that enraged the old lady:

> She was for some reason furious and said it was of no possible consequence how Flixy sat, and she saw no reason to bring it up. I felt hot blood pounding in my head. I was so angry that she should talk to me like that and I couldn't hold on to myself, and I'm afraid I said, in a fairly cold voice, that hardly anything was of any consequence that one could think of and that I had only said it because it seemed interesting to me. Mingie said I needn't speak to her as if I was the same age as my children. I hung on to myself and didn't say another word although I am still trembling. She has gone to her room. I know it was bad of me to answer her with any kind of an answer—I just should have sat still and let her say whatever she wanted to—but, dearest, I couldn't. What are we to do?

The New Hampshire vacation was cut short. If nothing else, it proved that my mother and Mingie couldn't get along with each other, and long spells together at close quarters would never again be attempted. But the visit also had another important consequence—it launched my mother toward what would be her most lasting creation.

IN THE FALL OF 1938, not long after the Mingie disaster, my mother began to imagine a revolutionary new kind of book for babies—but she just wasn't ready yet to set it down. The sudden bursts of fire that had brought on her first nonsense books were harder and harder to ignite.

She had moved her office from the little attic space to a large, bookcase-filled room in an office building in Morristown where she would hide away whenever both the nurse and the cook were at home and our schools were under way. She was growing more and more intrigued by historical literature. Her interest in Abraham Lincoln and in nineteenth-century America had begun to blossom and, instead of working on new children's books, she was more apt to be buying dusty volumes from a local secondhand book dealer named Turitz, hauling them to her office, and studying their contents. Notes from her reading of history and from her thinking on what children liked and how to interest and amuse them began piling up.

It was fortunate that she could juggle projects; she often had half a dozen going at one time. To work on one intensely, then set it aside for another quite different challenge, suited her nature. If she couldn't finish a book in the time her internal clock allotted to it, on she would charge to another idea, quite sure in her own mind that she would return to the project just shelved and finish it one day soon. It didn't always turn out that way. Her notes to herself describe many books that never saw the light of day.

We children laughed at our mother as she leapt from the dining room table to write down her thoughts. We wondered when she took a pillow to the office—was she going to sleep on the floor? We were aware that she haunted farms, zoos, and circuses—wherever there were animals; that she was drawn to libraries and schools and dealers—wherever there were books. No wonder she was perpetually tired; she crammed the work of two or more people into one life. Only later did I come to realize that in order to create something brilliant my mother also had to feel desperate, deserted, lonely. She had to lock herself away from her family. She needed the torture of a hotel room at 3:00 a.m. with the uncaring, sleeping city outside her windows, or at least territory she was unfamiliar with, that didn't reek of love. The comfort of her own house was no longer conducive to work.

In one note for *The Family Book,* my mother reported that little Ken had asked her, "When do you write, Mummy? You are always taking notes." In another, she recorded her husband's entreaties:

> Couldn't you just give me any little thing you've written to type-write? It doesn't have to be polished. You always say nothing is ready and that it will be soon. You arrange and lay out. You read other books and books on writing. Why don't you finish up one idea and make a book? You have dozens started.

In the next moment he had switched positions and was defending her, perhaps speaking for her, saying, "How long it takes to think and decide! How ideas have to brew and stew for a long time." In another revealing note, my mother wrote in the voice of Nancy, "Mum's getting awfully cross lately. I think she's going to try to write a book again."

The months leading up to the days when my mother actually put together her classic were filled with children, housework, answering requests, "love letters" from Kate, and making her final changes to *David's Birthday Party,* which was to be published by Rand McNally & Co. in the summer of 1939. Not until recently, when I came upon a letter written by Dorothy to my father that spring, did I realize how much she hated housework and how much her writing motivated her to escape it. "I am cursing myself," she wrote, "for being such an utter fool as to exhaust myself so over endless physical drudgery when my brain is teeming with ideas and I should be using them and earning the money to have this dirty job done."

Then again, my mother often took hours of her precious time to answer the children who had written her fan letters. "Dear Sylvia Ann," she wrote, printing the enlarged words slowly and carefully just as she had done with the text in her books, and parodying their tone:

One day not long ago I had a little postcard come to me which said there was a package in the main post office in New York addressed to me—that it did not have enough stamps on it but that if I really wanted it I could have it for eleven cents. If they did not hear from me before a reasonable length of time, they would destroy it. I let the days slip by until they almost, but not quite, amounted to a reasonable length of time. At first, I thought, that package does not interest me, it is probably something horrid that I do not want at all and this is a splendid chance for me to be rid of it. But as time went on I began to think and the package began to seem not as horrid as it had at first, and then I began to want it and then I began to want it badly and in the end I could hardly wait to have it come to me. In my mind this package had become something I simply could not do without, and the one thing that made my heart sink was that I had come within a breath, a single breath, probably one postman's sigh, of never having it at all.

Sylvia Ann's package had contained her copy of *Junket Is Nice* with a request for a signature. The little girl received back not only her signed book but also copies of *Brave Mr. Buckingham* and *Now Open the Box*.

In searching for what was on my mother's mind around the time she wrote her most famous book, I was not surprised to come upon a number of letters from Kate, who by now had a husband of her own, and three children, and was working for the Birth Control Federation in New York City.

One of Kate's letters dwelt on "how wonderfully you write":

I am more and more impressed with the sway and march of your writing. Your letters would be thrilling even if they didn't say anything. This one, however, said things that made me want to talk to you for hours and hours and hours. About the war. About where we belong in the world from now on, and the mistakes that were made when we were children that we can perhaps avoid for ours.

Another put how much Dorothy meant to Kate in vivid words:

My dearest Dorothy, I am glad you were born. Without you so many people's lives would have been less vivid and less poignant. I feel as though before I met you I lived in a round room with one or two little windows, and when I met you immediately the windows that were there got much bigger and soon there were more of them. Now there are great sweeps of plate glass and many of them were put there by you.

The two were so in the habit of sharing their ups and downs. Sometimes Kate had little or no reason to write, except that she wanted to feel she was touching her friend. "I am feeling terribly depressed tonight for absolutely no reason at all," one letter began—and soon ended:

Really ancestral voices prophesy on every side of the utter and complete decay of every faculty of my being. So the typewriter being open and the habit of writing you when I am gloomy deeply ingrained in me, here I sit and moan, with nothing to say but good night, Dorothy. I am very fond of you. Kate.

Dorothy and Kate were always brutally honest with each other, and sometimes Kate let Dot know that her criticism hurt:

Devil that you are, your letter destroyed most of the little peace that your visit had left with me. You hear of people called bad angels. I dub you my good devil, for good always comes of the battles you stir up in my heart. How we ever lived together for four years now seems to me a tribute to the toughness of youth. I can't see you or hear from you without being torn to shreds. It is a little like what a child does to one, tearing down your illusions and breaking your heart and giving you more solid satisfaction than anything else on earth. So please don't stop, but don't mind too much if I abuse you from time to time for my lost peace.

In her letters Kate spoke of Dorothy's "virtuous lack of virtue" and her "intolerant" nature: "Intolerant as you are, no one has the appetite for great qualities that you have or the perception of them. And that is more worthwhile than tolerance, although more exhausting." Kate once mentioned Dot's childhood fear of being alone: "But I think you told me once that you had got over that terror because you had too many things to be interested in."

One letter from Kate that had upset Dorothy talked about the fear of ending up an old maid, and a deep unhappiness that had lodged inside Kate during the years following Dot's marriage:

You know, during the years when I was not married, and wished to be, I went through the process of spinsterizing to such an extent that I have all the bitterness and hysteria and raw touchiness left, not very far beneath the happy exterior of my life, even now that every cause for it has been removed. That is why I run from old maids so convulsively. I will not pity them with a pity that opens those old wounds again, it springs so deep from my heart.

Kate felt that getting older and settling down was changing her:

I cannot resent the things that keep us apart for such long stretches at a time, for they are everything that we always longed for. One of our dearest bonds was moaning over the lack of them. Just at this moment I feel like someone that you never knew. I've settled down. I used to think that that was synonymous with giving up. I wonder if you still do. There has always been this essential difference between us—that you are eternally feminine and I feel perfectly neuter.

And Kate was also beginning to think of death:

Does one get increasingly tired as one gets older until one longs for nothing but death, and yet fears it at the same time, I wonder. Please promise to survive me; for to have to do without you would be like going without one of the dear senses—sight or the sense of smell or hearing. I should be lonely—not only for you—but for all the world that I know better and love more because of you.

THE SIGNATURE ILLUSTRATION for Dot's next book had been percolating for some time. The distinctive image of the bunny stretched as far back as 1928, when one-year-old Nancy had been given a stuffed rabbit—a cuddly white bunny made of crocheted wool. It was this adored object that first inspired Dorothy to make a simple, cutout silhouette of a bunny to illustrate the "B" page in an alphabet book she was planning. She even wrote the poem that would accompany the letter B:

B is for bunny so wistful and white
With shoebutton eyes that stay open all night—
He knows he is knit out of nothing but wool
And his ears would unravel if I were to pull,
But it's hard to be wool when you're aching to go
To the nice little places that all bunnies know—
Where bunnies are bounding and squeaking for joy
And there's welcome for even a silly old toy.
Perhaps he looks silly, but really he's not
And I think bunny knows that I love him a lot.

This was as far as the alphabet book got; it was to be banished to the bin of Dot's "never finished things." Dorothy's illustration of a bunny in profile, though, would be resurrected years later.

Her most celebrated creation evolved from literally thousands of notes on Edith's first years of life. It grew out of Dorothy's determination that a book needn't be just words on paper, and out of her understanding that for a growing child hands-on experience was primary to discovery. It came from protecting her time whenever she could. She had even taught Edith to call for her father during the night, instructing her to say from the bassinet beside their bed—"Daddy, dear, I need you." And Daddy would inevitably get up and tend his baby girl so that Mummy could either go on working or catch the little sleep she needed. Daddy was also the one who got Edith up in the morning—while my mother took notes.

She wrote the notes on anything she could grab at the time—on slips of paper, corners of envelopes, binder paper, ripped pieces of stationery, hunks of cardboard, laundry bills, the backs of the butcher's bills for the family's weekly meat supply. Sometimes the notes were pinned together with straight sewing pins. Some were written in ink, but most were in pencil, sometimes red pencil. The writing was rushed and often minuscule, often indecipherable. Sometimes she used a private shorthand code, illustrated with doodles or drawings.

The notes tried to capture my sister's baby talk and emerging use of language, her favorite words, and how Edith jumbled them up to be funny. Edith was almost two years old in the summer of 1939 when my mother noted, "Edith has become a great reader. She likes the *New Yorker* best and invents a stream of nonsense words as she turns the pages." Dorothy saw that while magazines and books interested Edith, she was more delighted by games like peek-a-boo. Even picture books didn't hold nearly the satisfaction of the simple magic of a mirror.

My mother's notes included written snapshots of Edith playing hide-and-seek, jumping, dancing, drawing pictures, playing with shadows, blowing dandelions and soap bubbles, watching her father shave, going to bed at night. The notes described the baby's moods—"joyous," "calm," "triumphant," "passionate," "almost in tears." My mother was looking for the humorousness, the honesty, the directness in her child. Often, in her note-taking, she would identify with Edith's innocence, her heartbreaking sweetness, her heartswelling devotion, her fantasies and wishes, her purity of heart. As Edith grew and the notes mounted, Dorothy knew she was going to make a book out of a few of the things her fourth baby had learned to do. The book would show in simple, realistic line drawings the child's family—the mother, the father, the sister, the brother. It would never show the baby herself, for the entire book would be aimed at her, her presence would be implicit, just outside the pages, her little eyes and hands and fingers participating in each familiar fun thing the book would ask her to do. The book would be called *Pat the Bunny* and it would have a white bunny on its pink cover and inside a soft bunny to pat. But the book was not about a rabbit, it was about a family's love and affection for its youngest member. And, in turn, it was about the youngest member's world of family, and her wonder at it.

Sometime early on, my mother made a list of delights that the baby reader would encounter in the eighteen pages of her unusual book. These included "comb hair," "eat spoon," "shake hands," "stand on head," "ride stick," "Daddy's big glove," "blow out match," "patty-cake." As the book evolved, she eliminated all of them, finding each one either not basic enough, or impractical, or hard to handle on a page. Instead, she chose eight simple activities that Edith adored and which could translate onto the page. The finished work would involve a bunny to pat, a peek-a-boo cloth, a squeaky ball, a mirror, Daddy's scratchy face, a tiny book, Mummy's ring, and waving "Bye-bye."

The first two pages were used to introduce the main characters—a brother and sister named Paul and Judy: "Here are Paul and Judy. They can do lots of things. You can do lots of things, too."

Then came a picture of sister Judy patting a white bunny: "Judy can pat the bunny." On the opposite page was a cutout shape of a bunny. Beneath the cutout was a soft, cottony piece of white fuzzy cloth. "Now YOU pat the bunny," the page gently commanded. It was as simple as that, throughout—somebody in the family doing something familiar, followed by a request that the little reader follow suit.

After patting the rabbit, the baby reader was offered a picture of Judy about to lift a polka-dotted handkerchief from in front of Paul's face: "Judy can play peek-a-boo with Paul." Over on the opposite page there was a picture of Paul with an actual piece of cotton material hanging down and hiding his face: "Now YOU play peek-a-boo with Paul."

My mother had figured out that the simplest, most fundamental game babies enjoy is peek-a-boo. In *The Family Book,* she had written:

When Edith was a tiny baby she used to think it was funny if you stuck your hand down suddenly on her tummy and said "Ah! Boo!" She would laugh like anything in quick baby giggles. When she was a few months older, she laughed hard when you put a handkerchief over her face and took it off suddenly.

Pat the Bunny's third surprise for baby readers dealt with the sense of hearing. On the left-hand page, a picture showed Judy with a beautiful, old-fashioned doll dressed in petticoats and a yellow, full-length dress, with button shoes and a painted face and a big red ball in her arms. "Judy can make the dolly's ball go squeak," the words above the picture said. And on the right, alongside a bigger picture of the doll holding the ball: "Now YOU make the dolly's ball go squeak." To the delight of the reader, hidden beneath the red ball was a real live squeaker which actually went "squeak!" when it was poked.

Unfortunately, the rubber in the squeaker used in the first edition came from Japan and the page was discontinued after Pearl Harbor. The "squeak" idea was first replaced by a button box that rattled. "Judy can shake Mummy's button box. Now you shake Mummy's button box. Rattle rattle rattle go the buttons." The trouble with the button box was that the whole book rattled whenever anyone touched it and the editors were also scared that the buttons might come loose and be swallowed. So before long, sound gave way to the sense of smell, with a new picture of Paul crouching down to smell the flowers. And opposite, "Now YOU smell the flowers," along with a drawing of a loopy patch of posies that had a sweet scent to them when sniffed. This new idea had grown out of *The Family Book:* "Edith likes to play hide-and-seek in her father's garden. She likes to pick Dad's flowers, just the flower part with no stems, and present them to her father." Imagine the thrill of being asked to smell your book for the very first time, and finding on the pages a whiff of flowers!

The fourth event in the book used a mirror. On the left was a picture of Judy kneeling down to see herself in a hand mirror that lay on the floor. On the right-hand page was a drawing of the hand mirror at the center of which was a real mirror. (In making the dummy of her book, my mother used a heavy little mirror she had picked up at the 1939 New York World's Fair that summer.) Until now, the baby reader had not been illustrated in any way. But suddenly, there she was in the circular mirror, right in the pages of her own book.

My mother's fifth wonder came to life with nothing more than a tiny swatch of sandpaper from the hardware store. Glued onto the drawing of Daddy's cheek, it created an instant beard. In the left-hand picture Judy reached up and touched Daddy's chin: "Judy can feel Daddy's scratchy face." On the right was a closer look at that father, who was about to shave off the sandpaper bristles: "Now YOU feel Daddy's scratchy face." It was a ritual that Edith and her father had gone through almost every morning of her young life.

The sixth treat was a tiny book within the book. On the left page a picture showed Judy engrossed in reading, with text underneath saying, "Judy can read her book." On the right, pasted onto the page, was a little book consisting of six miniature pages, with text saying "Now YOU read Judy's Book." It showed little pictures of the bunny come to life—listening to an alarm clock ticking, playing "How big is bunny?" eating his supper, and taking a nap.

My mother knew how much small children liked tiny things. So the tiny book was immediately appealing. But more so because in Dorothy's book-within-a-book the roles are switched. Bunny becomes the baby—eating, sleeping, growing. And the reader is now the big sister or brother. In *The Family Book*, when Edith was told, "You are such a big girl," her answer was, "And I'm not going to grow down again."

For delight number seven, my mother simply made a round hole in a page, encircled the hole with gold, and put it between the thumb and forefinger of a drawing of her own hand. On the left was a picture of Paul sticking his finger through his mother's ring: "Paul can put his finger through Mummy's ring." And on the right, with Mummy's hand holding the cutout hole, "Now YOU put your finger through Mummy's ring."

My mother knew what fascination her wedding ring held for Edith, how she liked to play with it, and to wear it on one of her tiny fingers. The two ring pages were all about family bonds, relationships, commitment, and endurance. Again, Dorothy's genius was in using the third dimension. Words and pictures did not have to lie flat and static on a page. Here, the page became part of the world, holding a ring to be worn.

And, finally, "Bye-bye"—one of the first expressions Edith ever learned: "That's all. Bye-bye. Can you say Bye-bye?" The last drawing showed the siblings waving: "Paul and Judy are waving Bye-bye to you." Edith would say bye-bye to her father every morning as he went off to business; they were the words that meant separation, and that conveyed the idea of things coming to an end, just as *Pat the Bunny* had come to its end.

Dorothy's original dummy for *Pat the Bunny* was made out of folded pink cards that had been produced for promotional mailings for her sister's business, "Helen Paton Wool Luxuries." The fold-over gave each 4 x 5¼-inch page the possibility of depth. The bunny on the cover was drawn, with "Pat the Bunny" written in India ink in a semicircle above the rabbit's ears, and below the rabbit "By Dorothy Kunhardt" was also rendered in India ink. A border design, looking like tiny rabbit footprints in blue watercolor, ran around the edges. The binding that held the pages together was string tied through two holes in the pages.

It was an extraordinary creation—cardboard, string, cotton, a little cloth, a squeaker, a mirror, a tiny strip of sandpaper, and a hole, plus fourteen illustrations and 132 words.

Mrs. Hamilton, an editor at Harcourt Brace, raved about the unlikely book, and my mother's letter to Kate describing the encounter said that Mrs. Hamilton would think about it for two weeks, "which is better news than I hoped for."

A week later, Kate replied and although she was excited, she was still hoping her friend would write for adults:

> We are so thrilled by the reception your book had at Harcourt. Of course, we knew it was good, but it was nice to have an editor say so, too. What wonderful satisfaction it must be, D! I keep wondering if, as your children grow up, your books will get older with them, until someday you write another *Of Human Bondage* and win your way single-handed into that Algonquin group into which Frank Adams wanted to usher you by the side door. Of course I still don't see why you don't let them accept you, as I think they are probably ready to do, as a good children's author, right now. Still, an adult book would clinch it. I think you could write for grown-ups the way Charlie Chaplin acts. Everything that happened would be funny and the sum total would wring your heart.

IN SEPTEMBER OF 1940, at age twelve, I was shipped off to the same boarding school to which my father had gone—Groton, in Massachusetts. So I was not home when *Pat the Bunny* was first published. And my mother kept no record of what happened to her little book after Harcourt Brace got its hands on it. I know they had to have turned it down. But I don't have any idea how the young company Simon & Schuster got involved. I do know that they held on to the dummy copy for a long time, trying to figure out how to produce it. At the beginning of June 1940, eleven months after the manuscript's completion, everybody had practically given up hope. Kate wrote, "I am deeply indignant about the fate of *Pat the Bunny.*" For my mother, it must have been an agonizing waiting game. On the same kind of card out of which she had fashioned her book, she now drew a little picture of Judy's hopeful face with a message addressed to the Simon & Schuster production chief, Tom Bevans: "Please Mr. Bevans, decide about me soon."

Bevans did. After being turned down by dozens of manufacturers, Simon & Schuster finally came up with a solution for making production of the book affordable—a coordination of the efforts of eleven industries, including makers of squeakers, sandpaper, fabric, metal mirrors, blanketing, and cotton cloth. Nothing like this had ever been attempted in the book industry before, but Simon & Schuster knew what they had—something groundbreaking and unique—a book aimed at a whole new age-group of "readers." They issued their contract, assembled a workforce of women, rushed through their orders, and were rolling out copies by November of 1940.

The book was not published exactly as my mother had first drawn it. Simon & Schuster had asked for more generic people than she had created. In her original dummy, the family had dark curly hair, and the brother was freckle-faced and carrot-topped. In Dorothy's original drawing of "Mummy" she was shown sitting on the floor with her feet tucked beneath a billowing, not-so-well-fitting dress. The father in her first drawings was rugged and earthy, modeled after my father. Bare-chested rather than wearing an undershirt, the original "Daddy" was intensely masculine with mischievous eyebrows, a strong jaw-line, and a tender smile for his daughter, whom he held in his muscled arms.

Simon & Schuster wanted a less realistic father and mother, with drawings without recognizable qualities. They wanted an innocence and lightness they considered just right for babies. And they wanted a blond, almost Scandinavian family. So that's what my mother gave them. Then, her drawings had to be copied to fit a slightly different page size, a tracing process that lost a whisper of Dorothy's intent.

In mid-November, *Pat the Bunny,* packaged in a hot pink cardboard box with the bunny imprinted on the front, hit America's bookstores.

The book's price of one dollar was high because so much of the book was assembled by hand. *Publishers Weekly* reported that "The binder, Russell-Rutter Company, rented an extra floor and had a force of eighty girls working on it. The girls had a wonderful time."

The orders flowed in and the books flowed out. The first edition of 15,000 copies was sold out within a week of publication. By Christmas, more than 100,000 copies had sold and there weren't nearly enough to go around. The *New York Herald Tribune* called *Pat the Bunny* "the find of the season." And Simon & Schuster advertised their achievement as, "A book you can press and it will squeak. You can put your finger through a page and have a ring on it. You can look at another page and see your own funny face." Simon & Schuster also promoted the book with ads about current adult best sellers: "*Oliver Wiswell* is a wonderful book—but it won't squeak if you press it. *For Whom the Bell Tolls* is magnificent—but it hasn't any bunny in it."

In just the five exciting weeks before Christmas of 1940, *Pat the Bunny* became the best-selling juvenile title of the year. And it has remained on the best-seller list for most of the sixty and more years since. "*The New York Times*" *Parent's Guide to the Best Books for Children* of that year describes it as, "The original babies' activities book . . . Babies love it and some eat several copies before they have even learned to walk." The first mass-market interactive children's book, it is now referred to by the industry as a "touch and feel" book, and it has inspired a host of imitations. Approaching eight million in total sales, it is one of the best-selling hardcover children's books of all time. Simon & Schuster, and then its offshoot Golden Press, and now Random House have gone on cutting and gluing and stamping out as many as a quarter of a million new copies of *Pat* each year, annually using up acres of sandpaper beard, six football fields of peek-a-boo cloth, and enough metalized polyester to mirror over a small lake. My mother's little book has not only delighted millions of little minds but has also opened them up to the infinite joy of reading.

Today, holding my mother's original dummy makes my spine tingle with pride and wonder and even fear—fear that I will drop these little, tied-together pages with the original squeaker making the book fat, its bellows enlarged by age, and the World's Fair souvenir mirror still too heavy on its page. The pink of the cards has faded to tan, but sixty-four years since this 132-word creation was first put together, the graying bunny is still soft to the touch and I can still play peek-a-boo with Judy. I don't like what I see in the mirror, but the tip of my little finger can just make it through Mummy's ring. And coming upon the last smudged page seems sad, as I can almost see my mother dip her pen in the ink, shake it once so there'd be no drops, then carefully write the final words: "Paul and Judy are waving Bye-bye to you."

"Write It Now"

The 1940s were Dorothy's most productive years.
Here, with the help of a kitchen spoon, she conducts
her family, displaying her joie de vivre.

P AT THE BUNNY is out today," my mother wrote to me in the middle of November of 1940, "and I have just seen it spread all over the counter at Macy's." I was twelve and into my second month at boarding school, reading the letter in my tiny room.

"It is really very cunning," my mother continued:

and now we are just hoping it will sell. It squeaks beautifully . . .
I would have mailed you a copy as I am crazy to have you see it
but I think perhaps Groton is not just the place to have a little
baby's book that squeaks and perhaps it is better to wait till you
get home.

While I was away at school, my mother always kept me informed of
what was happening back home, up to the minute, with news of each

member of the family, the health and happiness of our dog, and how the hill was doing as the seasons changed.

Personal mail, I remember, was delivered daily to us at 12:40, before lunch. My classmates and I clustered around the foot of a flight of stairs while the designated "mailman" stood near the top of the stairs, called out names, and sailed our envelopes and tossed our packages into a sea of eager hands. I never opened a letter from my mother on the spot. Instead, her offerings were kept for some quiet time alone, when the opening could be done without wisecracks and the reading without interruption. Actually, my classmates were jealous; no one else had a mother like mine. No one got bulging letters that took hours to read. Most of the other mothers seemed to have shipped their sons off to school and forgotten about them.

My mother's letters described the hill so vividly that I could practically smell its pine needles. Electricity leapt off her pages. She wrote on yellow legal pads, in dark inks that snaked from top to bottom, filling every square inch of space, with a voice as immediate as if she were talking to me. She made me laugh and she helped me whenever I turned to her and sometimes when I didn't. Depending on my mood, however, her letters could make me doubly homesick by the time I read her closing lines. "I miss you awfully," she would write in tiny script in the last corner of space on the page. Or, "Your letters give me very much joy." Or, "Goodnight sweetness. Mum."

My early letters home to her were written by someone I still recognize today—someone who didn't know how to finish a thought, who leapt from one funny, flighty subject to another:

The whole first form is rather nervous tonight because tomorrow is Bloody Sunday. Bloody Sunday is the day the second form beats up the new guys. I will write you about it. I have made a very good friend. He has a club. It is called the "red hand club." You see when you come out of the shower a club member whacks you on the back. It leaves a red mark of a hand. I joined it today. By the way I have learned to keep my napkin on my lap instead of under me.

Later that week I concluded the letter, adding:

It was down in the thirties this morning and my cold shower felt awful. Wait a minute, Peabody is making a face at me and I have to return it. There. Bloody Sunday wasn't bad at all, but it will be next year. Ha Ha.

In addition to not being prepared for the cold showers, I was not ready for the three-sided cubicle that was to be my room at Groton that first-form year; nor for the strict rules and regulations, demerits, black marks, and punishments. And I was especially not prepared for the heavy dose of God—chapel every single morning at 7:00, grace before meals, sacred studies, choir singing, bell ringing in the chapel tower, Holy Communion before dawn on Sundays followed by two long services, one in the morning, the other, vespers, in the evening. At home, my mother had once enrolled us in Sunday school classes at our Episcopal church, but that had lasted exactly one week because we all protested, including my father, who worked on Saturdays in those days and depended on Sundays for time in his garden and to be with his children. Granny had made me say prayers and she always said grace before meals, but we never did at home. As for singing, I couldn't carry a tune.

In essence, few children at the school were as unprepared as I was. I had hardly been away from home before, so homesickness overcame me. I wasn't used to being neat or on time or well-prepared in my studies, so I was constantly in trouble. Surrounded by opinionated, well-versed "brains," I knew next to nothing about national or world affairs. I knew absolutely nothing about the economy, or about poverty or wealth, yet I was surrounded by boys with names like Morgan, Davison, Peabody, and Auchincloss—wealthy and prominent families I had never heard of before. The school did its best to make everyone seem equal by issuing allowances of twenty-five cents a week to everyone. But I soon realized that while I had no additional income, my new friends always seemed to be flush.

I remember once when I was thirteen the whole Mali family came up to Groton to look it over for their three boys. Uncle Harry had, of course, gone there and was all for it, but Auntie Kate felt there was something twisted about the school and much preferred Milton Academy. I took all five of them off on a canoe ride. To confirm my memory, I was glad to come upon a 1941 letter from Kate to my mother:

We saw Philip at Groton and he was one great "smiling face." D, you really should be quite proud of him. He has charming manners, but is quite relaxed. I hate tense people. He had lunch with us and then took us canoeing on the lovely filthy river. Great heavens, he pulls more than his own weight in a canoe. There were five of us and you can imagine we were nearly down to the gunwales.

In the 1940s the letters between Kate and my mother slowed but they still, occasionally, asked each other for advice in personal matters.

"Source of all wisdom, advise me again," a grateful Kate wrote Dot after receiving a long, thoughtful epistle of counsel:

You might think that I profited nothing from rereading your beautiful and wise letter. Never has anyone taken the trouble to analyze another person's problem with such acute perception. You put before me exactly what I need to face, only I can't come to your conclusion—yet.

Neither my mother nor Kate got caught up in World War II, at least, their letters shied away from the terrible things that were happening overseas, instead dwelling on domestic subjects. Firing nurses and hiring new ones drove Kate crazy. It was:

> so cataclysmic a process that it makes me feel I have never known any happiness. I interviewed three boobs on Monday, decided Ruth was just as good as they on Tuesday; yesterday she let Derick fall off the dressing table onto the tile floor. He turned green, but she said he would be all right in a couple of hours—"they always were."

In earlier days Kate had written down each flurry of thought she was having and sent them along to Dot, and when she didn't write a letter, she pretended to: "Each day in my heart I write you a letter that tells you tediously all I have done and as ever how dearly I do love you. I hope you receive them faithfully."

Back then, it was as if the absence of husband and children had fanned the fires of correspondence: "I wish awfully someone would love me for myself alone; that being obviously the only thing I can be loved for." It was the kind of sentiment Kate had often confessed to a decade or so earlier:

> I have a sudden terror that I shall go to my grave without ever knowing the "flower and fruits of my birth" as the Hindoos say.

Suddenly I am afraid that I may never have any children. I want them desperately.

This was certainly not the same contented, middle-aged woman sitting on cushions in the bottom of my canoe in 1941, surrounded by her Groton-bound brood.

My father didn't make nearly enough money to cover school tuitions. Fortunately—and surprisingly—I had gotten a 100 on my mathematics entrance exam which had earned me a thousand-dollar scholarship for each of the six years I was there, leaving my father to struggle each year with the other thousand needed for tuition. So it was agreed between my parents that Dorothy would make up the difference with her writing. It was always hard for her to choose what to do next from the ever-expanding list of ideas she had for books for children. Which were too outrageous or too obvious? Which was original? Which would be most fun to work on? Her father's fascination with Abraham Lincoln was gripping her, too, and as her interest in and research on the sixteenth president increased, her lists of book ideas started including Lincoln. One list went like this:

- Read your book—and eat it, too—spiral binding of pink candy
- Wrist book
- Bathroom book—good little Dottie, sitting on her potty, good little Lloydie, sitting on the toidy
- Mask book
- Tad Lincoln
- Book of wishes
- Dressing-up book

- Magician's book—Mr. X's 3 best tricks
- Animal love story—koala?
- How to be good children book
- Amanda the Panda
- Little Jesus book
- Telephone book
- Measuring tape book
- Band-Aid book
- Tail book
- WRITE ONE THIS WEEK!!!

Having successfully created a new genre with *Pat the Bunny,* my mother went further and further afield, dreaming of transforming books into something not only readable but edible, wearable, washable—and on and on. Some books would have handles, others fur, others a lock and key and hiding place. Some could be hammered, some could be read in bed—in the dark, by "feeling" under the covers. In among the fantastic and the practical were ideas for history books that might appeal to the very young—a tiny book on the life of Tom Thumb, an Abraham Lincoln alphabet book. A book about Mary Lincoln's jewelry. My mother had ideas for a Christmas book, for a book about growing up, about dreams, about dying. And she was forever inspired by animals. She wanted to write an animal peek-a-boo book, a set of twelve circus animal books, a book about toys for animals and one about feeding the animals, one about the Scare Bunny, and another about Mummy Long Legs.

Some of her lists came in the guise of orders to herself to get to work; some were terse—a few enigmatic words; others had descriptions of what she had in mind; a number even sketched a plot and suggested dialogue, such as:

Face book—where's the lady's eye? There's the lady's eye. Now find the lady's other eye. There it is!—Same for goat's beard, cow's horn, bunny's ears, horsey's teeth, piggy's nose, doggy's tongue . . .

Once, she wrote Simon & Schuster about her "Bed book" idea:

I am submitting a model of a young child's Bed book. To be read in bed with the fingers either in the dark or under the covers or even at naptime in the daylight while the eyes are closed or look-ing dreamily at the ceiling. The toy animals, to be recognized by feel, must each have an instantly discoverable distinctive feature. The material of which the animals are composed must be invit-ingly, deliciously squishy, so that the child will want to examine them over and over. I don't believe I have found the right mate-rial yet but I know it exists in some laboratory—it must be tough and seductive to an eager forefinger as sponge rubber is, prefer-ably soft in the middle with a smooth, harder rim. I would also in-sert several that could be stroked, cut from a sort of high plush or teddy-bearish material, which is fun to fondle. This book would take the place of the beloved old crib blanket which finally wears down to a grayish and fiercely defended scrap, which babies and those just out of babyhood go to bed with every night and with-out which they are sleepless and inconsolable. Children like to rub and feel something soft in the loneliness and isolation that comes after being put to bed and leaving play, food, and people—so why not a cozy, comforting Bed book?

Another time, my mother paid a visit to one of her editors, Lucille Ogle, who later relayed her ideas to the rest of the Simon & Schuster staff:

Dorothy Kunhardt said she would like very much to go on record with the following book ideas so that she could work on them from time to time and feel there will be a spot for them when they crystallize: "Noah's Airplane; shoe book; a plastic book; rest book; belt book; beach book (using actual sand and shells); Daddy's Hat.

My mother was trying to safeguard her ideas, but she knew this was essentially impossible. Ideas simply swam around the world. Even though she was before her time with a dozen different, original book concepts, she once stated, "Don't ever think the idea you've had is new."

The 1940s were highly demanding and creative years in my mother's writing career. She needed to make money and she constantly put pressure on herself to produce. She must have been envious at times of Kate's wealth, her dress-buying binges, her soft, luxurious life. She must have felt miles from Kate's lifestyle at this point in their lives.

"The maids are hanging clean curtains in my windows," Kate wrote to Dot in 1941:

> reaching up miles above their heads while the rod wriggles like an eel and the material escapes and falls in a foam of cream-colored net. It is pretty to see them in their blue uniforms so sweetly working together and laughing, but I know they are ruining their insides stretching like that, and my own pampered misbehaving innards ache with guilty sympathy.

Another time Kate wrote: "Suddenly I have nothing to do. For the first time in years. Until lately that has been the signal to start having a baby." Dorothy could not imagine having a baby to fill time, nor could she imagine, in her overly-busy life, having time to fill.

My mother worked all the time. And somehow, she managed to focus on the best of her ideas long enough to execute them. Her next book for children came out in 1942. It was called *The Telephone Book*. It was the same size as *Pat the Bunny,* this time blue instead of pink. Inside the front and back covers were black, cradle-style, dial-telephones made of cardboard with cardboard receivers attached by strings which the reader could pick up and use, holding the phone to his ear close to the book, to talk to Paul and Judy of *Pat the Bunny* fame. Paul, however, is now tall and slim, and about eight years old, and Judy has left dimpled knees behind to become a big girl of seven. They have a little brother, curly-haired Timmy, whom they take care of, inviting the reader to join in. Together with the reader, they play hide-and-seek, they give naked Timmy a bath, in which he swims, and they put a Band-Aid on Timmy's knee. Even today I find it impossible to resist pulling up the miniature plastic strip and sneaking a peek at the tiny red scrape on Timmy's knee and then covering it back up again with the sticky bandage.

The Telephone Book was filled with other ingenious tricks, too, like a movable blanket at the bottom of a crib, which the reader could pull up to cover sleeping Timmy. The blanket would be returned to its starting place at the foot of the crib when on the next page the reader pulled open a bureau drawer full of Timmy's socks. At naptime, Timmy slept with a familiar-looking, oblong, stuffed-animal bunny.

Just as had happened with the illustrations for *Pat the Bunny,* Simon & Schuster had to alter my mother's work on *The Telephone Book* slightly to fit a different page size than they had been drawn for. This meant some skillful tracing—and the job befell Tom Bevans's wife, Margaret, an illustrator in her own right, who had worked on *Pat the Bunny* as well. After the tracing work had been done, my mother had a long meeting with Tom Bevans and then wrote Mrs. Bevans her thanks.

The letter, I think, sheds some interesting light on my mother's rather delicate sensibility.

"I do think they are much improved," she wrote of a second round of tracings:

But I am also now fully convinced that no person can trace another person's faces without destroying the personality placed there and substituting another—it's not done on purpose but you are dealing in lines where a hundredth of an inch on the end of a mouth means a lot. For instance, I think the baby's expression in the tub, through tracing, has become less lighted up, has become starey, but I don't think the whole should be done over because something might happen to Paul in the change and I think he is good now. In the last picture, page 18, Judy has come out again, your Judy with the long upper lip that I hoped we could change, but the other children are very sweet so I don't think we should risk a new doing.

In 1942, *The Telephone Book* sold for one dollar. On the back of the little blue cardboard box that contained it, the Simon & Schuster editors wrote, "Here is another wonderful little surprise book by Dorothy Kunhardt, author of *Pat the Bunny*. This one is for two to five year olds. Every page contains something that is fun to do. You can find a letter and mail it in a post box. You can do lots of other things, and THERE ARE TWO TELEPHONES TO TALK THROUGH."

The reviewers agreed that this was a wonderful little surprise book, and *The Telephone Book* was another instant success. But my mother didn't pause to enjoy it. By the spring of 1942, she had lighted upon one of the ideas on her ever-growing list—the story of Tad Lincoln. She was slowly reading the four volumes of Carl Sandburg's monumental, poetic *Abraham Lincoln: The War Years,* an exercise which put to rest the idea of one day writing her own biography of Lincoln. There were too many great ones out there already, she decided, and Sandburg's was simply overwhelming. Instead of trying to compete, she planned to shed new light on Lincoln by coming upon the great American story from the perspective of his appealing youngest son.

Consumed by the idea, my mother felt she must know everything about Springfield, Illinois, where Tad was brought up, everything about his father and mother and brothers in those prairie days, everything about their house, their neighbors, his playthings, his daily life, and also everything about Washington in the early 1860s, about the White House where Tad lived for over four years, about his pets, his pranks, and, in fact, about his every recorded move and word, including his sad wanderings with his mother after his father's assassination, until his early death at eighteen.

During a summer vacation at Lake George, she wrote to my father back in the city:

> I have been getting in constant reading on the Lincoln project and become more and more keyed up to start my real work of writing. I feel it is such a wonderful subject, so right for these times when young people need heroes, good ones, to look up to. I wish it were done now, it should be coming out this coming Christmas.

My mother was torn. Making children's books was a lonely, often painful affair. Working on *Tad* was exciting—calling for travel, the meeting of challenging new minds, endless immersion in old books and newspapers which left her beside herself with exhilaration. It was a new domain for Dorothy, and yet very familiar, and it linked her to her father's great interests. Still, the only way she knew how to make money was through her own kind of writing for children. She had a track record and she had all those ideas. Sometimes, her ambitious ideas filled her with dread. How to produce yet another best seller? In April of 1943, in a letter sent to the New York hotel to which my mother had retreated in hopes of conjuring up something magical, my father wrote:

> Dottie, I have tremendous confidence in you. You whipped that *Telephone Book* together in little over a week and it has been marvelously successful. You should recognize how wonderfully you have done with *Pat the Bunny* and *The Telephone Book* and attack this job with self-confidence and joy—not with fear that you can't do it and worry about being away. We shall be all right at home, so be happy that we have things set up so that you can get away and give some uninterrupted time to your writing. After all, when you really get going you love it.
>
> My advice is to attack one job at a time and to stick to the "Little Jesus Book" however hard it may be at the start. That is the only way you will finish anything. You do better under pressure, so let's have this book done when we go up to see the boys.
>
> And between times—you can't work all of the time—go and have a good time. See whoever you want and go to the movies or the theater—and don't feel guilty about it. You'll do better and be happier and more alive.

The good advice didn't work; weeks of frustration turned to months. She jumped between the "Little Jesus Book" and the Tad Lincoln idea—and back again. Maybe a complete change of scenery would help. In the summer of 1943 we accepted the generosity of Cousin Grace for a vacation at her large compound on the western shore of Lake George,

near Rogers Rock. From Lake George, Dorothy now wrote to her husband at work in New York City:

> Before I began this letter I was sitting reading *The War Years*, try-
> ing to keep my mind on it but thinking of my Tad Lincoln and
> how I am going to do it. I think about it most of the time. This
> winter is going to be a great test for me. I have made a long prep-
> aration now and I must, I must do something good. For Father's
> sake, and your sake and my own. If I can't, I don't know what I
> shall do. But I am going to.
>
> I try not to let myself get too wrought up over tiny matters,
> after all there are huge things like the world at war to be thought
> of—and our life, yours and mine together, as it stretches forward
> to be lived by us. So many things to be chosen and decided and
> striven for—to make it the best life for us and the children. The
> thing really boils down to the fact that I am not happy away from
> you. I need to be near you. Your strength and wisdom flow into
> me when I am with you and help me quickly. I do love you.
>
> Dottie

The Tad Lincoln book required an enormous amount of courage for
Dorothy to start. Through it she wanted to live up to her father's standards. "No one has ever had such a father," she had written him. "I want
to do Tad well, as much for you as for myself." For months she struggled with a beginning, but it seemed there was too much riding on it.
Too many expectations.

Then, in mid-November 1943, whether from a fall she had had at
Groton or simple biology at work, she was stricken by the very loss she
had years earlier more than wished upon herself. In the early stages of
pregnancy, hoping for a fifth child, she suffered a miscarriage. For the

next week her father wrote her daily at the Morristown Memorial Hospital:

> Another of your family is unhappy tonight—myself. Yet it is rather secondhand unhappiness compared to that of you and Phil, and in particular of you. Because you have the pain as well as the sorrow. But there is a better day coming and these days will pass and you will perhaps find comfort in them when you look backward and see what they might have brought. With Phil's hand in yours he can walk up any hill no matter how steep it is. He is such a tower of strength in my estimation and his day and night, his year and lifetime is centered in you. Try to keep your mind clear to be ready to approach the next hurdle because there are plenty of hurdles. But although they look high enough in the distance, sometimes they shrink up when we come nearer to them.

I don't know whether or not I was told why my mother had been hospitalized but my letters home didn't seem very concerned. I was almost fifteen and mostly I talked about the dances I was going to over Christmas vacation and the girls I had made plans to go out with. In a three-page letter to her dated December 6, 1943, I devoted exactly one sentence to my mother: "I hope you are home from the hospital and much better, Mum."

At forty-two years old, Dorothy knew this had been her last chance at a baby. With the loss of her pregnancy, her Tad Lincoln book, too, was miscarried. Sadness enveloped her, leaving her empty and collapsed. All the momentum that had launched her into that ambitious project now dissolved. Tad must have seemed too much to cope with and so Dorothy turned back to more familiar ground—a book for children, the one about Jesus as a little boy. It had been on her lists for years, and now the time was right. It's hard for me not to imagine that she found some sort of consolation writing the story of a child whose mother loves him and would also lose him.

Although my mother was never a serious churchgoer, she had always been stirred by Christianity, having watched her mother prayerfully worship every Sunday (her father went "tut-tut" and rolled his eyes). She loved parts of the church service—the psalms, the poetry of those prayers, the doxology, the reverberating organ, the uplifting hymns— but she could never accept the church's doctrine of the virgin birth or the divinity of the Christ child. She thought the young Jesus had probably been very much like her own children or any children for that matter, and so her story was about his humanity. Her idea for the "Little Jesus Book" was to have Jesus' mother tell her son his favorite story on the night of his fifth birthday. And what is any child's favorite story but the story of himself!

"I'll tell you a story about a boy," says Mary. "He is five years old on this very night. He lives in a village called Nazareth and his father is a carpenter."

As there is no Gospel mention of Jesus in his youth—they jump from the baby in the manger to the precocious young man in the temple instructing the elders—my mother took open artistic license. In her book, Mary tells Jesus how he helped his father with his work, played with his little brothers and sister, how he helped the shepherd with the sheep, filled the lamp with oil, carried the water from the well, rode a donkey, and watched the camels drink. My mother's description of animals was particularly vivid: "Jesus looked at the camels' floppy, soft lips. He looked at their white eyelashes and he looked at their long, whiskery eyebrows." And we learn why camels have tight noses—it's so when the sand blows in a desert storm, it can't blow up their noses. By the end of the book, Jesus says to his mother, "You're my best storyteller." And Mary tells her son, "I am happier every day I have my boy."

Well-researched, based on studies of the Bible, and filled with realistic details of the surroundings back then, the book never once mentions God. Instead, my mother's understanding of her own children brought Jesus into a familiar, human realm, into an engaging family story that might have happened. The finished book, illustrated with color drawings by the artist Helen Sewell, was called *Once There Was a Little Boy* and was published by the Viking Press in 1946. Dorothy dedicated it to her mother.

The *New York Times Book Review* reported that *Once There Was a Little Boy* was "told with luminous simplicity," claiming that readers, "will have the sense of knowing Jesus as a friend and will come to the Biblical story of His life with a deeper understanding of its background." The Roman Catholic press found the book charming, but too infused with humanity. "When will authors like this one realize," a Catholic critic asked, "that Jesus wasn't just another little boy but a divine being from his birth onwards and not someone to be treated casually or written about with such familiarity?" The *New York Post*, however, hailed the new book and got to its heart, saying, "With superb understatement in prose of quiet distinction, Mrs. Kunhardt captures the love of a mother for her son and the son for his mother."

After *Once There Was a Little Boy*, Dorothy concentrated on another *Pat the Bunny*–style book, this one called, *More Please, The Hungry Animal Book*. The book contained a little box of paper cutout foods—a peanut, a clump of grass, a lump of sugar, a bone, a carrot, a fish, a jam sandwich, and a worm. Each animal on the pages that followed had a big, red slot in its open mouth, so that the paper food could be swallowed in one gulp. When the elephant got his peanut, it disappeared down the little red lane and then conveniently dropped into a little cardboard trough which opened under all the pages of the book. Subsequently, when the cow got its grass from the reader, it was deposited in the trough as well, and the same for the horse, the doggy, the rabbit, the seal, the child, and the bird. On the last page, the reader was instructed to transfer all the "food" back into the food envelope pasted on the inside cover "so you can get it again when you are ready."

Simon & Schuster had another hit on their hands. My mother later commented on her publisher, "The sales amaze me, not that S. & S. can't sell plain white pages if they have a fancy to."

MY MOTHER'S PROJECTS were flowing steadily now. One idea she had come back to again and again, and finally fixed on, was to create miniature books that could fit in children's tiny hands. All through the 1940s, Dorothy collected from antiquarian bookshops dozens of miniature books in many languages—tiny hymnals, fables, and poems and rhymes with tiny type and instructional content from the eighteenth and nineteenth centuries. She began experimenting with her own carefully constructed, twenty-four page miniature books, approximately two inches wide and three inches tall. But instead of abridged and abbreviated versions of longer stories, Dorothy's tinies were conceived as complete books.

Simon & Schuster liked the idea of these tiny short books but insisted that their contents be animals. My mother started studying animals, looking for unusual and little-known traits for every animal from aardvark to zebra. Simon & Schuster began devising a package that resembled a little library in the shape of a brick, which could contain an even dozen of Dorothy's creations. An excellent young illustrator, Garth Williams, was hired to draw the little families of animals Dorothy was writing about. The illustrations had to be directly related to the

words, and Williams was a wonderful choice; his work was colorful, accurate, funny, and free from cartoonish sentimentality—qualities E. B.
White had first discovered in this *New Yorker* artist in the early 1940s
when he'd done illustrations for *Stuart Little*.

Tiny Animal Stories was published in 1948, followed in 1949 by *Tiny
Nonsense Stories*, each a grouping of twelve little books in boxes that resembled a library shelf. The stories had plots, were funny, and fully
formed. While her earliest books for children had contained a virtual
flood of words, thousands of them, matched by her own quirky illustrations, these books were sparse, witty, and concise. Although about animals, they involved teasing, spanking, getting underfoot, acting brave,
feeling lonely, paying attention, and other homely family matters. The
dialogue, albeit from the mouths of camels and whales, sounded natural. The tiny books appealed to early readers whose mothers bought the
libraries by the million. In addition to helping pay for school tuitions,
my mother claimed the profits from these tiny stories paid for Nancy's
not-so-tiny wedding.

I was twenty by the time the Tiny Golden libraries were published
and when I read the miniature books, the animal stories seemed vaguely
familiar to me, as if I had experienced what they were portraying in
some other life. In fact, each family in the *Tiny Nonsense Stories*, always
made up of a father, a mother, and a child, suspiciously resembled a
telescoped version of our own family—an often grumpy but devoted
provider father, a slightly kooky, easy to anger, overprotective but for-
giving mother, and a child who loved to play but who could get into a lot
of trouble. Little Raymond Frog and his mother played an April Fools'
trick on Mr. Frog by putting a "Pinch me" sign on his hat as he went off
to work; Little Robert Pig dressed like a witch to frighten his dad on
Halloween; Little Theodore Pussycat visited his grandma who hated his
pretend cowboy gun, made him wear snow pants on a spring day, tied a

bib on him at meals, and brushed his teeth at night; and Little Oliver Bull, who was sick and had to watch the snowstorm and the making of a snowman—no, a snowbull—from his window. Pretty soon, he couldn't tell the snowbull from his father, who was now almost a snow-bull himself.

Was my mother writing for me? Of course not, at least that was the answer she gave in response to a reader's similar question. "I never write for any particular child," she answered:

> but simply for myself, and what pleases me is likely to please the young. I think I am an especially suitable writer for the crib age. My son Ken's remark when he was five is indubitably founded— "Mummy, you have an awfully baby mind, haven't you?"

Something I noticed this time around, as I reread all two dozen of the Tiny books (each of my children heard each book read over and over) is that of the twenty-four stories, twenty-one feature little boys as their heroes and only three revolve around little girls. Of those three girls, one is a complex and naughty child and another is a crybaby. Only one girl is up for some fun, on par with the boys. And that Tiny Nonsense book heroine is named "Dorothy Donkey"—a polka-dotted, bathing-suited young donkey who does cartwheels down the beach after her father and pretends to fly like an airplane like her mother, and then later asks her father, "May I be the leader next time?" Reading it over, it now seems fairly clear that my mother was giving a knowing wink to her audience and to herself.

10.

The Collector

Lincoln biographer and poet Carl Sandburg visits
the Kunhardt house in 1943, and inspires Dorothy
to devote herself to the Lincoln story, both
as a scholar and as a collector.

AFTER A DECADE of "learning" away from home, life changed suddenly for me in 1950 when, in a one-month span, I graduated from college, got married, and started my first real job, as a cub reporter for *Life* magazine. That first year of employment I was assigned to the magazine's Entertainment department and, as its theater reporter I saw, with my wife Katharine, almost one hundred plays in one of Broadway's most exciting seasons. (The musicals included *The King and I* and *Guys & Dolls*.) Then, after a year in the Sports department, helping make picture stories out of prizefights and baseball games, the magazine shipped me off to California to be a correspondent in its Los Angeles bureau.

I was dizzy with excitement. I had watched my father almost drag himself to work, hating the monotony of the woolen business, and I had expected that whatever job I ended up with would be drudgery, too. But the work I was now being paid to do was nothing like any work I had imagined. In fact, it wasn't work at all—it was pure fun. *Life* magazine was in its heyday back then, fifty years ago, the biggest and most powerful weekly in the world; the name alone opened doors. And wherever I went during those youthful years representing the magazine, I was welcomed with open arms. It was often said of Henry Luce's two main publications that *Time* made enemies and *Life* made friends. It was true—most of the stories we did were positive rather than critical. The American people loved us because we loved them.

My mother and father were delighted by my career. Nobody in our wide family of conservative businessmen—with some lawyers and a doctor thrown in—had ever been sent by his company on a romantic, all-expense paid, five-year-long journey like the one my wife, our first child, and I were being treated to. For a sheltered, naïve, curious, and ambitious twenty-four-year-old, every moment was new and rewarding, with an office in Beverly Hills, a little house for my growing family underneath the end of the runway of the Santa Monica Airport, surf to ride on weekends, and stories about this new kind of living to think up and get photographed and write up and ship off. New York was so far away now, a place already in my distant past. On Thanksgiving Day, 1952, my mother wrote her first letter to us in California:

How I miss you and Katharine and your adorable little Phil, I can never tell you. I can still hardly believe that your company all of a sudden sent you off to California. I keep telling myself what a wonderful chance in business and opening of all kinds of doors into a more wonderful life this is for you. Dad says that on the day you left, he slipped into his sample room, which was deserted, and prayed for you. Dad is so proud of you. He says the move out there is a real feather in your cap, those are his very words. He

says handle everything that comes your way with brains and always with a smile. That's not quite the advice I'd give, but . . .

She stopped there, keeping her own particular advice to herself and
returned to family matters:

Here, on our hilltop, the darkness even at this early hour of four
is already beginning to gather about the house and warn Dad,
whose bending figure in the garden is so a part of all our lives,
that he must come in soon. This is not like any Thanksgiving Day
we have ever had, with you three so far away, but thank Heavens
minds and hearts have the power of reaching out and distance
vanishes.

Much as she had done while I was away at Groton and Princeton, my
mother wrote letters so vivid that they kept me connected to my old
world, which she didn't want me to lose. It was a world of family, of rit-
uals, of an ever-changing hill, a world of memories and close bonds
from my past, all of which I was in some ways trying to shed. Being on
my own, I was feeling alive and when still another of those fat letters arrived, I began rolling my eyes. But it was not long before her letters, as
they had captivated me at school, began to engulf me again, and keep
me, at least, from being totally seduced by my new world of pink houses
and palm trees.

My mother would keep a list of things she wanted to include in her
letters. Sometimes she would jot down three or four sentences and mail
those thin letters off one after another during a week. But most of the
time she would put off the writing until her list had grown so long there
was no room to add another thought and then she would find the time to
write, getting up at five in the morning and gulping two cups of coffee

before making her way in the darkness to her desk. Then she wrote compulsively, as if she were meeting some kind of deadline. And she was. The deadline was life itself, which seemed to her to be getting shorter all the time.

She filled her letters with rich and detailed accounts of the family back east, explaining what Ken and his bride were doing, and how his first job in the advertising business was going and what their apartment in New York City looked like. I learned all about Nancy and her growing family. And Edith—everything about what she had said and done and how young men were beginning to swarm about her, but what an impossible place the hill was for a young woman wishing to meet people:

> One thing Dad and I worry about is that in this house, so over-loaded with my dusty old books and with no room for her to bring her friends and have a good time, Dith has practically never had a friend inside these doors.

In these letters, everybody in the family seemed attached in special ways, my Meserve grandparents and their children—my Aunt Helen and Uncle Dick, Uncle Leighton and Aunt Kay, my cousins Joan, David, Pammy, Anne, Fred, and Marcia—the list was enormous. At first, I couldn't quite understand the intensity of feeling all these people had for each other. When I stumbled on a birthday letter from my grand-mother's sister, Ella Dunn, to my mother on her forty-fifth birthday, I began to understand that it was an almost genetic trait, passed on from one generation to the next:

> Dearest Dot,
>   My heart overflows with love and happiness because you are you, and you have brought so much rich happiness into my life.

From that first wonderful Sunday when Dads and I went up to see your mother and father and your father opened the door for us and excitedly said you were here. We were led upstairs to the library, and you, you precious mite, were carried in in a clothes basket. You were adorable. You had charm even at that moment and you waved your pretty hands about and then you slept through our adoration. Well, I've loved you ever since and long to some day have you all to myself for even just a little while.

That's the kind of letter that was common in our family; even the reticent members learned to be intensely affectionate on paper.

My mother, however, did not simply paint pretty nostalgic pictures of the hill or gush emotion. She addressed difficult, at times tragic, family matters straight on, with the honesty of a journalist and the ear of a playwright. In 1954, my "baby cousin," fourteen-year-old Pammy, drowned in an Adirondack lake accident and I could not make the trip for the funeral. My mother took it upon herself to relive the tragedy for me in a fifteen-page letter that began, "I will try and tell you some of the facts about Pam's loss." Nobody else would have chronicled the dramas that unfolded around my cousin's sudden, violent waterfall death and the exact path the awful news took on its way to her parents. Nobody else would have rendered a blow-by-blow account of everybody's reactions to the tragedy and their roles in the funeral so that we in California might understand each awful moment and share in the intimate family experience:

Pam's body was found after eight hours of searching—forty men from the community volunteered. Four men had been roped together to try to search under the falls but the rush of water was too strong and they finally had to put up sandbags at the falls to divert the current, and then they found her under a rock, directly in the center, which had under it a ten-foot-deep whirlpool which no one had known was there.

My mother's letter spoke in minutes, not hours or days, and it captured the humanity of our big family as it tried to cope with devastating loss.

"When the whole family came in Sunday afternoon," she wrote:

—all but Uncle Dick who stood pathetically on the sidewalk— Pam looked very sweet, but her face was not Pam's. All the elfin, joyous life that was Pam had left it, and one could see that she had put up a terrible struggle among the rocks.

And of her own mother she wrote:

I almost think poor Gran had the hardest time, alone in New York at the funeral parlor, putting a little nosegay of sweetheart roses each day in Pam's hands. I saw Gran say good-bye to Pam, and I never could imagine anything so noble or so touching. She looked at her a long time and then she said softly, "I can't spare her," but she walked away, head up, to help others.

THE 1950S SHOULD have been a decade of peace and quiet for my mother. There was enough money coming in and less going out, my father's business no longer tormented him, and by 1950 both Nancy and I were married, with Ken soon to follow, leaving only Edith at home.

But, instead, these were tempestuous years for Dorothy as the tug-of-war between work and family pulled her in opposite directions. A quarter of a century earlier her father had offered to start turning over his photograph collection to her but she had not been ready for it, opting, instead, to try her hand at writing.

Now, my mother was increasingly consumed by her work on Lincoln. It had become an obsession—to learn everything there was to learn about our sixteenth president, and then to hunt out facts about him and his family and those close to him that had not yet been uncovered. But then grandchildren arrived. At first it seemed perfectly natural for Dorothy to help out when Nancy and George had their first babies and when Katharine and I had ours. But Nancy was to have six children and Katharine and I had three in quick succession and then three more. According to Nancy, no one, and she meant no one, but her mother was allowed to take care of her children during her long hospital maternity stays. Or when she traveled abroad with her husband, or vacationed in Bermuda, or campaigned with him when he went into politics, certainly no one but Mum could possibly be in charge of her growing tribe while she was away. To my father's consternation, my mother made it clear that she was always there to take over in case of emergency or whenever some opportunity arose. When my mother was visiting us in California, Katharine and I were quick to accept her offer to stay with our three little children while we went off on a camping trip to Baja, a long weekend in Las Vegas, or a week's climb in the High Sierras. Mum always did it with a smile, waving us on our way, although we knew the days and nights ahead would be hard for her. The never-ending grind of caring for little children was hard enough for a mother in her twenties; for a grandmother in her fifties it was physically and emotionally exhausting. Yet we kept asking her, and she kept agreeing, knowing that saying good-bye to Lincoln for a week meant a month before she would really get back to him.

And as a grandmother, my mother amazed me. I could see by the extraordinary way she was with our children how she could create books that young people adored. She could tune into their wavelength and for a weekend or a week she lived as a child. What made them laugh made her laugh. What made them sad made her sad. When she pretended she was a rooster and crowed, they went wild with delight and begged her for more crowing. When a grandchild got into a crying jag and wouldn't stop, she would get in one, too, raising the roof with wails and sobs of her own. This so impressed the offending child that his own crying was soon forgotten, tears halted mid-track at the sight of his tantruming grandmother. She had a knack with children but distributing that knack to two or three little children twelve hours a day exhausted her, and when the lights were finally out, she retreated to her room to read, hoping there wouldn't be too many night calls, with fears to calm and diapers to change and stories to tell to bring sleep back to the house.

It was in the 1950s that I started to really know my mother. The very fact that we were separated most of the year gave the times we were together an intensity. I had always known that she liked to collect things, but now I began to see that this was no hobby but a matter of passion. She was a collector at heart. She endowed books, photographs, artifacts, jewelry, and the written word with power, luster, and spirit. In particular, her father's collection of nineteenth-century photographs emanated life for Dorothy, those historic images a part of her father's lifeblood and now of her own. She was not simply the caretaker of the collection, for she widened and deepened its scope, ingesting its contents until her knowledge was a valuable part of the collection itself.

She worked hard, all her children were aware of that; she helped our father pay the bills and we were proud of her for being so bright and truthful and filled with energy. But I, at least, had not yet come to realize that so much of what she gave to us was carefully thought out and came as a sacrifice. When she gave her time, it was a sacrifice because she wanted to be working on Lincoln round the clock. When she gave us an important family heirloom, she made a ceremony out of the presentation, whether it was a silver goblet from North Andover or a large, oriental coin with a secret compartment from her trip around the world, or a gold pen and pencil set handed down generation after generation, or an inscribed Sandburg book, which she cherished. Giving presents gave her joy and a sense of accomplishment, but the right words had to be said or written to go along with the giving and the new owner of whatever treasure was changing hands had to be aware of the history of what he was getting and its importance.

At the same time that I was beginning to understand my mother better, she was trying her hardest to understand her own father. She wanted to chronicle her father and his history, to fit his life and work into the time line of his photography collection and its place in American history. One of the letters my mother wrote to us in California told of a key weekend visit from her parents. Although her father had made himself into a celebrated Lincoln collector and scholar, not even his daughter knew all the details of his past. Frederick Hill Meserve was a man who was guarded with his words and told only what he wanted to tell about his early life.

"Dad and I tried to make the two days with them out here in Morristown as happy ones as possible," my mother wrote us:

What really pleased me is that on Sunday morning Gampy and I drove after breakfast to get the papers—and then I had a flash of inspiration and parked the car on McCulloch Avenue, and for about an hour and a half I questioned Gampy about the whole of his early life—beginning just as far back as he could remember—and as he spoke I wrote it all down. It was thrilling to me, and for the first time I really have a picture of the early part of his ex-

traordinary life. He kept saying, "Don't write that down. I'll stop
if you do." But he was enjoying it hugely. And when Dad in his
black car with Gran beside him passed and called, "We're going
to church," Gamps laughed that wonderful laugh of his and said,
"We've had a reprieve."

The Meserve name, my mother recorded, could be tracked back to the
Isle of Jersey, off the English coast, whence around 1640 Clement
Meservy sailed across the Atlantic. Settling in Portsmouth, New Hampshire, he soon became responsible for a growing tribe of Meserves (the "y"
had been dropped), who merged by marriage with people named Torr,
Hall, Gerrish, Mayo, Hill, Leighton, Neil, Walker, Waterhouse, Blood,
Shackford, Buzell, and Burnham. In 1840, in direct line from the original
Meservy, William Neal Meserve was born. He grew up to become Fred's
father, my mother's paternal grandfather and an important influence in her
life. The son of a produce merchant for whom he clerked at the family
shop in Boston near Faneuil Hall, William, at age twenty-two, enlisted in
the Union army. It was 1862, the Civil War was raging, and William had
responded to Lincoln's call for "three hundred thousand men."

Although his father thought him too soft for army life, during
William's four years of military service he showed remarkable sol-
dierly qualities, making do with inadequate equipment and scant rations,
undergoing backbreaking forced marches, and overcoming a severe
wound at Antietam to fight in a total of eleven major Civil War engage-
ments. Throughout his years as a soldier, William kept a diary. His
account was precise, romantic, often brutal, but never self-serving. In
its beautiful, rolling script, it offered an incredible insight into the
Civil War.

In 1864, home from the front for Thanksgiving, William married

Abby Hill from New Hampshire and less than a year later, the war over and the young couple back in Massachusetts, my grandfather, Frederick Hill Meserve, was born.

After leaving the army, William entered the Boston Dental College and then moved his little family to Norfolk, Virginia, and opened a practice. Pulling teeth didn't last long, for William soon heeded the call of the church and abandoned dentistry for the Congregational Seminary in Harwington, Connecticut. Once ordained, William was dispatched to the West. His son Frederick remembered the family's train trip across the country. He remembered watching hunters with rifles pick off buffalo by the score from the platform of the rear car. But William would see little of Fred's coming-of-age. He felt his family, which now included four children, was a burden a man of God couldn't afford. A few lines of one of the many poems William composed summed up his decision:

> Life's real business God directs,
> Marks out for each the rightful way;
> Too oft the man himself selects
> And takes the path that leads astray.

Following what he perceived as "the rightful way," William abandoned his family in the town of Colorado Springs and took off for points farther west.

My mother set all this down, and then she wrote about how Fred's mother and three little brothers sadly returned to her childhood home in New Hampshire, but Fred stayed in Colorado, determined, at sixteen, to earn what his family needed to live on. As a hunter he bagged antelope and wildcats at the edge of town. He shot ducks and sold them at market. In the summers, he stripped to the waist and worked with Mexican sheepshearers cutting fleece, mailing his cash earnings home, and living on little himself. While a student at Colorado College, he earned wages as assistant city engineer, laid out a huge extension of the town on the plains, helped design and build the Antlers Hotel, and surveyed a proposed road to the top of Pikes Peak, the great mountain that loomed over the growing city.

"In those days I held the record for the forty miles to the top of Pikes Peak and back," Fred told my mother:

> Eleven and a half hours. I frequently slept out during that road survey. Just wrapped in a blanket, under the stars. We had tents but we didn't bother putting them up on a nice night. I'd wake up in the morning covered with snow.

Once, Fred spent several winter months at the summit of Pikes Peak as a civilian weather observer for the United States Signal Service. In temperatures that sometimes dropped to thirty-nine degrees below zero, Fred wrote lonely poems from the mountaintop. Like his father, Fred was a compulsive writer—hardly a letter home did not contain a vivid description or a new poem with a romantic notion. But the fact that his father had ignored what Fred considered to be the most important obligation in a man's life—the care of wife and family—and instead had run off to California for a "higher calling" never ceased to incense the young man and made him cynical about the idea of God.

Fred left the West in 1888, traveling to Galveston, Texas, by train, then by the steamer *Alamo* through the Gulf and up the east coast to New York and thence to New England. Behind him he left his youth— he was now twenty-three years old—but it had been a youth well spent, he'd had over seven years of earning what he called "filthy lucre" in a long list of ways. When taken altogether, that variety of jobs and experiences in the West had helped fashion a fearless, tireless, dedicated, nineteenth-century American with vision; one who spoke the language of the pioneer, who enjoyed figures and maps and architectural plans and railroad lore, who thrived on the majestic scenery of the Rockies and liked to test himself running, climbing, hunting, and riding with cowboys, and working with day laborers. He had also inherited from his father, along with perseverance, an altogether different side to his nature—that of the observer, the writer, the poet, the romantic. Endowed with a sharp intellect coupled with an agility with words and a growing devotion to recording the American past, Fred embodied the robust and optimistic spirit of the country.

Returning east, my grandfather entered the Massachusetts Institute of Technology to become a full-fledged architect. He paid his room, board, and tuition by taking on a draftsman's job with a Boston engineering firm, and by writing columns for the *Boston Globe* and the *Boston Herald*. But the president of his class never graduated. By his senior year his mother needed money so badly Fred left MIT and took a job running a heating company in the Midwest. When that didn't last, he decided to talk about his future with Seth Milliken, an astute businessman in New York City who had married a sister of Fred's mother. Uncle Seth's interests and investments were far ranging and he hired his young nephew on the spot. Starting at a hundred dollars a month, Fred Meserve worked for the Milliken family (except for a few years when he held a seat on the New York Stock Exchange), right up to the day he died in 1962 at the age of ninety-six. It was an amicable and mutually satisfying relationship.

But business alone would never occupy my grandfather. A compact, restless man with a poetic cast of mind and high energy always on the low boil, he needed something creative to do. In the early 1890s, he began to wonder whether his energy might be best spent on a joint project

with his father—a project that might also heal what wounds the deser-
tion had left behind. They were in touch by letter and now Fred suggested that they do something with William's war diary. He proposed
illustrating his father's writing with photographs of the battlefields
where William had fought, thereby creating a unique history book.
With the same robust optimism with which he approached all projects,
Fred set about buying up photographs and matching them to his father's
experiences. It was not long before he had a small collection of war scenes
and the important people related—generals, statesmen, even Abraham
Lincoln himself (for William had shaken the president's hand once in
the field). All these images would one day be very valuable, but no one
knew it yet. No one had even recognized the virtue of preserving photographs of Lincoln.

At the time, my grandfather was living in New York City, working
for his Uncle Seth, and occasionally getting a glimpse of a pretty, teenage
schoolgirl named Edith Turner, who was accompanied each weekday
morning by her stockbroker father as she walked down Madison Avenue
to her school. Fred's heart was set on Edith but he knew he would have
to bide his time for quite a few years. Finally, when she was old enough,
he married her. It was 1899. She was nineteen, he was thirty-four. Their
wedding present from Uncle Seth was one of seven row houses uptown
on Edgecombe Avenue not far from the Harlem River, that Fred had
helped build, and it was here that he brought his young bride, and here,
two years later, that their first child, Dorothy, was born. Fred was so
pleased by his firstborn that he raised an American flag over the front
door of the skinny, four-story house and on that night of September 29,
1901, he wrote a poem:

That gift-giving biped, the spindly stork,
'Tis a habit he has, I've heard,

In his peregrinations found New York,—
The story may seem absurd,—
But whether intended for us or not,
He perched on the roof of our house and lot,
And gave us a baby upon the spot.
The stork is a wonderful bird.

From the beginning, Fred Meserve adored his daughter. The more he studied her—her darting, dark eyes, her thoughtful pursed lips, that dimple of a nose—the more he was convinced that she was just like him. He was so enchanted with her that whenever he could he recorded the stages of Dorothy's early life with his black box Kodak camera. And, much as he had done with his father, Fred created a photographic book dedicated to and for his firstborn child. Underneath, in his precise handwriting, he put down the pertinent details. He included a photo taken of Dorothy on May 11, 1902, at seven months, when she was christened at the Manhattan Congregational Church at Seventy-sixth Street and Broadway. Then there was one of her three days later, when her first tooth appeared. Her father listed the words she could say, including "book," "please, father," and "I love you." The miracle that was Dorothy even softened Fred's spiritual cynicism as she inspired little prayers for his daughter:

Father, keep me safe tonight
Bless thy child again
Make me always do the right
In Christ's name. Amen.

The same year that Dorothy was born—1901—Fred made an acquisition that transformed his ever-growing but still minor collection of nineteenth-century photographs centering on American poets, Lincoln, and the Civil War into a major holding. He tracked down and purchased a cache of fifteen thousand long-forgotten glass negatives made in the 1860s by the great photographer Mathew Brady. In the weeks to come, as he slowly extracted the negatives from the wooden boxes which housed them, he found original images of Lincoln, as well as of Mary Lincoln and their sons, the Lincoln cabinet, all the important statesmen of the time, officers of both the Union and Confederate armies during the Civil War, and thousands of other important personages, including the great writers, artists, and actors of the day. Mathew Brady had been the most famous photographer during the Civil War years; the famous and influential had flocked to his studio to have their likenesses made. Brady had also sent an army of photographers into the field to capture scenes of the war. But, overextended and unable to pay his bills, by the end of the Civil War Brady was in such deep debt that his photographic supply house impounded thousands of his fragile negatives. For decades they lay untouched in a warehouse in Hoboken, New Jersey, until Fred, through careful research, sniffed them out and bought them.

He was now a major collector of photographs. And the Meserve Collection, as it was formally called, grew with each passing year. He began buying whole collections—ten thousand *cartes de visite* here, five thousand stereographs there.

"For fifty years," he told my mother:

a clerk in a Christian organization in New York had collected photographs of the English and American stage. After he died, his executor sold the entire collection to me claiming there were seventy-five thousand items. All of this shows my folly in buying too much and too many to know all I have or to have time to enjoy their study.

My grandfather began to publish privately in small editions—and instantly the demand for his books and monographs was far greater than he had imagined. His crowning achievement was a handmade set of ten large volumes with actual photographs, tipped-in, of the eight thousand most important American men and women of the last half of the nineteenth century. It took him a year and a half to make a set and before calling it quits, he constructed seven of them. "But the friends I have made," Fred emphasized to my mother:

the artists and sculptors, the writers and publishers who have come to me for help, the collectors who perhaps started out by collecting too much, have remained to remind us that I made no mistake when I dedicated my collection to the use of students and writers of history.

SO IT WAS that my mother grew up surrounded by visual evidence of the Civil War and the country's sixteenth president. She remembered that she and her sister, Helen, and brother, Leighton, were careful not to call their parents after lights-out so that one or the other wouldn't have to make the long, four-flight trip from the cellar when work on the collection went on, overseen by my knitting grandmother. No wonder my mother, having grown up in a Lincoln cauldron, was drawn to it and to her father's work as sources for her own writing. Dorothy would never be able to shake the shadow of the tall man from Illinois. She had to know everything about him—the dimensions of his oversize nose, the way his left eye wandered, what made that mole in his right cheek, the high pitch to his voice, how he rocked with laughter after telling a joke, what he ate, who trimmed his beard, why he cried, where he bought his clothes, which bank he used, how his mind worked. Lincoln's marriage became of special interest to Dorothy, as did his children. Soon she found that Sandburg and other Lincoln biographers had not uncovered everything by a long shot. There were still plenty of unsolved Lincoln mysteries, plenty of revealing stories to be told.

One of the tributes Fred Meserve liked best occurred when Dorothy and he were honored guests at the opening of the Lincoln papers in the nation's capital in 1947. In the excitement and crush of important figures in the Lincoln world, Dorothy and Fred came upon a group of scholars arguing about the date of a particular Lincoln picture. When Fred broke in and put them straight, one turned to him and asked, "Who do you think you are, Frederick Hill Meserve?" So my grandfather informed them that that was exactly who he thought he was.

As the 1940s faded into the '50s, hardly a day went by that my mother didn't find a note from her father in the mail. They weren't letters, really, just tidbits of information, a discovery he had made, an identification of some long-unknown face, a tiny new piece in the Lincoln puzzle, a request from a magazine for use of his pictures. Gradually, Frederick relied more and more heavily on his daughter to make important decisions about the collection. He had struggled for half a century to put it in order and to identify the date, subject, and photographer of each picture. Dorothy, in turn, went much further in her research. She was making a careful study of all the known Lincoln photographs to determine what the man had most probably been thinking at the time each pose was made. It was during these years that Fred began to realize that his daughter had surpassed him in knowledge of his collection and that he certainly could not come close to her in articulating and dramatizing most of its mysteries and subtleties. Now the telephone, once such a pariah to the family, was used frequently—Dorothy and her father talked at least once a day to supplement their mail.

As the '50s began, my mother embarked on a series of articles based on photographs and research from the Meserve Collection and finds she had made on her own. She sold these pieces to national magazines—the *Saturday Evening Post, Life,* and *Collier's*—and although her articles were meticulously accurate and highly entertaining, she always wrote them much too long. The necessary cutting process drove her mad. How could the supposedly intelligent editors at these big magazines with circulations in the millions, she wanted to know, be so unfeeling when they carved up in minutes what she had spent months perfecting? And didn't they see that, in the wake of their callous pencils, were a host of editor-created inaccuracies?

My mother was used to a lot more control in the writing of her children's books. But even so, she was now gaining a national name in the field of American history. Her words concerning Lincoln were being read by millions. She was acquiring a reputation as an innovative and clear-speaking scholar of the great American story.

For *Life* magazine, she proposed and wrote an article ostensibly about Lincoln's dog, Fido, but also about Lincoln's transition from small-town lawyer to the nation's president. As was her way, she treated the 3,000-word project as if she were writing a full-length book. Ever since she had discovered the little picture of Fido among her father's files, she had been piling up research on Springfield and the friends that the Lincolns had left behind when they moved to Washington, discovering everything she could about Lincoln and dogs. Piles of books and research covered her bed in the daytime and had to be moved to the floor in the evening for sleep.

In November 1952, my mother wrote me in California of her Fido mania:

Today I walked down Fifth Avenue to the public library to spend three hours in the history room doing a little early Illinois research for something that fits in with Lincoln's woof-woof Fido. I'm such an idiot—the months drag on—I now have two whole rooms stacked with volumes of information, a thousand times too much material for the article—and I still crave finding out more. As Dad says, it is dope and I am its helpless, pathetic victim. I must rouse myself and fight back to reality.

Fido had been left behind in Springfield in 1861, with some of Tad's friends in charge until the Lincolns returned. Those Illinois boys were now old men, still alive, though, to tell the tale of Fido if anyone ever asked them. So Dorothy did. First, she met eighty-six-year-old Isaac Diller, who spent three days with her reminiscing about knowing the Lincoln family when he was a boy. Then she got in touch with John Linden Roll, who was also in his eighty-sixth year.

From the memories of these two aged men Dorothy painted a vivid picture of the president-elect's emotional departure from Springfield and the little dog left behind, along with a community so proud of its citizen. Less than a year after Lincoln's assassination, tragedy overcame Fido, too, as Johnny Roll documented to my mother in a shaky pencil scrawl:

> We possessed the dog for a number of years when one day, in a playful mood, he put his dirty paws upon a drunken man on the street curb who, in his drunken rage, thrust a knife into the body of poor old Fido. He was buried by loving hands. So Fido, just a poor yellow dog, met the fate of his illustrious master—assassination.

Only Johnny Roll spelled it "assination" and what a fight my mother had with the *Life* editors over that. "No one will understand," they told her. "They'll think we spelled it wrong."

It was one of the dozens of little changes and cuts and skirtings of the truth that my mother could not bear. After all, she had practically slept in the same bed as Fido for the last two years and now that his story was down on paper, it ought to be correct. "It will read fine," they told her, and, as she silently retreated in a sea of disgust, I vowed that if I ever got high enough on *Life's* editorial ladder to make decisions of this nature, they would lie on the side of the writer and the truth instead of the niceties of editing.

Way back in 1939, Dorothy's father showed one of his early photographs to Dr. McClellan, President of Lincoln Memorial University. The picture showed a rag doll that had been on the floor of the room where Lee surrendered to Grant and had been published as "The Silent Witness" many years before. Dr. McClellan said, "What a title for a moving story, a clever writer could make a great article out of it." Fred Meserve related this to his daughter and for over a decade Dorothy let the idea brew as she collected information about that moment in history and even tracked down the doll to its proud owner. Then she finally wrote the story for the *Saturday Evening Post* under the title of "The Lost Rag Doll of Appomattox." The article employed the same techniques as the Fido piece, using the premise of telling the story of a doll, but in truth shedding new light on the fabled surrender.

Dorothy was not only becoming an acclaimed author of nineteenth-century history, she was also busy putting together a collection of Lincoln artifacts of her own. As usual, my father backed her completely; they put whatever money they could toward acquiring treasures. Like her father's collection, it started with photographs. Whenever she came upon daguerreotypes, ambrotypes, or tintypes to her liking, she would buy them. Lithographs fascinated her, too, especially ones that had to do with the Lincoln family and, in particular, those that depicted Lincoln's death. There were dozens of these, each one differing not only in the placement of people in the death room but also in exactly who those people were. Along with a constant stream of little gifts from her father, mostly photographs he knew she would be interested in, Dorothy's collection grew. Her library expanded almost by the day as the secondhand bookshop in Morristown always seemed well supplied with Lincoln-related material—soon the books were blocking out the light from the three bedroom windows. Then, in January of 1956, in front of the Turitz bookshop, Dorothy came upon a scene she would never forget.

"The proprietor's truck was parked in front of the door," she later wrote:

> the back part still crammed with a thousand books and on the sidewalk was a scattered mountain of old leather-covered volumes. I hurried inside and there on the floor I saw pile upon pile of neatly unloaded books—Lincoln—I read. Lincoln, Lincoln, Lincoln, every title had Lincoln in it. Quickly I opened the covers. Here were the first editions of the most important Lincoln biographies. On the flyleaves was the signature of "Albert S. Edwards," and beneath, "The Lincoln Home, Springfield, Illinois." I knew Albert Edwards was the son of Mrs. Lincoln's sister. He had been custodian of Lincoln's house for many years. This must be his library. I suddenly felt sick with excitement. All around me there must be source material such as I could never find again.

My mother wasn't able to buy this surprise cache from her book dealer; he had already promised it to a dealer in New York City. But in the weeks to come she was able to follow it to the city shop and purchase all six hundred volumes from the library that Lincoln himself had often borrowed from, plus the books owned by the families closest to the prairie lawyer, with inscription after inscription by Lincoln's neighbors and friends. Dorothy was able to find out where all the books had come from, and then headed for Springfield to meet ninety-year-old Mary Edwards Brown, granddaughter of Mary Lincoln's sister, and custodian of the Lincoln home following her father. Mrs. Brown had decided to divest herself of the Lincoln library and her Lincoln possessions before she died and she was only too eager to meet Mr. Meserve's daughter, for she had some relics she wanted to sell, to the right person.

From her three trips to Springfield to see Mrs. Brown, Dorothy became the new owner of a quantity of Lincoln-related objects—the three sperm-oil lamps that had lighted the Lincoln wedding in the Edwards's home, five family scrapbooks filled with a record of the Lincolns over the years, Mary Lincoln's travel commode, which she kept beside her bed, the horsehair covering from the couch on which Lincoln courted Mary at her sister's house, a rare first printing of Lincoln's farewell address to the citizens of Springfield, nails from Lincoln's house and tin from its roof, strands of Lincoln's hair, plus dozens upon dozens of family pictures—never-before-seen daguerreotypes and ambrotypes and *cartes de visite* of the Springfield people closest to Lincoln during his lawyer days.

"My husband says that the drive back east was a nightmare," Dorothy later wrote:

> because at each motel I made him carry in four enormous shrouded objects and then he had to stagger out with them in the morning. The lamps are now on our mantelpiece, and the commode in an upstairs bedroom close beside a crib. And a sleepy child at ten o'clock hears: "Come, darling, time to sit on Mrs. Lincoln's potty."

Even more exciting than the acquisition of the Lincoln relics were the stories Mary Edwards Brown told my mother about Abe and Mary and all their relatives and friends in Springfield. Especially the ones about Mrs. Lincoln, whom Mrs. Brown as a young girl had helped care for during her final days. My mother took notes and wrote the story of her journey, which was later published in *Life* as an article called "Mission in Lincolnland," along with stunning pictures of the relics.

Out in California, I had no influence or control over my mother's articles. I heard about them from her, either by letter or on long-distance phone calls. I hardly knew the editors with whom she was working but I do remember shuddering more than once upon hearing of some harsh face-offs between her and them, hoping that my mother's involvement with my magazine would somehow mysteriously disappear but proud, at the same time, that she was becoming one of our star writers.

EARLY IN 1958, I was transferred back to New York and soon after, at age thirty, *Life* appointed me assistant picture editor. In 1960, the leadership of the editorial side of the magazine changed, and I was able to leapfrog into a major position on the new managing editor's team. Before long, I was an assistant managing editor running many of *Life*'s departments.

It was in the late '50s that my mother and I, in one of our many excited conversations about Lincoln, decided to write a book together. Our minds had always been close. But now, as a formal research and writing collaboration evolved, we grew even closer.

For years, my mother had been "interested in death." She kept piles of notes on things her children said about death. She wanted to write an obituary book and other stories that dealt with death. And perhaps the greatest American death story was that of Abraham Lincoln. Soon, we were both excited about telling the story of Lincoln's death—the drama and the horror of it, and the unprecedented funeral procession across the country to Springfield where he was entombed. The Meserve Collection had pictures from the many cities along the way, as, at each stop, Lincoln's body was removed from the special train, transferred onto an elaborately decorated hearse, viewed by thousands, prayed over, and put back on the train again, bound for the next stop. But that wasn't all. Our idea for the book included what happened to Lincoln's body over the years, how it was moved over and over again, how the coffin was cut into for viewing, how Lincoln's remains were almost stolen by outlaws who were after ransom money, how, after that, the body was hidden away in the bowels of the tomb in Springfield for many years before it was finally sunk underground at the base of the tomb in an enormous block of cement.

Gampy was so pleased with our project that in 1959 he paid for a trip to Springfield for us to do preliminary research for the book. My mother knew every Lincoln expert in the prairie lawyer's hometown; she had been there many times before, and so our path was cleared as we ranged over the Lincoln home, the law office, his city streets, and the tomb just outside of town. I even climbed up the inside of the monument to take a flash picture, looking down, at the spot where the coffin had been hidden for years among rotting discarded timbers.

My mother was alive with excitement the entire trip. And I came to appreciate the breadth and depth of her Lincoln knowledge, both the broad strokes and the quirky details that she knew. We worked well together. We both had ideas. She had an encyclopedic understanding of Lincoln and an incredible familiarity with the Meserve Collection. It was immensely fun to be with her as each of us sparked the other. We shared a dark sense of humor, a taste for adventure, and a love of history and words. I think it was the first time in my life I had spent that kind of time with my mother; it was certainly the first time I saw in person what reverence for Lincoln is all about. She cared so much for the walls of his house, the floors he walked on, the trees he planted; she even dug down in the earth a good foot to find some of the dirt that had actually been in his backyard in the 1850s. By the end of the trip we had all sorts of ideas for our book, and in 1960 we signed a contract with Harper & Brothers.

Although we would periodically meet to discuss the book and go over pictures, no real progress was made. The time wasn't right. My mother was being consumed, not with a new book, but with the approaching deaths of the two people she loved most in the world—her sixty-year-old husband and her ninety-four-year-old father.

1 1.

Beyond Words

Taken at the doorway of the Meserve house in
New York City, this picture shows
Dorothy with the two men she loved most in
the world—her father and her husband.

For my father, the 1950s were the first tension-free years since the 1920s—the years of his football fame at Harvard and his engagement and marriage to Dorothy. Whenever he could, he accompanied Mum on her trips west and loved every moment with us as we swam the Pacific together or climbed the high mountains. Money worries were a thing of the past. He had finally made peace with his job and worked at it if not joyously at least with some pleasure. Living on the hill in Morristown and tending his garden gave him quiet but constant satisfaction. And working for the people of his community in so many volunteer capacities made him beloved by everybody.

I was aware of all this, but I was so caught up in myself, I hardly saw that my father had begun to die. He had a chemical imbalance he was told, but, actually, it was his one failing kidney that was poisoning him. My mother shielded me from the truth so that nothing would interfere with my work.

When my family returned east from California, I began to have weekly lunches with my father at the Harvard Club, of which he was president. He covered up his failing health with loving good cheer. We ate cold salmon with mayonnaise and talked about my work. I knew my mother was taking special care of him now, not letting him get over-tired, seeing he kept to his salt-free diet, making sure he didn't work too long or hard in his garden on weekends. But I wouldn't believe that any-thing was seriously wrong.

Around Christmas of 1961, my father's doctor had carefully exam-ined his patient in the bedroom that had originally been Ken's and mine. Dr. Krusie came down the front steps slowly, signaled my mother and me into the dining room, closed the door, and told us we had to face the fact that my father had a year to live at most, probably less.

The following year was spent so privately by my mother and father, living alone together on the hill and sharing his collapse, that when it was over I hardly knew what had transpired. Six years later, when I was writing a book about my father's life, I asked my mother to write down all she remembered—for she had never mentioned any of the details of their last months together. My request seemed to have opened up a store of memories that must have been lurking there, maybe hoping to be released. Whether that was the motivation, or whether it was her desire to be of any help she could to me, my request brought forth a hand-written outpouring which filled twenty-six oversized pages—a carefully worded, meticulously-detailed, extraordinary letter about my father. A death letter:

Dear Phil,

You have asked me to set down for you how it was as Dad did things that were a part of his life, each for the last time, during the last year of his life—the year of 1962.

On January 1, 1962, he was wearing a heavy metal and leather brace that surrounded the swollen knee and proceeded the length of his leg to strap underneath his shoe. It made him limp and was painful and the back of his leg—that great muscular calf which his friends at college said contained *two* swelling muscles that reminded them of a baby's behind—was bleeding from the scraping of the brace. Also, he was taking almost daily injections for an excess of liquid which his body manufactured and which caused his ankles and other parts of his body to swell. This even rounded and puffed his face which had always been so lean and handsome—so that when I saw the finished portrait of Dad done by Bill Draper to hang at the entrance of the New York Harvard Club for the next two years, as an honor to him for having been president, I almost gave a little scream of horror. Mr. Draper, in his studio, proudly pulled the cloth from the canvas, and I felt I was looking at a complete stranger. He had never known Dad as he used to be, and the change had been so gradual and I loved him so much that I had not seen it come.

My father continued doing what he had been doing for the last thirty-five years that spring, going halfway down the hill through the arborvitae trees to our icy, spring-fed pool and playing in it like a seal. But now, my mother timed his every trip, making sure no more than ten minutes elapsed between the time of the loud shot and splash of his first dive to the time he reappeared at the foot of his garden, examining his scalloped flower beds. And the swimming didn't last much longer. My mother continued:

With no comment made by either of us, he now seemed to be content with his bath before dinner in the old-fashioned, lion claw–footed bathtub in our bathroom. I wanted so much to take that tub with me wherever I went, and when I moved to New York about a year and a half later, after Dad's death, I said good-bye to that bathtub with the greatest difficulty. I figured that he had taken 28,000 baths in that silly tub.

He had bad days when he could hardly get out of bed he felt so sick, but they were often followed by good days, as my mother's long letter described:

In May he was feeling marvelously well and he drove me into New York to see Gampy—as it happened, for the last time . . . Father was lying motionless on his bed, very pale, his features carven and handsomer than I have ever seen them. Phil struggled up to the third floor with his heavy brace and stood holding Gampy's thin waxlike hand in his broad, powerful one. I had come to believe that the reason Gampy never responded to Granny was that he had become almost totally deaf. I thought I would make a try at something and, stooping, I put my mouth right at Gampy's ear and shouted, "This is Dorothy, I love you!" A little, faraway voice answered, "Dear Dorothy," and I'll remember those two last words all my life.

I was thirty-four when Gampy died. My mother was sixty. My mother's letter described the scene:

On June 25, in the early morning Father quietly stopped breath-ing and Mother insisted that he lie in his open coffin in their bedroom, where they had slept together and talked over all the problems of their lives for so many years. This time I drove Phil in—for the funeral, and we stood in the church where we had been married, and listened to the words being said as one person.

Gampy wouldn't have cared about the words being said at his funeral, all he cared about was doing what he thought was right and being with the people he loved. I remember visiting "148" after he died, and trying to get out of going upstairs where he lay. But Granny and my mother insisted. There he was in his coffin in front of the fireplace looking as if he'd just come in from eighteen holes of golf. "Rufus," he always called me because of my red hair, and standing there beside him I felt like a small boy again. To divert my attention, I opened his top bureau drawer, at the foot of the coffin. Family members must have given him electric razors every Christmas and birthday because the drawer was full of them, unused. My mother's letter to me continued:

Mother seemed in a complete daze—not believing. She said only one thing to me—"Doesn't Father look sweet?" When the awful truth finally broke into her mind several months later, she had a complete stroke which never allowed her to utter a sound from that day forth, or to move even her little finger, though tears sometimes rolled down her cheeks.

Phil insisted on my driving him in from Morristown to see Mother, and he was now on crutches as well as having his brace to carry on each step—so it was a real struggle to get up to the same bedroom where Gampy had been, on the third floor. He stood beside her holding her hand and calling her by his special pet name for her—"Mutter" which he had always used since Dad and I first became engaged and Mother, noting the German name, "Kunhardt," of the boy I had met in Providence and whom I seemed to like quite a bit, asked if he could speak any English. So he called her Mutter. This time there was no response.

Although most of the letters between Dorothy and Kate in the first half of their lives had been jammed full of the shiver and joy of life, those that followed in the second half slowly quieted. They were not only more mature and reasoned, but their subject matter was more weighty—more often than not concerning death. Members of both their families had begun to die. Kate was particularly affected by the death of her Uncle Fred, who had accompanied the girls on their round-the-world trip:

> Every remembrance that I have of Uncle Fred is filled with pride and excitement. In that faith he had in people, he absolved them of the original sin of being young and clumsy, and as we grew older he blessed our lives with his approval and love. There are so many things I wanted to go on learning from him—but the chief one—charity—I have in my heart forever because of him.

Then, as World War II was being fought, Kate wrote Dorothy about the death of her parents:

> Sometimes I am even glad that my parents are dead and do not have to see the world collapsing, although I wish daily that I knew what Father would think and do now, but not as he would be now if he were alive and seventy-six! Think of it, but as he was at fifty-nine or sixty, still vigorous and afraid of nothing. I think he wouldn't sit around baying at the moon as so many of us are doing, but would be making a few plans for how to rescue this country. I used to feel so sure of what I thought and felt about things,

and now I realize it was because I just listened to Uncle Fred and Father, and even when I couldn't understand what they were talking about, I was so sure they were right it gave me the comfortable feeling of assurance that a child has, that perhaps a Catholic has.

And about Dorothy's family, Kate was equally emotional. She loved visiting Dot's family's house: "The atmosphere of love is like the smell of roses." Upon the death of Dorothy's father, Kate wrote:

You have been living this death in anguish for months and years, while the intensity of your tenderness has grown almost to bursting. For him it is the ending of a good life, rich in love and satisfactions. You were the one who shared and understood the historian's meticulous care and delight in sleuthing the mysteries of the past. How proud you must be, I can guess. How sad, I dare not think. I love you, DM. Katie.

My mother had lost both her parents almost simultaneously. And now she was determined to make the last months of her husband's life as happy and bearable as possible.

This meant making a serious withdrawal from society. All the time I was growing up, my mother had been one of the sparkling jewels of our town. Her clever sense of humor and her unpredictable, effervescent personality were felt by everyone she came in touch with, not only family and friends but all the workers and shopkeepers of Morristown. From the little old lady at the station where she bought her newspapers and magazines, to the man who ran the ice cream store, to the taciturn, white-coated druggist and the kindly lady at the hairdresser who did her hair once a week, to the shoe fitter, they all loved her. Even the garbage man loved her. She actually rode with him on his rounds several times in order to test the quality of his garbage for a book she was writing in a series of children's books about workers. Her curiosity was enormous; she focused on people and made them feel important. Faces perked up when she was spotted, people always wanted to take her on in conversation. My mother brightened up our town. But during the final year of my father's life all this changed. She kept to herself when she shopped, hardly spoke, nodded at her friends but rarely smiled. They knew something was gravely wrong. And they did not try to break into the shell she was building around her. It was to protect herself from unnecessary conversation so that her energies would be preserved for her husband. It was to help him say good-bye to all the things he loved so much—his fishing stream, his beehives, his fig tree, his sweetheart roses, each child as he or she came to visit, each grandchild—to say good-bye without ever saying it.

My mother's letter not only described her father's funeral and her mother's stroke, it also wandered back in time to her honeymoon, back even further, to the time when, at thirteen, she first started learning about sex. It was as if my mother was filling in the chinks for me. She knew what I already knew. Now she wanted me to learn what I didn't know:

During that last summer Dad was dressed in shorts, moccasins, and one of his old plaid cotton sports shirts—he had never worn an undershirt since I had known him. I discovered that on our honeymoon when he chose to take me to a small woodsy camp near Monticello in Virginia where I watched him splash like a huge, white tadpole in an outsized brook, where we had quite bad plain food cooked by the couple that owned the place and where we rode old jugging plugs of horses through the woods. I hated it—we had spent one night en route in a hotel in Washington, D.C., and I so longed to stay there—there was everything that excited and interested me, but Phil hated that, he longed to get on to the real heart of his week's honeymoon in the woods and fields. But we never discussed what I would like any more than Dad ever discussed sex. He brought himself to call on a Kunhardt doctor acquaintance in New York before our wedding—he was terribly innocent and pure but it occurred to him there might be something he should know, but the doctor only told him "just be a gentleman" and that was the end of that subject.

As for me, when, as a thirteen-year-old girl, wearing short, starched linen dresses and long black curls down my back, I noticed a slight brown stain in my starched white pants that were held up by innumerable large buttons I, in great embarrassment, went to my mother because I thought I had a dread disease. She looked, I thought, angry—marched to her bedroom bureau and returned with a pile of cotton "birds eye" baby's diapers, a narrow waist band and two safety pins. She said, "Here, wear one of these, this will happen every month. It has to do with having babies." I was in terror for literally years afterward. I thought I was having a baby, but no baby came. I had been told absolutely nothing about boys or their part in this. So on my wedding journey I was not only in a place I hated but my nightly position was that of an Egyptian mummy in its case. How Dad and I ever had any children so quickly I don't know. But the Lord performs his wonders. Later on, as our marriage settled into a tacit agreement each to give in to the other on the little things that did not matter, we let our sense of humor enter into the problems of daily life.

When, thirty-four years ago, I first read this description of my
mother's early sex life, I skipped over it fast, quite embarrassed that she
should reveal such intimate details to a son. Today, rereading her letter,
I am amazed at her frank honesty. She may never have spoken about
such things but, in writing, she could address just about anything. She
wanted me to know how naïve and innocent both of them were, and
how sleeping together was at first. I know from letters between them a
few years into their marriage, that things improved after the awkward
honeymoon year and that they yearned for each other and gave each
other great physical pleasure. But I doubt that my mother had ever told
the real story of the sorry beginnings to any living soul, not even to
Kate to whom she had painted her honeymoon as perfect bliss.

My mother's letter to me continued:

Dad was now unable to climb into a bathtub. Instead, he stood
docilely in front of the hand basin in our bathroom while I gave
him an old-fashioned sponge bath. He swayed a bit and waited
for the pleasure of a rough towel that I dried him with, a towel
that had been his father's in North Andover—he craved it because it was so great and scratchy but I hated to use it because the
skin on his back was as clear and delicate as a baby's and after a
rub with that favorite towel he looked as though he had been
beaten with twigs from a thornbush.

From then on, everything was pretty agonizing. My father's eyesight
was fading. At first, he insisted that new glasses would fix him up but it
was obvious soon that nothing could help. He was becoming incontinent, too. My mother kept a toilet chair by his bed at night. And she often slept on the floor of the bathroom; the hardness of the floor kept her
only very slightly asleep so that she could hear him call out to her at in-

tervals. Even with her round-the-clock vigilance, my mother now started to blame herself for things she hadn't done:

I began to have regrets about things that I had failed to do for Dad and to blame myself endlessly. One thing I have never gotten over is that about a month before Dr. Krusie said, "You haven't been out of the house for a long while, why don't you go in to New York?" I was too cowardly to ask him the question I feared above everything—"How much time is there, can I give up a day of being with him?" I don't know how I could have done it but I did go, leaving Dad only with a cleaning woman. It took me about an hour and three quarters to reach New York by train and by the tube underneath the Hudson River, and all the time my heart was pounding faster and faster and I could not get my breath. I was so frightened for him. I had left him in his big chair and I know that after the cleaning woman had brought him his luncheon tray he would make his way across the room to the sofa and lie down. The minute I reached New York at 33rd Street, I turned and ran down the stairs, took the first train to Hoboken, and ran with all my strength for the first train back to Morristown. I found him lying on the sofa. He had never complained that I left him but his heavenly smile of greeting and "I've missed you, Dottie, darling" broke me up into little pieces. I don't know how I could have done it.

The end was approaching. Once, Day's End had heralded the conclusion of my mother's search for the perfect man to marry and the beginning of a glorious, lifelong love affair. Now, thirty-seven years later, the phrase took on a new meaning—here was the dark, sad end as that bright light was being extinguished. For a long time since he had been so ill, my father had not been able to show physical affection to his wife, but one morning, he very timidly asked, "Could we lie down on the bed together for a few minutes?":

> He got himself somehow straight down in the center of the bed and I was lying close next to him. He lay there in silence for quite a while and then he said, "Dottie, dear, it is so wonderful for me to look down and see you there beside me." After a little while we got up and he hobbled to the top of the stairs to begin his down-ward struggle.

Finally, my mother's long, exhausting revelation was over and she was ready to sign it and send it off:

> Phil, I've got to stop this now because I should read it over before I send it to you. Perhaps if I read it I won't send it. Christmas you know about, because you were there, with Katharine and the chil-dren, and he died January 5. I gave Dad slippers for Christmas and for the first time since we were engaged, he gave me nothing. If he could have given me himself, to keep, I would have been the happiest woman in the world.

She signed the letter to me with, "I love you beyond words." It was a favorite phrase of hers, a way to stretch her feelings further than what she could write down. She was excited by life *beyond words*. She thought someone *beautiful beyond words*. She loved *beyond words*.

12.

A Life Alone

The author and his mother working on the
photographs that will be used in *Twenty Days*,
their book about the Lincoln assassination

T HE HOURS GO so slowly all alone," my mother wrote Nancy in January of 1963. She was back on the hill, for the first time truly by herself in the big, old house. I knew only too well the vivid picture that must have been playing in her tortured mind—the image of Mum, supported by her two sons on either arm, looking into the casket that lay in state in a side chapel in Morristown's St. Peter's Episcopal Church. It was not Dad lying there upon the white folds of satin. It was, instead, a man with a turned-down mouth and a drooping nose and gray skin. Only the forehead was familiar, with its large freckles and weak spray of hair, hair so endlessly rubbed by her strong hands all their years together but especially the last weeks, when all hope was gone. Leaning up close, she had touched that forehead and said, "So sweet."

Then my mother and Ken and I stood and looked at him some more. Her face was pained and her body shivered. "He's not in there anymore,

Mum," I managed to say. "I know," she replied. Then she turned us around and we left without looking back.

On the day of the funeral, when the service was over, my mother stood on the steps of the church and greeted every one of the vast assemblage of friends and family. Later, at the burial, she did not shed a tear or show any emotion as the casket was lowered into the ground, and for the next few days she stayed with Katharine and me. I never saw her cry. The time finally came for her to go back to Morristown, and I drove the hour-and-a-half trip and left her there, waving good-bye to me from the living room window next to my father's special chair, just as she had waved good-bye to my father each morning as he left for business. I had told her we would work together on our Lincoln book soon. Before my father had become so sick, she and I and Brendan Mulvey, an art director from one of the Time Inc. magazines, had been hiding away in my office every Friday, looking at pictures, and had laid out most of the book, putting the photographs in place and filling the areas around them with the proper amount of dummy type.

The book now became a form of healing for both of us. Most illustrated history books at the time were written first and then pictures were dropped into the text. But we started the other way around—using over three hundred photographs to tell the story of Lincoln's assassination and the nation's grief. We broke all the rules about cropping and focus and size, pushing the magnificent, century-old photographs for all they were worth. We created extreme enlargements of key scenes, magnifying details to reveal evidence, letting the photographs bleed over full pages, sometimes over two-page spreads, not worrying if the images got grainy and soft. Readers could look directly into the eyes of John Wilkes Booth, they could practically hold the assassin's derringer pistol or strain to see into the president's casket. My mother and I both thrilled at the power and emotion of the photographs. They assumed absolute, black-and-white authority. Once laid out, we would write the text to explain the remarkable drama.

For the first year of my mother's life alone and probably for the sixteen years that followed before her death, not a day went by when I didn't think of her, wondering how she was doing, sometimes feeling the pain she was in, and trying to figure out how I could make things better for her. I know she thought of me constantly, too, not wanting to drag me down with her sadness and yet needing my support.

I've often wondered why I felt her pain so sharply and why I felt so obligated to help her. Part of it was because our minds so often worked in the same way. I knew what and how she was thinking and, in this case, I could all too clearly imagine and feel her sinking spirits. I was deeply saddened by my father's death but I had my wife, my children, my work. My mother, I worried, hardly knew how to live without her husband and she was still mourning for her father as well. I felt I must support her now, and protect her, as my father had.

Part of my feeling of responsibility was the realization that I was where I was in life largely thanks to her. She had sacrificed and supported and encouraged. She had backed me in all my difficult decisions. She had inspired me with her devotion to intense work.

And part of it was that I never fully understood my mother's propensity for darkness and depression, or how self-destructive she could be. My mother began to try to tame her sadness with alcohol and pills long before I saw what was happening. So my efforts to cheer her up, to help give her life new purpose, would only work temporarily.

I knew hard work was one way to break her loneliness. I needed to get her into New York and engage her in an exciting project. But I tried to think of other ways, too. Outings. Family gatherings. Dreamed-up jobs to make sure she was busy and using her brain. Phone calls. Anything that kept her involved with the lives of her children and grandchildren would raise her spirits.

All that was forty years ago, and my memory of that year is one of a bleak landscape, with my mother going weeks without seeing or talking to anyone. When I study her calendar of 1963 now, I find how wrong I was.

Instead of a cold, silent first night at home on the hill, my mother spent a fiery Saturday afternoon and evening trying to settle a battle between her daughter Nancy and Nancy's husband, George. Nancy was on the verge of a breakdown by the time our father died. She had cried uncontrollably at the burial and later, in a New York hotel room, had succumbed to such hysterics that George had called upon a psychiatrist for help. Back home in Beverly, Massachusetts, there was talk of hospitalization.

After assessing the situation, Dorothy's first act back on the hill was to place calls to my father's Harvard roommate, Robert Bradford, an ex-governor of Massachusetts, and to her old friend Carl Binger, an eminent psychiatrist, both of whom lived in Massachusetts also. She outlined the dilemma and sought their help.

The entry on my mother's calendar for the next day—Sunday—simply said, "Alone," followed by "Many calls: great trouble!" In the days to follow, she lunched with her sister, Helen; had dinner with Edith and her husband, Ned; trained to Southampton on Long Island for the weekend with her sister; worked at *Life* all day on a Lincoln article; had a lunch meeting with our editor at Harper & Row; flew up to Boston to see Carl Binger, first alone, then with Nancy; flew down again to see her paralyzed mother before she was moved to a nursing home in Southampton; met with Kate and Harry Mali; and worked with Brendan Mulvey and me in my *Life* office. In other words, she wasn't just sitting around mourning. She was active. She was working. And she was worrying. She was trying to solve problems and she definitely was not alone.

Through all of this my mother and I proceeded with our book, tentatively titled *Lay Me in Some Quiet Place* after what Lincoln had said to his wife, Mary, while visiting a bucolic little graveyard outside of Washington shortly before his assassination. No one else liked the title much, probably because of its double entendre, but that easy observation never crossed our minds. I guess we were both a little naïve.

At the same time, trouble was brewing. My mother's 1963 calendar reads:

May 24: Ken gets job! May 26: Go on Librium. June 8: 40th Reunion dinner at Bryn Mawr. June 25: Anniversary of Father's death. Saw Mother. June 30: Phil and Katharine and children here. July 3–6: Dossy visits. July 11: In Southampton again—saw Mother—a doctor may try hypnotism to help her talk. July 19: Fly to Maine to work with Philip on our book. Aug. 23: Went on wagon.

Among this extraordinary line-up of events, "Go on Librium" and "Went on wagon" were dropped in like luncheons. Even now, with it staring at me in her own handwriting, it is difficult for me to take in my mother's blooming dependence on prescription drugs and alcohol. Librium, Valium, and Halcyon—all tranquilizers she was prescribed in the '60s and '70s in vast numbers to soothe nerves and help sleeplessness. My mother was an insomniac most of her adult life, but now that she was alone, the nights had become even worse. The Librium helped. Mum took it liberally. I remember the tiny pills she ate and to which over time she became addicted. Despite the pills, she became even more depressed, especially when alcohol or the codeine syrups she had taken for her cough ever since her breakdown in the '30s were added into the mix. Do the seemingly casual calendar entries suggest that my mother knew that alcohol and Librium was a risky combination, able to produce hallucinations, amnesia, and even death? Probably not. For it was not long before she returned to her evening cocktails. Looking back today I realize how desperate she was to mask the awful emptiness she felt, an ever-present loneliness that she had never known before.

Still, the pace of her life did not slow down, as her calendar attests:

Aug. 16–23: Work at *Life* with Philip and Brendan. Sept. 2: at Brookfield with Dith and Ned. Sept. 5, 6, 7: alone. Sept. 24: Columbus [her cat] has cancer—put to sleep. Oct. 2: Drive to Princeton, Civil War Centennial commission 5:00 p.m. at Nassau Inn. Spend night.

She had been chosen to be on a special commission of scholars to determine how the country would celebrate the hundredth anniversary of the Civil War. She was the only woman on the commission. And in the fall of 1963, *Life* assigned her another article, to commemorate the hundredth anniversary of the Gettysburg Address. By October 24, the article was done and my mother returned with me to my family's house in Chappaqua, New York. During that drive she told me that she couldn't bear to live on the hill without Dad anymore and that she had decided to move to her parents' Manhattan town house—148 East Seventy-eighth Street—we all just called it "148." Slowly she would start to move her possessions into the city, using her own car and an inexpensive professional moving company.

The Kennedy assassination, which took place in November, reinspired my mother in her work on our book. The recurrent national nightmare seemed to breathe fresh horror into our subject, to infuse it with a kind of reflected currency and, therefore, urgency. The name of the book was now changed to *Twenty Days*, the time between Booth's bullet thudding into the back of Lincoln's head and the final funeral on a hillside in Springfield's Oak Ridge Cemetery.

Before the writing was to start, I had to help move my mother out of Morristown. She herself had packed up her thousands of treasured books, but it was up to me to sift through the rest—the accumulation of treasures and junk in the attic, the closets, the cellar, the bathrooms. I remember all the clothes that hung in the closets dating back to my youth, and the piles of old magazines in the cellar—*Life* from the very first issue on, *Collier's*, *The Saturday Evening Post*, *The New Yorker*, *National Geographic*—piles that sometimes reached to the ceiling. And the bathroom shelves lined with bottles and tubes and brushes and powders. The Pond's cold cream and the tube of lipstick and an open box of pink powder with a puff in it and powder spilt everywhere from too hurried an application. Nothing ever got thrown away, even if it was dead empty, certainly not if it was half full.

Working away, weekend after weekend, digging my mother out, was a gigantic task. No hired help would have been able to make the judgment calls required—what would stay in her possession and get transferred to 148 and what went to the dump. Since I have the same problem as she did—of never throwing anything away—much of what I was doing was not only backbreaking but was also heartbreaking. I stuffed whatever small things I couldn't throw away in my pockets, but tons of minor treasures had to be bagged and boxed and slung onto Louis the garbage man's truck and carted who knows where. Anything in handwriting I kept.

Through it all, my mother practically hid. She stayed in her room and pretended to read. I knew she was pretending by the set of her jaw and the clench of her teeth. Whenever I took a break, I came into her room to give her words of encouragement. Sitting on the edge of the bed was a woman in her sixties whose face had little to do with the face that I re-

membered as a child. She had shed her soft, gamine look of youth for
the hard image of work. Some of this transition could be explained by
how poorly my mother took care of herself. She got little sleep, ate er-
ratically, and consumed all kinds of habit-forming pills and syrups to
calm her and to repress the deep, guttural coughs that were her constant
companions. Her one indulgence was her hair—she had it washed and
set once a week, wearing it short and soft atop her small head. Unlike
some women who sit in front of mirrors and carefully apply layers of
makeup, my mother hardly glanced at herself, and cosmetics were after-
thoughts at best. Always on the run, she tried to show a presentable face
by drawing red lipstick on her thin lips and smacking on powder.

So many things marked her change. The floating dresses of her
youth had given way first to wool skirts and sweater sets in browns and
greens, the cautionary colors her mother had taught her to wear, and
then, by the '60s, to stiff silk dresses. The dainty, short steps she took in
her youth had given way to strides, the better to get things done. Her
hands, once smooth, had become gnarled from gripping pencils and
pens, from washing dishes, from wrapping and carrying, from squeez-
ing steering wheels—from taking responsibility.

Sometimes my mother tried to affect the mannerisms of her earlier
days, twisting her mouth into a sly, coquettish smile, but it didn't work
anymore; it came out pinched and silly. The thousands of hours she had
spent lying on her side in bed, reading, always reading, absorbing history and interpreting it for herself and storing it in her memory, her jaw
always propped up and squeezed tight by her fist, had left her looking
severe, even angry. She was sixty-two but she seemed older.

WHEN THE MOVE from the hill into the city was finally completed, my
mother began her new life in her old house on East Seventy-eighth

Street, the five-story building bought by her parents when she was in college. 148 had been left to all three Meserve children, but her younger sister, Helen, and her still younger brother, Leighton, had generously given their shares to their sister. My father had left her very little—there was a small trust fund established for him by his father's brother, but no life insurance, no nest egg, not even a house—they had rented all those years. Her parents' estate was as yet to be worked out, but when it eventually was, there was little cash for the three children. The revenues from Dorothy's books were dwindling with each passing year.

Harper & Row had set a deadline for *Twenty Days* to be completed—the end of 1964, six months away. We split the work between us. My mother would produce the new "research" on the people and events in our story and I would shape it to the book, edit it, fit it to the allotted space, write the headlines and captions, and try to make the words sing. I was second in command. It was her scholarship—and her writing—that was to make the book unique. She would work night and day to put her vast knowledge down on paper and I would cut and paste and rewrite and stitch during the early mornings and on weekends. My work at *Life* was all-consuming so I had to get up at 2:00 a.m. to work on *Twenty Days* for four or five hours before leaving for the long commute to the office. My secretary would type what I brought to her each morning, and the book slowly took shape.

What my mother gave me on paper was usually remarkable. But she didn't make my job easy. Her pages of notes were wildly rambling. As she was writing she was also reading constantly, augmenting her knowledge. When she came upon some new detail or nuance, she was practically rabid with the fear that it might be left out. She wrote brushfire notes, chronicling new findings or emotional shadings that she said absolutely had to be included in order to do justice to the portraits we were presenting. She also did some first-rate sleuthing. She personally found the headbags that the conspirators who helped Booth in the assassination of Lincoln were made to wear during their trial. And she persuaded the reluctant government to photograph them for the book. She also was able to have the contents of Booth's pockets when he was captured—which included pictures of five women—unwrapped, spread out, and photographed.

Working straight through the dark hours of the nights, she wrote about Lincoln, Mary, and the politicians of the time as if they were lifelong neighbors whom she knew intimately and wanted to describe with heartfelt accuracy. She wanted, above all, to get all the details right, and would support her work with cross references and footnotes. She resisted my requests for orderly, disciplined completion of sections of the book. But despite herself she produced history of remarkable insight and palpable detail. The main trouble was that she could not keep to any schedule. To make our deadlines, I had to squeeze the writing out of her. I had to call her up two or three times a day and yell into the phone that what she was writing was too long, that only half of it could be used, and that she was to mail or bring me what she was working on immediately. Most of the time she brought it herself, coming down on the subway and walking crosstown to the Time & Life Building on Sixth Avenue.

The sight of my mother sitting outside my office waiting to see me while delegations of photographers, editors, writers, and art directors streamed in and out became an ongoing embarrassment. She would sit in a chair beside my secretary, sometimes for hours, waiting to get me to herself. And when she finally did, there was seldom any emergency; in fact, she often just wanted to see me and ask me a few questions about her finances—had I balanced her checkbook yet or paid such and such a bill? I should have put my foot down. But I couldn't.

Being in such close touch with me, working so hard on *Twenty Days*, making sure that everything she wrote was absolutely accurate, writing until her wrist gave out—all dispelled her loneliness and softened her grief. I kept on battering her with orders and deadlines, fearing that if I let up, what happened to her with the Tad Lincoln book would happen all over again—she just wouldn't finish. Taken as a whole, *Twenty Days* was too big for her to cope with, but breaking it down into concise, smaller parts made it do-able. Toward the end, a thick folder with her writing on Lincoln's extraordinary mind was delivered to me with the following printed on the outside:

If I had some more hours, I might cut and rewrite this for use—but this last stretch of working 29½ hours straight has killed me, as this heavy wad of paper will kill you. I have not read it over, am positive I have made a failure and my original idea has vanished.

But what she had given me was brilliant.

Slowly, out of the reams of beautifully conceived and stylishly written research, the book was fashioned. Although it would never have emerged without my work, *Twenty Days* was predominantly my mother's book. It was the Lincoln book she had always dreamed of, the one she thought she'd never write, and it demonstrated her fierce efforts to gather every last piece of information and her quirky, graphic way of seeing things:

At about ten thirty on the black night of April 14, 1865, a man signaled with a lighted candle from the stoop of Petersen's boarding house in Washington, D.C., and shouted four ordinary words, "Bring him in here." Opposite, across the street, something far out of the ordinary began to move. Monstrous and many-legged like a centipede, it had just squeezed itself out through a doorway of Ford's Theatre and now began to crawl in agonizingly slow motion toward the candle's flame, its many feet moving in weirdly unrelated, out-of-time steps, all struggling for stances in the wheel-rutted and hoof-chopped dirt.

This is how *Twenty Days* started, how Dorothy viewed the twenty-five soldiers and doctors and bystanders who together carried the unconscious president out of Ford's Theatre and across the street to the boardinghouse where, after a long night of horror, he died the next morning. Through vivid text and pictures, the book went on to chronicle twelve funerals in twelve cities as the Lincoln train made its way back to Springfield. It also told the story of Booth's capture and killing, of the trial of his conspirators, and of the hanging of four of them. It was our thesis that no generation since that time could feel the desolation of heart that the country had endured—until November 22, 1963, when "The frightful re-enactment of the awful event ninety-eight years before . . . brought the assassination of long ago to life for a whole new generation."

During the summer of 1965 our book was on the presses, I was on vacation in Maine, and my mother was worried. Worry was one of the things my mother did best. She inherited the habit of worry from her mother, who spent her whole life worrying that something in her far-flung family could go wrong. Day and night she had worried. My mother wasn't quite as bad—she picked her worry spots and then beat them to death, occasionally bordering on paranoia. And now she was convinced that Harper & Row had no plans to promote our book. Her worry turned neurotic at times, like when she dreamed up ways to punish the offending editors. She wanted me to write wrathful, accusatory letters complaining about what she termed, "their huge blanket of neglect."

When *Twenty Days* was finally published in the fall of 1965 with a wonderful foreword by the popular Civil War historian Bruce Catton, it was met with nothing but exuberant reviews. Scribner's Bookstore on Fifth Avenue in New York City turned over its window display to our book. My mother didn't have to worry that *Twenty Days* would quickly sink into oblivion, for today, almost forty years later, it is still in print and is considered a pioneering work in its field.

DURING THE SPRING of the following year—1966—I proposed that photography be the subject of the next year-end double issue of *Life*, and the idea was enthusiastically embraced. I wanted to start out the special issue with an extended picture essay about how photography began and what images its very earliest practitioners made. That called for a thorough and international research job. I remember talking to *Life's* picture editor, Dick Pollard, about the issue and what great photographers we could enlist to make it truly distinguished. Then, in discussing who might be qualified to do the research of early photography, Dick suddenly had an idea—"Why not," he offered, "your mother?" Dick knew of my mother, was familiar with the Meserve Collection, and, of course, with *Twenty Days*, which had been published six months before. At first I tried to dismiss the idea, not wanting her to get involved any more deeply than she already was in anything to do with my job. But when I thought it over, I began to realize what an opportunity such an assignment would be for her. Except for the stay in England and one short Bermuda vacation in the 1930s, my mother hadn't been out of the country since her traveling days before her marriage. The challenge and excitement of such a trip along with the exploration of many of the top museums of the world would certainly give her a fresh goal and purpose. I hadn't really thought it through before I heard myself saying, "Dick, why don't you ask her?"

So Dick Pollard offered my mother the assignment and with some encouragement from me, she accepted. Then Dick arranged what *Life* would pay her—$1,500 a month—and planned all the details of a three-month-long trip that would take her to England, Scotland, France, Italy, Germany, Austria, and Denmark. He insisted that she fly first class and stay at the best hotels. Wires went out to the bureaus enlisting their help and in late May, armed with letters of introduction, my mother, in a state of nervous excitement, took off for London. For the next months she worked like a fury in the daytime and at night she usually stayed in her hotel room, organized her notes, and took time to write me in great detail just what she had been doing. I was working so hard back in New York that summer that I skimmed her letters and laid them aside. Today, they sit in a pile on my desk, tissue-thin 1960s airmail paper from hotels in London, Paris, and Rome, my mother's tiny crowded handwriting, a cross between printing and script, spilling out her palpitating news. Taken as a whole these letters reveal a lot about her—the largeness of her mind, her capacity to make friends, the beguiling way she could get reticent people to drop their guard and cooperate, her love of gossip, her good judgment about new acquaintances, her astonishment over the big money being spent on her, her fear of paying out even a penny more than the *Life* expense account allotted to her (two dollars for breakfast, three dollars for lunch, six dollars for dinner) and her consistent expression of her pride in me. Even though she would live another thirteen years, it was the last time I would receive extended correspondence from her and it revealed her enormous energy and how she took the curators and experts of the photographic past of England and Europe by storm:

London, June 4

Mona Parrish is *Life*'s picture chief in London, pretty and so fragile-looking but actually strong as a precision machine and terribly capable and knowledgeable in the picture field—she has welcomed me as her special charge—has driven me to museums in London and to the Kodak Museum in Harrow, which was an all-day expedition. Mona has gone with me to most places and got me behind-the-scenes, to meet the top men, like C. Gibbs-Smith at the Victoria & Albert Museum where I've been three times. Yesterday, when we went to the Science Museum, we saw the curator D. B. Thomas, who was jolted during the first five minutes of showing his treasures to have me tell him that a daguerreotype displayed in a prominent case was not of Jenny Lind as marked. "That's not Jenny Lind" just popped out of my mouth and I was afraid for a minute I had made an enemy of Dr. Thomas whom I had met one minute before. I needn't have been afraid, Mr. Thomas is very shy, very sensitive, and very sweet, I must say. He began fumbling with his key to open the case and said, "I think I'll just remove this right now," but I begged him to leave it there till I can get home and send him pictures of Jenny Lind from the Meserve Collection.

London, June 11

I went alone to the Royal Photographic Society of London because the two heads there had been completely obstructive to Mona—endlessly saying the collection was in storage, in disorder, not in condition to be seen by visitors. I was told by the head, Mr. Hallett, and the curator, Mrs. Johnson, I could see nothing, but after I had described to them the condition of 148 and the Meserve Collection, spread over stairs and floors and on and under beds, their faces began to smile and they led me down to the basement where the disarray was, and while Mrs. Johnson unwrapped photographs by George Bernard Shaw and Rejlander (I got a photograph of him dressed up as Garibaldi in 1860) and a photographer named Keighly who snapped people unaware by wrapping up his camera in brown paper and string—like a casual parcel—Mr. Hallett himself bounded up the stairs and carried down with his own hands a pot of tea and three cups and saucers and some sweets, saying to me in the next hour, "Drink, Mrs. Kunhardt, your tea will be cold," and I told him the truth—"I can't drink, I'm too thrilled to be here and see all your treasures." When I went back to *Life* to report, everyone asked fearfully, "What happened?" It really was a piece of luck that I, the Mrs. Collier of New York City, could match the Royal Photographic Society in eccentric disarray.

I have to tell you about Scotland before I end. Going to Scotland with Dad had been something he had planned for us for many years. They asked me if I wanted to fly there—in one hour's time—and I said no, I would go by train, taking seven and a half hours, so that I could look out of the window at the countryside. I took a taxi last Sunday morning, alone, to King's Cross Station, settled myself in a window seat of my compartment, and watched in wonder and delight all day. It was a beautiful sunny day and when I went through Yorkshire, I thought I was right in the rolling, lovely hills of Ilkley where you and Nan spent that winter as babies. Everything passed so close to my eyes. I could see the pink cheeks and sturdy legs of children racing in their yards. I saw a white lilac bush covered with exquisite huge white clusters like a great bride's bouquet. There was flock after flock of sheep that had just been shorn, standing pale and suddenly small in the sunlight. Everything was so clean and pure and peaceful. Then when I got to Scotland there was the yellow gorse all over the hillside and in the city of Edinburgh that marvelous, dramatic castle high up on the broad street. I worked all the next day in the Royal Scottish Academy, flew home in the evening, and suddenly I was back in my hotel room. It was all a dream.

By the time my mother headed to Paris, she had gained confidence that she could manage this job, choose the hundreds upon hundreds of pictures she wanted printed for the *Life* editors, make a significant contribution to the year-end issue, and acquire a lot of friends along the way.

I knew many of the correspondents and photographers in the bureau well, all of whom paid her close attention. The trip was turning out to be better for her than I had hoped—a complete change, stimulating, invigorating people, exotic foreign places, a new challenge and very much up her professional alley. As I read them now, as if for the first time, my mother's letters from Europe at age sixty-five have much in common with the high-spirited, story-telling epistles she had written from abroad when she was in her early twenties:

Paris, June 18

At the Bibliothèque National I know what I want and what will tell the story of photography dramatically to *Life* readers— there are stereoscopic daguerreotypes of the moon taken in 1840, there are early pictures of people first trying to fly, with wings on their arms, and marvelous early balloon aerial views, lovely early nudes, etc., and I knew immediately when André Jammes showed me a picture taken by Bayard in the early 1840s of the Paris flea market that it was for us. I *really* am working and it is all you prophesied—a chance to meet new people and a chance to see new places and study a subject that fascinates me.

To visit the house in which the first photograph ever was taken, she traveled to the little town of Chalon-sur-Saône in a car driven, she said, by a madman:

> My chauffeur drove through the traffic of the outskirts of Paris at a speed that could only result from a mind demented, he clearly thought he was in orbit and free from all earthly obstructions which were all too visible to my sane eyes. In a word, *Life* had unwittingly placed me in the hands of a frustrated racing-car driver who made me think, "If this is the end, *Life* can probably get out a reasonably good issue with the pictures I already have." We made Chalon in about three and a half hours, an enormous distance from Paris. Somehow we didn't end up in the fields with the herds of milk-white cows, curiously delicate, feminine-looking cows as elegant and French-looking as my white telephone beside me which has just rung and someone from the *Life* office told me a cable has come from my son Phil.

Even though she was thousands of miles away, I could feel the rise and fall of my mother's moods. She was up one minute, down the next. She would be deliriously happy when good news arrived or she could be almost desperate over foiled plans or slights she imagined or any continued silence from me.

My mother's next flurry of letters came from Rome. She had been joined there by my younger sister, Edith, who would share the remaining part of the journey as assistant, companion, and conspirator. Her husband was taking care of their two children back in New York.

After the excitement of England and France, my mother found Italy a letdown. "The Italians have still to this day only the most mild interest in photography," she wrote, "early or present day." But just as in England and France, not all of Dorothy's time in Italy was consumed by work. She and Edith were taken to dinner at the fanciest places by members of the Time Inc. bureau, to cocktail parties, days at the Vatican, nights at the opera, lunch at the Villa Borghese, and on a trip to the Columbia Pictures set outside Rome to see Richard Burton and Elizabeth Taylor perform scenes for their movie *The Taming of the Shrew*.

After such gaiety, gloomy visits to Germany and Austria followed, and it was a relief to get to Denmark with its "cool, bright, sparkling countryside and young, yellow-haired, happy citizens equipped with bicycles instead of legs." Then came Amsterdam and the trip's end. My mother had winnowed an enormous number of important early photographs from the great collections of Europe. They included many firsts— the first image ever, the first studio still life, the first picture of a human being, the first street scene, the first human face, the first nudes, the first war pictures, the first studies of motion. Together with the best photographs the United States had to offer, this new *Life* collection would be made up of the most definitive look at the beginnings of the photograph ever assembled. My mother looked forward to the day she would go before *Life*'s editors and make a formal presentation of all her treasures, all her knowledge. Her heart would not only have sunk, it probably would have ceased beating completely, had she known then that that day would never come, that her plans for that important presentation would never take place nor would her involvement in the development of the story. Rather, as soon as she turned over all the properly identified prints she had ordered, the editors would consider her participation in the issue to be done and from then on they would take over.

Professionally, my mother had never learned the meaning of compromise—it was either all or nothing at all. And she had certainly never accepted the hierarchy of editors, the necessity of the editorial process, the space limitations of a magazine or the editors' job to create simple, bold stories, and in doing so, to eliminate most of the images she had worked so hard to collect.

At first, after she got home, my mother never complained to me about the people she had hoped to work with. But they were good, tough, seasoned editors, writers, and researchers, and they weren't about to have their special province invaded, especially by someone so closely connected to the person ultimately in charge. They considered Dorothy a researcher, a collector, and a scholar, and they treated her like the freelance outsider she was. When I did hear of my mother's dismay, I did nothing to correct the situation. I already felt guilty of nepotism and of taking work and foreign trips away from the *Life* staff. To have it known that *my mother* was working for me might have been something that could be ignored three thousand miles away. But now that she was just beyond my office door, I squirmed and let the chips fall where they may. I wasn't even sure how to refer to her to my colleagues. And when I finally told my mother that she should put everything she knew and felt in writing and submit it with the pictures, I knew she wouldn't.

Was it a betrayal not to force her into the inner circle of the magazine and let her perform? I don't think so. My real mistake was not explaining to my mother what a difficult situation I found myself in. Maybe she understood, because she silently pulled away. But even though the grand assignment ended poorly, I think the whole experience of travel and succeeding at a hard job steeled her, enriched her, gave her vitality, and helped make it possible for her to feel she could strike out on a new life.

Most encouraging to me was that my mother seemed to have gotten some of her self-confidence back. She was determined now to make it alone.

13.

The Vanished Dream

Even while lonely and discouraged
in her later years, Dorothy strove
to keep her sense of humor.

I N FRONT OF THE CHURCH after my father's funeral I promised Kate Mali that I would take care of my mother now that she was alone. Kate's eyes told me she would hold me to my promise. They told me a lot more, too. That Dot and she were different from others, that, as she had once written to my mother, they "felt more pain, more agony of mind." And that, therefore, life from here on for Dorothy would be especially difficult and that her sharp mind might now be a curse instead of a blessing. Auntie Kate wanted me to be especially vigilant. My sisters and brother would help when they could, but it was to me that my mother would turn for life support, especially when it came to her work and making big decisions, as well as for daily conversation, encouragement, and company.

After living at 148 for a few years, charging up and down its five flights of stairs, sleeping in the same third-floor room where her father had died, and creating a distinguished Lincoln room on the floor above, my mother was persuaded by her sister to sell the house and buy a two-bedroom apartment on Sixty-sixth and Lexington Avenue, where a mammoth two-story living room could house her library and Lincoln treasures properly. We had all gotten a scare when the building next to 148 burned to the ground. With the help of a grandchild, my mother made the move and transferred the Meserve Collection to her new quarters, pushing much of it herself in a supermarket shopping cart from place to place, with a couple of bundles of oranges slung on top for disguise during the twelve-block trip.

Her strength still seemed unlimited. She coughed a great deal, she drank moderately and overmedicated herself, but she seemed to have a clear eye on what she wanted, and enough physical strength to bring it about.

When Kate heard that my mother was making the move to a new apartment, she wrote her a typically gentle letter of praise and encouragement:

Dearest D,

I am glad you are tackling the giant job that must be done. Then you can devise a new life. It will be an interesting one—unique because it will be you that design it and lead it. Not the dream of youth—you've had that. This will be the dream of age and no carbon copy because there are few originals to copy.

Mum's new life was inaugurated by a housewarming party. Her friends and family were struck by the museum atmosphere of her apartment. Two walls were filled with thousands and thousands of books—a spectacular library of rare volumes that climbed from floor to ceiling.

Magnificent, sepia-colored photographic portraits of Abraham Lincoln looked out from gilt frames. On the gigantic, ornate mantel of the fireplace the Lincoln wedding lamps held forth. The bronze head and hands of Lincoln, one of the earliest castings made from Leonard W. Volk's plaster originals done from life, were exhibited on a central table, the deep features and tones of the bronze emphasized by the glow from the mahogany table they sat upon. A bronze statue of a seated Lincoln by Charles Keck graced another antique table. Both the Volk and the Keck had been the prized possessions of her father, now they were hers.

And when guests peeked into Dorothy's bedroom they were greeted by her menagerie of early American toys and antique dolls, her penny banks and music boxes and wind-up toys, her papier mâché lion, her drum, her giraffe on rollers, her rocking horse, her nest of dolls with real hair and real jewelry and glass eyes and painted cheeks, her tiny kitchen with its copper utensils, her cloth cat with painted paws, her wooden ark with a hundred animals lined up before it two-by-two, her jewel-tipped, foot-long hat pins thrust into giant pincushions, her ironing board as big as a finger, with a miniature iron on top, her baskets of old marbles, her jumping fish, her pirate's trunk, her tiny theater, her myriad flags.

Standing amid Dorothy's guests that evening, I remember thinking that this apartment, with all its magnificence, would surely launch her new life. I imagined she would finally complete her Tad Lincoln book, would write a biography of Mathew Brady, that here she would catalogue the contents of the Meserve Collection.

My mother loved to show the collection. Whether to friends like Kate or to interested scholars, she always did it with fascinating artistry. The tour would begin in her living room, then move to the seven storerooms she rented nearby, where the Brady negatives lived along with the bulk of the 200,000 items that made up the collection. Dorothy's final stop took place in the bowels of an east-side branch of Chase Manhattan.

Once downstairs in the bank, my mother would withdraw a bristle of keys from her large pocketbook and give them to her trusted friends, the guards for the safe deposit section, and, behind bars now, they would carefully remove three long drawers from the gleaming steel wall. My mother's voice would become low, almost a whisper, as she withdrew a glass negative of Lincoln about the size of a playing card, then another, and then another. The lucky guest would be allowed to pick up each negative and look at it against the light. My mother made the whole presentation into an almost religious experience, and when the steel drawers had been replaced and we had climbed up the marble stairs and were out onto the street again, it was as if we were coming out of a cat-acomb and had just taken part in a mystical service highlighted by the nonstop chant of my mother's elegant, erudite voodoo. It was all part of her new life, I thought at the time.

But unexpected sadnesses began to close in. Two of her children's mar-riages collapsed—first Ken's, then Edith's. Initially, Dorothy was alarmed, then she grew angry at the spouses of her unhappy children; finally, she tried to help with sympathy and understanding. Then there was a succes-sion of deaths—her mother's, her aunt's, and, finally, her brother's, which darkened her world even more. Kate wrote of Leighton's death:

Almost every day is laden with memories now. I remember fear-ing, in my youth, that we wouldn't have any. The happier they have been, the more poignant are the partings.

To make matters worse, Dorothy was besieged by repeated bouts of pneumonia. Throughout these travails, Kate kept an eye on her friend, recognizing her pain. Dorothy had once long ago told her, "If I only had the right person to share things with I could bear—and also dare—anything." She had always lived in a world of unfinished things where there was forever something new to learn, something fresh to write. Now, dreading life instead of cherishing it, she was turning to pills and alcohol to see her through.

Kate tried to bring my mother's spirits up by a flow of letters. In one, Kate suggested again that they rethink an old idea of theirs—to make a book out of their lifelong correspondence:

Dearest my Dorothy,

Two days ago I opened a box marked, "D. M. Kunhardt's Letters. Return to her," and thought I'd glance over them. But immediately I found myself reading every word, and I sit up late at night devouring them, and am hardly able to wait finishing one stack to start another.

It has taken me into the world of our lifelong (we were eleven when we first met at Brearley) companionship of mind and spirit that is truly extraordinary. You used to say that it was, but I think I never fully realized it until I started rereading your letters, beautifully handwritten—and with such wit and style and intensity of perception and feeling and such genius. Yes, you have it. Don't deny it.

Only get well again and use it again. And come and visit me for weeks of perfumed air, eggnogs, and total neglect. I love you.

Katie

At twenty-four, from Paris, DM had written Kate about her old-maid traveling companion, Cousin Nell:

Sip every minute of golden youth while you have it, Kate. Age is a cold, pitiful thing, if it isn't a warm and glorious one, and there's always just the chance that things will slip up and it will be the former.

Kate realized how "warm and glorious" Dot's life had been but things had slipped up all right and now her very existence was becoming "cold and pitiful." A few days later, Kate wrote again:

Dearest D,

Looking back it seems to me the letter I wrote you several days ago was sort of a callous one.

Although written in all love and tenderness it did say in effect "Hop up and be your wonderful old self because that self gives more delight to your friends than any other self can give"—and never mentioned the sorrows that make it so hard for you to get well.

Those sorrows are real and terrible, the worst being the oldest, Phil's death and your never-ending need for him. And now to this has been added Ken's and Edith's unhappiness. This letter is only to say I understand. Even though I am in a calm pool of happiness myself at this moment I do know through my great love for you what wretched churning waters you are in.

Kate tried to extend her "calm pool of happiness" in Winsted, Connecticut, to Dorothy whenever she could, and for a while it helped. In 1971, from her New York apartment, my mother wrote:

My heart and mind are in Winsted, where live my beloved Katie and Harry on the brow of that gentle slope edged with your lovely woods. I wish I could have walked with Harry, but my lungs seem to no longer function as a working bellows. Can you believe that I shall be seventy in September? Don't say yes. You are so young. Kate, I've been thinking of you so much since I've been home. I still find you the dearest, most electric, most wonderful to look at, most continually satisfying, rewarding, everything-nice person, reaching back almost sixty of my seventy years. This is a love letter.

But Kate could not solve everything. Coupled with divorce, alcoholism had begun to wreak havoc in our family. It was in our genes we would later discover, handed down from both sides of the family. My sister, Edith, suffered most, but she finally stopped drinking thirty years ago, and went on to build a full life for herself as an editor, a photographer, and a very successful children's book author in her own right. Ken kept on drinking heavily during the '70s. All this pained our mother almost as much as the divorces. She tried to help, as I did, but we were both drinkers, too, and could hardly cast the first stone.

THE YEAR 1972 was a turning point for me. Having worked at Time Inc. more than the twenty years that made me eligible for a sabbatical, I was now entitled to either a whole year off with half pay or a half-year with full pay. Out of necessity I chose the latter, and Katharine and I began planning a three-month stay in Spain and France with four of our children, the oldest two boys to be left behind in college. We would settle into houses for long stretches of time to really soak in the culture and I would have time to write as well. We would leave in August and return to the United States before Christmas. Then, late at night in early summer, my mother fell and broke her hip. Drinking and pills, as well as infirmity, had caused the fall. She, however, insisted nothing had happened, and kept walking on her broken hip and drinking, too, until Edith got her to New York Hospital by ambulance the next day. I was in Maine and heard about her subsequent hip replacement operation long distance.

In New York Hospital Dorothy was anything but an ideal patient. She was increasingly angered by the fact that she was losing control over her life. She argued with the doctors and attendants who knew that if they couldn't make her exercise and care for her new hip, she probably would never walk again. She screamed with pain every time she was forced to move. She threw a glass of milk at one of the nurses and cursed them all. The change in her character was as dramatic as Dr. Jekyll turning into Mr. Hyde and must have been triggered by a mixture of extreme pain and the absence of her usual drugs. The hospital was glad to see her go. Next, her sister, Helen, took her to her home in Southampton, Long Island, but my mother needed professional care so she was placed in a nursing home—rehabilitation center nearby.

"My dearest and most unpredictable of friends," Kate wrote:

> Why did you have to go and do anything so ghastly as to break your hip! I'm just hating to think of how you are suffering and just hoping and wishing to whatever gods there be, that you will soon be out of pain. Remember, dearest D, how precious you are to how many people—among them your loving Kate.

Before leaving on my European trip, my sister Nancy and I drove out to Long Island to pay our mother a visit. Mum was moved that we had come, disturbed that I would be away on another continent for so long, and, without saying it, she was distressed at being in unfamiliar surroundings. Although her sister visited her every day, my mother didn't like her present circumstances at all. She longed to go home. Wheelchair or no, she felt confined. The place felt more like a nursing home than a rehabilitation center, and she had always dreaded nursing homes. Once, I remember, while driving her out of New York City to Chappaqua for a weekend in the country, I had taken her on the Taconic Parkway instead of the Saw Mill River Parkway which she was more accustomed to. Struck by the unfamiliarity of the countryside, she asked me where we were going and, without thinking, I had fliply tossed off, "To a nursing home." She grasped my arm and begged me to tell her it wasn't so. I quickly told her it was just a joke, but she would not believe me until she was at our house and had her bags taken from the car. "Promise me you'll never put me in one of those," she said, unable to bring herself to say the words "nursing home." "You must promise me. It is the one thing I'm truly terrified of." So I promised.

Before leaving her that day in Southampton, Nancy and I assured her again that we would never abandon her in a nursing home, that, if it were ever necessary, we would take her into our own homes and let her live out her life among family. It was agreed that as soon as she could travel, she would go straight to Nancy's in Massachusetts. I left for Europe with a relatively peaceful conscience, grateful to Nan for taking on Mum's care while we were away.

After three months, my European trip was cut short by an urgent request from the powers at Time-Life to come back immediately. So we headed home, and one morning in early December, the reason behind this mysterious recall finally became clear. All of *Life*'s staff were summoned to the company auditorium. There, to a hushed, packed house, the announcement was made—*Life* was closing down. The older members of the staff, especially, were stunned. Everybody knew that advertising revenue was way down and the magazine had been losing money for the last few years. Still, it seemed impossible. *Life* was a national institution and it had been our life; many of us had never even had another job. We were tightly wedded to what we did and to each other, and we were proud of our product. We wandered out of the auditorium that day silent, confused, dumbfounded, many in tears.

Time Inc. helped find new jobs for the orphaned *Life* staff—new positions either on their other publications or in the outside world. I would stay with the company in a division called "magazine development." My salary was cut, and my spirits flagged. Then, late in that winter of 1973, I proposed a special *Life* issue on the twenty-fifth anniversary of the creation of the modern republic of Israel, which was to be celebrated in May. The go-ahead came almost immediately and I flew to Israel to set up the issue, assign writers, and scout picture stories. My little staff and I then proceeded at breakneck speed and the issue went to press in April. It turned out to be a huge success. We had taken the first step in bringing our magazine back to life.

In June I was asked to develop a magazine to be called *People*, a full-fledged expansion of what was then a single "people" page in the weekly *Time* magazine. In less than a week my staff of a few ex-*Life*-ers and I, using borrowed *Time* and *Sports Illustrated* writers and the worldwide *Time* bureau system, put together a first issue. The management of the company loved it. So for the next month we put out four more in-house issues and then a printed test issue which was sold at newsstands and supermarkets in a number of key cities. The test was a success; the new magazine was to become a reality. At first, I was expected to be its editor. But having survived a heart attack years earlier, I didn't want to risk my health by working on a new Time Inc. weekly with late nights and constant pressure.

Writing to me from Massachusetts where she had been recuperating for months at Nancy's, my mother did not agree with the decision I was making.

"I wish," she wrote:

I had said to you on the telephone that day to think more carefully before you turn down *People*. It sounds much too good an idea to pass up lightly. Is it too late for you to creep back on your knees and beg for it, saying you've had a change of heart?

This was an uncertain point in my life—I had to set a new course. I knew what I wanted and I also knew I had to bide my time for it. Nonetheless, I wrote my mother for more advice, wanting her to feel part of the decision.

On June 28, 1973, she answered my request:

Dearest Phil,

You are right. I do want the best possible life for you and I wish the most perfect possible health as well as the greatest happiness, as well as the most congenial and exciting occupation of your days. You touched indeed the most hurting subject with me when you said you wanted to live. I literally lose my breath, my heart pounds, and tears come to my eyes, as at this moment. If I were to lose you, a very large part of myself would die. So I do not think lightly of your future.

The first big question is your health. Is it so bad that you are forced to accept something that would be a bore for the rest of your years? Or are you fully recovered from your heart attack, or could be recovered if you used some sense, and if in fact you are only mortally overtired by the disaster of *Life*'s ending, overpowered with exhaustion, and a sort of mild despair at all that has happened, but have the power of renewing yourself body and soul, then maybe you ought to go directly to the one person you must ultimately go to—yourself.

What do you long to do?

Can you place yourself in a position to do such a thing?

Have you or can you summon the physical strength to do that?

You underestimate me and almost abase me when you say I want you to be successful and stop short at that. Truthfully, your success has been a thing of which I have been very proud, but it is very secondary to my seeing on your face as I search it, an expression of completion—a lively sense of your using your skills, all your ability, fully. I know the opposite demeanor and I dread it for you.

My mother went on to tell me of the many things she thought I could do successfully. At the end of her long list was what she really thought:

Maybe you should hang around for a little while doing odd jobs for Time Inc. until the old *Life* comes back into existence by nationwide request. I really can't conceive of the U.S. being permanently without that super-marvelous magazine. It's part of the nation and my bereavement is renewed every week.

Of course, the last suggestion is the one I took, the one I'd already taken. I didn't want to risk another heart attack and there was someone who could do the *People* job better than I could, anyway—my friend Dick Stolley who, like me, had been an assistant managing editor of the weekly *Life* and who had been taken into Time Inc.'s magazine development division upon its demise. I, in turn, would hang my hopes on a revival of *Life* in a monthly format sometime in the future while Stolley would begin to make *People* the most successful magazine in history. My mother's impassioned letter proved to me that she was sharper than I'd been giving her credit for. If she could advise me to stand back and look at myself, it showed me she could do the same for herself.

In another letter, she led me to believe she had done just that:

I know I am the oldest member of our whole family and I want you to look up to me, if possible, with pride as well as affection and I shall do my best with my remaining years. I need to talk to you about those years—receive your advice—give you my thoughts on what I hope to accomplish in that short time. This is of utmost importance to me and I know, too, how much you care.

I have very strong feelings on how I want to live until my death, which may not be far away. I do not want to live an unhappy life, chosen for me by others. It is *my* life, made up of bits and parts of all my dear family and my large group of friends that are quite wonderful to be able to claim.

I want to be worthy of them all. I intend to be.

She tried. Having mended herself with Nancy, she now moved back to her apartment on Lexington Avenue and Sixty-sixth Street and began to live an independent life once more.

BY THE END OF 1975, I had edited six special issues of *Life* which were sold on newsstands instead of through subscriptions; we printed about a million copies of each issue and they were virtual sell-outs, which told me the old magazine was still flickering. At the beginning of 1976, I was named head of the Time Inc. Magazine Development Group, but since no magazine idea needed developing just then, I asked for a leave of absence in order to write another book with my mother. It would be on the photographer Mathew Brady, whose great Civil War–era negatives were owned by the Library of Congress, the National Archives, and the Meserve Collection. We had more than five thousand of the original negatives, mostly portraits, and many more copy negatives. They had never been published as a group before. Time-Life Books was to be the publisher, my mother and I the authors.

At the very beginning of the project I asked Mum to start with some background for the book. Propped up in bed with a pad on her knee she began with the man who would become Brady's favorite photographic subject. Lincoln and his family were just leaving Springfield and heading for Washington four months after the election. She wrote:

> The Lincoln family was not entirely filled with joy over the results of the election. They were a close, devoted family who dreaded leaving the town of Springfield with all its western charms—the children had swarms of friends with whom they played daily and they had been told they could not take their dog, Fido, to Washington, but must choose a caretaker for him who would be kind, until their return. No one dreamed that this happy life was over, that Willie would die of pneumonia in his new home, that their father would be shot by an assassin, that Mrs. Lincoln and Tad would wander, lonely, from country to country, and that even Fido would lose his life, attacked by the knife of a drunken man on whose knee he had put his muddy paw. Mr. Lincoln had told one of his closest friends that he did not really want to leave Springfield: "My children were coming up and were interesting to me. I would be better off here than going east to play president."

The plan was to write the Brady book in much the same way we had taken on *Twenty Days*—my mother would provide the research and I would spin it into a book, the words coiling through hundreds of captioned pictures. But after finishing that short description on February 6,

1976, my mother never wrote another word about Lincoln or Brady or anyone else who existed in her vast treasure chest of knowledge. She claimed she could not remember anymore. At first I was annoyed; she certainly wasn't senile. But slowly I began to see that she wasn't well enough to do the work. Way back in her youth she had prophesied this moment. "There is something in me that burns and hurts," she had written Kate. "I surmise when that burning thing goes out, one is old and life is over." Life wasn't quite over, but that "burning thing" in my mother had definitely flickered out.

So I continued the book on my own. For a time, I showed what I was writing to my mother but soon I gave that up—she never even read my chapters, except for my long introductory chapter on her father and the Meserve Collection, which she read very slowly. She nodded politely at the end. Fortunately, I knew a good deal about Brady and Civil War–era photography myself; and our collection offered many insights into Brady's mind, his techniques, and his work habits. I also had the help of my mother's friend Josephine Cobb, the Civil War photography expert who had retired from the National Archives and was living in Maine. Compared to how *Twenty Days* was written, the Brady book went more quickly and easily. But the text had a different sensibility. It lacked my mother's unique brand of scholarship and flare.

Even so, retreating as she had, my mother believed she was by my side in everything I took on and always would be.

Dearest Philip,

On your forty-ninth birthday I want to say again how deeply proud of you I am. I want you to be proud of me however many failures I have made. You wrote me a year ago that "great things are going to happen and I want you to be by my side." I carry that letter with me.

As time passed, I tried to encourage my mother to take better care of herself, tried to convince her that she was needed by all of us. My younger sister, Edith, tried to send her the same message, as did Nancy and Ken, either by phone, letter, or visit. I wonder, though, whether it was a defensive measure on my part to keep her quiet and at arm's length or a genuine show of love that I wrote my mother all the little, intense, overstated notes of encouragement I did:

Mum, you are an absolute wonder. Keep strong. Get sleep.

Or:

Dear Mum,
How immensely proud I am of you. You are courageous and marvelous.

Or:

Dear Mum, I admire you greatly for what you have done in the past two weeks. You look ten years younger, your marvelous mind has returned, and some of your strength.

Or:

Dear Mum,
To wish you happy birthday today may seem only a family ritual to you, because of the strange, painful, uprooted year you have just finished, always with the loneliness of being without Dad. But what those simple two words mean to me today is that I

am happy because it is the day of your birth, grateful that you are here and blessed to have you as my mother.

By the end of 1978, after publishing our tenth *Life* special, the company was ready to bring *Life* back on a regular basis, as a monthly rather than a weekly, and I was named its managing editor. It was exactly what I had been hoping would happen for nearly six years. But just as the magazine was resurrected, my mother's health began to deteriorate rapidly. She started using more and more oxygen to breathe, her coughing fits increased, and her codeine consumption went unchecked. Forgoing the oxygen, sometimes doubling her dose of pills, her face almost turned black at times and her speech blurred. We accused her of taking overdoses of codeine. She first tried to make light of it, as if she were writing for children. "My hand," she explained, "just went over there and picked the pills up and put them in my mouth. I watched my hand do it." My mother was now on a constant downward spiral. Her increasing age was combined with a second hip operation, pneumonia, emphysema, dizzy spells, massive nosebleeds, memory loss, ulcers, bad eating habits, and too many pills. Periodic binges involved what she called her "moo-juice," a mixture of bourbon and milk.

On top of all this, she was always keenly aware of her mortality. "Let's make a code between you and me," I remember her saying, "in case I ever become completely paralyzed. There's usually something you can move—a toe, maybe, or an eye can be rolled. So stand very close and say very loud, 'Can you hear me, Mum?' and then look everywhere for any little movement. I'll communicate with you in some way. And remember, one wiggle of something means 'yes' and two means 'no,' so if you find the thing that I can move, we can actually talk." That's the way we would talk and laugh together.

My sister Nancy was driven crazy by all of this. Once, she had tried to reach Mum in her apartment by phone from Massachusetts. Over and over she had dialed the number. When Nancy couldn't reach me or Edith, either, she sped to the airport and got on a Boston-LaGuardia shuttle and taxied to Manhattan knowing by intuition that something was wrong. She arrived at Mum's apartment at three o'clock in the afternoon to find Mum unconscious on the floor with blood in her hair and caked on her face, blood on her nightgown, on the rug and floor and books and toys. Nancy told me, "I thought she was almost dead and I said, 'Mum, what have you done to yourself?' And she just stared at me and finally said, 'I don't know what you're talking about—done to myself? Done to myself?'" Nancy said, "I'm here, Mum, don't worry." And Mum said to her, "Go away."

That night in Chappaqua, I recorded in my diary the conversation Nancy had with Mum when she had begun to regain her senses:

"Why do you try to kill your beautiful self? Why?" Nancy moaned at Mum. "You are so lovely and valuable to us all and so wonderful and beautiful! How could you feel so badly about yourself that you drank so much or popped so many pills that you fell down again and cut your head and almost bled to death?"

Had my mother wanted to put herself to sleep forever? Was she angry that Nancy had saved her? Or was this episode a dramatized plea for us to take care of her, proof that she couldn't do it herself anymore? Or should we have believed her when she insisted it was an accident and that she wanted to go back to her apartment, wanted her independence, demanded it, in fact? Despite her weakened state, she was still formidable and we gave her a dozen second chances. But after that I was never sure what I would find when I unlocked the three locks in the front door to her apartment. "It's me," I'd call out as I entered the cavernous living room. Frequently there was no answer and I'd find her asleep in bed. I'd end up shaking her to rouse her from some pill and moo-juice slumber.

Once I left a long, thin note, pinned to her pillow:

Mum
I shook you
I beat you
And yelled
You didn't stir
You were either dead
But still breathing
Or so asleep
That you obviously
Didn't want to wake up.

When Edith and I hired kindly women to live with our mother, she screamed, "Witches! Witches! That's what you want to trap me with. A filthy witch who wants to kill me. I should die!"

As things got worse and worse, everybody advised us that a nursing home was the only answer. But recently, Katharine's father had been put into a very good one in New York City and after a sad and disoriented month there, he had been found abandoned in a hallway in the middle of the night, strapped into his wheelchair. We had gotten him out of there fast and he was able to die with quiet dignity in his own apartment several months later. No, a nursing home wasn't the answer. Besides, I had promised my mother.

But what was the answer? We waited to figure that out. And then one night my mother had another fall and Edith took her to the emergency room of New York's St. Clare's Hospital. When I found her the next day in the intensive care unit, she raised her hand to my cheek and tried to say good-bye. The attending doctor was not hopeful. When Nancy arrived she grabbed the doctor who was in charge and pleaded with him to save her mother's life. At first, the doctor just looked at Nancy as if she were crazy not to allow nature to simply take its course. Finally, though, her entreaties got through to him and he went into action. Two days later Mum opened her eyes again.

After that crisis it was agreed among us that Nancy would take our mother half the time in Massachusetts and Katharine and I would harbor her the other half. She could never go back to live alone in her apartment again. On the day of my fiftieth birthday, a blustery day in February, my mother was brought by ambulance to the hospital near us in Mount Kisco. That night, with the people I liked best in the world gathered to celebrate, I drank to the health of my most important missing guest, all the time knowing that toasts and good wishes and praise and even straight talk would not work for my mother anymore.

My mother was pleased with the treatment she received in Northern Westchester Hospital. "The doctors here treat me with dignity," she said. "I don't know why. They don't even know me. But they are interested— Dr. Clark came out of the operating room to see me. He spent an hour talking to me about the collection between operations."

We talked of future projects. Encouraged once again, she said, "I want to live. You cannot know how much. I want to stay alive. I want to help you and be part of what you do with the collection and your writing."

My mother always talked as if she would be getting back to her apartment, but her children knew better. Nancy and I had finally made the move we had promised to make and we should have made years earlier. After three months with us, my mother lived with Nancy and her family in Massachusetts for the next six months. She had her own room on the ground floor with a lot of her own furniture and we sent up her prized old toy collection so she could be surrounded by her beloved antique dolls and carriages and animals. Nurses were employed both for day and for night. When my mother's meager income couldn't pay for this, her children helped, and so did her most devoted friends, led by Kate.

On October 6, 1978, Mum returned to Chappaqua accompanied by an eight-page letter of instruction from Nancy about what Mum's pills were, how much oxygen she used, what she liked best to eat, and how and where she slept best. "I hope I don't imply," Nan's letter ended:

> that you won't take good care of Mum. I know you will. I am just so very much involved and care so much and you must forgive me. Keep her warm, lend her a TV, love her, and thank you! She is a wonderful person and a steadfastly loving mother.

My mother's return to our house coincided with the publication of the first issue of the monthly *Life*. To publicize that *Life* was back meant parties and presentations in New York, Chicago, Detroit, Los Angeles, San Francisco, Paris, and London. And when I returned from these travels, the pressure to put out new and spectacular issues was intense. Most of the care of my mother fell upon my wife's willing shoulders. She managed to balance raising our youngest two children with the care of my mother and helping me stay sane. My mother's bedroom was a large room on the ground floor at the back of our old stucco house which had originally been a barn. The room had housed a pool table but we had taken that down and installed a big, queen-size bed along with a telephone and a television. The room was cut off from the rest of the house. We thought about using the children's intercom system to hear her if she called, but when my mother objected to our "illegal, spy tactics," we gave her an antique metal cowbell instead. To summon one of us she shook the large cowbell and someone came running. Sometimes guests wondered what that clanking was and were taken aback when told it was my old mother in the back room trying to be heard.

The days of moo-juice were over. Mum would stay in her room most of the time. Katharine would check in on her and visit and sometimes coax her to put on her fur coat and sit on the porch in the sun. Our teenage daughter and nine-year-old son would dart in and out of her room. And by the time I got home at the end of the day we would gather for dinner. Gradually, she stayed in her room more and more, for she was on oxygen almost full-time now, and the huge metal tanks were too heavy to move.

Our first round of nurses, who were hired for twelve-hour shifts, seemed to work. But Mum hated them. Once, she complained that she had been forced into an unbearably hot, early morning bath. We assured her it was in her imagination but when her complaints persisted, I secretly slept in a room close to hers to keep watch. After a few nights I was awakened at 4:00 a.m. by running water, and when I got to the bathroom there was my mother being lowered into practically scalding water by a sadistic nurse who almost dropped her at the sight of me. Needless to say, the nurse was fired on the spot.

After that, we did our best to cope without professional help. Some nights turned horrific. If it wasn't for Katharine, I doubt that I would have held up. She and I became conspirators, doing what had to be done, often with muffled laughter between us. I remember one winter night after my mother had become incontinent, we put clean sheets on her bed and ran the soiled ones out into the snow, pitching them onto a snow bank and laughing hysterically together at the sudden turns in life and the accompanying smells.

Mum could still read and watch television but her mind wandered and she found herself getting more satisfaction fingering her jewelry or hiding it and almost immediately forgetting the hiding place. She kept the shades drawn, feeling more comfortable in the dark, closed off from the cheerful outdoor colors. Sarah, our thirteen-year-old, always tried to help when she got home from school. In an English assignment "about a family member" she wrote:

My grandmother lay on her side with her legs up close to her chest, her body leaning over the side of the bed. There was hardly any room for her because the bed was covered with books and papers and clothes and hundreds of other things. The air in the room felt thick and warm. Long oxygen tubes stretched out of her sore, red nostrils. Her hair was matted down from sleeping on it. She was always alone, in the back part of the house, when I got home from school. The door was cracked open a few inches and I could see her lying, still and quiet. I hesitated to peer inside, but I made myself do it. I opened the door and her eyes instantly lit up.

"Hello, my dear Sarah," she would say, with that little smirk on the side of her lips.

Sometimes that smile turned into a scary, crazy look. With a deadly, deep stare she gazed into my eyes, but she did not know who I was. She believed I was her daughter, Nancy, and that she was young again. She screeched at me.

"Catch that little man, hurry, catch him, he's running under the bureau."

She waved her hands high in the air and pointed to a spot in the corner of the room. I got down on my hands and knees and looked for the little man, but I told her he was nowhere to be seen.

In my memories, Mum was more lucid. Each month I brought her a new copy of *Life* which had just come out and she lost herself in its pages. Because I had been the editor of each issue, she felt she had taken part in the editing, too, and, actually, in a way she had. She also treasured the letters from Kate, which she kept in her huge, bottomless pocketbook. One of them began:

> A love letter from you is like no other epistle on earth and I cherish mine and read it over every day. Pretty soon I'll know it by heart but I'll keep on reading it because the handwriting is so beautiful.

As my mother's life ebbed, I wondered when she had last thought of God. In Paris, when Dorothy was twenty-three, she had described her childhood conception of the Almighty in the opening verses of her poem "The Dreaming Game":

> That special night we lay quite still, each in a wooden bed;
> I almost slept, when Nicolette sat up and softly said
> "What do you think of God as like, can you make him seem
> true?"
> I had to tell her, though it seemed a funny thing to do.

> I told her yes, God seemed to me a great head in the sky
> Just peeping over a stone wall, watching the birds go by—
> Watching the sparrows carefully to see they didn't fall—
> Gazing down at the world below, at children most of all.

> God watches all the ships that sail upon the restless sea—
> He knows just how much fruit will come on every apple tree—
> He guards the busy cities but he loves the country best.
> Any little spot of country, north south east and west.

He motions to the sun to shine on all the little farms
(I don't know how he manages, I've never seen his arms.)
I've only seen his head, and even that was a surprise,
Though sometimes when I'm dreaming, I can look into his eyes.

In the many decades since, Dorothy had searched for God's eyes over and over but she had not found them. Instead, her spiritual philosophy had become more and more rooted in the world and its people. When Kate's father died and Dorothy attended his funeral, she found the service dramatic and moving but not believable, and afterward she wrote Kate her deepest feeling, "Nothing else seems to matter in this world but love." That's what, after all, she had been trying to express in the last verse of "The Dreaming Game"—that dreams vanish, but never completely, if someone you love knows your dreams:

With snow, my lovely Nicolette, is ended this my dream
For snow, like many things, is not what it would seem:
It's only water in the end—my dream has vanished too—
But it will never leave me quite; for it has gone to you.

Even though my mother's dream had turned into a nightmare, she was leaving behind plenty of evidence of what it had been in its glory days. Almost everything she had ever written rang out with her message. That was her dreaming game with the world.

IN THE LATE SPRING of 1979, Katharine and I drove my mother halfway to Massachusetts where Nancy met us at a prearranged spot. The transfer of Mum was made from one station wagon to another, and we said good-bye.

I saw her twice more, once on her seventy-eighth birthday on September 29, when her four children assembled. Mum managed to get into her wheelchair and accept our gift of a color television. Then, in late October she fainted in her bedroom, was taken to the Beverly Hospital, running a high fever and suffering from heart fibrillations. A week later, she returned to Nancy's but no one, including the doctors, expected her to live long. I drove up to Massachusetts—this time to really say good-bye. My diary entry for November 11 reminds me now of the spirit that was left in her:

> It is hard for this solemn, quiet, gaunt, remnant of my mother to hear, to see, to speak. "Do you know who I am?" I ask her. This jolts her into trying to focus upon me, standing by her bedside. She smiles. "I certainly do," she says in her little voice. "And I think of you all the time and love you so much."

It was 8:45 on a Sunday morning, December 23, at the end of the final month of the decade and something must have told Mum not to start a new one because she just shut her eyes and her heart made its final beat. The nurse noted, "Changed position of patient, pulse very weak," but then only a few minutes later she wrote down, "No vital signs apparent. Doctor called." It was peaceful at the end. Nancy and her husband were away on a trip so it was up to the two nurses to make calls and to arrange for a death certificate and the undertaker.

That Sunday morning I was in bed at home in Chappaqua, reading the *New York Times* and drinking coffee with Katharine. The day before, I had called Mum twice but both times she was asleep and I had spoken to the nurses, instead. On Saturday night Katharine, the children, and I had all gone across our street to a party and we had danced past midnight. So life hadn't really started up again on Sunday in our house until the phone rang at 8:55 a.m. and the nurse told me, "Phil, your mother is gone." Before leaving for Massachusetts later in the day, I wrote in my diary:

> Well, it's over. All those long years and tight love suddenly over. With Nancy away and me sitting in bed and Mum dead with the medical examiner on the way. At 8:45 she just stopped existing. No pain. No horror.

After making a dozen calls and writing my mother's obituary, Katharine and I left at two o'clock in the afternoon for the drive to Nancy's house. The four-hour drive turned into an eight-hour one when our car broke down in Connecticut and Katharine and I abandoned it, hitched a ride to the Avis car rental place in New Haven, and finally arrived at Nancy's house in Beverly at 10:00 p.m. After eating Christmas turkey, which Nancy's youngest daughter had cooked for us, I went into my mother's empty room. There, on the bedside table I found some letters from Kate:

> Dearest D,
>   New York seems peculiar without you and I miss you awfully. Now if some book reviewer got hold of that statement it would be made to seem Lesbian. But we need hardly protest—it's not.

It wasn't the first time that one of them had observed how their declarations of love could be misunderstood.

"Stay with me," another of Kate's letters ended. She meant: "Do not die."

Just before leaving on a trip to Europe with her husband, Kate had driven up to Beverly for what would be their final visit together. Kate had sat by the bed and held my mother's hand and for an hour or so she did most of the talking. A few months later Kate's final letter arrived:

Dearest, my beloved Dorothy,

We are just back from Europe and, as always when I travel, I thought of you.

Not that any day ever goes by without my thinking of you, but travel intensifies and doubles the frequency of my recollections—of our first motor trip (and why our families ever allowed two such imbeciles to set off together I cannot understand). And, of course, "Around the World in the path of springtime." The amber from Ceylon, one of the first strings you ever bought and which you subsequently gave to me—and the jade and seed pearls which you got in Peking for my birthday—are constant reminders.

Edith gave me the photograph of you and Philip—so redolent of tenderness that I have to be careful about looking at it—or I'd never get anything done.

Take care my dearest. Remember how much I love you.

Katie

The next day my wife and I went to the undertaker with a dress we had picked out for Mum. She hated the idea of cremation, of flames consuming her, mostly, I think, because she wanted to lie beside her husband in the Kunhardt graveyard plot on Staten Island, lowered into the ground precisely as he had been, with a matching stone above.

The funeral was held on December 27 in New York City, in the same church where my parents had been married. Nancy, Ken, and many of her eighteen grandchildren all assembled the night before at our house in Chappaqua. That morning I got up very early—between 2:00 and 3:00—to think over the day ahead. We had decided that one grandchild from each of the four families would take part in the service, either doing a Bible reading or saying something from their hearts. Philip, our eldest, who would soon be ordained an Episcopal minister, had written a homily which he would give. The minister would make some remarks and read a prayer which I had yet to write.

Still, the approaching day wasn't quite right, I thought to myself as I moved around the dark house. There wasn't that swell of community feeling that had existed at my father's death. There wasn't that intense grief that ran through every last person in the Morristown church sixteen years earlier and which had seemed to cloak the very town. Yes, he had died before his time and his was the simple life of goodness, easy to mourn. My mother had run her time and she had grown old and difficult, could no longer bewitch a roomful with her odd ideas and her jabs of humor, could no longer make words and pictures sing on paper. For fifty years she had held her family together through sacrifice, hard work, imagination, humor, and love. She took on so many roles but at the end she was acutely aware she would play none of them any longer and that tormented her. Now many of her contemporaries were dead and few knew Dorothy as she had been. In the dark, then, it became even more clear to me that the time you die in life makes all the difference as to how you will be remembered. It's too bad. You should be able to call up your best face to die with, the years you were most vital, most alive, most filled with beauty and high moment, most in love with doing and the future. So that was my job; the hope of my prayer was to recall the Dorothy Kunhardt not yet fallen.

I made my way to the living room bookcase and in the dark I slipped behind the Christmas tree to the shelves where we keep all the children's books she wrote in the 1930s and '40s. I could not see them but I felt their different shapes and from their tattered, finger-softened feel could name each one. Is that where she is, I asked myself? Is that where she will remain long after this service today? Is that what made her life worthwhile, worth living, worth remembering? These simple drawings? These nonsense books for children? These toylike pages for the very little?

All the Christmases gone past, all the presents Mum had snuck down from their attic hiding places in the middle of the night and piled beneath how many trees came back to me as I smelled the evergreen and candy cane and ash from the fire the previous night. Morning light had just started to dawn through the windowpanes, turning them blue and black. I found a piece of paper and sat down at my desk, which had been my father's business desk for years.

In the past, Mum would have written the prayer. She would have known how to make the Episcopal service warmer, more personal, known how to make it come alive with the person it honored. Now she was gone and the job was mine. The minister would read it at the service so that the people on their knees would hear and say, "Yes, that was she."

I wrote quickly, without stopping. It was not merely for me that I wrote. I transformed myself into each of her children and into her sister, Helen, and her best friend, Kate, and into her friends and family everywhere, until the old man with the red beard and red slippers who kept on eating his Junket was part of me, too. And so was the spotted pig seeing how many minutes it takes for a cold bath and the daddy longlegs holding up its foot to be warmed by the sun. I was writing, too, for the teeniest weeniest teeny weeny little dog in all the world. And for a very thin old lady named Mrs. Ticklefeather and for Brave Mr. Buckingham who was made out of Nugg. I was writing for a soft white bunny and a paper telephone and a hundred tiny animals. I was writing for all her funny, nonsense characters and the special worlds she had created for children. And I was writing for me, too, of course, for the little boy on the tricycle who made the right guess and got to lick the bowl.

"Oh, Lord, remember your servant, Dorothy," the prayer began, "who enchanted the lives of her husband, her four children, her eighteen grandchildren, and her many friends with her clever, fanciful mind, her talent for drama, her insatiable curiosity, her sharp, eccentric wit, her extraordinary scholarship, and her fierce, infectious capacity for love." It went on for another eighteen lines, and closed with "for her triumphs, Oh, Lord, and for all the intense feelings of love she has left with us, and for her well-chosen words, her uncommon thoughts and for her unique humor, we especially thank you today. Amen."

My mother's body had been brought down from Massachusetts to New York City for the service but nobody had told the new undertaker that the coffin was to be closed. When we arrived at the crowded church, my mother was on view in a small enclosed chapel alcove of the church. Young grandchildren played games, opening the door to that alcove and claiming they were seeing inside something from *Planet of the Apes*. One teenager locked his brother in that tiny room. To make amends, I slipped a marble egg into her willow coffin—a gift from Nancy—along with a quickly scrawled note of love from me.

Our son Philip gave his homily from the pulpit. When our eyes met I could not keep from crying: "All of us are bound in some way. God knows Grandmummy was. Bound by the memory of her husband's too-early death, bound later by growing failure of body and mind, including loss of the ability to see well enough to read. And yet just days ago she could sit on her bed and giggle with her daughter."

Auntie Kate was there and thanked us for the prayer and the homily. "I like knowing," she said, "that some of DM's gifts are sprinkled among you."

That afternoon we buried our mother next to our father. Nancy's third child, who was named after her grandmother, read from *Junket Is Nice* as the coffin was lowered into the ground, and then we each threw a yellow rose on top of the coffin. It seemed fitting to be saying good-bye with Dad's favorite flower.

As the casket was being lowered, one of the graveyard men holding the rope that controlled the head of the box lost his grip for a moment so that his burden was on a slant, and I thought I heard Mum sliding to the front. Should I call a stop and have the thing hauled up again and opened and the contents straightened out? Or would she simply rest for posterity curled up like a pretzel the way she used to get comfortable before she went to sleep every night? It was never easy to say good-bye to her.

IT IS FITTING that as I write these words to finish this book I am sitting in the same room where my mother lived in her final year. It is a quarter of a century later and the room is now a library-workroom instead of a bedroom as it was then, but here a fight for life still goes on. The oxygen bottles that I am using are much smaller than her tanks; I can carry one around like a babe-in-arms, but they send forth the same life-preserving gas. It has been a year and a half since I wrote the introduction to this book and first mentioned the lung disease I have, which is called pulmonary fibrosis. Little more is known today about the disease except that the experimental interferon shots Katharine gives me three times a week are keeping people like me alive longer than those who don't take the shots. No one knows quite why, for the interferon does not halt or cure the scarring process in the lungs that eventually brings on death. In looking at the monthly X-rays, I'm sure the working sections of my lungs are getting smaller and smaller but my doctor says no, they're staying the same, about 40 percent efficient. Sometimes hope leads me to believe that I don't have this disease at all—that I have been misdiagnosed. My doctor shakes his head and asks, "Have you finished the book?" I say yes, except for a few pages, and he smiles.

It has been good for me to have been on this long journey at this time. It has made me worry a lot more about my book than about my health. But it has also brought me close again to my mother. Studying her as I have done, reading her most intimate thoughts, realizing her triumphs and agonies both little and big, I have drawn closer to her than when I was just a son. I probably loved her more back then, when love was often automatic, when I wasn't stepping back and trying to look at the total person.

The journey has not only led me through voluminous stacks of letters and manuscripts and diaries and books, but it has inspired me to get new, firsthand information as well. I revisited the house on the hill which was bought years ago from the Jenks estate and renovated. Although it seemed bigger and more comfortable today, I still recognized a thousand signposts of my childhood. I looked for Greytop in Chester but it had burned down. I visited Hardtcourt in North Andover, Massachusetts, wandered through the dark, boarded-up rooms, and talked with the son of Guppa's chauffeur who had been named Philip after my father. In search of letters and pictures, I visited Kate's eldest son in New York City and got, as well, some insights into my mother from her godson. The pieces of the puzzle were coming together.

I wonder now whether my mother would have been better off if she hadn't felt everything so intensely. Or whether leaving her children so often in her youth created flaws in us and in her—or whether the hill on which we grew up was less a paradise for her than for us, as she was shut off from the bouncy intellectual city life she loved. Or what heights she might have reached if my father had lived. Or what kind of a new life might have been in store for her if her long addiction to codeine and then to alcohol had not existed.

But these are literary questions. They can't be answered and don't need to be. What I take away from this endeavor is an enormous admiration for a true star of the twentieth century, one who shone brightly, but who was, at the same time, my own, my flesh-and-blood mother.

WHEN I THINK of my mother now, more often than not, I remember a weekend almost thirty years ago in Chappaqua. She used to come out regularly, to be filled with new vigor. Her loneliness relieved, I would drive her back to her apartment late Sunday afternoon. We would ride the elevator together and I would carry her overnight bag inside and help her switch on the lights. She would try to hold me there; there was always something new to show me, a piece of information she had noted, the discovery of a new face in an old familiar Civil War photograph. But after an hour or so, I had to go, my car would be towed away, my family would be worried. The parting was difficult for each of us, for I knew what emptiness awaited her after I disappeared. I would always try to give her an assignment—something to write or research, a goal to achieve before our next meeting, and when we settled on the task, she scribbled down her instructions on a long yellow pad and propped it beside her bed. When I got home, I would call her to make sure she had gotten through that first hour, that she had eaten something, and that she realized the importance of the project we had just cooked up together.

On the weekend I remember particularly, upon our return trip to the city, my mother asked me if I would mind taking her back to her apartment by a new route—via the house where she had grown up on Edgecombe Avenue. I had never been there before and she had never been back there, to my knowledge, since 1914 when she was thirteen and the house had been sold. My mother had often told me that her most vivid memory of growing up was going to bed at night and listening to the smack of her father's mallet from many floors below as he hit the head of his rectangular iron cutter to slice out photographs of the proper size for his limited-edition handmade books. The pounding happened about every ten seconds and was music to my mother's ears as she grew dizzy with sleep. I should have questioned her about it and other memories of her early life, just as she had questioned her father, but I didn't. Now, as we wound through the unfamiliar streets of upper Manhattan near the Harlem River, my mother grew anxious.

"This way," she said, spotting some landmark or other. "Now turn right. I think we're getting close."

Finally, we spotted the sign for Edgecombe and we proceeded slowly up an undistinguished street and yes, there was the row of houses my grandfather had helped build almost one hundred years before. It had been set in fields and country back then at the turn of the century, but now the row was just part of a run-down, built-up city.

"There, on the end. That's ours," my mother said, and we pulled over and parked across the street. Neither of us got out of the car. We just sat there and inhaled the sight.

"I skipped down those steps every morning," my mother said. "I roller-skated and played hopscotch on that sidewalk there. I loved to feel the smooth, brown stone with my hand as I sat on the stoop. Look! See! That was my room up there. Helen and I threw water bombs out of that window and hit a couple all dressed up for the opera."

As we sat there, transfixed, I could almost see a face in that upstairs window or a little girl dancing down those front steps. What stars, what thunderheads, what sun-drenched rooms would that little girl encounter,

I let myself wonder. What poems would she write, what songs sing, what games dream, what place of never finished things discover? For a moment only, the woman beside me came brightly clear—the child, the daughter, the debutante, the young wife, the mother, the writer, the collector, the collaborator, the grandmother, the widow, the lonely one. What joined them all, it struck me then, was the passionate belief in life itself and what could be made of it by living to the fullest. The secret was in the doing, and the immense energy and care and prickle she brought to bear on all she touched. That was her magic.

Then, my wonderment was suddenly, sharply broken by my mother at my side. Through the drowning dusk she simply said, "I want to go now."

— nothing has given me so much pleasure in a long time.

Tuesday
December 22

Dearest Kate —

The s... prov...
— just ... tell
I ha... are ...
Hennin ...
I ...

HARDTCOURT
NORTH ANDOVER, MASSACHU...

Beloved :—

While

installing

9. ...

...ord".

as a ...

tellin

...er whil...

...one ever...

...ed do

...sics, nice.

(Envelope, postmarked WALL ST. STA. N.Y. JUL 10.30 AM 1924, "ADDRESS YOUR MAIL TO STREET AND NUMBER", 2 CENTS stamp)

Miss Dorothy Moore
Graytop
Chester
New Jersey

Dot :—

I told you that me to
might would ... to think that ...
me. It was too about a week. I shall ...
perfect for me majority of my time thinking ...
hat you the most and of last night which needless to say
should treat me I shall never forget. Write me soon,
did happen, it Dot, my girl.
the fourth so
            Your Phil.
... and the ...
... like having dreams

Darling J :—
            I a...
Greeks thought ...
from the head of ...
several days this
and ...

HENRY J. MALI...
... STREET
YORK

...ng an idea.
...ing Eye at th...
...ing or literary
...e would rather hear...
...s always a virtue in...
...interest. Anyway you've...
...something even if only for...
...would feel cheated if you di...

        I wonder if it is the See...
itself or Morris Frank's personalit...
makes it so enthralling? Of course h...
ness lends a peculiar poignancy to h...
of mind; but what is really troublin...
Just what we were so unhappy about, I...
ago. I wanted to say to him Dear Lad...
and Jew to Gentiles. I know what it fe...
what it's like to be a Gentile to a...
like to be bursting with arrogance and...
ing with self-distrust at the same time...
wear to heaven that you will have noth...
not a jewel without flaw and yet nurs...
riction that you'll be lucky to get a...
tered pebble. By the way he was go...
he was going to regret having tr...
about himself. Be careful...
o that he can have the...
all to you again.

...ust go to Hi now.

...uch love my dearest ...

                Kate

ARVARD CLUB
WEST 44TH STREET

July 21st 1925.

I'm here at last and have
my first day of work in our
... as an underling. Its awfully
...resting to see this end of the
...wmess, very good for one who has
...manufacturing end drilled
... youth.

ON BOARD THE
CUNARD R.M.S. "SAMARIA"

Apri...
Shangh...
Cl...

Dearest Foppie —
I would give a...
this mornin to see you ...
— & sure son to ...
many kisse...